Weird Women

Weird Women

Classic Supernatural Fiction by Groundbreaking Female Writers

Volume 2: 1840–1925

EDITED BY

Lisa Morton AND Leslie S. Klinger

PEGASUS BOOKS
NEW YORK LONDON

WEIRD WOMEN

Pegasus Books, Ltd.
148 West 37th Street, 13th Floor
New York, NY 10018

Compilation and Introduction copyright © 2021 by Lisa Morton and Leslie S. Klinger

First Pegasus Books cloth edition September 2021

Interior design by Maria Fernandez

Library of Congress Cataloging-in-Publication Data is available.

ISBN: 978-1-64313-783-4

10 9 8 7 6 5 4 3 2 1

Printed in the United States of America
Distributed by Simon & Schuster
www.pegasusbooks.com

To my three mothers:

Madge Merriman

Dorothy Morton

. . . and of course Sheila Erickson, who let me be a weird

woman from early on

—Lisa

To Mary Shelley, mother of monsters

—Les

Contents

Introduction

by Lisa Morton and Leslie S. Klinger

Ask any woman who writes fiction meant to shock or disturb about response to her work, and she will no doubt offer up at least one anecdote involving something like, "You write *that?* But you look so nice!" It's certainly commonplace among modern female horror writers, and it seems likely that their sisters in the past occasionally endured similar responses. It's hard to say exactly *what* readers imagine a female horror writer looks like.

Women have been writing this sort of fiction more than even the most avid of readers may realize and for just as long—perhaps longer—than their male counterparts. Why aren't they as well-known today as their male contemporaries? Why did so many feel compelled to write under gender-neutral names or as "Mrs. XXX"? Some of them did achieve literary recognition—this book, for example, contains work by Edith Wharton, Harriet Beecher Stowe, George Eliot, and Zora Neale Hurston, writers certainly as highly regarded as any of their male peers; however, none of them are thought of primarily as writers of supernatural fiction, nor were their reputations enhanced by their horror credits. Those whose stories tended to center on more arcane themes—women like Mrs. Oliphant, Vernon Lee, or (arguably, given that she wrote in a number of genres but her best work was horror) Mary Elizabeth Braddon—are now less studied and anthologized than, say, Ambrose Bierce or M. R. James. Rhoda Broughton was a popular author during her lifetime (whose sharp tongue was said to have intimidated Oscar Wilde), but she's now far less known than her uncle Joseph Sheridan Le Fanu.

Why should that be? It seems too easy to simply cite sexism (although there's certainly more than a grain of truth in that as well). Perhaps they didn't fit readers' preconceived notions of what they should be.

Or maybe there's something subtler at work. Did they write about subjects or themes that were different from what men were writing about? Some did. Many of these women were deeply involved in social movements of their time—they were suffragettes, anti-vivisectionists, and labor advocates—and their work often involves contemporary issues that may seem unimportant to modern writers. Nineteenth-century tales of matrons fretting over parenthood or wrangling with their nursemaids or wives living in terror of being widowed may be harder for a reader in the twenty-first-century to relate to than, say, concerns about the appropriate bounds of science or the end of the world (themes that fascinated Mary Shelley, among others). Like many writers of the nineteenth century, these authors refused to be pigeonholed, confined to a "genre" (genres themselves probably being a twentieth-century invention); instead, they wrote stories about things that moved them, be the stories romantic or scary or mystifying. Today, we may look back and say "Mary Elizabeth Braddon wrote crime fiction" or "Louisa May Alcott wrote young-adult fiction." To a one, they would have rejected such classification—they wrote *stories*. And for many of these women, they wrote because it was their only possible livelihood, their only means to support a dependent family.

A good story doesn't have an expiration date. It's a snapshot of history, and if it's an accurate depiction, it reveals our past and reminds us of those elements that have endured into the present. Rhoda Broughton's "The Man With the Nose," for example, may at first seem to be (to put it mildly) old-fashioned, what with its plot revolving around a helpless wife and mesmerism, but it also captures the terror of being stalked by a stranger, a form of dread shared by people across the centuries. May Sinclair's "Where Their Fire is Not Quenched" and Edith Wharton's "The Fulness of Life" both capture the disappointments that many still experience when their relationships don't live up to their expectations. Zora Neale Hurston's "Spunk" shows a woman both wowed and cowed by a powerful man whose dangerously toxic masculinity will be instantly recognizable to readers from any age. And who doesn't feel some of the anguish of the mothers at the hearts of Josephine Daskam Bacon's "The Children" or Mrs. S. C. Hall's "The Drowned Fisherman"? Religion is brought into play in several of these stories, proving almost invariably ineffective against greater forces—for example, in Vernon Lee's "Marsyas in Flanders," Florence Marryat's "Little White Souls," and Alice Brown's "The Tryst," ancient mythology seems more powerful than modern Christianity. If the nineteenth-century was rushing forward at dizzying speeds that left many of those living through it consumed by existential fear and anxiety, surely our modern world isn't immune to those concerns.

Not all of these stories are about subjects that are traditionally "female." Some, like Mary Cholmondeley's terrifying "Let Loose," exist simply to entertain the reader with a roller coaster ride that leaves us turning the pages ever faster; others, like Harriet Beecher Stowe's "The Ghost in the Mill" or Gertrude Atherton's "The Dead and the Countess," offer gentler, more playful takes on folklore. Their charm is impossible to ignore even a century-and-a-half later.

It must also be admitted that parts of these stories may be difficult for modern readers to swallow. The narrators of the tales may be casually cruel to servants, people of different races or faiths; colonialism might rear its ugly head; and of course misogyny is on open display. A failure to be reflective of twenty-first century attitudes, however, should not be cause to consign a story to obscurity. If we are to change how we treat others, if we are to progress, we must look unblinkingly at our past and acknowledge our mistakes and wrong-headed attitudes. A gifted writer is one who can show us who we were, no matter how much we may deplore our own behaviors.

This anthology is not intended to serve as a memorial to forgotten women writers or to somehow apologize to them for their marginalization. It's not meant to be a history lesson about the birth and growth of supernatural fiction. Instead, it's meant to present to a modern audience important works by important writers—works that have been left too long in the shadows, with timeless insights into human nature and our basic fears. In a world where the voices of women continue to be ignored, we hope that readers will rejoice in rediscovering these echoes from the past two centuries, with messages that are as critical today as when penned.

—Lisa Morton and Les Klinger
Los Angeles

Anna Maria Hall was born in Dublin in 1800; although she moved with her mother to England in 1815 and stayed there until her death in 1881, her work often dealt with Irish lore. In 1824 she married Samuel Carter Hall and was a frequent contributor to *The Art Journal*, which he edited. She also produced nine novels, several successful plays, and a number of short story collections; both she and her husband were prolific, and one estimate puts their total number of published works at around five hundred. Later in life, she founded several charitable organizations and was involved in women's rights and temperance causes. This story, first published in 1840, was chosen to appear in *The Romancist, and Novelist's Library: The Best Works of the Best Authors, Volume III*.

The Drowned Fisherman

by Mrs. S. C. Hall

In the immediate neighbourhood of Duncannon Fort,[*] along that portion of the coast, which contracts into the Waterford river, there are a number of scattered cottages, standing either singly or in small clusters along a wild and picturesque sea shore—more wild, perhaps, than beautiful, although the infinite number of creeks and bays, and overhanging rocks, vary the prospect at every hundred yards; and I know nothing more delightful than to row, during a long summer evening, from the time that the sun abates her fierceness, until the moon has fairly risen upon the waters, nothing more delightful than to row—now in, now out, now under the hanging rocks,

---

[*] Duncannon Fort is a strategic military fort situated on a peninsula in County Wexford, Ireland, along the country's southeast coast.

now close upon the silver-sanded bays, where thousands of many-coloured shells form the most beautiful mosaic beneath the transparent waters.

"And what 'ud ail the boat but to do? Sure she's done, ay, and done a dale for us, this ten years; and as to the hold, Jemmy 'ill plug his hat into it, or stick in a piece of sail-cloth, and what 'ud ail her then, but sail, God bless her—like a swan or a curlew,* as she always does?"

"Dermot—Dermot, darling! listen to me for onc't—!"

"Faith!" replied Dermot to his better half, Kate Browne, while his keen, blue eye twinkled with that mixture of wit and humour so truly Irish, "faith, my dear, I'll accommodate you in any way I can, for I'll listen to you onc't for three speakings—come, out with it, and don't stand twisting your face that was onc't so purty as to win the heart and hand of the handsomest man in the parish, and that is—myself, Dermont Browne, at your sarvice, Mistress Kate Browne, madam! Don't keep lengthening your face to the length of a herring net, but out with it—at onc't!"

"Dermot, I've got the box of tools quite convanient; I brought it with me to the shore, and the last time I was in Waterford, I bought all sortings of nails, large and small; and there's plenty of boord in the shed—and Dermot, mend the hole, and God bless you!—sure it's the sore heart I'd have when you'd be on the wather, to think that any harm would happen you—it won't take you anything like an hour."

"An hour! God bless the woman, why, a body would think you had never been a fisherman's wife! An hour would turn the tide—and the luck!—an hour! Why, the herrings out yonder would miss my company if I waited; and all for what! To go to the trouble of nailing a bit o' boord on a mite of a hole, when it will be just as easy to stop it with a hat!"

"But not as safe, Dermot!"

"Be asy with your safety! You're always touching on that;—ay; will it, and as safe too: hav'nt I done it before?—Why, turn up every one of the boats along the shore, and I'll bet you the cod I mean to catch against a branyan† that there isn't as sound a boat as my own on the sands; doesn't Harrison's go without a rudder?—doesn't Micbau's go without a mast—barring a gag

---

* A curlew is a long-billed, wading shorebird.

† This probably refers to a type of cake or cookie.

of a gate-post that he pulled out of Lavery's field? I'm sure Michael Murphy's craft is bang full of dowshy holes, like a riddle; and a good noggin he won on that, for he betted Lanty Moore that, at the present time, the keel of his boat had more holes in it than Lanty's English sieve, which he had for winnowing corn; and sure enough he won; for the holes in the sieve were all stopped up with the dirt! Lend a hand, old girl, and help me and the boy to shove her off!" he continued, appealing to his wife—"What, you won't? Why then, Kate, agra what ails ye?—I've been your true and faithful husband, next Candlemas* will be seventeen years, and you never refused me a hand's turn before!" Still Kate Browne moved not; and her husband using, with his son, considerable exertion to push off the boat, became annoyed at her obstinacy.

Kate saw, but, contrary to her usual habit, heeded it not. She stood, with folded arms and tearful eyes, surveying the proceedings, without possessing the power of putting a stop to preparations, of the termination of which she had a fearful presentiment.

"Why, then, look at your mother, Benje," exclaimed Browne to his son; "sure, she's enough to set a man mad, and her's the help that's as good as five—she has such a knowledge of setting everything straight. Kate?" he exclaimed to his wife.

"Let her alone, father dear," interrupted the boy, "let her alone, and don't vex her more; don't ye see there's a tear in her eye?"

"And how can I help that?" expostulated the father, looking kindly towards his wife at the same time; "them women are ever so hard to manage and manage as ye will, ye can't find 'em out; there's the sun shining above her head, the waters dancing and capering like jewels at her feet, the herrings crying 'Come, catch me,' and Benje, between you and I, as handsome a husband, and as fine, ay, and for the matter of that, as good a boy as a woman's heart could wish, and yet the tears are in her eyes, and the corner of her mouth drawn as far down as if she did nothing but sup sorrow all her life." Benjamin, the fisher's only child, made no reply; and, after a moment's pause, his father looked at him, and said, "Why, boy, you look as much cast down as your mother—stay on shore, and good luck to you!"

---

* A Catholic day observing the presentation of Jesus at the Temple, held on February 2.

"No, father, that I won't! I'll not put more on the trouble she's in, by letting you go by yourself; I wish from my heart the boat was mended, if it would make her easy."

"Don't bother about the boat, boy," replied Browne; "I never meddle or make with her house, or land business; hasn't she got a back-door for the cabin—a sty for the poor pig—chaney dish for the pratees,* and a white table-cloth for saints' days and bonfire nights?—Can't she stay at home and mind them, and let me and the cobble alone?" Benjamin loved the wild and careless spirit of his father better than the prudence and forethought of his mother; yet did he not forget that the very arrangements and luxuries to which his father alluded, were solely the effects of her care and industry.

"Won't you say, God speed me, Kate?" inquired the fisherman as he pushed off his dangerous craft with a broken oar, "won't you say, God speed me and the boy?" The woman clasped her hands suddenly and fervently together, and dropping on her knees, without moving from the spot on which she had been standing, uttered a few earnest words of supplication for their safety. Benjamin sprang on the shingles, and raising his mother affectionately in his arms, whispered—

"Keep a good heart, we will be back with such bouncing fish, before morning, any how; and mother, darling, if you see Statia Byrne, here is the neckerchief she promised to hem for me; tell her not to forget her promise." The kisses Mrs. Browne bestowed on her son were mingled with tears. She watched the boat until it had dwindled to a small speck on the horizon. As she turned to ascend the cliff, she saw the round, laughing face of Statia Byrne peer from behind a rock, and withdraw itself instantly on being perceived. She called to her; and, after a little time, Statia came blushing, and smiling, and lingering by the way to pluck every sprig of samphire,† every root of sea-pink, that grew within her reach.

"I just came down to gather a few bits of herbs for the granny's cures, and a few shells to keep the children asy," said Statia—pulling her sea-pinks to pieces at the same time.

---

* "A china dish for the potatoes."

† A plant that grows on rocks beside the sea and is used in pickling.

"And what does the granny cure with these?" inquired Mrs Browne.

"Sorra a know I know," replied the girl, blushing still more deeply.

"Maybe," continued Mrs. Browne gravely, "maybe, Stacy honey, there's a charm in them like the yarrow you put under your pillow last holy-eve night."*

"Ah! thin, Mistress Browne, ma'am, let me alone about the yarrow—sure it was only out of innocent mirth I did it, and no harm; and, any way, I've no belief in such things at all, at all."

"And why do you disbelieve them?" inquired the fisherman's wife. Statia made no reply—"I can tell you," she continued; "because though you neither spoke nor laughed that blessed night, my poor girl, after you placed the yarrow under your pillow—still you did not dream of Benje Browne. Stacy, Stacy, I mind the time myself, when, if a spell worked contrary, I'd disbelieve it directly—it's only human natur, darling."

Statia Byrne flung her handful of sea-pinks upon the shingles, and passed the back of her hand across her eyes, for they were filled with tears.

"You have thrown away the granny's pinks," said Kate, pointing to the flowers that the sea-breeze was scattering far and wide.

"Ah, thin, let me alone, Mistress Browne dear!" exclaimed the girl, "And good by for the present, ma'am, I'm sure the child 'ill be woke before this, and mother is carding wool, so she'll want me now."

"Good by, Statia—but stop, child: Benje desired me to put you in mind that you promised to hem this handkerchief for him; and tell your mother, jewel, that if she'll let you come down to my cabin to-night, when the grawls† are all in bed, I'll be for ever obliged to her; Browne and the boy are out to sea, and there's something over me that I don't care to be quite alone this blessed night: so come down a lannan‡—and thin you can hem the neckerchief—before morning."

---

* It was once believed that if yarrow was place under the pillow, and if no words had been spoken between the time the yarrow was cut and when sleep came, then the sleeper would see their future beloved in a dream.

† Children.

‡ Dialect for "in your cloak."

"I will, I will," said the maiden, with whom smiles had already taken the place of tears, for she loved Mrs. Browne's cottage almost better than her own; "I will, and I've learnt a new song; oh, I shall be so happy," and she danced up the cliffs with all the light gaiety of fifteen.

The fisherman's wife set her house in order, and then commenced mending her husband's nets. It would have been evident to any observer that her mind was ill at ease; for instead of pursuing her occupation with her usual steadiness, she frequently suffered the hard meshes to drop from her bony fingers, and the wooden needle to lie idle on her lap. She would rise and peer from her small window, or more frequently still from the open door, into the heavens; but there was no cause for disquiet in their aspect—the moon was in her full, calm glory; and the stars, bright, glittering, and countless, waited round her throne as handmaids silently attending upon their mistress. She could see the reflection of the moon-beams on the far-away waters—but her ear, practised as it was, could hardly catch the murmur of the ocean, so profound was its repose; and yet Kate continued restless and feverish. Benjamin was her only surviving child, although five others had called her mother; and, indeed, while he was absent from her, she felt that undefined, but perfectly natural, dread, which steals over a sensitive mind for the welfare of a beloved object, whenever the one is separated from the other.

It was a great relief to her spirits when she heard the light foot of Statia Byrne on her threshold, and she felt new-sprung hope within her heart when she looked into the bright eyes, and observed the full smile of the joyous girl.

"They're all a-bed, and the baby went off to sleep without an hushow! and mother says, as you're all alone by yourself, I might stay with you all night, Mrs. Browne; and so I will, if you please—and I've brought my needle, and I'll hem the handkerchief, if you please—and then, maybe—maybe you'd show me how you mend nets—I should so like to mend Mister Browne's herring-net; he gave mother (God bless him!) as many herrings last year as lasted all Lent!—I'm sure we can never forget it to him."

"Pray for him then, Stacy—pray on your bended knees—for Dermot and Benjamin Browne this night."

"Why so I will," rejoined the girl—astonished at the woman's earnest-ness of manner—"but the night is fine, the sky is blue, the waters clear as chrysthal; they've been out many a night when the winds do be blowing the waves into the sky, and I've wondered to see you heart-easy about them—what then ails you to-night?"

"God knows," replied Kate Browne, with a heavy sigh, "I think I'll go over my bades a bit;* ough, Stacy darling, it's a fine thing to have the religion to turn to when the heart turns against everything else."—Kate sprinkled herself with holy water out of a small chalice, and knelt down, with a "decket" of beads in her hands, to "say her prayers;" almost unwittingly, she repeated them aloud, but they had, in a degree, lost their soothing power, and she mingled the anxieties of earth with her petitions, not to heaven but to its inhabitants; her "mingled yarn" ran thus:—"'Holy Mary, mother of God, pray for us'—Statia, open the door, agra and listen, myself thinks the wind's rising—'now, and in the hour'—the cat, avourneen,† don't you see the cat at the herring tub, bad luck to that cat'?—'now, and in the hour of our death'—" There was a long pause, and she continued murmuring her petitions, and speaking aloud her anxieties, while Statia went on hemming the handkerchief; at last she looked up at her young companion and inquired, "Where did I leave off, my darling, was it at 'Virgin most powerful,' or at 'Queen of Confessors'?"

"I did not hear," replied the industrious maiden.

"Hear what?" exclaimed Kate Browne, starting off her knees.

"Lord defend us, you startle the very life out of me—" ejaculated the girl, devoutly crossing herself.

"But what did you hear, Stacy?"

"Nothing. I told you I did not hear where you left off."

"Ough! ay! ay!" exclaimed Mrs. Browne; "God forgive me, I am a poor, sinful thing; quite full of sin; I must give up the prayers for to-night; I can't steady my heart to them, good nor bad: there! finish your work, and we'll go to bed, jewel—it is, as you say, a beautiful night, thanks be to God for his mercies! and I ought to have more faith."

---

* Her "beads"—that is, her rosary.

† "Darling."

Long did they both remain awake during that calm moonlight: the fisherman's wife muttering prayers and fears, and raising her eyes to the little window, which opened at the foot of her bed, and from which, as she lay, she could catch a view of the distant sea—at last, she fell off into a deep, deep sleep. But Statia, though free from all anxiety as to the fate of the absent, could not close her eyes—poor girl! her young imagination had passed a gulf of years, and she was thinking, that, perhaps, she might be to the young fisher what Kate what was to the old; and she thought how good he was, and how handsome; and how happy she should be to mend his nets, and watch the return of his boat from the highest cliff that "toppled o'er the deep." The grey morning was stealing on the night, yet still Kate slept—and still Statia Byrne continued with her eyes fixed on the window, creating—not castles, but—nets, and boats, and cottages in the air; when suddenly before the window stood Benjamin Browne—she had not seen his shadow pass—she had heard no step, no voice—no sound; nor did she see a figure, but there was his face almost pressed to the glass—his long, uncurled hair hung down either cheek—and his eyes were fixed on her with a cold, unmoving, rayless gaze—she endeavoured to sit up—she felt suddenly paralyzed—she could not move—she tried to speak, to call Mrs. Browne, who still slept heavily, heavier than before—she could make no sound—still her lover gazed—gazed on. And what occurred to her, (for she afterwards declared she never, for a moment, was deprived of consciousness) as most strange was, that though the room within was dark, and his head obscured the window, still she could see his features, (to use her own expressive phrase) "Clear like wax:" while, as he gazed, their beautiful form assumed the long, pale hue of death—by a sudden effort she closed her eyes, but only for a brief, brief moment. When she re-opened them he was gone—and she only looked upon the grey mingling of sea and sky; trembling and terror-stricken she at last succeeded in awakening her companion. Mrs. Browne heard her story with apparent calmness, and putting her lips close to the ear of the fainting girl, whispered—"HE IS DEAD!"

It was long, long before Statia recovered from her swoon, for when she did, the morning sun was shining on her face—and she was alone, quite alone in the fisherman's cottage; at first she thought she had fearfully dreamed, but the realities around her recalled her to herself; she flew to the same cliff where, the evening before, unconscious of the strong affection, which bound her almost childish heart to her young lover, she had watched his departure; and looking down on the beach, her painful vision was too truly realized—Dermot Browne was leading his wife from a group of persons who were bearing the corpse of the young fisherman to the shore; in the distance could be seen the keel of the doomed boat floating upwards, while crowds of sea birds overhead screamed the youth's funeral dirge.

It might be about two months after this occurrence—which plunged the warm-hearted people of the neighbouring villages into deep sorrow—that Kate Browne visited the cottage of Statia Byrne; it was the first time the bereaved mother had entered any cottage, save her own, since "her trouble." As soon as Statia saw her, she flung herself upon her neck and sobbed as if her heart would break; the fisherman's wife held her from her, and parting her hair from off her brow, said,

"Sorrow has worked with you, and left his mark upon your face, avourneen; and though, my darlint, you did not drame of him that's gone last Holy-eve, you've dramed of him often since."

The poor girl wept still more bitterly.

"You must have been very dear, very dear entirely, to him," continued Kate Browne, "for his blessed spirit found it harder quitting you than his own mother, who nursed him a babby at her breast; but whisht, darlint, don't I love you better for that now? Sure everything—let alone every one that he regarded—that his regard only rested on, is more to me than silver or goold, or the wealth of the whole world! Didn't the bright eyes of his spirit look from the heavens on you, my jewel? And what I'm come here for, Mistress Byrne, ma'am, is, that as you have so many children, (and God keep them to you!) may be you'd spare Statia to bind my heart from breaking, and let her bide entirely with us—we have prosperity enough, for when the Lord takes one thing away, why he gives another—blessed be his holy name! And sure, since the boy's gone, nothing can equal Dermot's industry and carefulness, stopping every hole in every fisherman's boat—when he's ashore the hammer and nails is never out of his hand. Let her be to me as my own child, Mistress Byrne, and you'll have a consolation that will never lave you, no! not on your death-bed. Sure you'll see her every day the sun rises—let her bide with me, for I am very desolate!"

The mother, as she looked round upon seven rosy, healthy children, felt that indeed her neighbour was desolate and in a voice hoarse with emotion, she said—

"Statia may go, and take our blessing with her, if she likes!"

Many little voices wept aloud in that cottage, although they knew they should see their sister daily; but the maiden was firm in her resolve, and that night greeted, as a father, the father of him whom her young heart had loved with an entireness of affection, which the heart can know but once.

Statia is now long past the age of girlhood, and it is pleasant to see how perfectly her simple life is an illustration of the pathetic exclamation of the Jewish damsel, "Thy people shall be my people, and thy God my God!"* She manages admirably between her two "mothers," as she calls them, so that the one may not be jealous of the other; but though she has had many suitors for her hand, she has never forgotten—the drowned fisherman!

---

* Ruth utters this in Ruth 1:16, when she decides to stay with her mother-in-law Naomi after her husband has died.

The British author **George Eliot** (1819–1880), born Mary Ann Evans (although as an adult she preferred Marian), was one of the literary sensations of her time. Her seven novels, which include *Middlemarch, Silas Marner*, and *The Mill on the Floss*, were masterworks of realistic drama and social commentary. However, her life garnered her far more notoriety among her peers than her books: From 1851 to his death in 1878, she had an unmarried relationship with the philosopher and critic George Henry Lewes (who was still married to another woman). Despite the disapproval that most Victorians had of the affair, Marian was a popular literary figure in London, and her Sunday gatherings at her home, the Priory, were attended by such luminaries as Charles Dickens, Henry James, and Lord Tennyson. "The Lifted Veil" is Eliot's only work of supernatural fiction, and she later hesitated to allow reprints of it, referring to its "painfulness" and "dismal loneliness." It first appeared in *Blackwood's Edinburgh Magazine* for July 1859, without Eliot's name.

The Lifted Veil

by George Eliot

Give me no light, great Heaven, but such as turns
To energy of human fellowship;
No powers beyond the growing heritage
That makes completer manhood.[*]

---

[*] Eliot composed these lines to add to the 1878 reprinting of "The Lifted Veil."

CHAPTER I

The time of my end approaches. I have lately been subject to attacks of *angina pectoris*;* and in the ordinary course of things, my physician tells me, I may fairly hope that my life will not be protracted many months. Unless, then, I am cursed with an exceptional physical constitution, as I am cursed with an exceptional mental character, I shall not much longer groan under the wearisome burthen of this earthly existence. If it were to be otherwise—if I were to live on to the age most men desire and provide for—I should for once have known whether the miseries of delusive expectation can outweigh the miseries of true provision. For I foresee when I shall die, and everything that will happen in my last moments.

Just a month from this day, on September 20, 1850, I shall be sitting in this chair, in this study, at ten o'clock at night, longing to die, weary of incessant insight and foresight, without delusions and without hope. Just as I am watching a tongue of blue flame rising in the fire, and my lamp is burning low, the horrible contraction will begin at my chest. I shall only have time to reach the bell, and pull it violently, before the sense of suffocation will come. No one will answer my bell. I know why. My two servants are lovers, and will have quarrelled. My housekeeper will have rushed out of the house in a fury, two hours before, hoping that Perry will believe she has gone to drown herself. Perry is alarmed at last, and is gone out after her. The little scullery-maid is asleep on a bench: she never answers the bell; it does not wake her. The sense of suffocation increases: my lamp goes out with a horrible stench: I make a great effort, and snatch at the bell again. I long for life, and there is no help. I thirsted for the unknown: the thirst is gone. O God, let me stay with the known, and be weary of it: I am content. Agony of pain and suffocation—and all the while the earth, the fields, the pebbly brook at the bottom of the rookery,† the fresh scent after the rain, the light of the morning through my chamber-window, the warmth of the hearth after the frosty air—will darkness close over them for ever?

---

* Chest pain due to coronary heart disease.

† A *rookery* is a bird colony.

Darkness—darkness—no pain—nothing but darkness: but I am passing on and on through the darkness: my thought stays in the darkness, but always with a sense of moving onward . . .

Before that time comes, I wish to use my last hours of ease and strength in telling the strange story of my experience. I have never fully unbosomed myself to any human being; I have never been encouraged to trust much in the sympathy of my fellow-men. But we have all a chance of meeting with some pity, some tenderness, some charity, when we are dead: it is the living only who cannot be forgiven—the living only from whom men's indulgence and reverence are held off, like the rain by the hard east wind. While the heart beats, bruise it—it is your only opportunity; while the eye can still turn towards you with moist, timid entreaty, freeze it with an icy unanswering gaze; while the ear, that delicate messenger to the inmost sanctuary of the soul, can still take in the tones of kindness, put it off with hard civility, or sneering compliment, or envious affectation of indifference; while the creative brain can still throb with the sense of injustice, with the yearning for brotherly recognition—make haste—oppress it with your ill-considered judgements, your trivial comparisons, your careless misrepresentations. The heart will by and by be still—"*ubi saeva indignatio ulterius cor lacerare nequit*";* the eye will cease to entreat; the ear will be deaf; the brain will have ceased from all wants as well as from all work. Then your charitable speeches may find vent; then you may remember and pity the toil and the struggle and the failure; then you may give due honour to the work achieved; then you may find extenuation for errors, and may consent to bury them.

That is a trivial schoolboy text; why do I dwell on it? It has little reference to me, for I shall leave no works behind me for men to honour. I have no near relatives who will make up, by weeping over my grave, for the wounds they inflicted on me when I was among them. It is only the story of my life that will perhaps win a little more sympathy from strangers when I am dead, than I ever believed it would obtain from my friends while I was living.

---

* "Where savage indignation can no longer tear his heart." —Jonathan Swift asked that this be part of the epitaph inscribed on his tomb.

My childhood perhaps seems happier to me than it really was, by contrast with all the after-years. For then the curtain of the future was as impenetrable to me as to other children: I had all their delight in the present hour, their sweet indefinite hopes for the morrow; and I had a tender mother: even now, after the dreary lapse of long years, a slight trace of sensation accompanies the remembrance of her caress as she held me on her knee—her arms round my little body, her cheek pressed on mine. I had a complaint of the eyes that made me blind for a little while, and she kept me on her knee from morning till night. That unequalled love soon vanished out of my life, and even to my childish consciousness it was as if that life had become more chill. I rode my little white pony with the groom by my side as before, but there were no loving eyes looking at me as I mounted, no glad arms opened to me when I came back. Perhaps I missed my mother's love more than most children of seven or eight would have done, to whom the other pleasures of life remained as before; for I was certainly a very sensitive child. I remember still the mingled trepidation and delicious excitement with which I was affected by the tramping of the horses on the pavement in the echoing stables, by the loud resonance of the groom's voices, by the booming bark of the dogs as my father's carriage thundered under the archway of the courtyard, by the din of the gong as it gave notice of luncheon and dinner. The measured tramp of soldiery, which I sometimes heard—for my father's house lay near a county town where there were large barracks—made me sob and tremble; and yet when they were gone past, I longed for them to come back again.

I fancy my father thought me an odd child, and had little fondness for me; though he was very careful in fulfilling what he regarded as a parent's duties. But he was already past the middle of life, and I was not his only son. My mother had been his second wife, and he was five-and-forty when he married her. He was a firm, unbending, intensely orderly man, in root and stem a banker, but with a flourishing graft of the active landholder, aspiring to county influence: one of those people who are always like themselves from day to day, who are uninfluenced by the weather, and neither know melancholy nor high spirits. I held him in great awe, and appeared more timid and sensitive in his presence than at other times; a circumstance, which, perhaps, helped to confirm him in the intention to educate me on a different plan from the prescriptive one with which he had complied in the case of my elder brother, already a tall youth at Eton. My brother was to be his representative and successor; he must go to Eton and Oxford, for the sake of making connexions, of course: my father was not a man to underrate the bearing of Latin satirists or Greek dramatists on the attainment of an aristocratic position. But, intrinsically, he had slight esteem for "those dead but sceptred spirits"; having qualified himself for forming an independent opinion by reading Potter's *Æschylus*,* and dipping into Francis's *Horace*.† To this negative view he added a positive one, derived from a recent connexion with mining speculations; namely, that a scientific education was the really useful training for a younger son. Moreover, it was clear that a shy, sensitive boy like me was not fit to encounter the rough experience of a public school. Mr. Letherall had said so very decidedly. Mr. Letherall was a large man in spectacles, who one day took my small head between his large hands, and pressed it here and there in an exploratory, auspicious manner—then placed each of his great thumbs on my temples, and pushed me a little way from him, and stared at me with glittering spectacles. The contemplation appeared to displease him, for he frowned sternly, and said to my father, drawing his thumbs across my eyebrows—

"The deficiency is there, sir—there; and here," he added, touching the upper sides of my head, "here is the excess. That must be brought out, sir, and this must be laid to sleep."‡

I was in a state of tremor, partly at the vague idea that I was the object of reprobation, partly in the agitation of my first hatred—hatred of this big, spectacled man, who pulled my head about as if he wanted to buy and cheapen it.

---

* The translations of the plays of Aeschylus by Reverend Robert Potter (1721–1804) were the standard translation from 1877 to the mid-nineteenth century.

† Philip Francis was an eighteenth-century scholar who translated the works of the Roman poet Horace.

‡ The practice of phrenology—diagnosing a patient's illnesses by reading the bumps on their skull—was much in vogue in Victorian England when Eliot wrote "The Lifted Veil."

I am not aware how much Mr. Letherall had to do with the system afterwards adopted towards me, but it was presently clear that private tutors, natural history, science, and the modern languages, were the appliances by which the defects of my organization were to be remedied. I was very stupid about machines, so I was to be greatly occupied with them; I had no memory for classification, so it was particularly necessary that I should study systematic zoology and botany; I was hungry for human deeds and humane motions, so I was to be plentifully crammed with the mechanical powers, the elementary bodies, and the phenomena of electricity and magnetism. A better-constituted boy would certainly have profited under my intelligent tutors, with their scientific apparatus; and would, doubtless, have found the phenomena of electricity and magnetism as fascinating as I was, every Thursday, assured they were. As it was, I could have paired off, for ignorance of whatever was taught me, with the worst Latin scholar that was ever turned out of a classical academy. I read Plutarch, and Shake-speare, and Don Quixote by the sly, and supplied myself in that way with wandering thoughts, while my tutor was assuring me that "an improved man, as distinguished from an ignorant one, was a man who knew the reason why water ran downhill." I had no desire to be this improved man; I was glad of the running water; I could watch it and listen to it gurgling among the pebbles, and bathing the bright green water-plants, by the hour together. I did not want to know *why* it ran; I had perfect confidence that there were good reasons for what was so very beautiful.

There is no need to dwell on this part of my life. I have said enough to indicate that my nature was of the sensitive, unpractical order, and that it grew up in an uncongenial medium, which could never foster it into happy, healthy development. When I was sixteen I was sent to Geneva to complete my course of education; and the change was a very happy one to me, for the first sight of the Alps, with the setting sun on them, as we descended the Jura,* seemed to me like an entrance into heaven; and the three years of my life there were spent in a perpetual sense of exaltation, as if from a draught of delicious wine, at the presence of Nature in all her awful loveliness. You will think, perhaps, that I must have been a poet, from

---

* The Jura mountains are a range located just to the north of the Western Alps.

this early sensibility to Nature. But my lot was not so happy as that. A poet pours forth his song and *believes* in the listening ear and answering soul, to which his song will be floated sooner or later. But the poet's sensibility without his voice—the poet's sensibility that finds no vent but in silent tears on the sunny bank, when the noonday light sparkles on the water, or in an inward shudder at the sound of harsh human tones, the sight of a cold human eye—this dumb passion brings with it a fatal solitude of soul in the society of one's fellow-men. My least solitary moments were those in which I pushed off in my boat, at evening, towards the centre of the lake; it seemed to me that the sky, and the glowing mountain-tops, and the wide blue water, surrounded me with a cherishing love such as no human face had shed on me since my mother's love had vanished out of my life. I used to do as Jean Jacques* did—lie down in my boat and let it glide where it would, while I looked up at the departing glow leaving one mountain-top after the other, as if the prophet's chariot of fire were passing over them on its way to the home of light. Then, when the white summits were all sad and corpse-like, I had to push homeward, for I was under careful surveillance, and was allowed no late wanderings. This disposition of mine was not favourable to the formation of intimate friendships among the numerous youths of my own age who are always to be found studying at Geneva. Yet I made *one* such friendship; and, singularly enough, it was with a youth whose intellectual tendencies were the very reverse of my own. I shall call him Charles Meunier; his real surname—an English one, for he was of English extraction—having since become celebrated. He was an orphan, who lived on a miserable pittance while he pursued the medical studies for which he had a special genius. Strange! that with my vague mind, susceptible and unobservant, hating inquiry and given up to contemplation, I should have been drawn towards a youth whose strongest passion was science. But the bond was not an intellectual one; it came from a source that can happily blend the stupid with the brilliant, the dreamy with the practical: it came from community of feeling. Charles was poor and ugly,

---

* Jean-Jacques Rousseau (1712–1778), the famed philosopher who espoused the virtues of leading a more natural life and who, *in Reveries of the Solitary Walker*, referred to his time drifting in a boat near the Island of St. Pierre as a "a sufficient, complete and perfect happiness which leaves no emptiness to be filled in the soul."

derided by Genevese *gamins*, and not acceptable in drawing-rooms. I saw that he was isolated, as I was, though from a different cause, and, stimulated by a sympathetic resentment, I made timid advances towards him. It is enough to say that there sprang up as much comradeship between us as our different habits would allow; and in Charles's rare holidays we went up the Salève* together, or took the boat to Vevey,† while I listened dreamily to the monologues in which he unfolded his bold conceptions of future experiment and discovery. I mingled them confusedly in my thought with glimpses of blue water and delicate floating cloud, with the notes of birds and the distant glitter of the glacier. He knew quite well that my mind was half absent, yet he liked to talk to me in this way; for don't we talk of our hopes and our projects even to dogs and birds, when they love us? I have mentioned this one friendship because of its connexion with a strange and terrible scene which I shall have to narrate in my subsequent life.

This happier life at Geneva was put an end to by a severe illness, which is partly a blank to me, partly a time of dimly-remembered suffering, with the presence of my father by my bed from time to time. Then came the languid monotony of convalescence, the days gradually breaking into variety and distinctness as my strength enabled me to take longer and longer drives. On one of these more vividly remembered days, my father said to me, as he sat beside my sofa—

"When you are quite well enough to travel, Latimer, I shall take you home with me. The journey will amuse you and do you good, for I shall go through the Tyrol and Austria, and you will see many new places. Our neighbours, the Filmores, are come; Alfred will join us at Basel, and we shall all go together to Vienna, and back by Prague" . . .

My father was called away before he had finished his sentence, and he left my mind resting on the word *Prague*, with a strange sense that a new and wondrous scene was breaking upon me: a city under the broad sunshine, that seemed to me as if it were the summer sunshine of a long-past century arrested in its course—unrefreshed for ages by dews of night, or the rushing

---

* A mountain in France that is known as "the balcony of Geneva," climbed by the Creature in Mary Shelley's *Frankenstein*.

† A Swiss town on the north shore of Lake Geneva.

rain-cloud; scorching the dusty, weary, time-eaten grandeur of a people doomed to live on in the stale repetition of memories, like deposed and superannuated kings in their regal gold-inwoven tatters. The city looked so thirsty that the broad river seemed to me a sheet of metal; and the blackened statues, as I passed under their blank gaze, along the unending bridge, with their ancient garments and their saintly crowns, seemed to me the real inhabitants and owners of this place, while the busy, trivial men and women, hurrying to and fro, were a swarm of ephemeral visitants infesting it for a day. It is such grim, stony beings as these, I thought, who are the fathers of ancient faded children, in those tanned time-fretted dwellings that crowd the steep before me; who pay their court in the worn and crumbling pomp of the palace, which stretches its monotonous length on the height; who worship wearily in the stifling air of the churches, urged by no fear or hope, but compelled by their doom to be ever old and undying, to live on in the rigidity of habit, as they live on in perpetual midday, without the repose of night or the new birth of morning.

A stunning clang of metal suddenly thrilled through me, and I became conscious of the objects in my room again: one of the fire-irons had fallen as Pierre opened the door to bring me my draught. My heart was palpitating violently, and I begged Pierre to leave my draught beside me; I would take it presently.

As soon as I was alone again, I began to ask myself whether I had been sleeping. Was this a dream—this wonderfully distinct vision—minute in its distinctness down to a patch of rainbow light on the pavement, transmitted through a coloured lamp in the shape of a star—of a strange city, quite unfamiliar to my imagination? I had seen no picture of Prague: it lay in my mind as a mere name, with vaguely-remembered historical associations—ill-defined memories of imperial grandeur and religious wars.

Nothing of this sort had ever occurred in my dreaming experience before, for I had often been humiliated because my dreams were only saved from being utterly disjointed and commonplace by the frequent terrors of nightmare. But I could not believe that I had been asleep, for I remembered distinctly the gradual breaking-in of the vision upon me, like the new images in a dissolving view, or the growing distinctness of the landscape as the sun lifts up the veil of the morning mist. And while I was conscious of this incipient vision, I was also conscious that Pierre came to tell my father Mr. Filmore was waiting for him, and that my father hurried out of the room. No, it was not a dream; was it—the thought was full of tremulous exultation—was it the poet's nature in me, hitherto only a troubled yearning sensibility, now manifesting itself suddenly as spontaneous creation? Surely it was in this way that Homer saw the plain of Troy, that Dante saw the abodes of the departed, that Milton saw the earthward flight of the Tempter. Was it that my illness had wrought some happy change in my organization—given a firmer tension to my nerves—carried off some dull obstruction? I had often read of such effects—in works of fiction at least. Nay; in genuine biographies I had read of the subtilizing or exalting influence of some diseases on the mental powers. Did not Novalis* feel his inspiration intensified under the progress of consumption?

When my mind had dwelt for some time on this blissful idea, it seemed to me that I might perhaps test it by an exertion of my will. The vision had begun when my father was speaking of our going to Prague. I did not for a moment believe it was really a representation of that city; I believed—I hoped it was a picture that my newly liberated genius had painted in fiery haste, with the colours snatched from lazy memory. Suppose I were to fix my mind on some other place—Venice, for example, which was far more familiar to my imagination than Prague: perhaps the same sort of result would follow. I concentrated my thoughts on Venice; I stimulated my imagination with poetic memories, and strove to feel myself present in Venice, as I had felt myself present in Prague. But in vain. I was only colouring the Canaletto engravings that hung in my old bedroom at home; the picture was a shifting one, my mind wandering uncertainly in search of more vivid images; I could see no accident of form or shadow without conscious labour after the necessary conditions. It was all prosaic effort, not rapt passivity, such as I had experienced half an hour before. I was discouraged; but I remembered that inspiration was fitful.

For several days I was in a state of excited expectation, watching for a recurrence of my new gift. I sent my thoughts ranging over my world of

---

* Novalis was the pen name of Georg Philipp Friedrich Freiherr von Hardenberg, an eighteenth-century German mystic and poet. He died of tuberculosis (then known as consumption) at the age of twenty-eight.

knowledge, in the hope that they would find some object which would send a reawakening vibration through my slumbering genius. But no; my world remained as dim as ever, and that flash of strange light refused to come again, though I watched for it with palpitating eagerness.

My father accompanied me every day in a drive, and a gradually lengthening walk as my powers of walking increased; and one evening he had agreed to come and fetch me at twelve the next day, that we might go together to select a musical box, and other purchases rigorously demanded of a rich Englishman visiting Geneva. He was one of the most punctual of men and bankers, and I was always nervously anxious to be quite ready for him at the appointed time. But, to my surprise, at a quarter past twelve he had not appeared. I felt all the impatience of a convalescent who has nothing particular to do, and who has just taken a tonic in the prospect of immediate exercise that would carry off the stimulus.

Unable to sit still and reserve my strength, I walked up and down the room, looking out on the current of the Rhone, just where it leaves the dark-blue lake; but thinking all the while of the possible causes that could detain my father.

Suddenly I was conscious that my father was in the room, but not alone: there were two persons with him. Strange! I had heard no footstep, I had not seen the door open; but I saw my father, and at his right hand our neighbour Mrs. Filmore, whom I remembered very well, though I had not seen her for five years. She was a commonplace middle-aged woman, in silk and cashmere; but the lady on the left of my father was not more than twenty, a tall, slim, willowy figure, with luxuriant blond hair, arranged in cunning braids and folds that looked almost too massive for the slight figure and the small-featured, thin-lipped face they crowned. But the face had not a girlish expression: the features were sharp, the pale grey eyes at once acute, restless, and sarcastic. They were fixed on me in half-smiling curiosity, and I felt a painful sensation as if a sharp wind were cutting me. The pale-green dress, and the green leaves that seemed to form a border about her pale blond hair, made me think of a Water-Nixie*—for my mind

---

* A shape-shifting water spirit from German folklore (also the subject of a fairy tale collected by the Brothers Grimm).

was full of German lyrics, and this pale, fatal-eyed woman, with the green weeds, looked like a birth from some cold sedgy stream, the daughter of an aged river.

"Well, Latimer, you thought me long,"* my father said . . .

But while the last word was in my ears, the whole group vanished, and there was nothing between me and the Chinese printed folding-screen that stood before the door. I was cold and trembling; I could only totter forward and throw myself on the sofa. This strange new power had manifested itself again. . . . But *was* it a power? Might it not rather be a disease—a sort of intermittent delirium, concentrating my energy of brain into moments of unhealthy activity, and leaving my saner hours all the more barren? I felt a dizzy sense of unreality in what my eye rested on; I grasped the bell convulsively, like one trying to free himself from nightmare, and rang it twice. Pierre came with a look of alarm in his face.

"Monsieur ne se trouve pas bien?"† he said anxiously.

"I'm tired of waiting, Pierre," I said, as distinctly and emphatically as I could, like a man determined to be sober in spite of wine; "I'm afraid something has happened to my father—he's usually so punctual. Run to the Hôtel des Bergues‡ and see if he is there."

Pierre left the room at once, with a soothing "Bien, Monsieur"; and I felt the better for this scene of simple, waking prose. Seeking to calm myself still further, I went into my bedroom, adjoining the *salon*, and opened a case of eau-de-Cologne; took out a bottle; went through the process of taking out the cork very neatly, and then rubbed the reviving spirit over my hands and forehead, and under my nostrils, drawing a new delight from the scent because I had procured it by slow details of labour, and by no strange sudden madness. Already I had begun to taste something of the horror that belongs to the lot of a human being whose nature is not adjusted to simple human conditions.

---

* "Long" here is used to refer to a long length of time.

† "Monsieur is not feeling well?"

‡ A luxury hotel founded in 1834 in Geneva and still in operation.

Still enjoying the scent, I returned to the salon, but it was not unoccupied, as it had been before I left it. In front of the Chinese folding-screen there was my father, with Mrs. Filmore on his right hand, and on his left—the slim, blond-haired girl, with the keen face and the keen eyes fixed on me in half-smiling curiosity.

"Well, Latimer, you thought me long," my father said . . .

I heard no more, felt no more, till I became conscious that I was lying with my head low on the sofa, Pierre, and my father by my side. As soon as I was thoroughly revived, my father left the room, and presently returned, saying—

"I've been to tell the ladies how you are, Latimer. They were waiting in the next room. We shall put off our shopping expedition to-day."

Presently he said, "That young lady is Bertha Grant, Mrs. Filmore's orphan niece. Filmore has adopted her, and she lives with them, so you will have her for a neighbour when we go home—perhaps for a near relation; for there is a tenderness between her and Alfred, I suspect, and I should be gratified by the match, since Filmore means to provide for her in every way as if she were his daughter. It had not occurred to me that you knew nothing about her living with the Filmores."

He made no further allusion to the fact of my having fainted at the moment of seeing her, and I would not for the world have told him the reason: I shrank from the idea of disclosing to any one what might be regarded as a pitiable peculiarity, most of all from betraying it to my father, who would have suspected my sanity ever after.

I do not mean to dwell with particularity on the details of my experience. I have described these two cases at length, because they had definite, clearly traceable results in my after-lot.

Shortly after this last occurrence—I think the very next day—I began to be aware of a phase in my abnormal sensibility, to which, from the languid and slight nature of my intercourse with others since my illness, I had not been alive before. This was the obtrusion on my mind of the mental process going forward in first one person, and then another, with whom I happened to be in contact: the vagrant, frivolous ideas and emotions of some uninteresting acquaintance—Mrs. Filmore, for example—would force themselves on my consciousness like an importunate, ill-played musical instrument, or the loud activity of an imprisoned insect. But this unpleasant sensibility was fitful, and left me moments of rest, when the souls of my companions were once more shut out from me, and I felt a relief such as silence brings to wearied nerves. I might have believed this importunate insight to be merely a diseased activity of the imagination, but that my prevision of incalculable words and actions proved it to have a fixed relation to the mental process in other minds. But this superadded consciousness, wearying and annoying enough when it urged on me the trivial experience of indifferent people, became an intense pain and grief when it seemed to be opening to me the souls of those who were in a close relation to me—when the rational talk, the graceful attentions, the wittily-turned phrases, and the kindly deeds, which used to make the web of their characters, were seen as if thrust asunder by a microscopic vision, that showed all the intermediate frivolities, all the suppressed egoism, all the struggling chaos of puerilities, meanness, vague capricious memories, and indolent make-shift thoughts, from which human words and deeds emerge like leaflets covering a fermenting heap.

At Basel we were joined by my brother Alfred, now a handsome, self-confident man of six-and-twenty—a thorough contrast to my fragile, nervous, ineffectual self. I believe I was held to have a sort of half-womanish, half-ghostly beauty; for the portrait-painters, who are thick as weeds at Geneva, had often asked me to sit for them, and I had been the model of a dying minstrel in a fancy picture. But I thoroughly disliked my own physique and nothing but the belief that it was a condition of poetic genius would have reconciled me to it. That brief hope was quite fled, and I saw in my face now nothing but the stamp of a morbid organization, framed for passive suffering—too feeble for the sublime resistance of poetic production. Alfred, from whom I had been almost constantly separated, and who, in his present stage of character and appearance, came before me as a perfect stranger, was bent on being extremely friendly and brother-like to me. He had the superficial kindness of a good-humoured, self-satisfied nature, that fears no rivalry, and has encountered no contrarieties. I am not sure that my disposition was good enough for me to have been quite free from envy towards him, even if our desires had not clashed, and if I had been in the healthy human condition, which admits of generous confidence and charitable construction. There must always have been an antipathy between our natures. As it was, he became in a few weeks an object of intense hatred to me; and when he entered the room, still more when he spoke, it was as if a sensation of grating metal had set my teeth on edge. My diseased consciousness was more intensely and continually occupied with his thoughts and emotions, than with those of any other person who came in my way. I was perpetually exasperated with the petty promptings of his conceit and his love of patronage, with his self-complacent belief in Bertha Grant's passion for him, with his half-pitying contempt for me—seen not in the ordinary indications of intonation and phrase and slight action, which an acute and suspicious mind is on the watch for, but in all their naked skinless complication.

For we were rivals, and our desires clashed, though he was not aware of it. I have said nothing yet of the effect Bertha Grant produced in me on a nearer acquaintance. That effect was chiefly determined by the fact that she made the only exception, among all the human beings about me, to my unhappy gift of insight. About Bertha I was always in a state of uncertainty: I could watch the expression of her face, and speculate on its meaning; I could ask for her opinion with the real interest of ignorance; I could listen for her words and watch for her smile with hope and fear: she had for me the fascination of an unravelled destiny. I say it was this fact that chiefly determined the strong effect she produced on me: for, in the abstract, no womanly character could seem to have less affinity for that of a shrinking, romantic, passionate youth than Bertha's. She was keen, sarcastic, unimaginative, prematurely cynical, remaining critical and unmoved in the most impressive scenes, inclined to dissect all my favourite poems, and especially contemptuous towards the German lyrics, which were my pet literature at that time. To this moment I am unable to define my feeling towards her: it was not ordinary boyish admiration, for she was the very opposite, even to the colour of her hair, of the ideal woman who still remained to me the type of loveliness; and she was without that enthusiasm for the great and good, which, even at the moment of her strongest dominion over me, I should have declared to be the highest element of character. But there is no tyranny more complete than that which a self-centred negative nature exercises over a morbidly sensitive nature perpetually craving sympathy and support. The most independent people feel the effect of a man's silence in heightening their value for his opinion—feel an additional triumph in conquering the reverence of a critic habitually captious and satirical: no wonder, then, that an enthusiastic self-distrusting youth should watch and wait before the closed secret of a sarcastic woman's face, as if it were the shrine of the doubtfully benignant deity who ruled his destiny. For a young enthusiast is unable to imagine the total negation in another mind of the emotions, which are stirring his own: they may be feeble, latent, inactive, he thinks, but they are there—they may be called forth; sometimes, in moments of happy hallucination, he believes they may be there in all the greater strength because he sees no outward sign of them. And this effect, as I have intimated, was heightened to its utmost intensity in me, because Bertha was the only being who remained for me in the mysterious seclusion of soul that renders such youthful delusion possible. Doubtless there was another sort of fascination at work—that subtle physical attraction which delights in cheating our psychological predictions, and in compelling the men who paint sylphs, to fall in love with some *bonne et brave femme,*[*] heavy-heeled and freckled.

Bertha's behaviour towards me was such as to encourage all my illusions, to heighten my boyish passion, and make me more and more dependent on her smiles. Looking back with my present wretched knowledge, I conclude that her vanity and love of power were intensely gratified by the belief that I had fainted on first seeing her purely from the strong impression her person had produced on me. The most prosaic woman likes to believe herself the object of a violent, a poetic passion; and without a grain of romance in her, Bertha had that spirit of intrigue, which gave piquancy to the idea that the brother of the man she meant to marry was dying with love and jealousy for her sake. That she meant to marry my brother, was what at that time I did not believe; for though he was assiduous in his attentions to her, and I knew well enough that both he and my father had made up their minds to this result, there was not yet an understood engagement—there had been no explicit declaration; and Bertha habitually, while she flirted with my brother, and accepted his homage in a way that implied to him a thorough recognition of its intention, made me believe,

---

[*] "Good and brave woman."

by the subtlest looks and phrases—feminine nothings, which could never be quoted against her—that he was really the object of her secret ridicule; that she thought him, as I did, a coxcomb,* whom she would have pleasure in disappointing. Me she openly petted in my brother's presence, as if I were too young and sickly ever to be thought of as a lover; and that was the view he took of me. But I believe she must inwardly have delighted in the tremors into which she threw me by the coaxing way in which she patted my curls, while she laughed at my quotations. Such caresses were always given in the presence of our friends; for when we were alone together, she affected a much greater distance towards me, and now and then took the opportunity, by words or slight actions, to stimulate my foolish timid hope that she really preferred me. And why should she not follow her inclination? I was not in so advantageous a position as my brother, but I had fortune, I was not a year younger than she was, and she was an heiress, who would soon be of age to decide for herself.

The fluctuations of hope and fear, confined to this one channel, made each day in her presence a delicious torment. There was one deliberate act of hers which especially helped to intoxicate me. When we were in Vienna her twentieth birthday occurred, and as she was very fond of ornaments, we all took the opportunity of the splendid jewellers' shops in that Teutonic Paris to purchase her a birthday present of jewellery. Mine, naturally, was the least expensive; it was an opal ring—the opal was my favourite stone, because it seems to blush and turn pale as if it had a soul. I told Bertha so when I gave it her, and said that it was an emblem of the poetic nature, changing with the changing light of heaven and of woman's eyes. In the evening she appeared elegantly dressed, and wearing conspicuously all the birthday presents except mine. I looked eagerly at her fingers, but saw no opal. I had no opportunity of noticing this to her during the evening; but the next day, when I found her seated near the window alone, after breakfast, I said, "You scorn to wear my poor opal. I should have remembered that you despised poetic natures, and should have given you coral, or turquoise, or some other opaque unresponsive stone." "Do I despise it?" she answered, taking hold of a delicate gold chain which she always

---

* A vain, conceited, or foolish man.

wore round her neck and drawing out the end from her bosom with my ring hanging to it; "it hurts me a little, I can tell you," she said, with her usual dubious smile, "to wear it in that secret place; and since your poetical nature is so stupid as to prefer a more public position, I shall not endure the pain any longer."

She took off the ring from the chain and put it on her finger, smiling still, while the blood rushed to my cheeks, and I could not trust myself to say a word of entreaty that she would keep the ring where it was before.

I was completely fooled by this, and for two days shut myself up in my own room whenever Bertha was absent, that I might intoxicate myself afresh with the thought of this scene and all it implied.

I should mention that during these two months—which seemed a long life to me from the novelty and intensity of the pleasures and pains I underwent—my diseased anticipation in other people's consciousness continued to torment me; now it was my father, and now my brother, now Mrs. Filmore or her husband, and now our German courier, whose stream of thought rushed upon me like a ringing in the ears not to be got rid of, though it allowed my own impulses and ideas to continue their uninterrupted course. It was like a preternaturally heightened sense of hearing, making audible to one a roar of sound where others find perfect stillness. The weariness and disgust of this involuntary intrusion into other souls was counteracted only by my ignorance of Bertha, and my growing passion for her; a passion enormously stimulated, if not produced, by that ignorance. She was my oasis of mystery in the dreary desert of knowledge. I had never allowed my diseased condition to betray itself, or to drive me into any unusual speech or action, except once, when, in a moment of peculiar bitterness against my brother, I had forestalled some words which I knew he was going to utter—a clever observation, which he had prepared beforehand. He had occasionally a slightly affected hesitation in his speech, and when he paused an instant after the second word, my impatience and jealousy impelled me to continue the speech for him, as if it were something we had both learned by rote. He coloured and looked astonished, as well as annoyed; and the words had no sooner escaped my lips than I felt a shock of alarm lest such an anticipation of words—very far from being words of course, easy to divine—should have betrayed me as an exceptional being, a

sort of quiet energumen,* whom every one, Bertha above all, would shudder
at and avoid. But I magnified, as usual, the impression any word or deed of
mine could produce on others; for no one gave any sign of having noticed
my interruption as more than a rudeness, to be forgiven me on the score of my
feeble nervous condition.

While this superadded consciousness of the actual was almost constant
with me, I had never had a recurrence of that distinct prevision, which I
have described in relation to my first interview with Bertha; and I was
waiting with eager curiosity to know whether or not my vision Prague
would prove to have been an instance of the same kind. A few days after
the incident of the opal ring, we were paying one of our frequent visits to the
Lichtenberg Palace.† I could never look at many pictures in succession;
for pictures, when they are at all powerful, affect me so strongly that one
or two exhaust all my capability of contemplation. This morning I had
been looking at Giorgione's picture of the cruel-eyed woman, said to be a
likeness of Lucrezia Borgia.‡ I had stood long alone before it, fascinated
by the terrible reality of that cunning, relentless face, till I felt a strange
poisoned sensation, as if I had long been inhaling a fatal odour, and was
just beginning to be conscious of its effects. Perhaps even then I should not
have moved away, if the rest of the party had not returned to this room,
and announced that they were going to the Belvedere Gallery to settle a bet
which had arisen between my brother and Mr. Filmore about a portrait. I
followed them dreamily, and was hardly alive to what occurred till they had
all gone up to the gallery, leaving me below; for I refused to come within
sight of another picture that day. I made my way to the Grand Terrace,
since it was agreed that we should saunter in the gardens when the dispute
had been decided. I had been sitting here a short space, vaguely conscious
of trim gardens, with a city and green hills in the distance, when, wishing
to avoid the proximity of the sentinel, I rose and walked down the broad
stone steps, intending to seat myself farther on in the gardens. Just as I

---

* Someone who is diabolically possessed.

† A ruined castle in Germany.

‡ This is probably a reference to Giorgione's famous painting "Laura," the only youthful
  female portrait by the Italian Renaissance artist.

reached the gravel-walk, I felt an arm slipped within mine, and a light hand gently pressing my wrist. In the same instant a strange intoxicating numbness passed over me, like the continuance or climax of the sensation I was still feeling from the gaze of Lucrezia Borgia. The gardens, the summer sky, the consciousness of Bertha's arm being within mine, all vanished, and I seemed to be suddenly in darkness, out of which there gradually broke a dim firelight, and I felt myself sitting in my father's leather chair in the library at home. I knew the fireplace—the dogs for the wood-fire— the black marble chimney-piece with the white marble medallion of the dying Cleopatra in the centre. Intense and hopeless misery was pressing on my soul; the light became stronger, for Bertha was entering with a candle in her hand—Bertha, my wife—with cruel eyes, with green jewels and green leaves on her white ball-dress; every hateful thought within her present to me. . . . "Madman, idiot! why don't you kill yourself, then?" It was a moment of hell. I saw into her pitiless soul—saw its barren worldliness, its scorching hate—and felt it clothe me round like an air I was obliged to breathe. She came with her candle and stood over me with a bitter smile of contempt; I saw the great emerald brooch on her bosom, a studded serpent with diamond eyes. I shuddered—I despised this woman with the barren soul and mean thoughts; but I felt helpless before her, as if she clutched my bleeding heart, and would clutch it till the last drop of life-blood ebbed away. She was my wife, and we hated each other. Gradually the hearth, the dim library, the candle-light disappeared—seemed to melt away into a background of light, the green serpent with the diamond eyes remaining a dark image on the retina. Then I had a sense of my eyelids quivering, and the living daylight broke in upon me; I saw gardens, and heard voices; I was seated on the steps of the Belvedere Terrace, and my friends were round me.

The tumult of mind into which I was thrown by this hideous vision made me ill for several days, and prolonged our stay at Vienna. I shuddered with horror as the scene recurred to me; and it recurred constantly, with all its minutiæ, as if they had been burnt into my memory; and yet, such is the madness of the human heart under the influence of its immediate desires, I felt a wild hell-braving joy that Bertha was to be mine; for the fulfilment of my former prevision concerning her first appearance before me, left me little hope that this last hideous glimpse of the future was the mere diseased play of my own mind, and had no relation to external realities. One thing alone I looked towards as a possible means of casting doubt on my terrible conviction—the discovery that my vision of Prague had been false—and Prague was the next city on our route.

Meanwhile, I was no sooner in Bertha's society again than I was as completely under her sway as before. What if I saw into the heart of Bertha, the matured woman—Bertha, my wife? Bertha, the *girl*, was a fascinating secret to me still: I trembled under her touch; I felt the witchery of her presence; I yearned to be assured of her love. The fear of poison is feeble against the sense of thirst. Nay, I was just as jealous of my brother as before—just as much irritated by his small patronizing ways; for my pride, my diseased sensibility, were there as they had always been, and winced as inevitably under every offence as my eye winced from an intruding mote. The future, even when brought within the compass of feeling by a vision that made me shudder, had still no more than the force of an idea, compared with the force of present emotion—of my love for Bertha, of my dislike and jealousy towards my brother.

It is an old story, that men sell themselves to the tempter, and sign a bond with their blood, because it is only to take effect at a distant day; then rush on to snatch the cup their souls thirst after with an impulse not the less savage because there is a dark shadow beside them for evermore. There is no short cut, no patent tram-road, to wisdom: after all the centuries of invention, the soul's path lies through the thorny wilderness which must be still trodden in solitude, with bleeding feet, with sobs for help, as it was trodden by them of old time.

My mind speculated eagerly on the means by which I should become my brother's successful rival, for I was still too timid, in my ignorance of Bertha's actual feeling, to venture on any step that would urge from her an avowal of it. I thought I should gain confidence even for this, if my vision of Prague proved to have been veracious; and yet, the horror of that certitude! Behind the slim girl Bertha, whose words and looks I watched for, whose touch was bliss, there stood continually that Bertha with the fuller form, the harder eyes, the more rigid mouth—with the barren, selfish soul laid bare; no longer a fascinating secret, but a measured fact, urging itself perpetually on my unwilling sight. Are you unable to give me your sympathy—you who react this? Are you unable to imagine this double consciousness at work within me, flowing on like two parallel streams which never mingle their waters and blend into a common hue? Yet you must have known something of the presentiments that spring from an insight at war with passion; and my visions were only like presentiments intensified to horror. You have known the powerlessness of ideas before the might of impulse; and my visions, when once they had passed into memory, were mere ideas—pale shadows that beckoned in vain, while my hand was grasped by the living and the loved.

In after-days I thought with bitter regret that if I had foreseen something more or something different—if instead of that hideous vision, which poisoned the passion it could not destroy, or if even along with it I could have had a foreshadowing of that moment when I looked on my brother's face for the last time, some softening influence would have been shed over my feeling towards him: pride and hatred would surely have been subdued into pity, and the record of those hidden sins would have been shortened. But this is one of the vain thoughts with which we men flatter ourselves. We try to believe that the egoism within us would have easily been melted, and that it was only the narrowness of our knowledge which hemmed in our generosity, our awe, our human piety, and hindered them from submerging our hard indifference to the sensations and emotions of our fellows. Our tenderness and self-renunciation seem strong when our egoism has had its day—when, after our mean striving for a triumph that is to be another's loss, the triumph comes suddenly, and we shudder at it, because it is held out by the chill hand of death.

Our arrival in Prague happened at night, and I was glad of this, for it seemed like a deferring of a terribly decisive moment, to be in the city for hours without seeing it. As we were not to remain long in Prague, but to go on speedily to Dresden, it was proposed that we should drive out the next morning and take a general view of the place, as well as visit some of its specially interesting spots, before the heat became oppressive—for we were in August, and the season was hot and dry. But it happened that the ladies were rather late at their morning toilet, and to my father's politely-repressed but perceptible annoyance, we were not in the carriage till the morning was far advanced. I thought with a sense of relief, as we entered the Jews' quarter, where we were to visit the old synagogue,* that we should be kept in this flat, shut-up part of the city, until we should all be too tired and too warm to go farther, and so we should return without seeing more than the streets through which we had already passed. That would give me another day's suspense—suspense, the only form in which a fearful spirit knows the solace of hope. But, as I stood under the blackened, groined arches of that old synagogue, made dimly visible by the seven thin candles in the sacred lamp, while our Jewish cicerone† reached down the Book of the Law, and read to us in its ancient tongue—I felt a shuddering impression that this strange building, with its shrunken lights, this surviving withered remnant of medieval Judaism, was of a piece with my vision. Those darkened dusty Christian saints, with their loftier arches and their larger candles, needed the consolatory scorn with which they might point to a more shrivelled death-in-life than their own.

As I expected, when we left the Jews' quarter the elders of our party wished to return to the hotel. But now, instead of rejoicing in this, as I had done beforehand, I felt a sudden overpowering impulse to go on at once to the bridge, and put an end to the suspense I had been wishing to protract. I declared, with unusual decision, that I would get out of the carriage and walk on alone; they might return without me. My father, thinking this merely a sample of my usual "poetic nonsense," objected that I should only do myself harm by walking in the heat; but when I persisted, he said angrily that I might follow my own absurd devices, but that Schmidt (our courier) must go with me. I assented to this, and set off with Schmidt towards the bridge. I had no sooner passed from under the archway of the grand old gate leading on to the bridge, than a trembling seized me, and I turned cold under the midday sun; yet I went on; I was in search of something—a small detail, which I remembered with special intensity as part of my vision. There it was—the patch of rainbow light on the pavement transmitted through a lamp in the shape of a star.

---

* "The Lifted Veil" was inspired by the author's own visit to the synagogue in Prague.

† A guide or docent.

CHAPTER II

Before the autumn was at an end, and while the brown leaves still stood thick on the beeches in our park, my brother and Bertha were engaged to each other, and it was understood that their marriage was to take place early in the next spring. In spite of the certainty I had felt from that moment on the bridge at Prague, that Bertha would one day be my wife, my constitutional timidity and distrust had continued to benumb me, and the words in which I had sometimes premeditated a confession of my love, had died away unuttered. The same conflict had gone on within me as before—the longing for an assurance of love from Bertha's lips, the dread lest a word of contempt and denial should fall upon me like a corrosive acid. What was the conviction of a distant necessity to me? I trembled under a present glance, I hungered after a present joy, I was clogged and chilled by a present fear. And so the days passed on: I witnessed Bertha's engagement and heard her marriage discussed as if I were under a conscious nightmare—knowing it was a dream that would vanish, but feeling stifled under the grasp of hard-clutching fingers.

When I was not in Bertha's presence—and I was with her very often, for she continued to treat me with a playful patronage that wakened no jealousy in my brother—I spent my time chiefly in wandering, in strolling, or taking long rides while the daylight lasted, and then shutting myself up with my unread books; for books had lost the power of chaining my attention. My self-consciousness was heightened to that pitch of intensity in which our own emotions take the form of a drama which urges itself imperatively on our contemplation, and we begin to weep, less under the sense of our suffering than at the thought of it. I felt a sort of pitying anguish over the pathos of my own lot: the lot of a being finely organized for pain, but with hardly any fibres that responded to pleasure—to whom the idea of future evil robbed the present of its joy, and for whom the idea of future good did not still the uneasiness of a present yearning or a present dread. I went dumbly through that stage of the poet's suffering, in which he feels the delicious pang of utterance, and makes an image of his sorrows.

I was left entirely without remonstrance concerning this dreamy wayward life: I knew my father's thought about me: "That lad will never be good for anything in life: he may waste his years in an insignificant way on the income that falls to him: I shall not trouble myself about a career for him."

One mild morning in the beginning of November, it happened that I was standing outside the portico patting lazy old Cæsar, a Newfoundland almost blind with age, the only dog that ever took any notice of me—for the very dogs shunned me, and fawned on the happier people about me—when the groom brought up my brother's horse which was to carry him to the hunt, and my brother himself appeared at the door, florid, broad-chested, and self-complacent, feeling what a good-natured fellow he was not to behave insolently to us all on the strength of his great advantages.

"Latimer, old boy," he said to me in a tone of compassionate cordiality, "what a pity it is you don't have a run with the hounds now and then! The finest thing in the world for low spirits!"

"Low spirits!" I thought bitterly, as he rode away; "that is the sort of phrase with which coarse, narrow natures like yours think to describe experience of which you can know no more than your horse knows. It is to such as you that the good of this world falls: ready dulness, healthy selfishness, good-tempered conceit—these are the keys to happiness."

The quick thought came, that my selfishness was even stronger than his—it was only a suffering selfishness instead of an enjoying one. But then, again, my exasperating insight into Alfred's self-complacent soul, his freedom from all the doubts and fears, the unsatisfied yearnings, the exquisite tortures of sensitiveness, that had made the web of my life, seemed to absolve me from all bonds towards him. This man needed no pity, no love; those fine influences would have been as little felt by him as the delicate white mist is felt by the rock it caresses. There was no evil in store for *him*: if he was not to marry Bertha, it would be because he had found a lot pleasanter to himself.

Mr. Filmore's house lay not more than half a mile beyond our own gates, and whenever I knew my brother was gone in another direction, I went there for the chance of finding Bertha at home. Later on in the day I walked thither. By a rare accident she was alone, and we walked out in the grounds together, for she seldom went on foot beyond the trimly-swept gravel-walks. I remember what a beautiful sylph she looked to me as the low November sun shone on her blond hair, and she tripped along teasing me with her usual light banter, to which I listened half fondly, half moodily; it was all the sign Bertha's mysterious inner self ever made to me. To-day perhaps, the moodiness predominated, for I had not yet shaken off the access of jealous hate, which my brother had raised in me by his parting patronage. Suddenly I interrupted and startled her by saying, almost fiercely, "Bertha, how can you love Alfred?"

She looked at me with surprise for a moment, but soon her light smile came again, and she answered sarcastically, "Why do you suppose I love him?"

"How can you ask that, Bertha?"

"What! your wisdom thinks I must love the man I'm going to marry? The most unpleasant thing in the world. I should quarrel with him; I should be jealous of him; our *ménage* would be conducted in a very ill-bred manner. A little quiet contempt contributes greatly to the elegance of life."

"Bertha, that is not your real feeling. Why do you delight in trying to deceive me by inventing such cynical speeches?"

"I need never take the trouble of invention in order to deceive you, my small Tasso," (that was the mocking name she usually gave me). "The easiest way to deceive a poet is to tell him the truth."

She was testing the validity of her epigram in a daring way, and for a moment the shadow of my vision—the Bertha whose soul was no secret to me—passed between me and the radiant girl, the playful sylph whose feelings were a fascinating mystery. I suppose I must have shuddered, or betrayed in some other way my momentary chill of horror.

"Tasso!" she said, seizing my wrist, and peeping round into my face, "are you really beginning to discern what a heartless girl I am? Why, you are not half the poet I thought you were; you are actually capable of believing the truth about me."

The shadow passed from between us, and was no longer the object nearest to me. The girl whose light fingers grasped me, whose elfish charming face looked into mine—who, I thought, was betraying an interest in my feelings that she would not have directly avowed,—this warm breathing presence again possessed my senses and imagination like a returning siren melody which had been overpowered for an instant by the roar of threatening waves. It was a moment as delicious to me as the waking up to a consciousness of youth after a dream of middle age. I forgot everything but my passion, and said with swimming eyes—

"Bertha, shall you love me when we are first married? I wouldn't mind if you really loved me only for a little while."

Her look of astonishment, as she loosed my hand and started away from me, recalled me to a sense of my strange, my criminal indiscretion.

"Forgive me," I said, hurriedly, as soon as I could speak again; "I did not know what I was saying."

"Ah, Tasso's mad fit has come on, I see," she answered quietly, for she had recovered herself sooner than I had. "Let him go home and keep his head cool. I must go in, for the sun is setting."

I left her—full of indignation against myself. I had let slip words, which, if she reflected on them, might rouse in her a suspicion of my abnormal mental condition—a suspicion which of all things I dreaded. And besides that, I was ashamed of the apparent baseness I had committed in uttering them to my brother's betrothed wife. I wandered home slowly, entering our park through a private gate instead of by the lodges. As I approached the house, I saw a man dashing off at full speed from the stable-yard across the park. Had any accident happened at home? No; perhaps it was only one of my father's peremptory business errands that required this headlong haste.

Nevertheless I quickened my pace without any distinct motive, and was soon at the house. I will not dwell on the scene I found there. My brother was dead—had been pitched from his horse, and killed on the spot by a concussion of the brain.

I went up to the room where he lay, and where my father was seated beside him with a look of rigid despair. I had shunned my father more than any one since our return home, for the radical antipathy between our natures made my insight into his inner self a constant affliction to me. But now, as I went up to him, and stood beside him in sad silence, I felt the presence of a new element that blended us as we had never been blent before. My father had been one of the most successful men in the money-getting world: he had had no sentimental sufferings, no illness. The heaviest trouble that had befallen him was the death of his first wife. But he married my mother soon after; and I remember he seemed exactly the same, to my keen childish observation, the week after her death as before. But now, at last, a sorrow had come—the sorrow of old age, which suffers the more from the crushing of its pride and its hopes, in proportion as the pride and hope are narrow and prosaic. His son was to have been married soon—would probably have stood for the borough at the next election. That son's existence was the best motive that could be alleged for making new purchases of land every year to round off the estate. It is a dreary thing to live on doing the same things year after year, without knowing why we do them. Perhaps the tragedy of disappointed youth and passion is less piteous than the tragedy of disappointed age and worldliness.

As I saw into the desolation of my father's heart, I felt a movement of deep pity towards him, which was the beginning of a new affection—an affection that grew and strengthened in spite of the strange bitterness with which he regarded me in the first month or two after my brother's death. If it had not been for the softening influence of my compassion for him—the first deep compassion I had ever felt—I should have been stung by the perception that my father transferred the inheritance of an eldest son to me with a mortified sense that fate had compelled him to the unwelcome course of caring for me as an important being. It was only in spite of himself that he began to think of me with anxious regard. There is hardly any neglected child for whom death has made vacant a more favoured place, who will not understand what I mean.

Gradually, however, my new deference to his wishes, the effect of that patience which was born of my pity for him, won upon his affection, and he began to please himself with the endeavour to make me fill my brother's place as fully as my feebler personality would admit. I saw that the prospect which by and by presented itself of my becoming Bertha's husband was welcome to him, and he even contemplated in my case what he had not intended in my brother's—that his son and daughter-in-law should make one household with him. My softened feelings towards my father made this the happiest time I had known since childhood;—these last months in which I retained the delicious illusion of loving Bertha, of longing and doubting and hoping that she might love me. She behaved with a certain new consciousness and distance towards me after my brother's death; and I too was under a double constraint—that of delicacy towards my brother's memory and of anxiety as to the impression my abrupt words had left on her mind. But the additional screen this mutual reserve erected between us only brought me more completely under her power: no matter how empty the adytum,* so that the veil be thick enough. So absolute is our soul's need of something hidden and uncertain for the maintenance of that doubt and hope and effort, which are the breath of its life, that if the whole future were laid bare to us beyond to-day, the interest of all mankind would be bent on the hours that lie between; we should pant after the uncertainties of our one morning and our one afternoon; we should rush fiercely to the Exchange for our last possibility of speculation, of success, of disappointment: we should have a glut of political prophets foretelling a crisis or a no-crisis within the only twenty-four hours left open to prophecy. Conceive the condition of the human mind if all propositions whatsoever were self-evident except one, which was to become self-evident at the close of a summer's day, but in the meantime might be the subject of question, of hypothesis, of debate. Art and philosophy, literature and science, would fasten like bees on that one proposition which had the honey of probability in it, and be the more eager because their enjoyment would end with sunset. Our impulses, our spiritual activities, no more adjust themselves to the idea of their future nullity, than the beating of our heart, or the irritability of our muscles.

Bertha, the slim, fair-haired girl, whose present thoughts and emotions were an enigma to me amidst the fatiguing obviousness of the other minds around me, was as absorbing to me as a single unknown to-day—as a single hypothetic proposition to remain problematic till sunset; and all the cramped, hemmed-in belief and disbelief, trust and distrust, of my nature, welled out in this one narrow channel.

And she made me believe that she loved me. Without ever quitting her tone of *badinage* and playful superiority, she intoxicated me with the sense that I was necessary to her, that she was never at ease, unless I was near her, submitting to her playful tyranny. It costs a woman so little effort to beset us in this way! A half-repressed word, a moment's unexpected silence, even an easy fit of petulance on our account, will serve us as *hashish* for a long while. Out of the subtlest web of scarcely perceptible signs, she set me

---

* The innermost or hidden sanctuary in an ancient Greek temple.

weaving the fancy that she had always unconsciously loved me better than Alfred, but that, with the ignorant fluttered sensibility of a young girl, she had been imposed on by the charm that lay for her in the distinction of being admired and chosen by a man who made so brilliant a figure in the world as my brother. She satirized herself in a very graceful way for her vanity and ambition. What was it to me that I had the light of my wretched provision on the fact that now it was I who possessed at least all but the personal part of my brother's advantages? Our sweet illusions are half of them conscious illusions, like effects of colour that we know to be made up of tinsel, broken glass, and rags.

We were married eighteen months after Alfred's death, one cold, clear morning in April, when there came hail and sunshine both together; and Bertha, in her white silk and pale-green leaves, and the pale hues of her hair and face, looked like the spirit of the morning. My father was happier than he had thought of being again: my marriage, he felt sure, would complete the desirable modification of my character, and make me practical and worldly enough to take my place in society among sane men. For he delighted in Bertha's tact and acuteness, and felt sure she would be mistress of me, and make me what she chose: I was only twenty-one, and madly in love with her. Poor father! He kept that hope a little while after our first year of marriage, and it was not quite extinct when paralysis came and saved him from utter disappointment.

I shall hurry through the rest of my story, not dwelling so much as I have hitherto done on my inward experience. When people are well-known to each other, they talk rather of what befalls them externally, leaving their feelings and sentiments to be inferred.

We lived in a round of visits for some time after our return home, giving splendid dinner-parties, and making a sensation in our neighbourhood by the new lustre of our equipage, for my father had reserved this display of his increased wealth for the period of his son's marriage; and we gave our acquaintances liberal opportunity for remarking that it was a pity I made so poor a figure as an heir and a bridegroom. The nervous fatigue of this existence, the insincerities and platitudes, which I had to live through twice over—through my inner and outward sense—would have been maddening to me, if I had not had that sort of intoxicated callousness, which came from the delights of a first passion. A bride and bridegroom, surrounded by all the appliances of wealth, hurried through the day by the whirl of society, filling their solitary moments with hastily-snatched caresses, are prepared for their future life together as the novice is prepared for the cloister—by experiencing its utmost contrast.

Through all these crowded excited months, Bertha's inward self remained shrouded from me, and I still read her thoughts only through the language of her lips and demeanour: I had still the human interest of wondering whether what I did and said pleased her, of longing to hear a word of affection, of giving a delicious exaggeration of meaning to her smile. But I was conscious of a growing difference in her manner towards me; sometimes strong enough to be called haughty coldness, cutting and chilling me as the hail had done that came across the sunshine on our marriage morning; sometimes only perceptible in the dexterous avoidance of a *tête-à-tête* walk or dinner to which I had been looking forward. I had been deeply pained by this—had even felt a sort of crushing of the heart, from the sense that my brief day of happiness was near its setting; but still I remained dependent on Bertha, eager for the last rays of a bliss that would soon be gone for ever, hoping and watching for some after-glow more beautiful from the impending night.

I remember—how should I not remember?—the time when that dependence and hope utterly left me, when the sadness I had felt in Bertha's growing estrangement became a joy that I looked back upon with longing as a man might look back on the last pains in a paralysed limb. It was just after the close of my father's last illness, which had necessarily withdrawn us from society and thrown us more on each other. It was the evening of father's death. On that evening the veil which had shrouded Bertha's soul from me—had made me find in her alone among my fellow-beings the blessed possibility of mystery, and doubt, and expectation—was first withdrawn. Perhaps it was the first day since the beginning of my passion for her, in which that passion was completely neutralized by the presence of an absorbing feeling of another kind. I had been watching by my father's deathbed: I had been witnessing the last fitful yearning glance his soul had cast back on the spent inheritance of life—the last faint consciousness of love he had gathered from the pressure of my hand. What are all our personal loves when we have been sharing in that supreme agony? In the first moments when we come away from the presence of death, every other relation to the living is merged, to our feeling, in the great relation of a common nature and a common destiny.

In that state of mind I joined Bertha in her private sitting-room. She was seated in a leaning posture on a settee, with her back towards the door; the great rich coils of her pale blond hair surmounting her small neck, visible above the back of the settee. I remember, as I closed the door behind me, a cold tremulousness seizing me, and a vague sense of being hated and lonely—vague and strong, like a presentiment. I know how I looked at that moment, for I saw myself in Bertha's thought as she lifted her cutting grey eyes, and looked at me: a miserable ghost-seer, surrounded by phantoms in the noonday, trembling under a breeze when the leaves were still, without appetite for the common objects of human desires, but pining after the moon-beams. We were front to front with each other, and judged each other. The terrible moment of complete illumination had come to me, and I saw that the darkness had hidden no landscape from me, but only a blank prosaic wall: from that evening forth, through the sickening years which followed, I saw all round the narrow room of this woman's soul—saw petty artifice and mere negation where I had delighted to believe in coy sensibilities and in wit at war with latent feeling—saw the light floating vanities of the girl defining themselves into the systematic coquetry, the scheming selfishness, of the woman—saw repulsion and antipathy harden into cruel hatred, giving pain only for the sake of wreaking itself.

For Bertha, too, after her kind, felt the bitterness of disillusion. She had believed that my wild poet's passion for her would make me her slave; and that, being her slave, I should execute her will in all things. With the essential shallowness of a negative, unimaginative nature, she was unable to conceive the fact that sensibilities were anything else than weaknesses. She had thought my weaknesses would put me in her power, and she found them unmanageable forces. Our positions were reversed. Before marriage she had completely mastered my imagination, for she was a secret to me; and I created the unknown thought before which I trembled as if it were hers. But now that her soul was laid open to me, now that I was compelled to share the privacy of her motives, to follow all the petty devices that preceded her words and acts, she found herself powerless with me, except to produce in me the chill shudder of repulsion—powerless, because I could be acted on by no lever within her reach. I was dead to worldly ambitions, to social vanities, to all the incentives within the compass of her narrow imagination, and I lived under influences utterly invisible to her.

She was really pitiable to have such a husband, and so all the world thought. A graceful, brilliant woman, like Bertha, who smiled on morning callers, made a figure in ball-rooms, and was capable of that light repartee, which, from such a woman, is accepted as wit, was secure of carrying off all sympathy from a husband who was sickly, abstracted, and, as some suspected, crack-brained. Even the servants in our house gave her the balance of their regard and pity. For there were no audible quarrels between us; our alienation, our repulsion from each other, lay within the silence of our own hearts; and if the mistress went out a great deal, and seemed to dislike the master's society, was it not natural, poor thing? The master was odd. I was kind and just to my dependents, but I excited in them a shrinking, half-contemptuous pity; for this class of men and women are but slightly determined in their estimate of others by general considerations, or even experience, of character. They judge of persons as they judge of coins, and value those who pass current at a high rate.

After a time I interfered so little with Bertha's habits that it might seem wonderful how her hatred towards me could grow so intense and active as it did. But she had begun to suspect, by some involuntary betrayal of mine, that there was an abnormal power of penetration in me—that fitfully, at least, I was strangely cognizant of her thoughts and intentions, and she began to be haunted by a terror of me, which alternated every now and then with defiance. She meditated continually how the incubus could be shaken off her life—how she could be freed from this hateful bond to a being whom she at once despised as an imbecile, and dreaded as an inquisitor. For a long while she lived in the hope that my evident wretchedness would drive me to the commission of suicide; but suicide was not in my nature. I was too completely swayed by the sense that I was in the grasp of unknown forces, to believe in my power of self-release. Towards my own destiny I had become entirely passive; for my one ardent desire had spent itself, and impulse no longer predominated over knowledge. For this reason I never thought of taking any steps towards a complete separation, which would have made our alienation evident to the world. Why should I rush for help to a new course, when I was only suffering from the consequences of a deed which had been the act of my intensest will? That would have been the logic of one who had desires to gratify, and I had no desires. But Bertha and I lived more and more aloof from each other. The rich find it easy to live married and apart.

That course of our life, which I have indicated in a few sentences, filled the space of years. So much misery—so slow and hideous a growth of hatred and sin, may be compressed into a sentence! And men judge of each other's lives through this summary medium. They epitomize the experience of their fellow-mortal, and pronounce judgment on him in neat syntax, and feel themselves wise and virtuous—conquerors over the temptations they define in well-selected predicates. Seven years of wretchedness glide glibly over the lips of the man who has never counted them out in moments of chill disappointment, of head and heart throbbings, of dread and vain wrestling, of remorse and despair. We learn *words* by rote, but not their meaning; *that* must be paid for with our life-blood, and printed in the subtle fibres of our nerves.

But I will hasten to finish my story. Brevity is justified at once to those who readily understand, and to those who will never understand.

Some years after my father's death, I was sitting by the dim firelight in my library one January evening—sitting in the leather chair that used to be my father's—when Bertha appeared at the door, with a candle in her hand, and advanced towards me. I knew the ball-dress she had on—the white ball-dress, with the green jewels, shone upon by the light of the wax candle, which lit up the medallion of the dying Cleopatra on the mantel-piece. Why did she come to me before going out? I had not seen her in the library, which was my habitual place for months. Why did she stand before me with the candle in her hand, with her cruel contemptuous eyes fixed on me, and the glittering serpent, like a familiar demon, on her breast? For a moment I thought this fulfilment of my vision at Vienna marked some dreadful crisis in my fate, but I saw nothing in Bertha's mind, as she stood before me, except scorn for the look of overwhelming misery with which I sat before her. . . . "Fool, idiot, why don't you kill yourself, then?"—that was her thought. But at length her thoughts reverted to her errand, and she spoke aloud. The apparently indifferent nature of the errand seemed to make a ridiculous anticlimax to my prevision and my agitation.

"I have had to hire a new maid. Fletcher is going to be married, and she wants me to ask you to let her husband have the public-house and farm at Molton. I wish him to have it. You must give the promise now, because Fletcher is going to-morrow morning—and quickly, because I'm in a hurry."

"Very well; you may promise her," I said, indifferently, and Bertha swept out of the library again.

I always shrank from the sight of a new person, and all the more when it was a person whose mental life was likely to weary my reluctant insight with worldly ignorant trivialities. But I shrank especially from the sight of this new maid, because her advent had been announced to me at a moment to which I could not cease to attach some fatality: I had a vague dread that I should find her mixed up with the dreary drama of my life—that some new sickening vision would reveal her to me as an evil genius. When at last I did unavoidably meet her, the vague dread was changed into definite disgust. She was a tall, wiry, dark-eyed woman, this Mrs. Archer, with a face handsome enough to give her coarse hard nature the odious finish of bold, self-confident coquetry. That was enough to make me avoid her, quite apart from the contemptuous feeling with which she contemplated me. I seldom saw her; but I perceived that she rapidly became a favourite with her mistress, and, after the lapse of eight or nine months, I began to be aware that there had arisen in Bertha's mind towards this woman a mingled feeling of fear and dependence, and that this feeling was associated with ill-defined images of candle-light scenes in her dressing-room, and the locking-up of something in Bertha's cabinet. My interviews with my wife had become so brief and so rarely solitary, that I had no opportunity of perceiving these images in her mind with more definiteness. The recollections of the past become contracted in the rapidity of thought till they sometimes bear hardly a more distinct resemblance to the external reality than the forms of an oriental alphabet to the objects that suggested them.

Besides, for the last year or more a modification had been going forward in my mental condition, and was growing more and more marked. My insight into the minds of those around me was becoming dimmer and more fitful, and the ideas that crowded my double consciousness became less and less dependent on any personal contact. All that was personal in me seemed to be suffering a gradual death, so that I was losing the organ through which the personal agitations and projects of others could affect me. But along with this relief from wearisome insight, there was a new development of what I concluded—as I have since found rightly—to be a provision of external scenes. It was as if the relation between me and my fellow-men was more and more deadened, and my relation to what we call the inanimate was quickened into new life. The more I lived apart from society, and in proportion as my wretchedness subsided from the violent throb of agonized passion into the dulness of habitual pain, the more frequent and vivid became such visions as that I had had of Prague—of strange cities, of sandy plains, of gigantic ruins, of midnight skies with strange bright constellations, of mountain-passes, of grassy nooks flecked with the afternoon sunshine through the boughs: I was in the midst of such scenes, and in all of them one presence seemed to weigh on me in all these mighty shapes—the presence of something unknown and pitiless. For continual suffering had annihilated religious faith within me: to the utterly miserable—the unloving and the unloved—there is no religion possible, no worship but a worship of devils. And beyond all these, and continually recurring, was the vision of my death—the pangs, the suffocation, the last struggle, when life would be grasped at in vain.

Things were in this state near the end of the seventh year. I had become entirely free from insight, from my abnormal cognizance of any other consciousness than my own, and instead of intruding involuntarily into the world of other minds, was living continually in my own solitary future. Bertha was aware that I was greatly changed. To my surprise she had of late seemed to seek opportunities of remaining in my society, and had cultivated that kind of distant yet familiar talk, which is customary between a husband and wife who live in polite and irrevocable alienation. I bore this with languid submission, and without feeling enough interest in her motives to be roused into keen observation; yet I could not help perceiving something triumphant and excited in her carriage and the expression of her face—something too subtle to express itself in words or tones, but giving one the idea that she lived in a state of expectation or hopeful suspense.

My chief feeling was satisfaction that her inner self was once more shut out from me; and I almost revelled for the moment in the absent melancholy that made me answer her at cross purposes, and betray utter ignorance of what she had been saying. I remember well the look and the smile with which she one day said, after a mistake of this kind on my part: "I used to think you were a clairvoyant, and that was the reason why you were so bitter against other clairvoyants, wanting to keep your monopoly; but I see now you have become rather duller than the rest of the world."

I said nothing in reply. It occurred to me that her recent obtrusion of herself upon me might have been prompted by the wish to test my power of detecting some of her secrets; but I let the thought drop again at once: her motives and her deeds had no interest for me, and whatever pleasures she might be seeking, I had no wish to baulk her. There was still pity in my soul for every living thing, and Bertha was living—was surrounded with possibilities of misery.

Just at this time there occurred an event which roused me somewhat from my inertia, and gave me an interest in the passing moment that I had thought impossible for me. It was a visit from Charles Meunier, who had written me word that he was coming to England for relaxation from too strenuous labour, and would like to see me. Meunier had now a European reputation; but his letter to me expressed that keen remembrance of an early regard, an early debt of sympathy, which is inseparable from nobility of character: and I too felt as if his presence would be to me like a transient resurrection into a happier pre-existence.

He came, and as far as possible, I renewed our old pleasure of making *tête-à-tête* excursions, though, instead of mountains and glaciers and the wide blue lake, we had to content ourselves with mere slopes and ponds and artificial plantations. The years had changed us both, but with what different result! Meunier was now a brilliant figure in society, to whom elegant women pretended to listen, and whose acquaintance was boasted of by noblemen ambitious of brains. He repressed with the utmost delicacy all betrayal of the shock which I am sure he must have received from our meeting, or of a desire to penetrate into my condition and circumstances, and sought by the utmost exertion of his charming social powers to make our reunion agreeable. Bertha was much struck by the unexpected fascinations of a visitor whom she had expected to find presentable only on the score of his celebrity, and put forth all her coquetries and accomplishments. Apparently she succeeded in attracting his admiration, for his manner towards her was attentive and flattering. The effect of his presence on me was so benignant, especially in those renewals of our old *tête-à-tête* wanderings, when he poured forth to me wonderful narratives of his professional experience, that more than once, when his talk turned on the psychological relations of disease, the thought crossed my mind that, if his stay with me were long enough, I might possibly bring myself to tell this man the secrets of my lot. Might there not lie some remedy for me, too, in his science? Might there not at least lie some comprehension and sympathy ready for me in his large and susceptible mind? But the thought only flickered feebly now and then, and died out before it could become a wish. The horror I had of again breaking in on the privacy of another soul, made me, by an irrational instinct, draw the shroud of concealment more closely around my own, as we automatically perform the gesture we feel to be wanting in another.

When Meunier's visit was approaching its conclusion, there happened an event which caused some excitement in our household, owing to the surprisingly strong effect it appeared to produce on Bertha—on Bertha, the self-possessed, who usually seemed inaccessible to feminine agitations, and did even her hate in a self-restrained hygienic manner. This event was the sudden severe illness of her maid, Mrs. Archer. I have reserved to this moment the mention of a circumstance which had forced itself on my notice shortly before Meunier's arrival, namely, that there had been some quarrel between Bertha and this maid, apparently during a visit to a distant family, in which she had accompanied her mistress. I had overheard Archer speaking in a tone of bitter insolence, which I should have thought an adequate reason for immediate dismissal. No dismissal followed; on the contrary, Bertha seemed to be silently putting up with personal inconveniences from the exhibitions of this woman's temper. I was the more astonished to observe that her illness seemed a cause of strong solicitude to Bertha; that she was at the bedside night and day, and would allow no one else to officiate as head-nurse. It happened that our family doctor was out on a holiday, an accident which made Meunier's presence in the house doubly welcome, and he apparently entered into the case with an interest, which seemed so much stronger than the ordinary professional feeling, that one day when he had fallen into a long fit of silence after visiting her, I said to him—

"Is this a very peculiar case of disease, Meunier?"

"No," he answered, "it is an attack of peritonitis, which will be fatal, but which does not differ physically from many other cases that have come under my observation. But I'll tell you what I have on my mind. I want to make an experiment on this woman, if you will give me permission. It can do her no harm—will give her no pain—for I shall not make it until life is extinct to all purposes of sensation. I want to try the effect of transfusing blood into her arteries after the heart has ceased to beat for some minutes. I have tried the experiment again and again with animals that have died of this disease, with astounding results, and I want to try it on a human subject. I have the small tubes necessary, in a case I have with me, and the rest of the apparatus could be prepared readily. I should use my own blood—take it from my own arm. This woman won't live through the night, I'm convinced, and I want you to promise me your assistance in making the experiment. I can't do without another hand, but it would perhaps not be well to call in a medical assistant from among your provincial doctors. A disagreeable foolish version of the thing might get abroad."

"Have you spoken to my wife on the subject?" I said, "because she appears to be peculiarly sensitive about this woman: she has been a favourite maid."

"To tell you the truth," said Meunier, "I don't want her to know about it. There are always insuperable difficulties with women in these matters, and the effect on the supposed dead body may be startling. You and I will sit up together, and be in readiness. When certain symptoms appear I shall take you in, and at the right moment we must manage to get every one else out of the room."

I need not give our farther conversation on the subject. He entered very fully into the details, and overcame my repulsion from them, by exciting in me a mingled awe and curiosity concerning the possible results of his experiment.

We prepared everything, and he instructed me in my part as assistant. He had not told Bertha of his absolute conviction that Archer would not survive through the night, and endeavoured to persuade her to leave the patient and take a night's rest. But she was obstinate, suspecting the fact that death was at hand, and supposing that he wished merely to save her nerves. She refused to leave the sick-room. Meunier and I sat up together in the library, he making frequent visits to the sick-room, and returning with the information that the case was taking precisely the course he expected. Once he said to me, "Can you imagine any cause of ill-feeling this woman has against her mistress, who is so devoted to her?"

"I think there was some misunderstanding between them before her illness. Why do you ask?"

"Because I have observed for the last five or six hours—since, I fancy, she has lost all hope of recovery—there seems a strange prompting in her to say something, which pain and failing strength forbid her to utter; and there is a look of hideous meaning in her eyes, which she turns continually towards her mistress. In this disease the mind often remains singularly clear to the last."

"I am not surprised at an indication of malevolent feeling in her," I said. "She is a woman who has always inspired me with distrust and dislike, but she managed to insinuate herself into her mistress's favour." He was silent after this, looking at the fire with an air of absorption, till he went upstairs again. He stayed away longer than usual, and on returning, said to me quietly, "Come now."

I followed him to the chamber where death was hovering. The dark hangings of the large bed made a background that gave a strong relief to Bertha's pale face as I entered. She started forward as she saw me enter, and then looked at Meunier with an expression of angry inquiry; but he lifted up his hand as it to impose silence, while he fixed his glance on the dying woman and felt her pulse. The face was pinched and ghastly, a cold perspiration was on the forehead, and the eyelids were lowered so as to conceal the large dark eyes. After a minute or two, Meunier walked round to the other side of the bed where Bertha stood, and with his usual air of gentle politeness towards her begged her to leave the patient under our care—everything should be done for her—she was no longer in a state to be conscious of an affectionate presence. Bertha was hesitating, apparently almost willing to believe his assurance and to comply. She looked round at the ghastly dying face, as if to read the confirmation of that assurance, when for a moment the lowered eyelids were raised again, and it seemed as if the eyes were looking towards Bertha, but blankly. A shudder passed through Bertha's frame, and she returned to her station near the pillow, tacitly implying that she would not leave the room.

The eyelids were lifted no more. Once I looked at Bertha as she watched the face of the dying one. She wore a rich *peignoir*, and her blond hair was half covered by a lace cap: in her attire she was, as always, an elegant woman, fit to figure in a picture of modern aristocratic life: but I asked myself how that face of hers could ever have seemed to me the face of a woman born of woman, with memories of childhood, capable of pain, needing to be fondled? The features at that moment seemed so preternaturally sharp, the eyes were so hard and eager—she looked like a cruel immortal, finding her spiritual feast in the agonies of a dying race. For across those hard features there came something like a flash when the last hour had been breathed out, and we all felt that the dark veil had completely fallen. What secret was there between Bertha and this woman? I turned my eyes from her with a horrible dread lest my insight should return, and I should be obliged to see what had been breeding about two unloving women's hearts. I felt that Bertha had been watching for the moment of death as the sealing of her secret: I thanked Heaven it could remain sealed for me.

Meunier said quietly, "She is gone." He then gave his arm to Bertha, and she submitted to be led out of the room.

I suppose it was at her order that two female attendants came into the room, and dismissed the younger one who had been present before. When they entered, Meunier had already opened the artery in the long thin neck that lay rigid on the pillow, and I dismissed them, ordering them to remain at a distance till we rang: the doctor, I said, had an operation to perform—he was not sure about the death. For the next twenty minutes I forgot everything but Meunier and the experiment in which he was so absorbed, that I think his senses would have been closed against all sounds or sights which had no relation to it. It was my task at first to keep up the artificial respiration in the body after the transfusion had been effected, but presently Meunier relieved me, and I could see the wondrous slow return of life; the breast began to heave, the inspirations became stronger, the eyelids quivered, and the soul seemed to have returned beneath them. The artificial respiration was withdrawn: still the breathing continued, and there was a movement of the lips.

Just then I heard the handle of the door moving: I suppose Bertha had heard from the women that they had been dismissed: probably a vague fear had arisen in her mind, for she entered with a look of alarm. She came to the foot of the bed and gave a stifled cry.

The dead woman's eyes were wide open, and met hers in full recognition—the recognition of hate. With a sudden strong effort, the hand that Bertha had thought for ever still was pointed towards her, and the haggard face moved. The gasping eager voice said—

"You mean to poison your husband . . . the poison is in the black cabinet . . . I got it for you . . . you laughed at me, and told lies about me behind my back, to make me disgusting . . . because you were jealous . . . are you sorry . . . now?"

The lips continued to murmur, but the sounds were no longer distinct. Soon there was no sound—only a slight movement: the flame had leaped out, and was being extinguished the faster. The wretched woman's heart-strings had been set to hatred and vengeance; the spirit of life had swept the chords for an instant, and was gone again for ever. Great God! Is this what it is to live again . . . to wake up with our unstilled thirst upon us, with our unuttered curses rising to our lips, with our muscles ready to act out their half-committed sins?

Bertha stood pale at the foot of the bed, quivering and helpless, despairing of devices, like a cunning animal whose hiding-places are surrounded by swift-advancing flame. Even Meunier looked paralysed; life for that moment ceased to be a scientific problem to him. As for me, this scene seemed of one texture with the rest of my existence: horror was my familiar, and this new revelation was only like an old pain recurring with new circumstances. *

---

* The editor John Blackwood, who first published this story in his *Blackwood's Magazine*, found the revivification of Mrs. Archer out of step with the rest of the story and even urged the author to consider deleting it.

Since then Bertha and I have lived apart—she in her own neighbourhood, the mistress of half our wealth, I as a wanderer in foreign countries, until I came to this Devonshire nest to die. Bertha lives pitied and admired; for what had I against that charming woman, whom every one but myself could have been happy with? There had been no witness of the scene in the dying room except Meunier, and while Meunier lived his lips were sealed by a promise to me.

Once or twice, weary of wandering, I rested in a favourite spot, and my heart went out towards the men and women and children whose faces were becoming familiar to me; but I was driven away again in terror at the approach of my old insight—driven away to live continually with the one Unknown Presence revealed and yet hidden by the moving curtain of the earth and sky. Till at last disease took hold of me and forced me to rest here—forced me to live in dependence on my servants. And then the curse of insight—of my double consciousness, came again, and has never left me. I know all their narrow thoughts, their feeble regard, their half-wearied pity.

It is the 20th of September, 1850. I know these figures I have just written, as if they were a long familiar inscription. I have seen them on this pace in my desk unnumbered times, when the scene of my dying struggle has opened upon me . . .

If George Eliot was the late-nineteenth-century cause célèbre of England, **Harriet Beecher Stowe** was surely her American equivalent. In 1851, at the age of forty, the first magazine installment of her 1852 novel *Uncle Tom's Cabin* was published; the novel portrayed slavery in a more realistic light and created a sensation, selling three hundred thousand copies in its first year. The book embroiled Stowe in controversy, and Abraham Lincoln was said to have told Stowe that her book "started this great war." Aside from abolitionism, Stowe was also a vocal proponent of women's rights. Although the two never met, she kept up a personal correspondence with George Eliot for many years; in her letters she not only commented on her friend's books but also offered criticism of them. Stowe died in 1896 after suffering from dementia or Alzheimer's disease for nearly a decade. "The Ghost in the Mill" first appeared in the June 1870 issue of *The Atlantic Monthly*.

The Ghost in the Mill

by Harriet Beecher Stowe

"Come, Sam, tell us a story," said I, as Harry and I crept to his knees, in the glow of the bright evening firelight; while Aunt Lois was busily rattling the tea-things, and grandmamma, at the other end of the fireplace, was quietly setting the heel of a blue-mixed yarn stocking.

In those days we had no magazines and daily papers, each reeling off a serial story. Once a week, "The Columbian Sentinel" came from Boston* with its slender stock of news and editorial; but all the multiform devices—pictorial, narrative, and poetical—which keep the mind of the

---

* The *Columbian Centinel* [sic], founded in 1790, ceased publication in 1840.

present generation ablaze with excitement, had not then even an existence. There was no theatre, no opera; there were in Oldtown* no parties or balls, except, perhaps, the annual election, or Thanksgiving festival; and when winter came, and the sun went down at half-past four o'clock, and left the long, dark hours of evening to be provided for, the necessity of amusement became urgent. Hence, in those days, chimney-corner story-telling became an art and an accomplishment. Society then was full of traditions and narratives, which had all the uncertain glow and shifting mystery of the firelit hearth upon them. They were told to sympathetic audiences, by the rising and falling light of the solemn embers, with the hearth-crickets filling up every pause. Then the aged told their stories to the young—tales of early life; tales of war and adventure, of forest-days, of Indian captivities and escapes, of bears and wild-cats and panthers, of rattlesnakes, of witches and wizards, and strange and wonderful dreams and appearances and providences.

In those days of early Massachusetts, faith and credence were in the very air. Two-thirds of New England was then dark, unbroken forests, through whose tangled paths the mysterious winter wind groaned and shrieked and howled with weird noises and unaccountable clamors. Along the iron-bound shore, the stormful Atlantic raved and thundered, and dashed its moaning waters, as if to deaden and deafen any voice that might tell of the settled life of the old civilized world, and shut us forever into the wilderness. A good story-teller, in those days, was always sure of a warm seat at the hearthstone, and the delighted homage of children; and in all Oldtown there was no better story-teller than Sam Lawson.

"Do, do, tell us a story," said Harry, pressing upon him, and opening very wide blue eyes, in which undoubting faith shone as in a mirror; "and let it be something strange, and different from common."

---

* Oldtown, Massachusetts, is Stowe's fictionalized version of Natick, Massachusetts, where her husband was born. Her first book of Oldtown, *Oldtown Folks*, was published in 1869; Sam Lawson was a lesser character in that novel. In 1872 she published the collection *Sam Lawson's Oldtown Fireside Tales*, which elevated Sam Lawson to a principal character. "The Ghost in the Mill" is the first tale in that collection.

"Wal, I know lots o' strange things," said Sam, looking mysteriously into the fire. "Why, I know things, that ef I should tell,—why, people might say they wa'n't so; but then they *is* so for all that."

"Oh, *do*, do, tell us!"

"Why, I should scare ye to death, mebbe," said Sam doubtingly.

"Oh, pooh! no, you wouldn't," we both burst out at once.

But Sam was possessed by a reticent spirit, and loved dearly to be wooed and importuned; and so he only took up the great kitchen-tongs, and smote on the hickory forestick, when it flew apart in the middle, and scattered a shower of clear bright coals all over the hearth.

"Mercy on us, Sam Lawson!" said Aunt Lois in an indignant voice, spinning round from her dishwashing.

"Don't you worry a grain, Miss Lois," said Sam composedly. "I see that are stick was e'en a'most in two, and I thought I'd jest settle it. I'll sweep up the coals now," he added, vigorously applying a turkey-wing to the purpose, as he knelt on the hearth, his spare, lean figure glowing in the blaze of the firelight, and getting quite flushed with exertion.

"There, now!" he said, when he had brushed over and under and between the fire-irons, and pursued the retreating ashes so far into the red, fiery citadel that his finger-ends were burning and tingling, "that are's done now as well as Hepsy herself could 'a' done it. I allers sweeps up the haarth: I think it's part o' the man's bisness when he makes the fire. But Hepsy's so used to seein' me a-doin' on't, that she don't see no kind o' merit in't. It's just as Parson Lothrop said in his sermon—folks allers overlook their common marcies"—

"But come, Sam, that story," said Harry and I coaxingly, pressing upon him, and pulling him down into his seat in the corner.

"Lordy massy, these 'ere young uns!" said Sam. "There's never no contentin' on 'em: ye tell 'em one story, and they jest swallows it as a dog does a gob o' meat; and they're all ready for another. What do ye want to hear now?"

Now, the fact was, that Sam's stories had been told us so often, that they were all arranged and ticketed in our minds. We knew every word in them, and could set him right if he varied a hair from the usual track; and still the interest in them was unabated. Still we shivered, and clung to his knee, at the mysterious parts, and felt gentle, cold chills run down our spines at appropriate places. We were always in the most receptive and sympathetic condition. To-night, in particular, was one of those thundering stormy ones, when the winds appeared to be holding a perfect mad carnival over my grandfather's house. They yelled and squealed round the corners; they collected in troops, and came tumbling and roaring down chimney; they shook and rattled the buttery-door and the sinkroom-door and the cellar-door and the chamber-door, with a constant undertone of squeak and clatter, as if at every door were a cold, discontented spirit, tired of the chill outside, and longing for the warmth and comfort within.

"Wal, boys," said Sam confidentially, "what'll ye have?"

"Tell us 'Come down, come down!'" we both shouted with one voice. This was, in our mind, an "A No. 1" among Sam's stories.

"Ye mus'n't be frightened now," said Sam paternally.

"Oh, no! we ar'n't frightened ever," said we both in one breath.

"Not when ye go down the cellar arter cider?" said Sam with severe scrutiny. "Ef ye should be down cellar, and the candle should go out, now?"

"I ain't," said I: "I ain't afraid of any thing. I never knew what it was to be afraid in my life."

"Wal, then," said Sam, "I'll tell ye. This 'ere's what Cap'n Eb Sawin told me when I was a boy about your bigness, I reckon.

"Cap'n Eb Sawin was a most respectable man. Your gran'ther knew him very well; and he was a deacon in the church in Dedham afore he died. He was at Lexington when the fust gun was fired agin the British. He was a dreffle smart man, Cap'n Eb was, and driv team a good many years atween here and Boston. He married Lois Peabody, that was cousin to your gran'ther then. Lois was a rael sensible woman; and I've heard her tell the story as he told her, and it was jest as he told it to me—jest exactly; and I shall never forget it if I live to be nine hundred years old, like Mathuselah.

"Ye see, along back in them times, there used to be a fellow come round these 'ere parts, spring and fall, a-peddlin' goods, with his pack on his back; and his name was Jehiel Lommedieu. Nobody rightly knew where he come from. He wasn't much of a talker; but the women rather liked him, and kind o' liked to have him round. Women will like some fellows, when men can't see no sort o' reason why they should; and they liked this 'ere Lommedieu, though he was kind o' mournful and thin and shad-bellied,* and hadn't nothin' to say for himself. But it got to be so, that the women would count and calculate so many weeks afore 'twas time for Lommedieu to be along; and they'd make up ginger-snaps and preserves and pies, and make him stay to tea at the houses, and feed him up on the best there was: and the story went round, that he was a-courtin' Phebe Ann Parker, or Phebe Ann was a-courtin' him—folks didn't rightly know which. Wal, all of a sudden, Lommedieu stopped comin' round; and nobody knew why—only jest he didn't come. It turned out that Phebe Ann Parker had got a letter from him, sayin' he'd be along afore Thanksgiving; but he didn't come, neither afore nor at Thanksgiving time, nor arter, nor next spring: and finally the women they gin up lookin' for him. Some said he was dead; some said he was gone to Canada; and some said he hed gone over to the Old Country.

"Wal, as to Phebe Ann, she acted like a gal o' sense, and married 'Bijah Moss, and thought no more 'bout it. She took the right view on't, and said she was sartin that all things was ordered out for the best; and it was jest as well folks couldn't always have their own way. And so, in time, Lommedieu was gone out o' folks's minds, much as a last year's apple-blossom.

"It's relly affectin' to think how little these 'ere folks is missed that's so much sot by. There ain't nobody, ef they's ever so important, but what the world gets to goin' on without 'em, pretty much as it did with 'em, though there's some little flurry at fust. Wal, the last thing that was in anybody's mind was, that they ever should hear from Lommedieu agin. But there ain't nothin' but what has its time o' turnin' up; and it seems his turn was to come.

"Wal, ye see, 'twas the 19th o' March, when Cap'n Eb Sawin started with a team for Boston. That day, there come on about the biggest snow-storm that there'd been in them parts sence the oldest man could remember. 'Twas this 'ere fine, siftin' snow, that drives in your face like needles, with a wind to cut your nose off: it made teamin' pretty tedious work. Cap'n Eb was about the toughest man in them parts. He'd spent days in the woods a-loggin', and he'd been up to the deestrict o' Maine a-lumberin', and was about up to any sort o' thing a man gen'ally could be up to; but these 'ere

---

* Another way of saying he was thin.

March winds sometimes does set on a fellow so, that neither natur' nor grace can stan' 'em. The cap'n used to say he could stan' any wind that blew one way 't time for five minutes; but come to winds that blew all four p'ints at the same minit,—why, they flustered him.

"Wal, that was the sort o' weather it was all day: and by sundown Cap'n Eb he got clean bewildered, so that he lost his road; and, when night came on, he didn't know nothin' where he was. Ye see the country was all under drift, and the air so thick with snow, that he couldn't see a foot afore him; and the fact was, he got off the Boston road without knowin' it, and came out at a pair o' bars nigh upon Sherburn,* where old Cack Sparrock's mill is.

"Your gran'ther used to know old Cack, boys. He was a dreful drinkin' old crittur, that lived there all alone in the woods by himself a-tendin' saw and grist mill. He wasn't allers jest what he was then. Time was that Cack was a pretty consid'ably likely young man, and his wife was a very respectable woman—Deacon Amos Petengall's dater from Sherburn.

"But ye see, the year arter his wife died, Cack he gin up goin' to meetin' Sundays, and, all the tithing-men and selectmen could do, they couldn't get him out to meetin'; and, when a man neglects means o' grace and sanctuary privileges, there ain't no sayin' *what* he'll do next. Why, boys, jist think on't!—an immoral crittur lyin' round loose all day Sunday, and not puttin' on so much as a clean shirt, when all 'spectable folks has on their best close, and is to meetin' worshippin' the Lord! What can you spect to come of it, when he lies idlin' round in his old week-day close, fishing, or some sich, but what the Devil should be arter him at last, as he was arter old Cack?"

Here Sam winked impressively to my grandfather in the opposite corner, to call his attention to the moral which he was interweaving with his narrative.

"Wal, ye see, Cap'n Eb he told me, that when he come to them bars and looked up, and saw the dark a-comin' down, and the storm a-thickenin' up, he felt that things was gettin' pretty consid'able serious. There was a dark piece o' woods on ahead of him inside the bars; and he knew, come to get in there, the light would give out clean. So he jest thought he'd

---

* This probably refers to Sherborn, Massachusetts, which is located eighteen miles from Boston.

take the hoss out o' the team, and go ahead a little, and see where he was. So he driv his oxen up ag'in the fence, and took out the hoss, and got on him, and pushed along through the woods, not rightly knowin' where he was goin'.

"Wal, afore long he see a light through the trees; and, sure enough, he come out to Cack Sparrock's old mill.

"It was a pretty consid'able gloomy sort of a place, that are old mill was. There was a great fall of water that come rushin' down the rocks, and fell in a deep pool; and it sounded sort o' wild and lonesome: but Cap'n Eb he knocked on the door with his whip-handle, and got in.

"There, to be sure, sot old Cack beside a great blazin' fire, with his rum-jug at his elbow. He was a drefful fellow to drink, Cack was! For all that, there was some good in him, for he was pleasant-spoken and 'bliging; and he made the cap'n welcome.

"'Ye see, Cack,' said Cap'n Eb, 'I'm off my road, and got snowed up down by your bars,' says he.

"'Want ter know!' says Cack. 'Calculate you'll jest have to camp down here till mornin',' says he.

"Wal, so old Cack he got out his tin lantern, and went with Cap'n Eb back to the bars to help him fetch along his critturs. He told him he could put 'em under the mill-shed. So they got the critturs up to the shed, and got the cart under; and by that time the storm was awful.

"But Cack he made a great roarin' fire, 'cause, ye see, Cack allers had slab-wood a plenty from his mill; and a roarin' fire is jest so much company. It sort o' keeps a fellow's spirits up, a good fire does. So Cack he sot on his old teakettle, and made a swingeing lot o' toddy; and he and Cap'n Eb were havin' a tol'able comfortable time there. Cack was a pretty good hand to tell stories; and Cap'n Eb warn't no way backward in that line, and kep' up his end pretty well: and pretty soon they was a-roarin' and haw-hawin' inside about as loud as the storm outside; when all of a sudden, 'bout midnight, there come a loud rap on the door.

"'Lordy massy! what's that?' says Cack. Folks is rather startled allers to be checked up sudden when they are a-carryin' on and laughin'; and it was such an awful blowy night, it was a little scary to have a rap on the door.

"Wal, they waited a minit, and didn't hear nothin' but the wind a-screechin' round the chimbley; and old Cack was jest goin' on with his story, when the rap come ag'in, harder'n ever, as if it'd shook the door open.

"'Wal,' says old Cack, 'if 'tis the Devil, we'd jest as good's open, and have it out with him to onst,' says he; and so he got up and opened the door, and, sure enough, there was old Ketury there. Expect you've heard your grandma tell about old Ketury. She used to come to meetin's sometimes, and her husband was one o' the prayin' Indians; but Ketury was one of the rael wild sort, and you couldn't no more convert *her* than you could convert a wild-cat or a painter.* Lordy massy! Ketury used to come to meetin', and sit there on them Indian benches; and when the second bell was a-tollin', and when Parson Lothrop and his wife was comin' up the broad aisle, and everybody in the house ris' up and stood, Ketury would sit there, and look at 'em out o' the corner o' her eyes; and folks used to say she rattled them necklaces o' rattlesnakes' tails and wild-cat teeth, and sich like heathen trumpery, and looked for all the world as if the spirit of the old Sarpent himself was in her. I've seen her sit and look at Lady Lothrop out o' the corner o' her eyes; and her old brown baggy neck would kind o' twist and work; and her eyes they looked so, that 'twas enough to scare a body. For all the world, she looked jest as if she was a-workin' up to spring at her. Lady Lothrop was jest as kind to Ketury as she always was to every poor crittur. She'd bow and smile as gracious to her when meetin' was over, and she come down the aisle, passin' oot o, meetin'; but Ketury never took no notice. Ye see, Ketury's father was one o' them great powwows down to Martha's Vineyard; and people used to say she was set apart, when she was a child, to the sarvice o' the Devil: any way, she never could be made nothin' of in a Christian way. She come down to Parson Lothrop's study once or twice to be catechised; but he couldn't get a word out o' her, and she kind o' seemed to sit scornful while he was a-talkin'. Folks said, if it was in old times, Ketury wouldn't have been allowed to go on so; but Parson Lothrop's so sort o' mild, he let her take pretty much her own way. Everybody thought that Ketury was a witch: at least, she knew

---

* Panther.

consid'able more'n she ought to know, and so they was kind o' 'fraid on her. Cap'n Eb says he never see a fellow seem scareder than Cack did when he see Ketury a-standin' there.

"Why, ye see, boys, she was as withered and wrinkled and brown as an old frosted punkin-vine; and her little snaky eyes sparkled and snapped, and it made yer head kind o' dizzy to look at 'em; and folks used to say that anybody that Ketury got mad at was sure to get the worst of it fust or last. And so, no matter what day or hour Ketury had a mind to rap at anybody's door, folks gen'lly thought it was best to let her in; but then, they never thought her coming was for any good, for she was just like the wind—she came when the fit was on her, she staid jest so long as it pleased her, and went when she got ready, and not before. Ketury understood English, and could talk it well enough, but always seemed to scorn it, and was allers mowin' and mutterin' to herself in Indian, and winkin' and blinkin' as if she saw more folks round than you did, so that she wa'n't no way pleasant company; and yet everybody took good care to be polite to her. So old Cack asked her to come in, and didn't make no question where she come from, or what she come on; but he knew it was twelve good miles from where she lived to his hut, and the snow was drifted above her middle: and Cap'n Eb declared that there wa'n't no track, nor sign o' a track, of anybody's coming through that snow next morning."

"'How did she get there, then?' said I.

"'Didn't ye never see brown leaves a-ridin' on the wind? Well,' Cap'n Eb he says, 'she came on the wind,' and I'm sure it was strong enough to fetch her. But Cack he got her down into the warm corner, and he poured her out a mug o' hot toddy, and give her: but ye see her bein' there sort o' stopped the conversation; for she sot there a-rockin' back'ards and for'ards, a-sippin her toddy, and a-mutterin', and lookin' up chimbley.

"Cap'n Eb says in all his born days he never hearn such screeches and yells as the wind give over that chimbley; and old Cack got so frightened, you could fairly hear his teeth chatter.

"But Cap'n Eb he was a putty brave man, and he wa'n't goin' to have conversation stopped by no woman, witch or no witch; and so, when he see her mutterin', and lookin' up chimbley, he spoke up, and says he, 'Well, Ketury, what do you see?' says he. 'Come, out with it; don't keep it to yourself.' Ye see Cap'n Eb was a hearty fellow, and then he was a leetle warmed up with the toddy.

"Then he said he see an evil kind o' smile on Ketury's face, and she rattled her necklace o' bones and snakes' tails; and her eyes seemed to snap; and she looked up the chimbley, and called out, 'Come down, come down! let's see who ye be.'

"Then there was a scratchin' and a rumblin' and a groan; and a pair of feet come down the chimbley, and stood right in the middle of the haarth, the toes pi'ntin' out'rds, with shoes and silver buckles a-shinin' in the fire-light. Cap'n Eb says he never come so near bein' scared in his life; and, as to old Cack, he jest wilted right down in his chair.

"Then old Ketury got up, and reached her stick up chimbley, and called out louder, 'Come down, come down! let's see who ye be.' And, sure enough, down came a pair o' legs, and j'ined right on to the feet: good fair legs they was, with ribbed stockings and leather breeches.

"'Wal, we're in for it now,' says Cap'n Eb. 'Go it, Ketury, and let's have the rest on him.'

"Ketury didn't seem to mind him: she stood there as stiff as a stake, and kep' callin' out, 'Come down, come down! let's see who ye be.' And then come down the body of a man with a brown coat and yellow vest, and j'ined right on to the legs; but there wa'n't no arms to it. Then Ketury shook her stick up chimbley, and called, *Come down, come down!* And there came down a pair o' arms, and went on each side o' the body; and there stood a man all finished, only there wa'n't no head on him.

"'Wal, Ketury,' says Cap'n Eb, 'this 'ere's getting serious. I 'spec' you must finish him up, and let's see what he wants of us.'

"Then Ketury called out once more, louder'n ever, 'Come down, come down! let's see who ye be.' And, sure enough, down comes a man's head, and settled on the shoulders straight enough; and Cap'n Eb, the minit he sot eyes on him, knew he was Jehiel Lommedieu.

"Old Cack knew him too; and he fell flat on his face, and prayed the Lord to have mercy on his soul: but Cap'n Eb he was for gettin' to the bottom of matters, and not have his scare for nothin'; so he says to him, 'What do you want, now you hev come?'

"The man he didn't speak; he only sort o' moaned, and p'inted to the chimbley. He seemed to try to speak, but couldn't; for ye see it isn't often that his sort o' folks is permitted to speak: but just then there came a screechin' blast o' wind, and blowed the door open, and blowed the smoke and fire all out into the room, and there seemed to be a whirlwind and darkness and moans and screeches; and, when it all cleared up, Ketury and the man was both gone, and only old Cack lay on the ground, rolling and moaning as if he'd die.

"Wal, Cap'n Eb he picked him up, and built up the fire, and sort o' comforted him up, 'cause the crittur was in distress o' mind that was drefful. The awful Providence, ye see, had awakened him, and his sin had been set home to his soul; and he was under such conviction, that it all had to come out,—how old Cack's father had murdered poor Lommedieu for his money, and Cack had been privy to it, and helped his father build the body up in that very chimbley; and he said that he hadn't had neither peace nor rest since then, and that was what had driv' him away from ordinances; for ye know sinnin' will always make a man leave prayin'. Wal, Cack didn't live but a day or two. Cap'n Eb he got the minister o' Sherburn and one o' the selectmen down to see him; and they took his deposition. He seemed railly quite penitent; and Parson Carryl he prayed with him, and was faithful in settin' home the providence to his soul: and so, at the eleventh hour, poor old Cack might have got in; at least it looks a leetle like it. He was distressed to think he couldn't live to be hung. He sort o' seemed to think, that if he was fairly tried, and hung, it would make it all square. He made Parson Carryl promise to have the old mill pulled down, and bury the body; and, after he was dead, they did it.

"Cap'n Eb he was one of a party o' eight that pulled down the chimbley; and there, sure enough, was the skeleton of poor Lommedieu.

"So there you see, boys, there can't be no iniquity so hid but what it'll come out. The Wild Indians of the forest, and the stormy winds and tempests, j'ined together to bring out this 'ere."

"For my part," said Aunt Lois sharply, "I never believed that story."

"Why, Lois," said my grandmother, "Cap'n Eb Sawin was a regular church-member, and a most respectable man."

"Law, mother! I don't doubt he thought so. I suppose he and Cack got drinking toddy together, till he got asleep, and dreamed it. I wouldn't believe such a thing if it did happen right before my face and eyes. I should only think I was crazy, that's all."

"Come, Lois, if I was you, I wouldn't talk so like a Sadducee,"* said my grandmother. "What would become of all the accounts in Dr. Cotton Mather's 'Magnilly'† if folks were like you?"

"Wal," said Sam Lawson, drooping contemplatively over the coals, and gazing into the fire, "there's a putty consid'able sight o' things in this world that's true; and then ag'in there's a sight o' things that ain't true. Now, my old gran'ther used to say, 'Boys,' says he, 'if ye want to lead a pleasant and prosperous life, ye must contrive allers to keep jest the *happy medium* between truth and falsehood.' Now, that are's my doctrine."

Aunt Lois knit severely.

"Boys," said Sam, "don't you want ter go down with me and get a mug o' cider?"

Of course we did, and took down a basket to bring up some apples to roast.

"Boys," says Sam mysteriously, while he was drawing the cider, "you jest ask your Aunt Lois to tell you what she knows 'bout Ruth Sullivan."

"Why, what is it?"

"Oh! you must ask her. These 'ere folks that's so kind o' toppin' about sperits and sich, come sift 'em down, you gen'lly find they knows one story that kind o' puzzles 'em. Now you mind, and jist ask your Aunt Lois about Ruth Sullivan."‡

---

* The Sadducees were a Jewish sect that denied the resurrection of the dead or the existence of spirits.

† Puritan minister and historian Cotton Mather's *Magnalia Christi Americana* includes Mather's account of the Salem Witch Trials, in which he was heavily involved (Mather praised the executions of the so-called witches).

‡ This abrupt ending leads into the second story in *Sam Lawson's Oldtown Fireside Stories*, "The Sullivan Looking-Glass," about a young woman with second sight who locates a missing will.

Rhoda Broughton (1840–1920) was a popular Welsh author of sensational novels and short stories. The niece of the well-known publisher Joseph Sheridan LeFanu, himself the author of many fantastic stories—including the oft-anthologized and filmed "Carmilla"—her novels won praise from critics who saw Broughton as an important bridge between George Eliot and Virginia Woolf. The following story first appeared in the *Temple Bar* magazine for October 1872 and was later collected in *Tales for Christmas Eve* (1873), also known as *Twilight Stories*, a collection of five supernatural stories. It is unfair to characterize the story as a ghost story, as it was later labelled—but it will nonetheless haunt the reader.

The Man with the Nose

by Rhoda Broughton

[The details of this little story are of course imaginary, but the main incidents are, to the best of my belief, facts. They happened twenty, or more than twenty years ago.]

CHAPTER ONE

Let us get a map and see what places look pleasantest," says she.

"As for that," reply I, "on a map, most places look equally pleasant."

"Never mind; get one."

I obey.

"Do you like the seaside?" asks Elizabeth, lifting her little brown head and her small, happy, white face from the English sea-coast, along which her forefinger is slowly travelling.

"Since you ask me, distinctly *no*," reply I, for once venturing to have a decided opinion of my own, which, during the last few weeks of imbecility, I can be hardly said to have had. "I broke my last wooden spade five and twenty years ago. I have but a poor opinion of cockles*—sandy, red-nosed things, are not they? And the air always makes me bilious."

"Then we certainly will not go there," says Elizabeth, laughing. "A bilious bridegroom! Alliterative but horrible! None of our friends show the least eagerness to lend us their country house."

"Oh, that God would put it into the hearts of men to take their wives straight home, as their fathers did!" say I, with a cross groan.

"It is evident, therefore, that we must go somewhere," returns she, not heeding the aspiration contained in my last speech, making her forefinger resume its employment, and reaching Torquay.†

"I suppose so," say I, with a sort of sigh; "for once in our lives we must resign ourselves to having the finger of derision pointed at us by waiters and landlords."

"You shall leave your new portmanteau at home, and I will leave all my best clothes, and nobody will guess that we are bride and bridegroom; they will think that we have been married—oh, ever since the world began," (opening her eyes very wide).

I shake my head. "With an old portmanteau and in rags, we shall still have the mark of the beast upon us."

"Do you mind much? Do you hate being ridiculous?" asks Elizabeth, meekly, rather depressed by my view of the case; "because, if so, let us go somewhere out of the way, where there will be very few people to laugh at us."

"On the contrary," return I, stoutly, "we will betake ourselves to some spot where such as we do chiefly congregate—where we shall be swallowed up and lost in the multitude of our fellow-sinners." A pause devoted to reflection. "What do you say to Killarney?"‡ say I, cheerfully.

---

* Cockles are edible shellfish that are somewhat similar to scallops.

† Torquay is a seaside town in Devon, England.

‡ Killarney is a town in County Kerry, Ireland.

"There are a great many fleas there, I believe," replies Elizabeth, slowly; "flea-bites make large lumps on me; you would not like me if I were covered with large lumps."

At the hideous ideal picture thus presented to me by my little beloved I relapse into inarticulate idiocy; emerging from which by-and-by, I suggest "The Lakes."* My arm is round her, and I feel her supple body shiver, though it is mid July, and the bees are booming about in the still and sleepy noon-garden outside.

"Oh, no—no—not *there!*"

"Why such emphasis?" I ask, gayly; "more fleas? At this rate, and with this *sine qua non*,† our choice will grow limited."

"Something dreadful happened to me there," she says, with another shudder. "But, indeed, I did not think there was any harm in it—I never thought any thing would come of it."

"What the devil was it?" cry I, in a jealous heat and hurry; "what the mischief *did* you do, and why have not you told me about it before?"

"I did not *do* much," she answers, meekly, seeking for my hand, and, when found, kissing it in timid deprecation of my wrath; "but I was ill—very ill—there; I had a nervous fever. I was in a bed hung with a chintz, with a red and green fern-leaf pattern on it. I have always hated red and green fern-leaf chintzes ever since."

"It would be possible to avoid the obnoxious bed, would not it?" say I, laughing a little. "Where does it lie? Windermere? Ullswater? Wastwater?‡ Where?"

"We were at Ullswater," she says, speaking rapidly, while a hot colour grows on her small white cheeks—"Papa, mamma, and I; and there came

---

* The Lake District or "the Lakes" is a mountainous region in England famed for its scenic lakes and forests.

† Something that is absolutely essential.

‡ These are all lakes in the Lake District; Ullswater is the second largest.

a mesmeriser* to Penrith,† and we went to see him—everybody did—and he asked leave to mesmerise me—he said I should be such a good medium, and—and—I did not know what it was like. I thought it would be quite good fun, and—and—I let him."

She is trembling exceedingly; even the loving pressure of my arms cannot abate her shivering.

"Well?"

"And after that I do not remember anything; I believe I did all sorts of extraordinary things that he told me—sang and danced, and made a fool of myself—but when I came home I was very ill, very—I lay in bed for five whole weeks, and—and was off my head, and said odd and wicked things that you would not have expected me to say—that dreadful bed! shall I ever forget it?"

"We will *not* go to the Lakes," I say, decisively, "and we will not talk any more about mesmerism."

"That is right," she says, with a sigh of relief; "I try to think about it as little as possible; but sometimes, in the dead black of the night, when God seems a long way off, and the devil near, it comes back to me so strongly—I feel, do not you know, as if he were *there*—somewhere in the room, and I *must* get up and follow him."

"Why should not we go abroad?" suggest I, abruptly turning the conversation.

"Why, indeed?" cries Elizabeth, recovering her gayety, while her pretty blue eyes begin to dance. "How stupid of us not to have thought of it before!—only *abroad* is a big word. *What* abroad?"

"We must be content with something short of Central Africa," I say, gravely, "as I think our one hundred and fifty pounds would hardly take us that far."

---

* *Mesmerism* is named for Franz Anton Mesmer (1734–1815), a German physician who created the theory of animal magnetism, which suggested that all bodies contain magnetic poles, and that sickness results when the poles are out of alignment. One of Mesmer's disciples conducted the first experiments in hypnotism, and the practice of putting willing subjects into hypnotic trance states was originally referred to as mesmerism.

† A town located just outside the Lake District National Park.

"Wherever we go, we must buy a dialogue-book," suggests my little bride elect, "and I will learn some phrases before we start."

"As for that, the Anglo-Saxon tongue takes one pretty well round the world," reply I, with a feeling of complacent British swagger, putting my hands in my breeches pockets.

"Do you fancy the Rhine?" says Elizabeth, with a rather timid suggestion; "I know it is the fashion to run it down nowadays, and call it a cocktail river; but—but after all it cannot be so *very* contemptible, or Byron could not have said such noble things about it."

> "The castled crag of Drachenfals
>   Frowns o'er the wide and winding Rhine,
> Whose breast of waters broadly swells
>   Between the banks which bear the vine,"*

say I, spouting. "After all, that proves nothing, for Byron could have made a silk purse out of a sow's-ear."

"The Rhine will not do, then?" says she, resignedly, suppressing a sigh.

"On the contrary, it will do admirably; it *is* a cocktail river, and I do not care who says it is not," reply I, with illiberal positiveness; "but everybody should be able to say so from his own experience, and not from hearsay; the Rhine let it be, by all means."

So the Rhine it is.

CHAPTER TWO

I have got over it; we have both got over it tolerably, creditably; but, after all, it is a much severer ordeal for a man than a woman, who, with a bouquet to occupy her hands, and a veil to gently shroud her features, need merely be prettily passive. I am alluding, I need hardly say, to the religious ceremony of marriage, which I flatter myself I have gone through with a stiff sheepishness not unworthy of my country. It is a three-days-old event

---

* From Canto III of Byron's "Childe Harold's Pilgrimage."

now, and we are getting used to belonging to one another, though Elizabeth still takes off her ring twenty times a day to admire its bright thickness; still laughs when she hears herself called "Madame." Three days ago we kissed all our friends, and left them to make themselves ill on our cake, and criticise our bridal behaviour, and now we are in Brussels, she and I, feeling oddly, joyfully free from any chaperone. We have been mildly sight-seeing—very mildly, most people would say, but we have resolved not to take our pleasure with the railway speed of Americans, or the hasty sadness of our fellow Britons. Slowly and gayly we have been taking ours. To-day we have been to visit Wiertz's pictures.* Have you ever seen them, oh reader? They are known to comparatively few people, but, if you have a taste for the unearthly terrible—if you wish to sup full of horrors, hasten thither. We have been peering through the appointed peep-hole at the horrible cholera-picture—the man buried alive by mistake, pushing up the lid of his coffin, and stretching a ghastly face and livid hands out of his winding-sheet toward you, while awful grey-blue coffins are piled around, and noisome toads and giant spiders crawl damply about.† On first seeing it, I have reproached myself for bringing one of so nervous a temperament as Elizabeth to see so haunting and hideous a spectacle; but she is less impressed than I expected—less impressed than I myself am.

"He is very lucky to be able to get his lid up," she says, with a half-laugh; "we should find it hard work to burst our brass nails, should not we? When you bury me, dear, fasten me down very slightly, in case there may be some mistake."

And now all the long and quiet July evening we have been prowling together about the streets. Brussels is the town of towns for *flâner*-ing‡— have been flattening our noses against the shop-windows, and making each other imaginary presents. Elizabeth has not confined herself to imagination, however; she has made me buy her a little bonnet with

---

* Antoine Wiertz (1806–1865) was a Belgian painter known for both his huge canvasses and his macabre sensibilities. The Wiertz Museum still operates in Brussels, in what was once Wiertz's studio.

† Wiertz's painting "The Premature Burial," painted in 1854.

‡ *Flâner* is the French verb for strolling.

feathers—"in order to look married," as she says, and the result is such a delicious picture of a child playing at being grown up, having practised a theft on its mother's wardrobe, that for the last two hours I have been in a foolish ecstasy of love and laughter over her and it. We are at the "Bellevue,"* and have a fine suite of rooms, *au premier*, evidently specially devoted to the English, to the gratification of whose well-known loyalty the Prince and Princess of Wales are simpering from the walls. Is there any one in the three kingdoms† who knows his own face as well as he knows the faces of Albert Victor and Alexandra?‡ The long evening has at last slidden into night—night far advanced—night melting into earliest day. All Brussels is asleep. One moment ago I also was asleep, soundly as any log.

What is it that has made me take this sudden headlong plunge out of sleep into wakefulness? Who is it that is clutching at and calling upon me? What is it that is making me struggle mistily up into a sitting posture, and try to revive my sleep-numbed senses? A summer night is never wholly dark; by the half-light that steals through the closed *persiennes*§ and open windows I see my wife standing beside my bed; the extremity of terror on her face, and her fingers digging themselves, with painful tenacity into my arm.

"Tighter, tighter!" she is crying, wildly. "What are you thinking of? You are letting me go!"

"Good heavens!" say I, rubbing my eyes, while my muddy brain grows a trifle clearer. "What is it? What has happened? Have you had a nightmare?"

"You saw him," she says, with a sort of sobbing breathlessness; "you know you did! You saw him as well as I."

"I!" cry I, incredulously—"not I. Till this second I have been fast asleep. *I* saw nothing."

"You did!" she cries, passionately. "You know you did. Why do you deny it? You were as frightened as I?"

---

* The Hôtel Bellevue is still in operation today, located in Brussels next to the Royal Palace.

† England, Scotland, and Ireland.

‡ Broughton's timeline is a bit off here, since this story is supposed to have occurred twenty years prior to 1870, but Prince Albert Edward, the oldest son of Queen Victoria, didn't wed Alexandra of Denmark until 1863.

§ Persian blinds; window shutters with horizontal, movable slats.

"As I live," I answer, solemnly, "I know no more than the dead what you are talking about; till you woke me by calling me and catching hold of me, I was as sound asleep as the seven sleepers."*

"Is it possible that it can have been a *dream*?" she says, with a long sigh, for a moment loosing my arm, and covering her face with her hands. "But no—in a dream I should have been somewhere else, but I was here—*here*—on that bed, and he stood there (pointing with her forefinger)—just *there*, between the foot of it and the window!"

She stops, panting.

"It is all that brute Wiertz," say I, in a fury. "I wish I had been buried alive myself, before I had been fool enough to take you to see his beastly daubs."

"Light a candle," she says, in the same breathless way, her teeth chattering with fright. "Let us make sure that he is not hidden somewhere in the room."

"How could he be?" say I, striking a match; "the door is locked."

"He might have got in by the balcony," she answers, still trembling violently.

"He would have had to have cut a very large hole in the *persiennes*," say I, half-mockingly. "See, they are intact and well fastened on the inside."

She sinks into an arm-chair, and pushes her loose, soft hair from her white face.

"It *was* a dream, then, I suppose?"

She is silent for a moment or two, while I bring her a glass of water, and throw a dressing-gown round her cold and shrinking form.

"Now tell me, my little one," say I, coaxingly, sitting down at her feet, "what it was—what you thought you saw?"

"*Thought* I saw!" echoes she, with indignant emphasis, sitting upright, while her eyes sparkle feverishly. "I am as certain that I saw him standing

---

* "The Seven Sleepers" is a traditional story of seven youths who fled to a cave outside Ephesus to escape Roman persecution of Christians; after the Romans sealed the cave, the youths fell asleep and were finally freed over two hundred years later.

there as I am that I see that candle burning—that I see this chair—that I see you."

"*Him!* But who is *him*?"

She falls forward on my neck, and buries her face in my shoulder.

"That—dreadful—man!" she says, while her whole body is one tremor.

"*What* dreadful man?" cry I, impatiently.

She is silent.

"Who was he?"

"I do not know."

"Did you ever see him before?"

"Oh, no—no, never! I hope to God I may never see him again!"

"What was he like?"

"Come closer to me," she says, laying hold of my hand with her small and chilly fingers; "stay *quite* near me, and I will tell you" (after a pause)—"he had a *nose*!"

"My dear soul," cry I, bursting out with a loud laugh in the silence of the night, "do not most people have noses? Would not he have been much more dreadful if he had had *none*?"

"But it was *such* a nose!" she says, with perfect trembling gravity.

"A bottle-nose?" suggest I, still cackling.

"For heaven's sake, don't laugh!" she says, nervously; "if you had seen his face, you would have been as little disposed to laugh as I."

"But his nose?" return I, suppressing my merriment; "what kind of nose was it? See, I am as grave as a judge."

"It was very prominent," she answers, in a sort of awe-struck half-whisper, "and very sharply chiselled; the nostrils very much cut out." A little pause. "His eyebrows were one straight black line across his face, and under them his eyes burnt like dull coals of fire, that shone and yet did not shine; they looked like dead eyes, sunken, half-extinguished, and yet sinister."

"And what did he do?" ask I, impressed, despite myself, by her passionate earnestness; "when did you first see him?"

"I was asleep," she said—"at least I thought so—and suddenly I opened my eyes, and he was *there—there*"—pointing again with trembling finger—"between the window and the bed."

"What was he doing? Was he walking about?"

"He was standing as still as stone—I never saw any live thing so still—*looking* at me; he never called or beckoned, or moved a finger, but his eyes *commanded* me to come to him, as the eyes of the mesmeriser at Penrith did." She stops, breathing heavily. I can hear her heart's loud and rapid beats.

"And you?" I say, pressing her more closely to my side, and smoothing her troubled hair.

"I *hated* it," she cries, excitedly; "I loathed it—abhorred it. I was ice-cold with fear and horror, but—I *felt* myself going to him."

"Yes?"

"And then I shrieked out to you, and you came running, and caught fast hold of me, and held me tight at first—quite tight—but presently I felt your hold slacken—slacken—and, though I *longed* to stay with you, though I was *mad* with fright, yet I felt myself pulling strongly away from you—going to him; and he—he stood there always looking—looking—and then I gave one last loud shriek, and I suppose I woke—and it was a dream!"

"I never heard of a clearer case of nightmare," say I, stoutly; "that vile Wiertz! I should like to see his whole *Musée* burnt by the hands of the hangman to-morrow."

She shakes her head. "It had nothing to do with Wiertz; what it meant I do not know, but—"

"It meant nothing," I answer, reassuringly, "except that for the future we will go and see none but good and pleasant sights, and steer clear of charnel-house fancies."

CHAPTER THREE

Elizabeth is now in a position to decide whether the Rhine is a cocktail river or no, for she is on it, and so am I. We are sitting, with an awning over our heads, and little wooden stools under our feet. Elizabeth has a small sailor's hat and blue ribbon on her head. The river breeze has blown it rather away; has tangled her plenteous hair; has made a faint pink stain on her pale cheeks. It is some fete-day, and the boat is crowded.

Tables, countless camp-stools, volumes of black smoke pouring from the funnel, as we steam along. "Nothing to the Caledonian Canal!"* cries a burly Scotchman in leggings, speaking with loud authority, and surveying, with an air of contempt, the eternal vine-clad slopes, that sound so well, and look so *sticky* in reality. "Cannot hold a candle to it!" A rival bride and bridegroom opposite, sitting together like love-birds under an umbrella, looking into each other's eyes instead of at the Rhine scenery.

"They might as well have stayed at home, might not they?" says my wife, with a little air of superiority. "Come, we are not so bad as that, are we?"

A storm comes on: hailstones beat slantwise and reach us—stone and sting us right under our awning. Everybody rushes down below, and takes the opportunity to feed ravenously. There are few actions more disgusting than eating *can* be made. A handsome girl close to us—her immaturity evidenced by the two long tails of black hair down her back—is thrusting her knife halfway down her throat.

"Come on deck again," says Elizabeth, disgusted and frightened at this last sight. "The hail was much better than this!"

So we return to our camp-stools, and sit alone under one mackintosh in the lashing storm, with happy hearts and empty stomachs.

"Is not this better than any luncheon?" asks Elizabeth, triumphantly, while the raindrops hang on her long and curled lashes.

"Infinitely better," reply I, madly struggling with the umbrella to prevent its being blown inside out, and gallantly ignoring a species of gnawing sensation at my entrails.

The squall clears off by and by, and we go steaming, steaming on past the unnumbered little villages by the water's edge with church-spires and pointed roofs; past the countless rocks, with their little pert castles perched on the top of them; past the tall, stiff poplar rows. The church-bells are ringing gayly as we go by. A nightingale is singing from a wood. The black eagle of Prussia droops on the stream behind us,† swish-swish through the

---

* The Caledonian Canal, completed in 1822, connects Scotland's east and west coasts, a distance of about sixty miles.

† The Prussian flag showed a black eagle clutching a sword in one claw and a scepter in the other.

dull-green water. A fat woman, who is interested in it, leans over the back of the boat, and, by some happy effect of crinoline, displays to her fellow passengers two yards of thick, white cotton legs. She is, fortunately for herself, unconscious of her generosity.

The day steals on; at every stopping place more people come on. There is hardly elbow-room; and, what is worse, almost every lady is drunk. Rocks, castles, villages, poplars, slide by, while the paddles churn always the water, and the evening draws greyly on. At Bingen,* a party of big blue Prussian soldiers,† very drunk, "glorious" as Tam o' Shanter,‡ come and establish themselves close to us. They call for Lager Beer; talk at the tip-top of their strong voices; two of them begin to spar; all seem inclined to sing. Elizabeth is frightened. We are two hours late in arriving at Biebrich.§ It is half an hour more before we can get ourselves and our luggage into a carriage and set off along the winding road to Wiesbaden. The night is chilly, but not dark. There is only a little shabby bit of a moon, but it shines as hard as it can. Elizabeth is quite worn out, her tired head droops in uneasy sleep on my shoulder. Once she wakes up with a start.

"Are you sure that it meant nothing?" she asks, looking me eagerly in my face; "do people often have such dreams?"

"Often, often," I answer, reassuringly.

"I am always afraid of falling asleep now," she says, trying to sit upright and keep her heavy eyes open, "for fear of seeing him standing there again. Tell me, do you think I shall? Is there any chance, any probability of it?"

"None, none!"

---

* Bingen is a German town situated on the Rhein (or, in Broughton's spelling, Rhine); until 1871 it was on the border between Prussia and Germany.

† The Prussian soldier's uniform circa 1870 consisted notably of a heavy blue jacket.

‡ In Robert Burns's poem "Tam O'Shanter," the title character is out riding his horse late one night after drinking for hours at the pub, and Burns describes Tam's inebriated state by saying, "Kings may be blest, but Tam was glorious."

§ Biebrich is now a borough of the city of Wiesbaden, Germany, but prior to 1926 it was an independent city located near Wiesbaden.

We reach Wiesbaden at last, and drive up to the Hôtel des Quatre Saisons.* By this time it is full midnight. Two or three men are standing about the door. Morris, the maid, has got out—so have I, and I am holding out my hand to Elizabeth, when I hear her give one piercing scream, and see her with ash-white face and starting eyes point with her forefinger—

"There he is!—there—there!"

I look in the direction indicated, and just catch a glimpse of a tall figure, standing half in the shadow of the night, half in the gaslight from the hotel. I have not time for more than one cursory glance, as I am interrupted by a cry from the bystanders, and, turning quickly round, am just in time to catch my wife, who falls in utter insensibility into my arms. We carry her into a room on the ground floor; it is small, noisy, and hot, but it is the nearest at hand. In about an hour she reopens her eyes. A strong shudder makes her quiver from head to foot.

"Where is he?" she says, in a terrified whisper, as her senses come slowly back. "He is somewhere about—somewhere near. I feel that he is!"

"My dearest child, there is no one here but Morris and me," I answer, soothingly.

"Look you yourself. See."

I take one of the candles and light up each corner of the room in succession.

"You saw him!" she says, in trembling hurry, sitting up and clinching her hands together. "I know you did—I pointed him out to you—you *cannot* say that it was a dream *this* time."

"I saw two or three ordinary-looking men as we drove up," I answer, in a commonplace, matter-of-fact tone. "I did not notice any thing remarkable about any of them; you know the fact is, darling, that you have had nothing to eat all day, nothing but a biscuit, and you are over-wrought, and fancy things."

"Fancy!" echoes she, with strong irritation. "How you talk! Was I ever one to fancy things? I tell you that as sure as I sit here—as sure as you stand there—I saw him—*him*—the man I saw in my dream, if it was a dream.

---

* The Hôtel des Quatre Saisons (Four Seasons Hotel) was popular with nineteenth-century travelers but is no longer in existence.

There was not a hair's-breadth of difference between them—and he was looking at me—looking—"

She breaks off into hysterical sobbing.

"My dear child!" say I, thoroughly alarmed, and yet half angry, "for God's sake do not work yourself up into a fever; wait till to-morrow, and we will find out who he is, and all about him; you yourself will laugh when we discover that he is some harmless bagman."

"Why not *now*?" she says, nervously; "why cannot you find out *now—this minute*?"

"Impossible! Everybody is in bed! Wait till to-morrow, and all will be cleared up."

The morrow comes, and I go about the hotel, inquiring. The house is so full, and the data I have to go upon are so small, that for some time I have great difficulty in making it understood to whom I am alluding. At length one waiter seems to comprehend.

"A tall and dark gentleman, with a pronounced and very peculiar nose? Yes; there has been such a one, certainly, in the hotel, but he left at 'grand matin'* this morning; he remained only one night."

"And his name?"

The garçon shakes his head. "That is unknown, monsieur; he did not inscribe it in the visitor's book."

"What countryman was he?"

Another shake of the head. "He spoke German, but it was with a foreign accent."

"Whither did he go?"

"That also is unknown. Nor can I arrive at any more facts about him."

CHAPTER FOUR

A fortnight has passed; we have been hither and thither; now we are at Lucerne. Peopled with better inhabitants, Lucerne might well do for Heaven. It is drawing toward eventide, and Elizabeth and I are sitting,

* "At daybreak."

hand in hand, on a quiet bench, under the shady linden trees, on a high hill up above the lake. There is nobody to see us, so we sit peaceably hand in hand. Up by the still and solemn monastery we came, with its small and narrow windows, calculated to hinder the holy fathers from promenading curious eyes on the world, the flesh, and the devil, tripping past them in blue gauze veils: below us grass and green trees, houses with high-pitched roofs, little dormer-windows, and shutters yet greener than the grass; below us the lake in its rippleless peace, calm, quiet, motionless as Bethesda's pool before the coming of the troubling angel.*

"I said it was too good to last," say I, doggedly, "did not I, only yesterday? Perfect peace, perfect sympathy, perfect freedom from nagging worries—when did such a state of things last more than two days?"

Elizabeth's eyes are idly fixed on a little steamer, with a stripe of red along its side and a tiny puff of smoke from its funnel, gliding along and cutting a narrow, white track on Lucerne's sleepy surface.

"This is the fifth false alarm of the gout having gone to his stomach within the last two years,"† continue I, resentfully. "I declare to Heaven that, if it has not really gone there this time, I'll cut the whole concern."

Let no one cast up his eyes in horror, imagining that it is my father to whom I am thus alluding; it is only a great-uncle by marriage, in consideration of whose wealth and vague promises I have dawdled professionless through twenty-eight years of my life.

"You *must* not go," says Elizabeth, giving my hand an imploring squeeze. "The man in the Bible said, 'I have married a wife, and therefore I cannot come;'‡ why should it be a less valid excuse nowadays?"

"If I recollect rightly, it was considered rather a poor one even then," reply I, dryly.

---

* Bethesda's pool is in Jerusalem, where Jesus reportedly healed a paralyzed man. The Bible records that the sick went to this pool for healing, believing that at certain times an angel would descend to stir the waters, and the first person to enter the pool immediately thereafter would be healed.

† Gout is a form of arthritis caused by a build-up of urate crystals. It attacks joints, so it can't move to the stomach; however, it may be associated with kidney stones, which can cause great pain near the stomach.

‡ From a parable related in Luke 14:20, where it is used as a reason for not attending a banquet.

Elizabeth is unable to contradict this, she therefore only lifts two pouted lips (Monsieur Taine objects to the redness of English-women's mouths,* but I do not) to be kissed, and says, "Stay." I am good enough to comply with her unspoken request, though I remain firm with regard to her spoken one.

"My dearest child," I say, with an air of worldly experience and superior wisdom, "kisses are very good things—in fact, there are few better—but one cannot live upon them."

"Let us try," she says, coaxingly.

"I wonder which would get tired first?" I say, laughing. But she only goes on pleading, "Stay, stay."

"How *can* I stay?" I cry impatiently; "you talk as if I *wanted* to go! Do you think it is any pleasanter to me to leave you than to you to be left? But you know his disposition, his rancorous resentment of fancied neglects. For the sake of two days' indulgence, must I throw away what will keep us in ease and plenty to the end of our days?"

"I do not care for plenty," she says, with a little petulant gesture. "I do not see that rich people are any happier than poor ones. Look at the St. Clairs;† they have £40,000 a-year, and she is a miserable woman, perfectly miserable, because her face gets red after dinner."

"There will be no fear of *our* faces getting red after dinner," say I, grimly; "for we shall have no dinner for them to get red after."

A pause. My eyes stray away to the mountains. Pilatus on the right, with his jagged peak and slender snow-chains about his harsh neck; hill after hill rising silent, eternal, like guardian spirits standing hand-in-hand around their child, the lake. As I look, suddenly they have all flushed, as at some noblest thought, and over all their sullen faces streams an ineffable, rosy joy—a solemn and wonderful effulgence, such as Israel saw reflected from the features of the Eternal in their prophet's transfigured eyes.‡ The

---

* Hippolyte Adolphe Taine (1828–1893) was a French critic and author who wrote about literature and history. In his book *Thomas Graindorge*, he decried the folly of women.

† The St. Clair family was established in England by William St. Clair in 1066; in 1801, Alexander St. Clair was named 1st Earl of Rosslyn, a title the current head of the family, Peter St. Clair-Erskine, still holds.

‡ In the Biblical story of the prophet Elisha (2 Kings 6), the Arameans attack Israel, but Elisha opens the eyes of his servant, who sees chariots of fire protecting them.

unutterable peace and stainless beauty of earth and sky seem to lie softly on my soul. "Would God I could stay! Would God all life could be like this!" I say devoutly, and the aspiration has the reverent earnestness of a prayer.

"Why do you say, '*Would God*?'" she cries, passionately, "when it lies with yourself. Oh, my dear love" (gently sliding her hand through my arm, and lifting wetly-beseeching eyes to my face), "I do not know why I insist upon it so much—I cannot tell you myself—I dare say I seem selfish and unreasonable—but I feel as if your going now would be the end of all things—as if—" She breaks off suddenly.

"My child," say I, thoroughly distressed, but still determined to have my own way, "you talk as if I were going forever and a day; in a week, at the outside, I shall be back, and then you will thank me for the very thing for which you now think me so hard and disobliging."

"Shall I?" she answers, mournfully. "Well, I hope so."

"You will not be alone, either; you will have Morris."

"Yes."

"And every day you will write me a long letter, telling me every single thing that you do, say, and think?"

"Yes."

She answers me gently and obediently; but I can see that she is still utterly unreconciled to the idea of my absence.

"What is it that you are afraid of?" I ask, becoming rather irritated. "What do you suppose will happen to you?"

She does not answer; only a large tear falls on my hand, which she hastily wipes away with her pocket-handkerchief, as if afraid of exciting my wrath.

"Can you give me any good reason why I *should* stay?" I ask, dictatorially.

"None—none—only—stay—stay!"

But I am resolved *not* to stay. Early the next morning I set off.

CHAPTER FIVE

This time it is not a false alarm; this time it really has gone to his stomach, and, declining to be dislodged thence, kills him. My return is therefore retarded until after the funeral and the reading of the will. The latter is so satisfactory, and my time is so fully occupied with a multiplicity of attendant business, that I have no leisure to regret the delay. I write to Elizabeth, but receive no letters from her. This surprises and makes me rather angry, but does not alarm me. If she had been ill, if any thing had happened, Morris would have written. She never was great at writing, poor little soul. What dear little babyish notes she used to send me during our engagement! Perhaps she wishes to punish me for my disobedience to her wishes. Well, *now* she will see who was right.

I am drawing near her now; I am walking up from the railway-station at Lucerne. I am very joyful as I march along under an umbrella, in the grand, broad shining of the summer afternoon. I think with pensive passion of the last glimpse I had of my beloved—her small and wistful face looking out from among the thick, fair fleece of her long hair-winking away her tears and blowing kisses to me. It is a new sensation to me to have any one looking tearfully wistful over my departure. I draw near the great, glaring Schweizerhof,* with its colonnaded, tourist-crowded porch; here are all the pomegranates as I left them, in their green tubs, with their scarlet blossoms, and the dusty oleanders in a row. I look up at our windows; nobody is looking out from them: they are open, and the curtains are alternately swelled out and drawn in by the softly-playful wind. I run quickly upstairs and burst noisily into the sitting-room. Empty, perfectly empty! I open the adjoining door into the bedroom, crying, "Elizabeth! Elizabeth!" but I receive no answer. Empty too. A feeling of indignation creeps over me as I think, "Knowing the time of my return, she might have managed to be in-doors." I have returned to the silent sitting-room, where the only noise is the wind still playing hide-and-seek with the curtains. As I look vacantly round, my eye catches sight of a letter lying on the table. I pick it up mechanically and look at the address. Good Heavens! What can this mean? It is my own, that I sent her two days ago, unopened, with the seal unbroken. Does she carry her resentment so far as not even to open my letters? I spring at the bell and violently ring it. It is answered by the waiter who has always especially attended us.

"Is madame gone out?"

The man opens his mouth and stares at me.

---

* The Hotel Schweizerhof in Lucerne has been in operation since 1859.

"Madame! Is monsieur then not aware that madame is no longer at the hotel?"

"*What*?"

"On the same day as monsieur, madame departed."

"*Departed!* Good God! what are you talking about?"

"A few hours after monsieur's departure—I will not be positive as to the exact time, but it must have been between one and two o'clock, as the midday *table d'hôte** was in progress—a gentleman came and asked for madame—"

"Yes—be quick."

"I demanded whether I should take up his card, but he said 'No,' that was unnecessary, as he was perfectly well known to madame; and, in fact, a short time afterward, without saying any thing to any one, she departed with him."

"And did not return in the evening?"

"No, monsieur; madame has not returned since that day."

I clench my hands in an agony of rage and grief. "So this is it! With that pure child-face, with that divine ignorance—only three weeks married—this is the trick she has played me!" I am recalled to myself by a compassionate suggestion from the garçon.

"Perhaps it was the brother of madame."

Elizabeth has no brother, but the remark brings back to me the necessity of self-command. "Very probably," I answer, speaking with infinite difficulty. "What sort of looking gentleman was he?"

"He was a very tall and dark gentleman, with a most peculiar nose—not quite like any nose that I ever saw before—and most singular eyes. Never have I seen a gentleman who at all resembled him."

I sink into a chair, while a cold shudder creeps over me as I think of my poor child's dream—of her fainting fit at Wiesbaden—of her unconquerable dread of and aversion from my departure. And this happened twelve days ago! I catch up my hat, and prepare to rush like a madman in pursuit.

"How did they go?" I ask, incoherently; "by train?—driving?—walking?"

"They went in a carriage."

"What direction did they take? Whither did they go?"

---

* A fixed-price hotel meal offered with few choices.

He shakes his head. "It is not known."

"It *must* be known!" I cry, driven to frenzy by every second's delay. "Of course, the driver could tell. Where is he? where can I find him?"

"He did not belong to Lucerne, neither did the carriage; the gentleman brought them with him."

"But madame's maid," say I, a gleam of hope flashing across my mind— "did she go with her?"

"No, monsieur; she is still here. She was as much surprised as monsieur at madame's departure."

"Send her at once!" I cry, eagerly; but, when she comes, I find that she can throw no light on the matter. She weeps noisily, and says many irrelevant things; but I can obtain no information from her beyond the fact that she was unaware of her mistress's departure until long after it had taken place, when, surprised at not being rung for at the usual time, she had gone to her room and found it empty, and, on inquiring in the hotel, had heard of her sudden departure; that, expecting her to return at night, she had sat up waiting for her till two o'clock in the morning, but that, as I knew, she had not returned, neither had any thing since been heard of her.

Not all my inquiries, not all my cross-questionings of the whole staff of the hotel, of the visitors, of the railway-officials, of nearly all the inhabitants of Lucerne and its environs, procure me a jot more knowledge. On the next few weeks I look back as on a hellish and insane dream. I can neither eat nor sleep; I am unable to remain one moment quiet; my whole existence, my nights and my days, are spent in seeking, seeking. Everything that human despair and frenzied love can do is done by me. I advertise, I communicate with the police, I employ detectives; but that fatal twelve days' start forever baffles me. Only on one occasion do I obtain one tittle of information. In a village a few miles from Lucerne, the peasants, on the day in question, saw a carriage driving rapidly through their little street. It was closed, but through the windows they could see the occupants—a dark gentleman, with the peculiar physiognomy, which has been so often described, and on the opposite seat a lady, lying apparently in a state of utter insensibility.

But even this leads to nothing.

Oh, reader, these things happened twenty years ago; since then, I have searched sea and land, but never have I seen my little Elizabeth again.

Florence Marryat (1833–1889) had art and a fascination with exotic plàces in her blood. Her father, Captain Frederick Marryat, was a well-known author of naval fiction, he wrote *The Phantom Ship* (1839), which was hailed by S. T. Joshi as an early important work of weird fiction. Florence travelled to India with her first husband, an officer in the British Army, where they stayed for seven years. She soon turned to writing herself, her first novel being published in 1865, written while she was nursing her children over scarlet fever (Marryat had eight children by him, three of them born in India). This was the first of what would be more than seventy novels, as well as countless short stories, essays, and plays. She returned to England alone in 1870 and was soon living with another man; her first husband divorced her in 1879. By the mid-1870s, she took to the stage to perform some of her own work, and she continued to be a popular performer and lecturer until 1890, when Marryat retired from the stage. She continued to write, including several works on Spiritualism, until her death from diabetes and pneumonia in 1899. "Little White Souls" first appeared in her collection *The Ghost of Charlotte Cray and Other Stories* in 1883.

Little White Souls

by Florence Marryat

I am going to tell you a story, which is as improbable a one as you have ever heard. I do not expect anybody to believe it; yet it is perfectly true. The ignorant and bigoted will read it to the end perhaps, and then fling it down with the assertion that it is all nonsense, and there is not one word of truth in it. The wiser and more experienced may say it is very wonderful and incredible, but still they know there are more things in heaven and earth than are dreamt of in their philosophy. But no one will credit it with a hearty, uncompromising belief. And yet neither ridicule nor incredulity can alter the fact that this is a true history of circumstances that occurred but a few years since, and to persons who are living at the present time.

The scene is laid in India and to India,[*] therefore, I must transplant you in order that you may be introduced to the actors in this veracious[†] drama, premising that the names I give, not only of people but of places, are all fictitious.

It is Christmas time in a single station on the frontiers of Bengal,[‡] and a very dull Christmas the members of the 145th Bengal Muftis[§] find it in consequence. For to be quartered in a single station means to be compelled to associate with the same people day after day and month after month and year after year; and to carry on that old quarrel with Jones, or to listen to the cackle of Mrs. Robinson, or be bored with the twaddle of Major Smith, without any hope of respite or escape, and leaving the gentlemen out of the question, the ladies of the 145th Bengal Muftis are not in the best frame of mind at the time my story opens to spend the day of peace and goodwill towards men together. Regimental ladies seldom are. They are quarrelsome and interfering, and back-biting enough towards each other in an English garrison town, but that is a trifle compared to the way in which they carry on in our outlying stations in India. And yet, the ladies of the 145th Bengal Muftis are not bad specimens of the sex, taken individually. It is only when they come in contact that their Christian love and charity make themselves conspicuous. Mrs. Dunstan, the wife of the colonel, is the most important of them all, and the most important personage, too,

---

[*] At the time this story was written, India was under the rule of the British Raj.

[†] Truthful or honest.

[‡] Bengal is an area currently divided between India and Bangladesh, located at the northeastern edge of India. Under the Raj, it was one of three administrative regions and was known as the Bengal Presidency.

[§] Marryat did warn us at the start of the story that she had changed names, and "145th Bengal Muftis" is not a real name, since in the 1880s there were only 130 regiments in the British Indian Army, and none of them were known as Muftis (*muftis* are experts in Islamic law, or *sharia*, who are qualified to write opinions, or *fatwa*).

in this little story of a misfortune that involved herself, therefore let Mrs. Dunstan be the first to advance for inspection.

As we meet her, she is seated in a lounging chair in her own drawing-room at Mudlianah,* with a decided look of discontent or unhappiness upon her countenance. The scene around her would seem fair enough in the eyes of those who were not condemned to live in it. Her room is surrounded by a broad verandah, which is so covered by creepers as to be a bower of greenery. Huge trumpet-shaped blossoms of the most gorgeous hues of purple, scarlet, and orange, hang in graceful festoons about the windows and open doorways, whilst the starry jessamine and Cape honeysuckle fill the air with sweetness. Beyond the garden, which is laid out with much taste, though rather in a wild and tangled style, owing to the luxuriance of the vegetation, lie a range of snowy hills, which appear quite close in the transparent atmosphere, although in reality they are many miles away.

Mrs. Dunstan's room is furnished, too, with every luxury as befits the room of a colonel's wife, even in an up country station. The chairs and sofas are of carved ebony wood, and cane work from Benares;† the table is covered with flowers, books, and fancy work; a handsome piano stands in one corner; the floor is covered with coloured matting, and in the verandah are scattered toys from various countries, a token that this comfortable home does not lack the chief of married joys, a child-angel in the house.

The mistress, too, is still young and still handsome, not wanting the capacity for intellectual nor the health for physical enjoyment, there must be some deeper reason than outward discomfort therefore for that sad far-away look in her eyes and the pain, which has knitted her brow. Yes, "Mees Margie MacQueerk" (as she would style herself), has been giving Mrs. Dunstan an hour of her company that morning, and as usual left her trail behind her.

---

* Another name Marryat has created.

† Benares, also known as Varanasi, is a city located near India's northern edge, between New Delhi and Kolkata (Calcutta). Benares is known for its textiles, sculpture, and ivory; it is also considered to be the holiest of the seven sacred cities in Hinduism and Jainism.

"Mees Margie" is a tall, quaint, ill-favoured Scotchwoman on the wrong side of fifty, who has come out to India to keep the house of her brother, the doctor of the 145th. She is a rigid Presbyterian, with a brogue as uncompromising as her doctrine and a judgment as hard as nails. Never having been tempted to do anything wrong, she is excessively virtuous, and has an eye like a hawk for the misdoings of others; indeed she is so excellent a detective that she discovers the sins before the sinners have quite made up their minds to commit them. She is the detestation of the regiment, and the colonel's wife has been compelled in consequence to show Miss Mac-Quirk more attention than she would otherwise have done to make up for the neglect of the others. For never does Miss Maggie pass half-an-hour without hinting at a fresh peccadillo on the part of somebody else. She has a rooted conviction that all soldiers are libertines, not fit to be trusted out of sight of their wives or sisters, and if she has no new misdemeanour to relate on the part of the masters, the servants are sure to come in for their share of abuse, and so Miss Maggie MacQuirk manages to find food for scandal all the year round. Ethel Dunstan ought to know her foibles well enough to mistrust her by this time, and had the doctor's sister come in with some new story of young Freshfield's flirting, or Mr. Masterman's card playing, she would have been as ready as ever to laugh at the old Scotchwoman's mountainous molehills, and to assure her she was utterly mistaken. But Miss MacQuirk's discourse this morning had taken a different turn. She had talked exclusively of the latest arrival in Mudlianah; lovely Mrs. Lawless, who has just returned with her husband, Jack Lawless, from staff duty in the northwest provinces, and how her beauty seemed to have addled the heads of all the men of the 145th Bengal Muftis. And there was a great deal of truth in Miss MacQuirk's assertions, and that is what has made them go home to the heart of Ethel Dunstan. We are all so ready to believe anything that affects our own happiness.

"Deed, and it's jeest fretful," said Miss Margie, in her provincial twang, "to see a set of dunderheeds tairned the wrang way for the sake of a wee bit of a pasty face wi' two beeg eyes in the meedle of it. It's eno' to mak' a God-fearing woman praise the Laird that has kept her in the straight path. For I'll no affairm that it's by mee ain doin' that I can hand up my heed the day with the Queen o' England herself if need be."

"But Mrs. Lawless is very, *very* lovely—there cannot be two opinions on that subject," cried generous-hearted Mrs. Dunstan. "For my own part I never saw a more beautiful face than hers, and my husband says just the same thing."

"Eh! I nae doot it! The Cairnal's heed is tairned like all the rest o' them. But he cannot ca' it reet that men should rin after a leddy that has a lawfu' meeried husband of her ain."

"But you have such strange notions, Miss MacQuirk. If a gentleman shows a lady the least attention you call it 'running after her.' We are like one family shut up in this little station by ourselves. If we are not to be on friendly terms with each other, we are indeed to be pitied."

"Friendly tairms," exclaimed Miss Margie. "Do you call it 'friendly tairms' to be walking in the dairk with anither mon's wife? An' that's jeest what my gude brother saw yester e'en as he was comin' hame fra' mess."*

"What man! Whose wife?" asked Ethel Dunstan, for once interested in Miss MacQuirk's scandal.

"Aye! I dinna ken the mon, but the leddy was Mrs. Lawless hersel'. And her husband was at the mess the while, for Andrew left him at the table, and he was comin' home in the dark and he saw Mrs. Lawless in her garden at the dead o' neet walkin' with a strange mon—a tall mon, and stout, and not unlike the Cairnal, Andrew says."

"What nonsense, Charlie was back from mess by eleven o'clock," said Mrs. Dunstan, with an air of annoyance. "When you repeat such stories, Miss MacQuirk, be good enough to keep my husband's name out of them, or you may get into trouble."

"Ah, well, Mrs. Dunstan, I only mentioned that it was like the Cairnal. Doubtless he was at mess or at home the while. It was half-past ten when Andrew retairned. But it is hairdly reet that Mrs. Lawless should be walking in her gairden at that hour o' neet and with anither mon than her husband. I doot but one should infairm Mr. Lawless of the caircumstance."

---

* Although *mess* usually refers to an area where military men meet, in the British model it is a place where they socialize and hold events, essentially a military club; as such, it had its own dress uniform.

"Well, I advise you not to be the one," replied Ethel Dunstan, tartly. "Jack Lawless is considered a fire-eater amongst men, and I don't think he would spare the woman even who tried to take away his wife's character."

"Eh, Mrs. Doonstan, who talks of takin' awa' her character? I doot it's but little she's got, puir thing, and it 'twould be a sin to rob her of it. But it's a terrible thing to see how gude luiks air rated abuve guid deeds, and enough to mak' all honest men thank the Laird who has presairved them fra the wiles of the enemy. And now I'll wish you the gude mairnin', Mrs. Doonstan, for I have several other calls to pay before tiffin."*

And so the old scandal-monger had left the colonel's wife in the condition in which we found her.

Of course if there had been no more truth in it than in the generality of Miss MacQuirk's stories Ethel Dunstan would have laughed at and forgotten it. But there is just sufficient probability of its being a fact to give a colouring to the matter.

For Mrs. Lawless is not a woman that the most faithful husband in creation could look at without some degree of interest, and Colonel Dunstan being guileless of harm, has expressed his admiration of her in the most open manner. She is a graceful, fairy-like creature, of two or three-and-twenty, in the flush of youth and beauty, and yet with sufficient knowledge of the world to render her the most charming companion. She has a complexion like a rose leaf, a skin as white as milk, large limpid hazel eyes, a pert nose, a coaxing mouth, and hair of a sunny brown. Fancy such a woman alighting suddenly in an out-of-the-way, dull, dried up little hole of a station like Mudlianah, and in the midst of some twenty inflammable British officers. You might as well have sent a mitrailleuse† amongst them for the amount of damage she did. They were all alight at the first view of her, and hopelessly burned up before the week was over. She is devoted to her Jack, and has in reality no eyes nor thoughts except for him; but he has become a little used to her charms, after the manner of husbands, and so she flirts with the rest of the regiment indiscriminately, and sheds the

---

* An Indian English word for meal or snack.

† A volley or "machine" gun, predating the Gatling gun by at least ten years.

light of her countenance on all alike, from the colonel downwards. The wives of the 145th Bengal Muftis have received Mrs. Lawless but coldly. How can they look into her heart and see how entirely it is devoted to her husband? All they see is her lovely, smiling face, and contrasting it with their own less beautiful and somewhat faded countenances, they imagine that no man can be proof against her fascinations, and jealousy reigns supreme in the 145th with regard to Cissy Lawless.

Ethel Dunstan has no need to fear a rival in her colonel's heart, because she possesses every atom of his affection, and he has proved it by years of devotion and fidelity, but when a woman is once jealous of another, she forgets everything except the fear of present loss. Colonel Dunstan is vexed when he comes in that morning from regimental duty to find his wife pale and dispirited, still more so to hear the tart replies she makes to all his tender questioning.

"Are you not well, my darling?" he asks.

"Quite well, thank you; at least as well as one can be in a hole like Mudlianah. Charlie! where have you been this morning?"

"Been, dear! Why, to mess and barracks, to be sure! Where else should I have been?"

"There are plenty of houses to call at, I suppose. What is the use of pretending to be so dull? You made a call late last night, if I am not much mistaken!"

"Last night! What, after mess? I only went home with Jack Lawless for a minute or two."

"Did you go home with Mr. Lawless?"

"Yes; at least—he didn't walk home with me exactly; but he came in soon afterwards."

"Of course she was in bed?"

"Oh no, she wasn't. She was as brisk as a bee. We talked together for a long time."

"So I have heard! In the garden," remarks Mrs. Dunstan pointedly.

"Yes! Was there any harm in that?" replies her husband. "Our talk was solely on business. Is anything the matter, Ethel, darling? You are not at all like yourself this morning."

But the only answer Mrs. Dunstan gives him is indicated by her suddenly rising and leaving the room. She is not the sort of woman to tell her husband frankly what she feels. She thinks—and perhaps she is right—that to openly touch so delicate a matter as a dereliction from the path of marital duty, is to add fuel to the flame. But she suffers terribly, and in her excited condition Colonel Dunstan's open avowal appears an aggravation of his offence.

"He is too noble to deceive me," she thinks, "and so he will take refuge in apparent frankness. He confesses he admires her, and he will tell me every time he goes there, and then he will say—'How can you suspect me of any wrong intention when I am so open with you?'

"Business indeed! As if he could have any business with a doll like Mrs. Lawless. It is shameful of her to flirt with married men in this disgraceful way."

Yet Mrs. Dunstan and Mrs. Lawless meet at the band that evening, and smile and bow to and talk with one another as if they were the best friends in the world; but the colonel is prevented by duty from doing more than arrive in time to take his wife home to dinner, and so Ethel's heart is for the while at rest. But during dinner a dreadful blow falls upon her. A note is brought to the colonel, which he reads in silence and puts into the pocket of his white drill waistcoat.

"From Mr. Hazlewood, dear?" says Ethel interrogatively.

"No, my love, purely on business," replies the colonel, as he helps himself to wine. But when the meal is concluded he walks into his dressing-room, and re-appears in his mess uniform.

"Going to mess, Charlie?" exclaims his wife, in a tone of disappointment.

"No, my darling—business! I may be late. Good-night!" and he kisses her and walks out of the house.

"Business," repeats Mrs. Dunstan emphatically; and as soon as his back is turned, she is searching his suit of drill. Colonel Dunstan has not been careful to conceal or destroy the note he received at dinner. It is still in his waistcoat pocket. His wife tears it open and reads:—

"Dear Colonel—Do come over this evening if possible. I have had another letter, which you must see. I depend upon you for everything. You are the only friend I have in the world. Pray don't fail me—Ever yours gratefully,
"Cissy Lawless."

"Cat!" cries Mrs. Dunstan indignantly, "deceitful, fawning, hypocritical cat! This is the way she gets over the men—pretending to each one that he is the only friend she has in the world—a married woman, too! It's disgusting! Miss MacQuirk is quite right, and some one ought to tell poor Jack Lawless of the way she is carrying on. And Charlie is as bad as she is! It was only to-day he told me as bold as brass that that creature's eyes are so innocent and guileless-looking they reminded him of little Katie's—and not ten minutes afterwards, he said my new bonnet from England was a fright, and made me look as yellow as a guinea.* Oh! what is this world coming to, and where will such wickedness end? I wish that I was dead and buried with poor mamma." And so Mrs. Dunstan cries herself to sleep, and when her husband comes home and kisses her fondly as she lies upon the pillow, he decides that she is feverish, and has not been looking well lately and must require change, and remains awake for some time thinking how he can best arrange to let her have it.

In the middle of that night, however, something occurs to occupy the minds of both father and mother to the exclusion of everything else. Little Katie, their only child, a beautiful little girl of three years old, is taken suddenly and dangerously ill with one of those violent disorders that annually decimate our British possessions in the east. The whole household is roused—Dr. MacQuirk summoned from his bed—and for some hours the parents hang in mental terror over the baby's cot, fearing every minute lest their treasure should be taken from them. But the crisis passes. Little Katie is weak but out of danger, and then the consideration arises what is the best thing to facilitate her recovery. Dr. MacQuirk lets a day or two pass to allow the child to gain a little strength, and then he tells the colonel emphatically that she must be sent away at once—to England if possible—or he will not answer for her life. This announcement is a sad blow to Colonel Dunstan, but he knows it is imperative, and prepares to break the news to his wife.

"Ethel, my dear, I am sorry to tell you that MacQuirk considers it quite necessary that Katie should leave Mudlianah for change of air, and he wishes her, if possible, to go to England at once."

---

* Guineas were British coins that contained enough gold to give them a yellowish color.

"But it is *not* possible, Charlie. We could never consent to send the child home alone, and you cannot get leave again so soon. Surely it is not absolutely necessary she should go to England."

"Not absolutely necessary, perhaps but very advisable, not only for Katie, but for yourself. You are not looking at all well, Ethel. Your dispirited appearance worries me sadly, and in your condition you should take every care of yourself. I hardly like to make the proposal to you, but if you would consent to take Katie home to your sister's, say for a twelvemonth, I think it would do your own health a great deal of good."

But Colonel Dunstan's allusion to her want of spirits has recalled all her jealousy of Mrs. Lawless to Ethel's mind, and the journey to England finds no favour in her eyes.

"You want me to go away for a twelvemonth," she says sharply, "and pray what is to become of you meanwhile?"

"I must stay here. You know I cannot leave India."

"You will stay with Mrs.—I mean with the regiment, whilst I go home with the child."

"Yes. What else can I do?"

"Then I shall *not* go. I refuse to leave you."

"Not even for Katie's sake?"

"We will take her somewhere else. There are plenty of places in India where we can go for change of air; and if you *cared* for me, Charlie, you would never contemplate such a thing as a whole year's separation."

"Do you think I *like* the idea, Ethel? What should I do left here all by myself? I only proposed it for your sake and the child's."

"I will not go," repeats Mrs. Dunstan firmly, and she sends for Dr. MacQuirk and has a long talk with him.

"Dr. MacQuirk, is it an absolute necessity that Katie should go to England?"

"Not an absolute necessity, my dear leddy, but, from a mee-dical point of view, advisable. And your own hee-alth also—"

"Bother my health!" she cries irreverently. "What is the nearest place to which I could take the child for change?"

"You might take her to the Heels, Mrs. Doonstan—to the heels of Mandalinati,* which are very salubrious at this time of the year."

"And how far off are they?"

"A matter of a coople of hundred miles. Ye canna get houses there, but there is a cairs-tle on the broo' o' the Heel that ye may have for the airsking."

"A castle, that sounds most romantic? And whom must we ask, doctor?"

"The cairs-tle is the property of Rajah Mati Singh, and he bee-lt it for his ain plee-sure, but he doesna' ceer to leeve there, and so he will lend it to any Europeans who weesh for a change to the Heels of Mandalinati."

"Rajah Mati Singh! That horrid man! There will be no chance of seeing him, will there?"

"No, no, Mrs. Doonstan! the Rajah will not trouble ye! He never goes near the cairs-tle noo, and ye will have the whoole place to yersel' in peace and quietude."

"I will speak to the colonel about it directly he comes in. Thank you for your information, Dr. MacQuirk. If we must leave Mudlianah, I shall be delighted to stay for a while at this romantic castle on the brow of the hill.

"Yes," she says to herself, when the doctor is gone, "we shall be alone there, I and my Charlie, and it will seem like the dear old honeymoon time, before we came to live amongst these horrid flirting cats of women, and perhaps some of the old memories will come back to him, and we shall be happy, foolish lovers again as we used to be long ago before I was so miserable."

But when Colonel Dunstan hears of the proposed visit to the Mandalinati Hills he does not seem to approve of it half so much as he did of the voyage to England.

"I am not at all sure if the climate will suit you or the child," he says, "it is sometimes very raw and misty up on those hills. And then it is very wild and lonely. I know the castle MacQuirk means—a great straggling building standing quite by itself, and in a most exposed position. I really think you will be much wiser to go to England, Ethel."

"Oh, Charlie! how unkind of you, and when you know the separation will kill me!"

---

* Another fictitious name.

"It would be harder, just at first, but I should feel our trouble would be repaid. But I shall always be in a fidget about you at Mandalinati."

"But, Charlie, what harm can happen when you are with us?"

"My dear girl, I can't go with you to the castle."

"Why not?"

"Because business will detain me here. How do you suppose I can leave the regiment?"

"But you will come up very often to see us—every week at least; won't you, Charlie?"

"On a four days' journey! Ethel, my dear, be reasonable. If you go to Mandalinati, the most I can promise is to get a fortnight's leave after a time, and run up to see how you and the dear child are getting on. But I don't like your going, and I tell you so plainly. Suppose you are taken ill before your time, or Katie has another attack, how are you to get assistance up on those beastly hills? Think better of it, Ethel, and decide on England. If you go, Captain Lewis says he will send his wife at the same time, and you would be nice company for each other on the way home."

"Mrs. Lewis, indeed! an empty-headed noodle! Why, she would drive me crazy before we were half-way there. No, Charlie; I am quite decided. If *you* cannot accompany me to England, I refuse to go. I shall get the loan of the castle, and try what four weeks there will do for the child."

And thus it came to pass that Mrs Dunstan's absurd jealousy of Mrs. Lawless drives her to spend that fatal month at the lonely castle on the Mandalinati Hills, instead of going in peace and safety to her native land. For a brief space Hope leads her to believe that she may induce Mrs. Lawless to pass the time of exile with her. If her woman's wit can only induce the fatal beauty to become her guest, she will bear the loss of Charlie's society with equanimity. But though Cissy Lawless seems for a moment almost to yield, she suddenly draws back, to Mrs. Dunstan's intense annoyance.

"The old castle on the hills!" she exclaimed. "Are you and Colonel Dunstan really going there? How delightfully romantic! I believe no end of murders have been committed there, and every room is haunted. Oh, I should like to go, too, of all things in the world! I long to see a real ghost, only you must promise never to leave us alone, Colonel, for I should die of fright if I were left by myself."

"But I shall not be there, I am sorry to say," replies the colonel. "My wife and Katie are going for change of air, but I must simmer meanwhile at Mudlianah."

Pretty Cissy Lawless looks decidedly dumfoundered, and begins to back out of her consent immediately. "I pity you," she answers, "and I pity myself too, for I expect we shall have to simmer together. I should like it of all things, as I said before, but Jack would never let me leave him. He is such a dear, useless body without me. Besides, as you know, Colonel, I have business to keep me in Mudlianah."

Business again! Ethel turns away in disgust; but it is with difficulty she can keep the tears from rushing to her eyes. However, there is no help for it, and she must go. Her child is very dear to her, and at all risks it requires mountain air. She must leave her colonel to take his chance in the plains below—only as he puts her and the child into the transit that is to convey them to the hills, and bids her farewell with a very honest falter in his voice he feels her hot tears upon his cheek.

"Oh, Charlie, Charlie, be true to me! Think how I have loved you. I am so very miserable."

"Miserable, my love, and for this short parting? Come, Ethel, you must be braver than this. It will not be long before we meet again, remember."

"And, till then, you will be careful, won't you, Charlie, for my sake, and think of me, and don't go too much from home? and remember how treacherous women are; and I am not beautiful, I know, my darling; I never was, you know," with a deep sob, "like—like Mrs. Lawless and others. But I love you, Charlie, I love you with all my heart, and I have always been faithful to you in thought as well as deed." And so, sobbing and incoherent, Ethel Dunstan drives away to the Mandalinati Hills, whilst the good colonel stands where she left him, with a puzzled look upon his honest sunburnt face.

"What does she mean?" he ponders, "by saying she is not beautiful like Cissy Lawless, and telling me to remember how treacherous women are, as if I didn't know the jades.* Is it possible Ethel can be jealous—jealous of that poor, pretty little creature who is breaking her heart about her Jack?

---

* *Jade* is old slang for a hussy or prostitute.

No! that would be too ridiculous, and too alarming into the bargain; for even if I can get the boy out of the scrape, it is hardly a matter to trust to a woman's discretion. Well, well, I must do the best I can, and leave the rest to chance. Ethel to be jealous! the woman I have devoted my life to! It would be too absurd if anything the creatures do can possibly be called so."

And then he walks off to breakfast with the Lawlesses, though his heart is rather heavy, and his spirits are rather dull for several days after his wife starts for the castle on the hill. Ethel, on the other hand, gets on still worse than her husband. As she lies in her transit, swaying about from side to side over the rough country roads, she is haunted by the vision of Charlie walking about the garden till the small hours of the morning, hand in hand with Cissy Lawless, with a mind entirely oblivious of his poor wife and child, or indeed of anything except his beautiful companion. Twenty times would she have decided that she could bear the strain no longer, and given the order to return to Mudlianah, had it not been for the warning conveyed in the fretful wailing of her sickly child—his child—the blossom of their mutual love. So, for Katie's sake. poor Ethel keeps steadfastly to her purpose, and soon real troubles take the place of imaginary ones, and nearly efface their remembrance. She is well protected by a retinue of native servants, and the country through which she travels is a perfectly safe one; yet, as they reach the foot of the hills up which they must climb to reach the celebrated castle, she is surprised to hear that her nurse (or Dye*), who has been with her since Katie's birth, refuses to proceed any further, and sends in her resignation.

"What do you mean, Dye?" demands her mistress with a natural vexation, "you are going to leave Katie and me just as we require your services most. What can you be thinking of? You, who have always professed to be so fond of us both. Are you ill?"

"No, missus, I not ill, but I cannot go up the hill. That castle very bad place, very cold and big, and bad people live there and many noises come, and I want to go back to Mudlianah to my husband and little children."

"What nonsense, Dye! I didn't think you were so foolish. Who has been putting such nonsense into your head? The castle is a beautiful place, and

---

* A *dai* is a nurse, wet-nurse, or midwife.

you will not feel at all cold with the warm clothes I have given you, and we have come here to make Miss Katie well, you know, and you will surely never leave her until she is quite strong again."

But the native woman obstinately declares that she will not go on to the Mandalinati hills, and it is only upon a promise of receiving double pay that she at last complainingly consents to accompany her mistress to the castle. Ethel has to suffer, however, for descending to bribery, as before the ascent commences every servant in her employ has bargained for higher wages, and unless she wishes to remain in the plains she is compelled to comply with their demands. But she determines to write and tell Charlie of their extortion by the first opportunity, and hopes that the intelligence may bring him up, brimming with indignation, to set her household in order. Her first view of the castle, however, repays her for the trouble she has had in getting there. She thinks she has seldom seen a building that strikes her with such a sense of importance. It is formed of a species of white stone that glistens like marble in the sunshine, and it is situated on the brow of a jutting hill that renders it visible for many miles round. The approach to it is composed of three terraces of stone, each one surrounded by mountainous shrubs and hill-bearing flowers, and Ethel wonders why the Rajah Mati Singh, having built himself such a beautiful residence, should ever leave it for the use of strangers. She understands very little of the native language, but from a few words dropt here and there she gathers that the castle was originally intended for a harem, and supposes the rajah's wives found the climate too cold for susceptible natures. If they disliked the temperature as much as her native servants appear to do, it is no wonder that they deserted the castle, for their groans and moans and shakings of the head quite infect their mistress, and make her feel more lonely and nervous than she would otherwise have done, although she finds the house is so large that she can only occupy a small portion of it. The dining hall, which is some forty feet square, is approached by eight doors below, two on each side, whilst a gallery runs round the top of it, supported by a stone balustrade, and containing eight more doors to correspond with those on the ground floor. These upper doors open into the sleeping chambers, which all look out again upon open-air verandahs commanding an extensive view over the hills and plains below. Mrs. Dunstan feels very dismal and isolated as she sits down to her first meal in this splendid dining hall, but after a few days she gets reconciled to the loneliness and sits with Katie on the terraces and amongst the flowers all day long, praying that the fresh breeze and mountain air may restore the roses to her darling's cheeks. One thing, however, she cannot make up her mind to, and that is to sleep upstairs. All the chambers are furnished, for the Rajah Mati Singh is a great ally of the British throne, and keeps up this castle on purpose to ingratiate himself with the English by lending it for their use; but Ethel has her bed brought downstairs, and occupies two rooms that look out upon the moonlit terraces. She cannot imagine why the natives are so averse to this proceeding on her part. They gesticulate and chatter—all in Double Dutch,* as far as she is concerned—but she will have her own way, for she feels less lonely when her apartments are all together. Her Dye goes on her knees to entreat her mistress to sleep upstairs instead of down; but Ethel is growing tired of all this demonstration about what she knows nothing, and sharply bids her do as she is told. Yet, as the days go on, there is something unsatisfactory—she cannot tell what—about the whole affair. The servants are gloomy and discontented, and huddle together in groups, whispering to one another. The Dye is always crying and hugging the child, while she drops mysterious hints about their never seeing Mudlianah again, which make Ethel's heart almost stop beating, as she thinks of native insurrections and rebellions, and wonders if the servants mean to murder her and Katie in revenge for having been forced to accompany them to Mandalinati.

Meanwhile, some mysterious circumstances occur for which Mrs. Dunstan cannot account. One day, as she is sitting at her solitary dinner with two natives standing behind her chairs, she is startled by hearing a sudden rushing wind, and, looking up, sees the eight doors in the gallery open and slam again, apparently of their own accord, whilst simultaneously the eight doors on the ground floor which were standing open shut with a loud noise. Ethel looks round; the two natives are green with fright; but she believes that it is only the wind, though the evening is as calm as can be. She orders them to open the lower doors again, and having done so, they have hardly returned to their station behind her chair before the sixteen doors open and

---

* Slang for a language one cannot understand.

shut as before. Mrs. Dunstan is now very angry; she believes the servants are playing tricks upon her, and she is not the woman to permit such an impertinence with impunity. She rises from table majestically and leaves the room, but reflection shows her that the only thing she can do is to write to her husband on the subject, for she is in the power of her servants so long as she remains at the castle, where they cannot be replaced.

She stays in the garden that evening, thinking over this occurrence and its remedy, till long after her child has been put to bed—and as she re-enters the castle she visits Katie's room before she retires to her own, and detects the Dye in the act of hanging up a large black shawl across the window that looks out upon the terrace.

"What are you doing that for?" cries Ethel impetuously, her suspicions ready to be aroused by anything, however trivial.

The woman stammers and stutters, and finally declares she cannot sleep without a screen drawn before the window.

"Bad people's coming and going at night here!" she says in explanation, "and looking in at the window upon the child; and if they touch missy she will die. Missus had better let me put up curtain to keep them out. They can't do me any harm. It is the child they come for."

"Bad people coming at night! What on earth do you mean, Dye? What people come here but our own servants? If you go on talking such nonsense to me I shall begin to think you drink too much arrack."[*]

"Missus, please!" replies the native with a deprecatory shrug of the shoulders; "but Dye speaks the truth! A white woman walks on this terrace every night looking for her child, and if she sees little missy, she will take her away, and then you will blame poor Dye for losing her. Better let me put up the curtain so that she can't look in at window."

Ethel calls the woman some opprobrious epithet, but walks away nevertheless, and lets her do as she will; only the next day she writes a full account to Charlie of what she has gone through, and tells him she thinks all the servants are going mad. In which opinion he entirely agrees with her.

---

[*] Arrack is a fermented liquor (also spelled arak) common in Turkey and the Middle East; its ingredients depend on the country of origin.

"For 'mad' read 'bad,'" he writes back again, "and I'm with you. There is no doubt upon the matter, my dear girl. The brutes don't like the cold, and are playing tricks upon you to try and force you to return to the plains. It is a common thing in this country. Don't give way to them, but tell them I'll stop their pay all round if anything unpleasant happens again. I think now you must confess it would have been better to take my advice and try a trip home instead. However, as you are at Mandalinati, don't come back until your object in going there is accomplished. I wish I could join you, but it is impossible just yet. Jack Lawless is obliged to go north on business, and I have promised to accompany him. Keep up a good heart, dearest, and don't let those brutes think they have any power to annoy or frighten you."

"Going north on business!" exclaims Ethel bitterly; "and she is going too, I suppose; and Charlie can find time to go with them, though he cannot come to me. Oh, it is too hard. It is more than any woman can be expected to bear! I'm sure I wish I had gone to England instead. Then I should at least have had my dear sister to tell my troubles to, and he—he would have been free to flirt with that wretched woman as much as ever he chose."

And the poor wife lies in her bed that night too unhappy to sleep, while she pictures her husband doing all sorts of dishonourable things, instead of snoring as he really is in his own deserted couch. Her room adjoins that in which the Dye is sleeping with her little girl, and the door between them stands wide open. From where she lies, Ethel can see part of the floor of Katie's bedroom, from which the moonlight is excluded in consequence of the great black shawl, which the nurse continues to pin nightly across the window-pane. Suddenly, as she watches the shaded floor without thinking of it, a streak of moonshine darts right athwart it, as if a corner of the curtain had been raised. Always full of fears for her child, Ethel slips off her own bed, and with noiseless, unslippered feet runs into the next room, only in time to see part of a white dress upon the terrace as some unseen hand hastily drops the shawl again. She crosses the floor, and opening the window, looks out. Nobody is in sight. From end to end of the broad terraces the moon light lies undisturbed by any shadow, though she fancies her ear can discern the rustling of a garment sweeping the stone foundation. As she turns to the darkened chamber again, she finds the Dye is sitting up awake and trembling.

"Who raised that shawl just now, Dye? Tell me—I will know!" says Mrs. Dunstan.

"Oh, mam! How can poor Dye tell? Perhaps it was the English lady come to take my little missy! Oh! when shall we go back to Mudlianah and be safe again?"

"English fiddlesticks! Don't talk such rubbish to me. I am up to all your tricks, but you won't frighten me, and so you may tell the others. And I shall not go back to Mudlianah one day sooner for anything you may say or do—"

Yet Mrs. Ethel does not feel quite comfortable, even though her words are so brave. But shortly afterwards her thoughts are turned into another direction, whether agreeably or otherwise, we shall see. As she is sitting at breakfast the next morning, a shouting of natives and a commotion in the courtyard warns her of a new arrival. She imagines it is her husband, and rushes to meet him. But, to her surprise and chagrin, the figure that emerges from the transit is that of Mrs. Lawless looking as lovely in her travelling dress and rumpled hair as ever she did in the most extravagant *costume de bal*.

"Are you surprised to see me?" she cries, as she jumps to the ground. "Well, my dear, you can hardly be more surprised than I am to find myself here. But the fact is, Jack and the colonel are off to Hoolabad* on business, so I thought I would take advantage of their absence to pay you a visit. And I hope you are glad to see me?"

Of course Mrs. Dunstan says she *is* glad, and in a measure her words are true. She is glad to keep this fascinating wicked flirt under her eye, where it is impossible she can tamper with the affections of her beloved Charlie, and she is glad of her company and conversation, which is as sociable and bright as a clever little woman can make it. Mrs. Lawless is full of sympathy, too, with Mrs. Dunstan's fears and the bad behaviour of her servants, and being a very good linguist, she promises to obtain all the information she can from them, and make them fully understand their mistress's intentions in return.

"It's lucky I came, my dear," she says brightly, "or they might have made themselves still more offensive to you. But you have the dear

---

* Another name that's fictitious.

colonel and Jack to thank for that, for I shouldn't have left home if they had not done so."

"Ah, just as I imagined," thinks Ethel, "she would not have left him unless she had been obliged, and she has the impudence to tell me so to my very face. However, she is here, and I must make the best of it, and be thankful it has happened so." And so she lays herself out to please her guest in order to keep her by her as long as she possibly can.

But a few days after Cissy's arrival she receives a letter that evidently discomposes her. She keeps on exclaiming, "How provoking," and "How annoying," as she peruses it, and folds it up with an unmistakable frown on her brow.

"What is the matter?" demands Ethel. "I hope it is not bad news."

"Yes, it is very bad news. They have never gone after all, Mrs. Dunstan, and Jack is so vexed I should have left Mudlianah before he started."

"But now you are here, you will not think of returning directly, I hope," says Ethel, in an anxious voice.

"Oh no, I suppose not—it would be so childish—that is, unless Jack wishes me to do so. But I have hardly recovered from the effects of the journey yet; those transits shake so abominably. No, I shall certainly stay here for a few weeks, unless my husband orders me to return."

Yet Mrs. Lawless appears undecided and restless from that moment, which Mrs. Dunstan ascribes entirely to her wish to return to Mudlianah, and her flirtation with the colonel, and the suspicion makes her receive any allusions to such a contingency with marked coolness. Cissy Lawless busies herself going amongst the natives and talking with them about the late disturbances at the castle, and her report is not satisfactory.

"Are you easily frightened, Mrs. Dunstan?" she asks her one day suddenly.

"No, I think not. Why?"

"Because you must think me a fool if you like, but I am; and the stories your servants have told me have made me quite nervous of remaining at the castle."

"A good excuse to leave me and go back to Mudlianah," thinks Mrs. Dunstan; and then she draws herself up stiffly, and says, "Indeed! You must be very credulous if you believe what natives say. What may these dreadful stories consist of?"

"Oh! I daresay you will turn them into ridicule, because, perhaps, you don't believe in ghosts."

"Ghosts! I should think not, indeed. Who does?"

"I do, Mrs. Dunstan, and for the good reason that I have seen more than one."

"You have seen a spirit? What will you tell me next?"

"That I hope you never may, for it is not a pleasant sight. But that has nothing to do with the present rumours. I find that your servants are really frightened of remaining at the castle. They say there is not a native in the villages round about who would enter it for love or money, and that the reason the Rajah Mati Singh has deserted it is on account of its reputation for being haunted."

"Every one has heard of that," replies Ethel, with a heightened colour, "but no one believes it. Who should it be haunted by?"

"You know what a bad character the rajah bears for cruelty and oppression. They say he built this castle for a harem, and kidnapped a beautiful English woman, a soldier's daughter, and confined her here for some years. But, finding one day that she had been attempting to communicate with her own people, he had her most barbarously put to death, with her child and the servants he suspected of conniving with her. Then he established a native harem here, but was obliged to remove it, for no infant born in the house ever lived. They say that as soon as a child is born under this roof, the spirit of the white woman* appears to carry it away in place of her own. But the natives declare that she is not satisfied with the souls of black children, and that she will continue to appear until she has secured a white child like the one that was murdered before her eyes. And your servants assure me that she has been seen by several of them since coming here, and they feel certain that she is waiting for your baby to be born that she may carry it away."

---

* Marryat may have been inspired by the Indian legend of the Churel, said to be the ghost of a woman who either died in childbirth or was beaten to death by relatives. The Churel is a shapeshifter that can present itself as a beautiful woman dressed in white, although they preferred to tempt men to their doom rather than kidnapping children.

"What folly!" cries Mrs. Dunstan, whose cheeks have nevertheless grown very red. "It's all a *ruse* in order to make me go home again. In the first place, I should be ashamed to believe in such nonsense, and in the second, I do not expect my baby to be born until I am back in Mudlianah."

"But accidents happen some times, you know, dear Mrs. Dunstan, and it would be a terrible thing if you were taken ill up here. Don't you think, all things considered, it would be more prudent for you to go home again?"

"No, I do not," replied Mrs. Dunstan, decidedly. "I came here for my child's health, and I shall stay until it is re-established."

"But you must feel so lonely by yourself."

"I have plenty to do and to think of," says Ethel, "and I never want company whilst I am with my little Katie."

She is determined to take neither pity nor advice from the woman who is so anxious to join the colonel again.

"I am glad to hear you say so," replied Mrs. Lawless, somewhat timidly, "because it makes it easier for me to tell you that I am afraid I must leave you. I daresay you will think me very foolish, but I am too nervous to remain any longer at Mandalinati. I have not slept a wink for the last three nights. I must go back to Jack."

"Oh! You must go back to Jack!" repeats Mrs. Dunstan, with a sneer at Mrs. Lawless. "I hate duplicity! Why can't you tell the truth at once?"

"Mrs. Dunstan! What do you mean?"

"I mean that I know why you are going back to Mudlianah as well as you do yourself. It's all very well to lay it upon 'Jack,' or this ridiculous ghost; but you don't deceive me. I have known your treachery for a long time past. It is not 'Jack' you go back to cantonment* for—but my husband, and you are a bad, wicked woman."

"For your husband!" cried Cissy Lawless, jumping to her feet. "How dare you insult me in this manner! What have I ever done to make you credit such an absurdity?"

"You may call it an absurdity, madam, if you choose, but I call it a diabolical wickedness. Haven't you made appointments with him, and walked at night in the garden with him, and done all you could to make

* A military camp.

him faithless to his poor, trusting wife? And you a married woman, too. You ought to be ashamed of yourself!"

"Mrs. Dunstan, I will not stand this language any longer. I, flirt with your husband—a man old enough to be my father! You must be out of your senses! Why, he must be fifty if he's a day!"

"He's not fifty," screams Ethel, in her rage. "He was only forty-two last birth-day."

"I don't believe it. His hair is as grey as a badger. Flirt with the colonel, indeed. When I want to flirt I shall look for a younger and a handsomer man than your husband, I can tell you."

"You'd flirt with him if he were eighty, you bold, forward girl, and I shall take good care to inform Mr. Lawless of the way you have been carrying on with him."

"I shall go down at once, and tell him myself. You don't suppose I would remain your guest after what has happened for an hour longer than is absolutely necessary. I wish you good morning, Mrs. Dunstan, and a civil tongue for the future."

"Oh, of course, you'll go to Mudlianah. I was quite prepared for that, and an excellent excuse you have found to get back again. Good day, madam, and the less we meet before you start the better. Grey haired, indeed! Why, many men are grey at thirty, and I've often been told that he used to be called 'Handsome Charlie' when he first joined the service."

But the wife's indignant protests do not reach the ears of Cissy Lawless, who retires to her own apartments and does not leave them until she gets into the transit again and is rattled back to Mudlianah. When she is fairly off there is no denying that Ethel feels very lonely and very miserable. She is not so brave as she pretends to be, and she is conscious that she has betrayed her jealous feelings in a most unladylike manner, which will make Charlie very angry with her when he comes to hear of it. So what between her rage and her despair, she passes the afternoon and evening in a very hysterical condition of weeping and moaning, and the excitement and fatigue, added to terror at the stories she has heard, bring on the very calamity against which Mrs. Lawless warned her. In the middle of the night she is compelled by illness to summon her Dye to her assistance, and two frightened women do their best to alarm each other still more, until with the morning's light a poor little baby is born into the world, who had no business, strictly speaking, to have entered it till two months later, and the preparations for whose advent are all down at Mudlianah. Poor Ethel has only strength after the event to write a few faint lines in pencil to Colonel Dunstan, telling him she is dying, and begging him to come to her at once, and then to lie down in a state of utter despair, which would assail most women under the circumstances. She has not sufficient energy even to reprove the Dye, who laments over the poor baby as if it were a doomed creature, and keeps starting nervously, as night draws on again, at every shadow, as though she expected to see the old gentleman at her elbow.

She wears out Ethel's patience at last, for the young mother is depressed and feeble and longs for sleep. So she orders the nurse to lay her little infant on her arm, and to go into the next room as usual and lie down beside Katie's cot; and after some expostulation, and many shakings of her head, the Dye complies with her mistress's request. For some time after she is left alone, Ethel lies awake, too exhausted even to sleep, and as she does so, her mind is filled with the stories she has heard, and she clasps her little fragile infant closer to her bosom as she recalls the history of the poor murdered mother, whose child was barbarously slaughtered before her eyes. But she has too much faith in the teaching of her childhood quite to credit such a marvellous story, and she composes herself by prayer and holy thoughts until she sinks into a calm and dreamless slumber. When she wakes some hours after, it is not suddenly, but as though some one were pulling her back to consciousness. Slowly she realises her situation, and feels that somebody, the Dye she supposes, is trying to take the baby from her arms without disturbing her.

"Don't take him from me, Dye," she murmurs, sleepily; "he is so good—he has not moved all night."

But the gentle pressure still continues, and then Ethel opens her eyes and sees not the Dye but a woman, tall and finely formed, and fair as the day, with golden hair floating over her shoulders, and a wild, mad look in her large blue eyes, who is quietly but forcibly taking the baby from her. Already she has one bare arm under the child, and the other over him—and her figure is bent forward, so that her beautiful face is almost on a level with that of Mrs. Dunstan's.

"Who are you? What are you doing?" exclaims Ethel in a voice of breathless alarm, although she does not at once comprehend why she should experience it. The woman makes no answer, but with her eyes fixed on the child with a sort of wild triumph draws it steadily towards her.

"Leave my baby alone! How dare you touch him?" cries Ethel, and then she calls aloud, "Dye! Dye! come to me!"

But at the sound of her voice the woman draws the child hastily away, and Ethel sees it reposing on her arm, whilst she slowly folds her white robes about the little form, and hides it from view.

"Dye, Dye," again screams the mother, and as the nurse rushes to her assistance the spirit woman slowly fades away, with a smile of success upon her lips.

"Bring a light. Quick," cries Ethel. "The woman has been here; she has stolen my baby. Oh, Dye, make haste; help me to get out of bed. I will get it back again if I die in the attempt."

The Dye runs for a lamp, and brings it to the bedside as Mrs. Dunstan is attempting to leave it.

"Missus dreaming!" she exclaims quickly, as the light falls on the pillow. "The baby is there—safe asleep. Missus get into bed again, and cover up well, or she will catch cold!"

"Ah! my baby," cries Ethel, hysterically, as she seizes the tiny creature in her arms, "is he really there? Thank God! It was only a dream! But, Dye, what is the matter with him, and why is he so stiff and cold? He cannot—he cannot be—dead!"

Yes, it was true! It was not a dream after all. The white woman has carried the soul of the white child away with her, and left nothing but the senseless little body behind. As Ethel realises the extent of her misfortune, and the means by which it has been perpetrated, she sinks back upon her pillow in a state of utter unconsciousness.

⚬—♦—⚬

When she once more becomes aware of all that is passing around her, she finds her husband by her bedside, and Cissy Lawless acting the part of the most devoted of nurses.

"It was so wrong of me to leave you, dear, in that hurried manner," she whispers one day when Mrs. Dunstan is convalescent, "but I was so angry to think you could suspect me of flirting with your dear old husband. I ought to have told you from the first what all those meetings and letters meant, and I should have done so only they involved the character of my darling Jack. The fact is, dear, my boy got into a terrible scrape up country—and the colonel says the less we talk of it the better—however, it had something to do with that horrid gambling that men will indulge in, and it very nearly lost Jack his commission, and would have done so if it hadn't been for the dear colonel. But he and I plotted and worked together till we got Jack out of his scrape, and now we're as happy as two kings; and you will be so too, won't you, dear Mrs. Dunstan, now that you are well again, and know that your Charlie has flirted no more than yourself?"

"I have been terribly to blame," replies poor Ethel. "I see that now, and I have suffered for it too, bitterly."

"We have all suffered, my darling," says the colonel, tenderly; "but it may teach us a valuable lesson, never to believe that which we have not proved."

"And never to disbelieve that which we have not disproved," retorts Ethel. "If I had only been a little more credulous and a little less boastful of my own courage, I might not have lived to see my child torn from my arms by the spirit of the white woman."

And whatever Ethel Dunstan believed or not, I have only, in concluding her story, to reiterate my assertion that the circumstances of it are *strictly true*.

Like her friend Rhoda Broughton and many of her contemporaries, **Mary Cholmondeley** (1859–1925) did not confine her writing to what twentieth-century publishers labelled genres. The daughter of a Shropshire clergymen, she took up writing in her teens, publishing some short stories. Her first success was *The Danvers Jewels* (1887), a detective novel, and it was followed by several other works of what is now called crime fiction. Cholmondeley never married and lived with her sister Diana most of her life. Her 1899 novel *Red Pottage* satirized country life and explored women's sexuality, an important topic in women's literature at the end of the century. This story first appeared in the *Temple Bar* magazine (Broughton had introduced her to the editor) for April 1890 and was included in Cholmondeley's collection *Moth and Rust* (1902).

Let Loose *

by Mary Cholmondeley

The dead abide with us! Though stark and cold Earth seems
to grip them, they are with us still. †

S ome years ago I took up architecture, and made a tour through Holland, studying the buildings of that interesting country. I was not then

---

* [Author's note:] Since this story was written I have been told that what was related as a personal experience was partially derived from a written source. Every effort has been made, but in vain, to discover this written source. If, however, it does exist, I hope the unintentional plagiarism will be forgiven. It has been suggested to me that a story, which I have not read, called "The Tomb of Sara," by T. G. Loring (which I am told appeared in the December number of the *Pall Mall* magazine for 1900), must be the written source from which my story is taken. But this is impossible, as "Let Loose" was published in an English magazine before that date.

† From the poem "The Dead" by Mathilde Blind.

aware that it is not enough to take up art. Art must take you up, too. I never doubted but that my passing enthusiasm for her would be returned. When I discovered that she was a stern mistress, who did not immediately respond to my attentions, I naturally transferred them to another shrine. There are other things in the world besides art. I am now a landscape gardener.

But at the time of which I write I was engaged in a violent flirtation with architecture. I had one companion on this expedition, who has since become one of the leading architects of the day. He was a thin, determined-looking man with a screwed-up face and heavy jaw, slow of speech, and absorbed in his work to a degree which I quickly found tiresome. He was possessed of a certain quiet power of overcoming obstacles which I have rarely seen equalled. He has since become my brother-in-law, so I ought to know; for my parents did not like him much and opposed the marriage, and my sister did not like him at all, and refused him over and over again; but, nevertheless, he eventually married her.

I have thought since that one of his reasons for choosing me as his travelling companion on this occasion was because he was getting up steam for what he subsequently termed "an alliance with my family," but the idea never entered my head at the time. A more careless man as to dress I have rarely met, and yet, in all the heat of July in Holland, I noticed that he never appeared without a high, starched collar, which had not even fashion to commend it at that time.

I often chaffed him about his splendid collars, and asked him why he wore them, but without eliciting any response. One evening, as we were walking back to our lodgings in Middelburg,* I attacked him for about the thirtieth time on the subject.

"Why on earth do you wear them?" I said.

"You have, I believe, asked me that question many times," he replied, in his slow, precise utterance; "but always on occasions when I was occupied. I am now at leisure, and I will tell you."

And he did.

I have put down what he said, as nearly in his own words as I can remember them.

---

* Middelburg is a small city in the southwestern part of the Netherlands (or Holland) and is over a thousand years old.

Ten years ago, I was asked to read a paper on English Frescoes at the Institute of British Architects. I was determined to make the paper as good as I could, down to the slightest details, and I consulted many books on the subject, and studied every fresco I could find. My father, who had been an architect, had left me, at his death, all his papers and note-books on the subject of architecture. I searched them diligently, and found in one of them a slight unfinished sketch of nearly fifty years ago that specially interested me. Underneath was noted, in his clear, small hand—*Frescoed east wall of crypt. Parish Church. Wet Waste-on-the-Wolds, Yorkshire (via Pickering).*[*]

The sketch had such a fascination for me that I decided to go there and see the fresco for myself. I had only a very vague idea as to where Wet Waste-on-the-Wolds was, but I was ambitious for the success of my paper; it was hot in London, and I set off on my long journey not without a certain degree of pleasure, with my dog Brian, a large nondescript brindled creature, as my only companion.

I reached Pickering, in Yorkshire, in the course of the afternoon, and then began a series of experiments on local lines which ended, after several hours, in my finding myself deposited at a little out-of-the-world station within nine or ten miles of Wet Waste. As no conveyance of any kind was to be had, I shouldered my portmanteau, and set out on a long white road that stretched away into the distance over the bare, treeless wold. I must have walked for several hours, over a waste of moorland patched with heather, when a doctor passed me, and gave me a lift to within a mile of my destination. The mile was a long one, and it was quite dark by the time I saw the feeble glimmer of lights in front of me, and found that I had reached Wet Waste. I had considerable difficulty in getting any one to take me in; but at last I persuaded the owner of the public-house to give me a bed, and, quite tired out, I got into it as soon as possible, for fear he should change his mind, and fell asleep to the sound of a little stream below my window.

---

[*] If this was a real village, it apparently no longer exists, although there is an area called Wetwang Slack on the Yorkshire Wolds, which is host to a large Iron Age cemetery, and the town of Pickering is known for the medieval wall paintings in its parish church.

I was up early next morning, and inquired directly after breakfast the way to the clergyman's house, which I found was close at hand. At Wet Waste everything was close at hand. The whole village seemed composed of a straggling row of one-storeyed grey stone houses, the same colour as the stone walls that separated the few fields enclosed from the surrounding waste, and as the little bridges over the beck* that ran down one side of the grey wide street. Everything was grey.

The church, the low tower of which I could see at a little distance, seemed to have been built of the same stone; so was the parsonage when I came up to it, accompanied on my way by a mob of rough, uncouth children, who eyed me and Brian with half-defiant curiosity.

The clergyman was at home, and after a short delay I was admitted. Leaving Brian in charge of my drawing materials, I followed the servant into a low panelled room, in which, at a latticed window, a very old man was sitting. The morning light fell on his white head bent low over a litter of papers and books.

"Mr. er—?" he said, looking up slowly, with one finger keeping his place in a hook.

"Blake."

"Blake," he repeated after me, and was silent.

I told him that I was an architect; that I had come to study a fresco in the crypt of his church, and asked for the keys.

"The crypt," he said, pushing up his spectacles and peering hard at me. "The crypt has been closed for thirty years. Ever since—" and he stopped short.

"I should be much obliged for the keys," I said again.

He shook his head.

"No," he said. "No one goes in there now."

"It is a pity," I remarked, "for I have come a long way with that one object"; and I told him about the paper I had been asked to read, and the trouble I was taking with it.

He became interested. "Ah!" he said, laying down his pen, and removing his finger from the page before him, "I can understand that. I also was

---

* A word commonly found in parts of England that refers to a brook or stream.

young once, and fired with ambition. The lines have fallen to me in some-what lonely places, and for forty years I have held the cure of souls in this place, where, truly, I have seen but little of the world, though I myself may be not unknown in the paths of literature. Possibly you may have read a pamphlet, written by myself, on the Syrian version of the Three Authentic Epistles of Ignatius?"*

"Sir," I said, "I am ashamed to confess that I have not time to read even the most celebrated books. My one object in life is my art. Ars longa, vita brevis,† you know."

"You are right, my son," said the old man, evidently disappointed, but looking at me kindly.

"There are diversities of gifts, and if the Lord has entrusted you with a talent, look to it. Lay it not up in a napkin."‡

I said I would not do so if he would lend me the keys of the crypt. He seemed startled by my recurrence to the subject and looked undecided.

"Why not?" he murmured to himself. "The youth appears a good youth. And superstition! What is it but distrust in God!"

He got up slowly, and taking a large bunch of keys out of his pocket, opened with one of them an oak cupboard in the corner of the room.

"They should be here," he muttered, peering in; "but the dust of many years deceives the eye.

"See, my son, if among these parchments there be two keys; one of iron and very large, and the other steel, and of a long thin appearance."

I went eagerly to help him, and presently found in a back drawer two keys tied together, which he recognised at once.

---

* Ignatius was a Christian martyr who was killed by the Romans in 108 CE, and who wrote a number of letters now considered to be among the most important Early Christian documents. At the time this story was written, it was believed that three epistles discovered in 1845 were the original text, but this was later disproven.

† This phrase was coined by Hippocrates and means, "Art lasts forever, but life is short."

‡ Probably a reference to a parable that Jesus tells in *Luke* about a nobleman who berates a servant for keeping money in a napkin rather than investing it; the nobleman takes the money and gives it to someone who already has money, saying, "That unto every one which hath shall be given; and from him that hath not, even that he hath shall be taken away from him."

"Those are they," he said. "The long one opens the first door at the bottom of the steps which go down against the outside wall of the church hard by the sword graven in the wall. The second opens (but it is hard of opening and of shutting) the iron door within the passage leading to the crypt itself. My son, is it necessary to your treatise that you should enter this crypt?"

I replied that it was absolutely necessary.

"Then take them," he said, "and in the evening you will bring them to me again."

I said I might want to go several days running, and asked if he would not allow me to keep them till I had finished my work; but on that point he was firm.

"Likewise," he added, "be careful that you lock the first door at the foot of the steps before you unlock the second, and lock the second also while you are within. Furthermore, when you come out lock the iron inner door as well as the wooden one."

I promised I would do so, and, after thanking him, hurried away, delighted at my success in obtaining the keys. Finding Brian and my sketching materials waiting for me in the porch, I eluded the vigilance of my escort of children by taking the narrow private path between the parsonage and the church which was close at hand, standing in a quadrangle of ancient yews.

The church itself was interesting, and I noticed that it must have arisen out of the ruins of a previous building, judging from the number of fragments of stone caps and arches, bearing traces of very early carving, now built into the walls. There were incised crosses, too, in some places, and one especially caught my attention, being flanked by a large sword. It was in trying to get a nearer look at this that I stumbled, and, looking down, saw at my feet a flight of narrow stone steps green with moss and mildew. Evidently this was the entrance to the crypt. I at once descended the steps, taking care of my footing, for they were damp and slippery in the extreme.

Brian accompanied me, as nothing would induce him to remain behind. By the time I had reached the bottom of the stairs, I found myself almost in darkness, and I had to strike a light before I could find the keyhole and the proper key to fit into it. The door, which was of wood, opened inwards fairly easily, although an accumulation of mould and rubbish on the ground outside showed it had not been used for many years. Having got through it, which was not altogether an easy matter, as nothing would induce it to open more than about eighteen inches, I carefully locked it behind me, although I should have preferred to leave it open, as there is to some minds an unpleasant feeling in being locked in anywhere, in case of a sudden exit seeming advisable.

I kept my candle alight with some difficulty, and after groping my way down a low and of course exceedingly dank passage, came to another door. A toad was squatting against it, who looked as if he had been sitting there about a hundred years. As I lowered the candle to the floor, he gazed at the light with unblinking eyes, and then retreated slowly into a crevice in the wall, leaving against the door a small cavity in the dry mud, which had gradually silted up round his person. I noticed that this door was of iron, and had a long bolt, which, however, was broken.

Without delay, I fitted the second key into the lock, and pushing the door open after considerable difficulty, I felt the cold breath of the crypt upon my face. I must own I experienced a momentary regret at locking the second door again as soon as I was well inside, but I felt it my duty to do so. Then, leaving the key in the lock, I seized my candle and looked round. I was standing in a low vaulted chamber with groined roof, cut out of the solid rock. It was difficult to see where the crypt ended, as further light thrown on any point only showed other rough archways or openings, cut in the rock, which had probably served at one time for family vaults.

A peculiarity of the Wet Waste crypt, which I had not noticed in other places of that description, was the tasteful arrangement of skulls and bones, which were packed about four feet high on either side. The skulls were symmetrically built up to within a few inches of the top of the low archway on my left, and the shin bones were arranged in the same manner on my right. But the fresco! I looked round for it in vain. Perceiving at the further end of the crypt a very low and very massive archway, the entrance to which was not filled up with bones, I passed under it, and found myself in a second smaller chamber. Holding my candle above my head, the first object its light fell upon was—the fresco, and at a glance I saw that it was unique. Setting down some of my things with a trembling hand on a rough stone shelf hard by, which had evidently been a credence table, * I examined the

---

* A small side table used in celebration of the Eucharist.

work more closely. It was a reredos* over what had probably been the altar at the time the priests were proscribed.† The fresco belonged to the earliest part of the fifteenth century, and was so perfectly preserved that I could almost trace the limits of each day's work in the plaster, as the artist had dashed it on and smoothed it out with his trowel. The subject was the Ascension, gloriously treated. I can hardly describe my elation as I stood and looked at it, and reflected that this magnificent specimen of English fresco painting would be made known to the world by myself. Recollecting myself at last, I opened my sketching bag, and, lighting all the candles I had brought with me, set to work.

Brian walked about near me, and though I was not otherwise than glad of his company in my rather lonely position, I wished several times I had left him behind. He seemed restless, and even the sight of so many bones appeared to exercise no soothing effect upon him. At last, however, after repeated commands, he lay down, watchful but motionless, on the stone floor.

I must have worked for several hours, and I was pausing to rest my eyes and hands, when I noticed for the first time the intense stillness that surrounded me. No sound from me reached the outer world. The church clock which had clanged out so loud and ponderously as I went down the steps, had not since sent the faintest whisper of its iron tongue down to me below. All was silent as the grave. This was the grave. Those who had come here had indeed gone down into silence. I repeated the words to myself, or rather they repeated themselves to me.

Gone down into silence.

I was awakened from my reverie by a faint sound. I sat still and listened. Bats occasionally frequent vaults and underground places.

The sound continued, a faint, stealthy, rather unpleasant sound. I do not know what kinds of sounds bats make, whether pleasant or otherwise. Suddenly there was a noise as of something falling, a momentary pause—and then—an almost imperceptible but distant jangle as of a key.

---

* An ornamental screen covering the back wall behind an altar.

† In 1534 Henry VIII officially separated England and the Holy See, banning any official observance of Catholicism.

I had left the key in the lock after I had turned it, and I now regretted having done so. I got up, took one of the candles, and went back into the larger crypt—for though I trust I am not so effeminate as to be rendered nervous by hearing a noise for which I cannot instantly account; still, on occasions of this kind, I must honestly say I should prefer that they did not occur. As I came towards the iron door, there was another distinct (I had almost said hurried) sound. The impression on my mind was one of great haste. When I reached the door, and held the candle near the lock to take out the key, I perceived that the other one, which hung by a short string to its fellow, was vibrating slightly. I should have preferred not to find it vibrating, as there seemed no occasion for such a course; but I put them both into my pocket, and turned to go back to my work. As I turned, I saw on the ground what had occasioned the louder noise I had heard, namely, a skull which had evidently just slipped from its place on the top of one of the walls of bones, and had rolled almost to my feet. There, disclosing a few more inches of the top of an archway behind, was the place from which it had been dislodged. I stooped to pick it up, but fearing to displace any more skulls by meddling with the pile, and not liking to gather up its scattered teeth, I let it lie, and went back to my work, in which I was soon so completely absorbed that I was only roused at last by my candles beginning to burn low and go out one after another.

Then, with a sigh of regret, for I had not nearly finished, I turned to go. Poor Brian, who had never quite reconciled himself to the place, was beside himself with delight. As I opened the iron door he pushed past me, and a moment later I heard him whining and scratching, and I had almost added, beating, against the wooden one. I locked the iron door, and hurried down the passage as quickly as I could, and almost before I had got the other one ajar there seemed to be a rush past me into the open air, and Brian was bounding up the steps and out of sight. As I stopped to take out the key, I felt quite deserted and left behind. When I came out once more into the sunlight, there was a vague sensation all about me in the air of exultant freedom.

It was already late in the afternoon, and after I had sauntered back to the parsonage to give up the keys, I persuaded the people of the public-house to let me join in the family meal, which was spread out in the kitchen. The inhabitants of Wet Waste were primitive people, with the frank, unabashed manner that flourishes still in lonely places, especially in the wilds of

Yorkshire; but I had no idea that in these days of penny posts and cheap newspapers such entire ignorance of the outer world could have existed in any corner, however remote, of Great Britain.

When I took one of the neighbour's children on my knee—a pretty little girl with the palest aureole of flaxen hair I had ever seen—and began to draw pictures for her of the birds and beasts of other countries, I was instantly surrounded by a crowd of children, and even grown-up people, while others came to their doorways and looked on from a distance, calling to each other in the strident unknown tongue which I have since discovered goes by the name of "Broad Yorkshire."

The following morning, as I came out of my room, I perceived that something was amiss in the village. A buzz of voices reached me as I passed the bar, and in the next house I could hear through the open window a high-pitched wail of lamentation.

The woman who brought me my breakfast was in tears, and in answer to my questions, told me that the neighbour's child, the little girl whom I had taken on my knee the evening before, had died in the night.

I felt sorry for the general grief that the little creature's death seemed to arouse, and the uncontrolled wailing of the poor mother took my appetite away.

I hurried off early to my work, calling on my way for the keys, and with Brian for my companion descended once more into the crypt, and drew and measured with an absorption that gave me no time that day to listen for sounds real or fancied. Brian, too, on this occasion seemed quite content, and slept peacefully beside me on the stone floor. When I had worked as long as I could, I put away my books with regret that even then I had not quite finished, as I had hoped to do. It would be necessary to come again for a short time on the morrow. When I returned the keys late that afternoon, the old clergyman met me at the door, and asked me to come in and have tea with him.

"And has the work prospered?" he asked, as we sat down in the long, low room, into which I had just been ushered, and where he seemed to live entirely.

I told him it had, and showed it to him.

"You have seen the original, of course?" I said.

"Once," he replied, gazing fixedly at it. He evidently did not care to be communicative, so I turned the conversation to the age of the church.

"All here is old," he said. "When I was young, forty years ago, and came here because I had no means of mine own, and was much moved to marry at that time, I felt oppressed that all was so old; and that this place was so far removed from the world, for which I had at times longings grievous to be borne; but I had chosen my lot, and with it I was forced to be content. My son, marry not in youth, for love, which truly in that season is a mighty power, turns away the heart from study, and young children break the back of ambition. Neither marry in middle life, when a woman is seen to be but a woman and her talk a weariness, so you will not be burdened with a wife in your old age."

I had my own views on the subject of marriage, for I am of opinion that a well-chosen companion of domestic tastes and docile and devoted temperament may be of material assistance to a professional man. But, my opinions once formulated, it is not of moment to me to discuss them with others, so I changed the subject, and asked if the neighbouring villages were as antiquated as Wet Waste. "Yes, all about here is old," he repeated. "The paved road leading to Dyke Fens* is an ancient pack road, made even in the time of the Romans. Dyke Fens, which is very near here, a matter of but four or five miles, is likewise old, and forgotten by the world. The Reformation never reached it. It stopped here. And at Dyke Fens they still have a priest and a bell, and bow down before the saints. It is a damnable heresy, and weekly I expound it as such to my people, showing them true doctrines; and I have heard that this same priest has so far yielded himself to the Evil One that he has preached against me as withholding gospel truths from my flock; but I take no heed of it, neither of his pamphlet touching the Clementine Homilies,† in which he vainly contradicts that which I have plainly set forth and proven beyond doubt, concerning the word Asaph."‡

---

* Dyke Fens is likely a fictitious place; the Fens—a marshy coastal plain—is located to the south of Yorkshire.

† A collection of twenty books in Greek that recount the travels of Clement with the Apostle Peter.

‡ The Psalms of Asaph are twelve psalms found in the Book of Psalms; "Asaph" is still debated by modern Biblical scholars, who believe it could be the name of an author, a transcriber, a group, or a style.

The old man was fairly off on his favourite subject, and it was some time before I could get away. As it was, he followed me to the door, and I only escaped because the old clerk hobbled up at that moment, and claimed his attention.

The following morning I went for the keys for the third and last time. I had decided to leave early the next day. I was tired of Wet Waste, and a certain gloom seemed to my fancy to be gathering over the place. There was a sensation of trouble in the air, as if, although the day was bright and clear, a storm were coming.

This morning, to my astonishment, the keys were refused to me when I asked for them. I did not, however, take the refusal as, final—I make it a rule never to take a refusal as final—and after a short delay I was shown into the room where, as usual, the clergyman was sitting, or rather, on this occasion, was walking up and down.

"My son," he said with vehemence, "I know wherefore you have come, but it is of no avail. I cannot lend the keys again."

I replied that, on the contrary, I hoped he would give them to me at once.

"It is impossible," he repeated. "I did wrong, exceeding wrong. I will never part with them again."

"Why not?"

He hesitated, and then said slowly:

"The old clerk, Abraham Kelly, died last night." He paused, and then went on: "The doctor has just been here to tell me of that which is a mystery to him. I do not wish the people of the place to know it, and only to me he has mentioned it, but he has discovered plainly on the throat of the old man, and also, but more faintly on the child's, marks as of strangulation. None but he has observed it, and he is at a loss how to account for it. I, alas! can account for it but in one way, but in one way!"

I did not see what all this had to do with the crypt, but to humour the old man, I asked what that way was.

"It is a long story, and, haply, to a stranger it may appear but foolishness, but I will even tell it; for I perceive that unless I furnish a reason for withholding the keys, you will not cease to entreat me for them.

"I told you at first when you inquired of me concerning the crypt, that it had been closed these thirty years, and so it was. Thirty years ago a certain

Sir Roger Despard departed this life, even the lord of the manor of Wet Waste and Dyke Fens, the last of his family, which is now, thank the Lord, extinct. He was a man of a vile life, neither fearing God nor regarding man, nor having compassion on innocence, and the Lord appeared to have given him over to the tormentors even in this world, for he suffered many things of his vices, more especially from drunkenness, in which seasons, and they were many, he was as one possessed by seven devils,* being an abomination to his household and a root of bitterness to all, both high and low.

"And, at last, the cup of his iniquity being full to the brim, he came to die, and I went to exhort him on his death-bed; for I heard that terror had come upon him, and that evil imaginations encompassed him so thick on every side, that few of them that were with him could abide in his presence. But when I saw him I perceived that there was no place of repentance left for him, and he scoffed at me and my superstition, even as he lay dying, and swore there was no God and no angel, and all were damned even as he was. And the next day, towards evening, the pains of death came upon him, and he raved the more exceedingly, inasmuch as he said he was being strangled by the Evil One. Now on his table was his hunting knife, and with his last strength he crept and laid hold upon it, no man withstanding him, and swore a great oath that if he went down to burn in hell, he would leave one of his hands behind on earth, and that it would never rest until it had drawn blood from the throat of another and strangled him, even as he himself was being strangled. And he cut off his own right hand at the wrist, and no man dared go near him to stop him, and the blood went through the floor, even down to the ceiling of the room below, and thereupon he died.

"And they called me in the night, and told me of his oath, and I counselled that no man should speak of it, and I took the dead hand, which none had ventured to touch, and I laid it beside him in his coffin; for I thought it better he should take it with him, so that he might have it, if haply some day after much tribulation he should perchance be moved to stretch forth his hands towards God. But the story got spread about, and the people were affrighted, so, when he came to be buried in the place of his fathers, he being the last of his family, and the crypt likewise full, I had it

---

* In Mark 16:9 Jesus casts seven devils out of Mary Magdalene.

closed, and kept the keys myself, and suffered no man to enter therein any more; for truly he was a man of an evil life, and the devil is not yet wholly overcome, nor cast chained into the lake of fire. So in time the story died out, for in thirty years much is forgotten. And when you came and asked me for the keys, I was at the first minded to withhold them; but I thought it was a vain superstition, and I perceived that you do but ask a second time for what is first refused; so I let you have them, seeing it was not an idle curiosity, but a desire to improve the talent committed to you, that led you to require them."

The old man stopped, and I remained silent, wondering what would be the best way to get them just once more.

"Surely, sir," I said at last, "one so cultivated and deeply read as yourself cannot be biased by an idle superstition."

"I trust not," he replied, "and yet—it is a strange thing that since the crypt was opened two people have died, and the mark is plain upon the throat of the old man and visible on the young child. No blood was drawn, but the second time the grip was stronger than the first. The third time, perchance—"

"Superstition such as that," I said with authority, "is an entire want of faith in God. You once said so yourself."

I took a high moral tone which is often efficacious with conscientious, humble-minded people.

He agreed, and accused himself of not having faith as a grain of mustard seed; but even when I had got him so far as that, I had a severe struggle for the keys. It was only when I finally explained to him that if any malign influence had been let loose the first day, at any rate, it was out now for good or evil, and no further going or coming of mine could make any difference, that I finally gained my point. I was young, and he was old; and, being much shaken by what had occurred, he gave way at last, and I wrested the keys from him.

I will not deny that I went down the steps that day with a vague, indefinable repugnance, which was only accentuated by the closing of the two doors behind me. I remembered then, for the first time, the faint jangling of the key and other sounds, which I had noticed the first day, and how one of the skulls had fallen. I went to the place where it still lay. I have already said these walls of skulls were built up so high as to be within a few inches of the top of the low archways that led into more distant portions of the vault. The displacement of the skull in question had left a small hole just large enough for me to put my hand through. I noticed for the first time, over the archway above it, a carved coat-of-arms, and the name, now almost obliterated, of Despard. This, no doubt, was the Despard vault. I could not resist moving a few more skulls and looking in, holding my candle as near the aperture as I could. The vault was full. Piled high, one upon another, were old coffins, and remnants of coffins, and strewn bones. I attribute my present determination to be cremated to the painful impression produced on me by this spectacle. The coffin nearest the archway alone was intact, save for a large crack across the lid. I could not get a ray from my candle to fall on the brass plates, but I felt no doubt this was the coffin of the wicked Sir Roger. I put back the skulls, including the one which had rolled down, and carefully finished my work. I was not there much more than an hour, but I was glad to get away.

If I could have left Wet Waste at once I should have done so, for I had a totally unreasonable longing to leave the place; but I found that only one train stopped during the day at the station from which I had come, and that it would not be possible to be in time for it that day.

Accordingly I submitted to the inevitable, and wandered about with Brian for the remainder of the afternoon and until late in the evening, sketching and smoking. The day was oppressively hot, and even after the sun had set across the burnt stretches of the wolds, it seemed to grow very little cooler. Not a breath stirred. In the evening, when I was tired of loitering in the lanes, I went up to my own room, and after contemplating afresh my finished study of the fresco, I suddenly set to work to write the part of my paper bearing upon it. As a rule, I write with difficulty, but that evening words came to me with winged speed, and with them a hovering impression that I must make haste, that I was much pressed for time. I wrote and wrote, until my candles guttered out and left me trying to finish by the moonlight, which, until I endeavoured to write by it, seemed as clear as day.

I had to put away my MS., and, feeling it was too early to go to bed, for the church clock was just counting out ten, I sat down by the open window and leaned out to try and catch a breath of air. It was a night of exceptional beauty; and as I looked out my nervous haste and hurry of mind were allayed. The moon, a perfect circle, was—if so poetic an expression be permissible—as it were, sailing across a calm sky. Every detail of the little village was as clearly illuminated by its beams as if it were broad day; so, also, was the adjacent church with its primeval yews, while even the wolds beyond were dimly indicated, as if through tracing paper.

I sat a long time leaning against the window-sill. The heat was still intense. I am not, as a rule, easily elated or readily cast down; but as I sat under that light in the lonely village on the moors, with Brian's head against my knee, how, or why, I know not, a great depression gradually came upon me.

My mind went back to the crypt and the countless dead who had been laid there. The sight of the goal to which all human life, and strength, and beauty, travel in the end, had not affected me at the time, but now the very air about me seemed heavy with death.

What was the good, I asked myself, of working and toiling, and grinding down my heart and youth in the mill of long and strenuous effort, seeing that in the grave folly and talent, idleness and labour lie together, and are alike forgotten? Labour seemed to stretch before me till my heart ached to think of it, to stretch before me even to the end of life, and then came, as the recompense of my labour—the grave. Even if I succeeded, if, after wearing my life threadbare with toil, I succeeded, what remained to me in the end? The grave. A little sooner, while the hands and eyes were still strong to labour, or a little later, when all power and vision had been taken from them; sooner or later only—the grave.

I do not apologise for the excessively morbid tenor of these reflections, as I hold that they were caused by the lunar effects, which I have endeavoured to transcribe. The moon in its various quarterings has always exerted a marked influence on what I may call the sub-dominant, namely, the poetic side of my nature.

I roused myself at last, when the moon came to look ill upon me where I sat, and, leaving the window open, I pulled myself together and went to bed.

I fell asleep almost immediately, but I do not fancy I could have been asleep very long when I was wakened by Brian. He was growling in a low, muffled tone, as he sometimes did in his sleep, when his nose was buried in his rug. I called out to him to shut up; and as he did not do so, turned in bed to find my match box or something to throw at him. The moonlight was still in the room, and as I looked at him I saw him raise his head and evidently wake up. I admonished him, and was just on the point of falling asleep when he began to growl again in a low, savage manner that waked me most effectually. Presently he shook himself and got up, and began prowling about the room. I sat up in bed and called to him, but he paid no attention. Suddenly I saw him stop short in the moonlight; he showed his teeth, and crouched down, his eyes following something in the air. I looked at him in horror. Was he going mad? His eyes were glaring, and his head moved slightly as if he were following the rapid movements of an enemy. Then, with a furious snarl, he suddenly sprang from the ground, and rushed in great leaps across the room towards me, dashing himself against the furniture, his eyes rolling, snatching and tearing wildly in the air with his teeth. I saw he had gone mad. I leaped out of bed, and rushing at him, caught him by the throat. The moon had gone behind a cloud; but in the darkness I felt him turn upon me, felt him rise up, and his teeth close in my throat. I was being strangled. With all the strength of despair, I kept my grip of his neck, and, dragging him across the room, tried to crush in his head against the iron rail of my bedstead. It was my only chance. I felt the blood running down my neck. I was suffocating. After one moment of frightful struggle, I beat his head against the bar and heard his skull give way. I felt him give one strong shudder, a groan, and then I fainted away.

When I came to myself I was lying on the floor, surrounded by the people of the house, my reddened hands still clutching Brian's throat. Someone was holding a candle towards me, and the draught from the window made it flare and waver. I looked at Brian. He was stone dead. The blood from his battered head was trickling slowly over my hands. His great jaw was fixed in something that—in the uncertain light—I could not see.

They turned the light a little.

"Oh, God!" I shrieked. "There! Look! Look!"

"He's off his head," said some one, and I fainted again.

I was ill for about a fortnight without regaining consciousness, a waste of time of which even now I cannot think without poignant regret. When I did recover consciousness, I found I was being carefully nursed by the old clergyman and the people of the house. I have often heard the unkindness of the world in general inveighed against, but for my part I can honestly say that I have received many more kindnesses than I have time to repay. Country people especially are remarkably attentive to strangers in illness.

I could not rest until I had seen the doctor who attended me, and had received his assurance that I should be equal to reading my paper on the appointed day. This pressing anxiety removed, I told him of what I had seen before I fainted the second time. He listened attentively, and then assured me, in a manner that was intended to be soothing, that I was suffering from an hallucination, due, no doubt, to the shock of my dog's sudden madness.

"Did you see the dog after it was dead?" I asked.

He said he did. The whole jaw was covered with blood and foam; the teeth certainly seemed convulsively fixed, but the case being evidently one of extraordinarily virulent hydrophobia,* owing to the intense heat, he had had the body buried immediately.

My companion stopped speaking as we reached our lodgings, and went upstairs. Then, lighting a candle, he slowly turned down his collar.

"You see I have the marks still," he said, "but I have no fear of dying of hydrophobia. I am told such peculiar scars could not have been made by the teeth of a dog. If you look closely you see the pressure of the five fingers. That is the reason why I wear high collars."

---

* Rabies.

It's not possible to do justice to the career of **Edith Wharton** (1862–1937) in a brief paragraph. Born Edith Newbold Jones into one of the wealthiest families in New York, Wharton was not satisfied with a life of idleness and took up writing at an early age, though her first novel was not published until she was forty. Her novel *The Age of Innocence* (1920) perfectly captures the milieu of the Gilded Age of Manhattan and won Wharton the Pulitzer Prize for literature. *Ethan Frome* (1911) is a staple of high-school and college curricula. Wharton wrote fifteen novels, more than thirty other books, and countless short stories. She was nominated three times for the Nobel Prize for Literature. This story, one of her earliest published works, first appeared in *Scribner's Magazine* in December 1893.

The Fulness of Life

by Edith Wharton

I.

For hours she had lain in a kind of gentle torpor, not unlike that sweet lassitude which masters one in the hush of a midsummer noon, when the heat seems to have silenced the very birds and insects, and, lying sunk in the tasselled meadow-grasses, one looks up through a level roofing of maple-leaves at the vast shadowless, and unsuggestive blue. Now and then, at ever-lengthening intervals, a flash of pain darted through her, like the ripple of sheet-lightning across such a midsummer sky; but it was too transitory to shake her stupor, that calm, delicious, bottomless stupor into which she felt herself sinking more and more deeply, without a disturbing impulse of resistance, an effort of reattachment to the vanishing edges of consciousness.

The resistance, the effort, had known their hour of violence; but now they were at an end. Through her mind, long harried by grotesque visions, fragmentary images of the life that she was leaving, tormenting lines of verse, obstinate presentments of pictures once beheld, indistinct impressions of rivers, towers, and cupolas, gathered in the length of journeys half forgotten—through her mind there now only moved a few primal sensations of colorless well-being; a vague satisfaction in the thought that she had swallowed her noxious last draught of medicine . . . and that she should never again hear the creaking of her husband's boots—those horrible boots—and that no one would come to bother her about the next day's dinner . . . or the butcher's book. . . .

At last even these dim sensations spent themselves in the thickening obscurity which enveloped her; a dusk now filled with pale geometric roses, circling softly, interminably before her, now darkened to a uniform blue-blackness, the hue of a summer night without stars. And into this darkness she felt herself sinking, sinking, with the gentle sense of security of one upheld from beneath. Like a tepid tide it rose around her, gliding ever higher and higher, folding in its velvety embrace her relaxed and tired body, now submerging her breast and shoulders, now creeping gradually, with soft inexorableness, over her throat to her chin, to her ears, to her mouth. . . . Ah, now it was rising too high; the impulse to struggle was renewed; . . . her mouth was full; . . . she was choking. . . . Help!

"It is all over," said the nurse, drawing down the eyelids with official composure.

The clock struck three. They remembered it afterward. Someone opened the window and let in a blast of that strange, neutral air which walks the earth between darkness and dawn; someone else led the husband into another room. He walked vaguely, like a blind man, on his creaking boots.

II.

She stood, as it seemed, on a threshold, yet no tangible gateway was in front of her. Only a wide vista of light, mild yet penetrating as the gathered glimmer of innumerable stars, expanded gradually before her eyes, in blissful contrast to the cavernous darkness from which she had of late emerged.

She stepped forward, not frightened, but hesitating, and as her eyes began to grow more familiar with the melting depths of light about her, she distinguished the outlines of a landscape, at first swimming in the opaline uncertainty of Shelley's vaporous creations,* then gradually resolved into distincter shape—the vast unrolling of a sunlit plain, aerial forms of mountains, and presently the silver crescent of a river in the valley, and a blue stencilling of trees along its curve—something suggestive in its ineffable hue of an azure background of Leonardo's, strange, enchanting, mysterious, leading on the eye and the imagination into regions of fabulous delight. As she gazed, her heart beat with a soft and rapturous surprise; so exquisite a promise she read in the summons of that hyaline† distance.

"And so death is not the end after all," in sheer gladness she heard herself exclaiming aloud. "I always knew that it couldn't be. I believed in Darwin, of course. I do still; but then Darwin himself said that he wasn't sure about the soul‡—at least, I think he did—and Wallace was a spiritualist;§ and then there was St. George Mivart¶—"

Her gaze lost itself in the ethereal remoteness of the mountains.

"How beautiful! How satisfying!" she murmured. "Perhaps now I shall really know what it is to live."

As she spoke she felt a sudden thickening of her heart-beats, and looking up she was aware that before her stood the Spirit of Life.

---

* A reference to Percy Shelley, whose poetry Wharton had admired since her youth, and not (sadly) Mary Shelley.

† Translucent or glassy.

‡ Throughout his life, Charles Darwin—who usually declared himself to be an agnostic—wavered in his thoughts on the existence of the soul. In 1876 he wrote, of a moment in the Brazilian jungle that had inspired him to believe, ". . . I well remember my conviction that there is more in man than the mere breath of his body. But now, the grandest scenes would not cause any such convictions and feelings to rise in my mind."

§ The great British scientist Alfred Russel Wallace, who developed a theory of natural selection independently of Darwin and who was indeed a dedicated Spiritualist.

¶ St. George Jackson Mivart was a nineteenth-century British biologist who tried to reconcile Christianity and Darwin's theories on evolution.

"Have you never really known what it is to live?" the Spirit of Life asked her.

"I have never known," she replied, "that fulness of life which we all feel ourselves capable of knowing; though my life has not been without scattered hints of it, like the scent of earth which comes to one sometimes far out at sea."

"And what do you call the fulness of life?" the Spirit asked again.

"Oh, I can't tell you, if you don't know," she said, almost reproachfully. "Many words are supposed to define it—love and sympathy are those in commonest use, but I am not even sure that they are the right ones, and so few people really know what they mean."

"You were married," said the Spirit, "yet you did not find the fulness of life in your marriage?"

"Oh, dear, no," she replied, with an indulgent scorn, "my marriage was a very incomplete affair."

"And yet you were fond of your husband?"

"You have hit upon the exact word; I was fond of him, yes, just as I was fond of my grandmother, and the house that I was born in, and my old nurse. Oh, I was fond of him, and we were counted a very happy couple. But I have sometimes thought that a woman's nature is like a great house full of rooms: there is the hall, through which everyone passes in going in and out; the drawing-room, where one receives formal visits; the sitting-room, where the members of the family come and go as they list; but beyond that, far beyond, are other rooms, the handles of whose doors perhaps are never turned; no one knows the way to them, no one knows whither they lead; and in the innermost room, the holy of holies, the soul sits alone and waits for a footstep that never comes."

"And your husband," asked the Spirit, after a pause, "never got beyond the family sitting-room?"

"Never," she returned, impatiently; "and the worst of it was that he was quite content to remain there. He thought it perfectly beautiful, and sometimes, when he was admiring its commonplace furniture, insignificant as the chairs and tables of a hotel parlor, I felt like crying out to him: 'Fool, will you never guess that close at hand are rooms full of treasures and wonders, such as the eye of man hath not seen, rooms that no step has crossed, but that might be yours to live in, could you but find the handle of the door?'"

"Then," the Spirit continued, "those moments of which you lately spoke, which seemed to come to you like scattered hints of the fulness of life, were not shared with your husband?"

"Oh, no—never. He was different. His boots creaked, and he always slammed the door when he went out, and he never read anything but railway novels and the sporting advertisements in the papers—and—and, in short, we never understood each other in the least."

"To what influence, then, did you owe those exquisite sensations?"

"I can hardly tell. Sometimes to the perfume of a flower; sometimes to a verse of Dante or of Shakespeare; sometimes to a picture or a sunset, or to one of those calm days at sea, when one seems to be lying in the hollow of a blue pearl; sometimes, but rarely, to a word spoken by someone who chanced to give utterance, at the right moment, to what I felt but could not express."

"Someone whom you loved?" asked the Spirit.

"I never loved anyone, in that way," she said, rather sadly, "nor was I thinking of any one person when I spoke, but of two or three who, by touching for an instant upon a certain chord of my being, had called forth a single note of that strange melody, which seemed sleeping in my soul. It has seldom happened, however, that I have owed such feelings to people; and no one ever gave me a moment of such happiness as it was my lot to feel one evening in the Church of Or San Michele, in Florence."*

"Tell me about it," said the Spirit.

"It was near sunset on a rainy spring afternoon in Easter week. The clouds had vanished, dispersed by a sudden wind, and as we entered the church the fiery panes of the high windows shone out like lamps through the dusk. A priest was at the high altar, his white cope† a livid spot in the incense-laden obscurity, the light of the candles flickering up and down like fireflies about

---

* Orsanmichele in Florence was originally built in 1337 as a grain market, but was converted to a church less than a century later, when it served principally as the chapel for the city's powerful guilds. It is still standing and is now known chiefly for fourteen statues that commemorate the patron saints of the guilds.

† A cope is a cloak-like vestment worn by priests for occasions (like processions) other than the Mass.

his head; a few people knelt near by. We stole behind them and sat down on a bench close to the tabernacle of Orcagna.*

"Strange to say, though Florence was not new to me, I had never been in the church before; and in that magical light I saw for the first time the inlaid steps, the fluted columns, the sculptured bas-reliefs and canopy of the marvellous shrine. The marble, worn and mellowed by the subtle hand of time, took on an unspeakable rosy hue, suggestive in some remote way of the honey-colored columns of the Parthenon, but more mystic, more complex, a color not born of the sun's inveterate kiss, but made up of cryptal twilight, and the flame of candles upon martyrs' tombs, and gleams of sunset through symbolic panes of chrysoprase† and ruby; such a light as illumines the missals in the library of Siena,‡ or burns like a hidden fire through the Madonna of Gian Bellini in the Church of the Redeemer, at Venice;§ the light of the Middle Ages, richer, more solemn, more significant than the limpid sunshine of Greece.

"The church was silent, but for the wail of the priest and the occasional scraping of a chair against the floor, and as I sat there, bathed in that light, absorbed in rapt contemplation of the marble miracle which rose before me, cunningly wrought as a casket of ivory and enriched with jewel-like incrustations and tarnished gleams of gold, I felt myself borne onward along a mighty current, whose source seemed to be in the very beginning of things, and whose tremendous waters gathered as they went all the mingled streams of human passion and endeavor. Life in all its varied manifestations of beauty and strangeness seemed weaving a rhythmical dance around me

---

* Orcagna is the common name of Andrea di Cione di Arcangelo (ca. 1308–1368), an artist who was hired to create the Tabernacle of Orsanmichele, for which he created a relief depicting the *Dormition and Assumption of the Virgin Mary*.

† A greenish variety of chalcedony.

‡ The Piccolomini Library adjoins the Siena Cathedral and is renowned for both its collection of illuminated manuscripts and its frescoes painted by Bernardino di Betto, called Pinturicchio, probably based on designs by Raphael.

§ The Church of the Redeemer in Venice (Santissimo Redentore, usually known as Il Redentore) does not currently contain any works by the great Venetian artist Giovanni Bellini, although it does contain a famous Madonna and Child by Alise Vivarini (to whom Bellini is sometimes compared).

as I moved, and wherever the spirit of man had passed I knew that my foot had once been familiar.

"As I gazed the mediaeval bosses of the tabernacle of Orcagna seemed to melt and flow into their primal forms so that the folded lotus of the Nile and the Greek acanthus were braided with the runic knots and fish-tailed monsters of the North, and all the plastic terror and beauty born of man's hand from the Ganges to the Baltic quivered and mingled in Orcagna's apotheosis of Mary. And so the river bore me on, past the alien face of antique civilizations and the familiar wonders of Greece, till I swam upon the fiercely rushing tide of the Middle Ages, with its swirling eddies of passion, its heaven-reflecting pools of poetry and art; I heard the rhythmic blow of the craftsmen's hammers in the goldsmiths' workshops and on the walls of churches, the party-cries of armed factions in the narrow streets, the organ-roll of Dante's verse, the crackle of the fagots around Arnold of Brescia,* the twitter of the swallows to which St. Francis preached,† the laughter of the ladies listening on the hillside to the quips of the Decameron,‡ while plague-struck Florence howled beneath them—all this and much more I heard, joined in strange unison with voices earlier and more remote, fierce, passionate, or tender, yet subdued to such awful harmony that I thought of the song that the morning stars sang together and felt as though it were sounding in my ears. My heart beat to suffocation, the tears burned my lids, the joy, the mystery of it seemed too intolerable to be borne. I could not understand even then the words of the song; but I knew that if there had been someone at my side who could have heard it with me, we might have found the key to it together.

"I turned to my husband, who was sitting beside me in an attitude of patient dejection, gazing into the bottom of his hat; but at that moment he rose, and stretching his stiffened legs, said, mildly: 'Hadn't we better

---

* Arnold of Brescia (1090–1155) was hanged by the papacy after calling on the Church to renounce property ownership; he was burned posthumously.

† St. Francis of Assisi was once said to have asked noisy swallows to be quiet so he could preach to the village of Alviano, and the swallows complied.

‡ *The Decameron* is the fourteenth-century masterpiece by Giovanni Boccaccio, about a group of ten people who shelter outside of Florence to escape the Black Death.

be going? There doesn't seem to be much to see here, and you know the table d'hote dinner is at half-past six o'clock.'"

Her recital ended, there was an interval of silence; then the Spirit of Life said: "There is a compensation in store for such needs as you have expressed."

"Oh, then you *do* understand?" she exclaimed. "Tell me what compensation, I entreat you!"

"It is ordained," the Spirit answered, "that every soul which seeks in vain on earth for a kindred soul to whom it can lay bare its inmost being shall find that soul here and be united to it for eternity."

A glad cry broke from her lips. "Ah, shall I find him at last?" she cried, exultant.

"He is here," said the Spirit of Life.

She looked up and saw that a man stood near whose soul (for in that unwonted light she seemed to see his soul more clearly than his face) drew her toward him with an invincible force.

"Are you really he?" she murmured.

"I am he," he answered.

She laid her hand in his and drew him toward the parapet, which overhung the valley.

"Shall we go down together," she asked him, "into that marvellous country; shall we see it together, as if with the self-same eyes, and tell each other in the same words all that we think and feel?"

"So," he replied, "have I hoped and dreamed."

"What?" she asked, with rising joy. "Then you, too, have looked for me?"

"All my life."

"How wonderful! And did you never, never find anyone in the other world who understood you?"

"Not wholly—not as you and I understand each other."

"Then you feel it, too? Oh, I am happy," she sighed.

They stood, hand in hand, looking down over the parapet upon the shimmering landscape which stretched forth beneath them into sapphirine space, and the Spirit of Life, who kept watch near the threshold, heard now and then a floating fragment of their talk blown backward like the stray swallows, which the wind sometimes separates from their migratory tribe.

"Did you never feel at sunset—"

"Ah, yes; but I never heard anyone else say so. Did you?"

"Do you remember that line in the third canto of the 'Inferno?'"

"Ah, that line—my favorite always. Is it possible—"

"You know the stooping Victory in the frieze of the Nike Apteros?"*

"You mean the one who is tying her sandal? Then you have noticed, too, that all Botticelli and Mantegna are dormant in those flying folds of her drapery?"†

"After a storm in autumn have you never seen—"

"Yes, it is curious how certain flowers suggest certain painters—the perfume of the incarnation, Leonardo; that of the rose, Titian; the tuberose, Crivelli‡—"

"I never supposed that anyone else had noticed it."

"Have you never thought—"

"Oh, yes, often and often; but I never dreamed that anyone else had."

"But surely you must have felt—"

"Oh, yes, yes; and you, too—"

"How beautiful! How strange—"

Their voices rose and fell, like the murmur of two fountains answering each other across a garden full of flowers. At length, with a certain tender impatience, he turned to her and said: "Love, why should we linger here? All eternity lies before us. Let us go down into that beautiful country together and make a home for ourselves on some blue hill above the shining river."

As he spoke, the hand she had forgotten in his was suddenly withdrawn, and he felt that a cloud was passing over the radiance of her soul.

---

* The Temple of Athena Nike in Athens, built around 420 BCE, honors the goddesses Athena and Nike (goddess of victory). The frieze referred to depicts Nike wingless, hence it is sometimes referred to as Apteros Nike, or Wingless Victory. The frieze itself was moved to the Acropolis Museum in 2009 while a copy remains in the temple.

† Sandro Boticelli (1445–1510) and Andrea Mantegna (1431–1506) were two of the great Italian artists of the early Renaissance, and both were heavily influenced by Roman and Greek art.

‡ Carlo Crivelli (1430–1495) is one of the lesser known early Renaissance painters, although interest in his work was revived by the pre-Raphaelite artists.

"A home," she repeated, slowly, "a home for you and me to live in for all eternity?"

"Why not, love? Am I not the soul that yours has sought?"

"Y-yes—yes, I know—but, don't you see, home would not be like home to me, unless—"

"Unless?" he wonderingly repeated.

She did not answer, but she thought to herself, with an impulse of whimsical inconsistency, "Unless you slammed the door and wore creaking boots."

But he had recovered his hold upon her hand, and by imperceptible degrees was leading her toward the shining steps which descended to the valley.

"Come, O my soul's soul," he passionately implored; "why delay a moment? Surely you feel, as I do, that eternity itself is too short to hold such bliss as ours. It seems to me that I can see our home already. Have I not always seen it in my dreams? It is white, love, is it not, with polished columns, and a sculptured cornice against the blue? Groves of laurel and oleander and thickets of roses surround it; but from the terrace where we walk at sunset, the eye looks out over woodlands and cool meadows where, deep-bowered under ancient boughs, a stream goes delicately toward the river. Indoors our favorite pictures hang upon the walls and the rooms are lined with books. Think, dear, at last we shall have time to read them all. With which shall we begin? Come, help me to choose. Shall it be 'Faust' or the 'Vita Nuova,'* the 'Tempest' or 'Les Caprices de Marianne,'† or the thirty-first canto of the 'Paradise,' or 'Epipsychidion'‡ or "Lycidas'?§ Tell me, dear, which one?"

As he spoke he saw the answer trembling joyously upon her lips; but it died in the ensuing silence, and she stood motionless, resisting the persuasion of his hand.

"What is it?" he entreated.

---

* *La Vita Nuova,* or *The New Life,* is a work by Dante Alighieri published in 1294, some years before he began work on *The Divine Comedy.*

† *The Moods of Marianne,* an 1833 play by Alfred de Musset.

‡ An 1821 poetical work by Percy Shelley.

§ A 1637 pastoral poem by John Milton.

"Wait a moment," she said, with a strange hesitation in her voice. "Tell me first, are you quite sure of yourself? Is there no one on earth whom you sometimes remember?"

"Not since I have seen you," he replied; for, being a man, he had indeed forgotten.

Still she stood motionless, and he saw that the shadow deepened on her soul.

"Surely, love," he rebuked her, "it was not that which troubled you? For my part I have walked through Lethe.* The past has melted like a cloud before the moon. I never lived until I saw you."

She made no answer to his pleadings, but at length, rousing herself with a visible effort, she turned away from him and moved toward the Spirit of Life, who still stood near the threshold.

"I want to ask you a question," she said, in a troubled voice.

"Ask," said the Spirit.

"A little while ago," she began, slowly, "you told me that every soul which has not found a kindred soul on earth is destined to find one here."

"And have you not found one?" asked the Spirit.

"Yes; but will it be so with my husband's soul also?"

"No," answered the Spirit of Life, "for your husband imagined that he had found his soul's mate on earth in you; and for such delusions eternity itself contains no cure."

She gave a little cry. Was it of disappointment or triumph?

"Then—then what will happen to him when he comes here?"

"That I cannot tell you. Some field of activity and happiness he will doubtless find, in due measure to his capacity for being active and happy."

She interrupted, almost angrily: "He will never be happy without me."

"Do not be too sure of that," said the Spirit.

She took no notice of this, and the Spirit continued: "He will not understand you here any better than he did on earth."

"No matter," she said; "I shall be the only sufferer, for he always thought that he understood me."

---

* In Greek mythology the river Lethe was found in the Underworld and induced forgetfulness in those who drank from it.

"His boots will creak just as much as ever—"

"No matter."

"And he will slam the door—"

"Very likely."

"And continue to read railway novels—"

She interposed, impatiently: "Many men do worse than that."

"But you said just now," said the Spirit, "that you did not love him."

"True," she answered, simply; "but don't you understand that I shouldn't feel at home without him? It is all very well for a week or two—but for eternity! After all, I never minded the creaking of his boots, except when my head ached, and I don't suppose it will ache *here*; and he was always so sorry when he had slammed the door, only he never *could* remember not to. Besides, no one else would know how to look after him, he is so helpless. His inkstand would never be filled, and he would always be out of stamps and visiting-cards. He would never remember to have his umbrella re-covered, or to ask the price of anything before he bought it. Why, he wouldn't even know what novels to read. I always had to choose the kind he liked, with a murder or a forgery and a successful detective."

She turned abruptly to her kindred soul, who stood listening with a mien of wonder and dismay.

"Don't you see," she said, "that I can't possibly go with you?"

"But what do you intend to do?" asked the Spirit of Life.

"What do I intend to do?" she returned, indignantly. "Why, I mean to wait for my husband, of course. If he had come here first *he* would have waited for me for years and years; and it would break his heart not to find me here when he comes." She pointed with a contemptuous gesture to the magic vision of hill and vale sloping away to the translucent mountains. "He wouldn't give a fig for all that," she said, "if he didn't find me here."

"But consider," warned the Spirit, "that you are now choosing for eternity. It is a solemn moment."

"Choosing!" she said, with a half-sad smile. "Do you still keep up here that old fiction about choosing? I should have thought that *you* knew better than that. How can I help myself? He will expect to find me here when he comes, and he would never believe you if you told him that I had gone away with someone else—never, never."

"So be it," said the Spirit. "Here, as on earth, each one must decide for himself."

She turned to her kindred soul and looked at him gently, almost wistfully. "I am sorry," she said. "I should have liked to talk with you again; but you will understand, I know, and I dare say you will find someone else a great deal cleverer—"

And without pausing to hear his answer she waved him a swift farewell and turned back toward the threshold.

"Will my husband come soon?" she asked the Spirit of Life.

"That you are not destined to know," the Spirit replied.

"No matter," she said, cheerfully; "I have all eternity to wait in."

And still seated alone on the threshold, she listens for the creaking of his boots.

Margaret Oliphant Wilson (1828–1897) was a Scot who wrote historical and supernatural fiction, as well as historical and literary scholarship—more than 120 books—under the name "Mrs. Oliphant." She published her first novel at the age of twenty-one and soon made a connection with publisher William Blackwood that would last her lifetime, becoming a frequent contributor to the prestigious *Blackwood's Magazine*. She lost several children at a young age and her husband died when she was in her early thirties, so Oliphant was forced to turn to writing to support herself and her remaining family. In the 1880s she began to write supernatural fiction, including the oft-anthologized story "The Open Door." This tale—not quite a ghost story—first appeared in January 1896 in *Blackwood's Magazine*.

The Library Window
by Mrs. Oliphant

CHAPTER I

I was not aware at first of the many discussions which had gone on about that window. It was almost opposite one of the windows of the large old-fashioned drawing-room of the house in which I spent that summer, which was of so much importance in my life. Our house and the library were on opposite sides of the broad High Street of St Rule's,* which is a fine street, wide and ample, and very quiet, as strangers think who come from noisier places; but in a summer evening there is much coming and

---

* This is a fictitious town. St Rule's Church is in St. Andrews, Scotland, and in light of the Scot heritage of some of the characters, made evident shortly, this may be a disguised St. Andrews (which indeed has a college, though it lacks a High Street).

going, and the stillness is full of sound—the sound of footsteps and pleasant voices, softened by the summer air. There are even exceptional moments when it is noisy: the time of the fair, and on Saturday nights sometimes, and when there are excursion trains. Then even the softest sunny air of the evening will not smooth the harsh tones and the stumbling steps; but at these unlovely moments we shut the windows, and even I, who am so fond of that deep recess where I can take refuge from all that is going on inside, and make myself a spectator of all the varied story out of doors, withdraw from my watch-tower. To tell the truth, there never was very much going on inside. The house belonged to my aunt, to whom (she says, thank God!) nothing ever happens. I believe that many things have happened to her in her time; but that was all over at the period of which I am speaking, and she was old, and very quiet. Her life went on in a routine never broken. She got up at the same hour every day, and did the same things in the same rotation, day by day the same. She said that this was the greatest support in the world, and that routine is a kind of salvation. It may be so; but it is a very dull salvation, and I used to feel that I would rather have incident, whatever kind of incident it might be. But then at that time I was not old, which makes all the difference. At the time of which I speak the deep recess of the drawing-room window was a great comfort to me. Though she was an old lady (perhaps because she was so old) she was very tolerant, and had a kind of feeling for me. She never said a word, but often gave me a smile when she saw how I had built myself up, with my books and my basket of work. I did very little work, I fear—now and then a few stitches when the spirit moved me, or when I had got well afloat in a dream, and was more tempted to follow it out than to read my book, as sometimes happened. At other times, and if the book were interesting, I used to get through volume after volume sitting there, paying no attention to anybody. And yet I did pay a kind of attention. Aunt Mary's old ladies came in to call, and I heard them talk, though I very seldom listened; but for all that, if they had anything to say that was interesting, it is curious how I found it in my mind afterwards, as if the air had blown it to me. They came and went, and I had the sensation of their old bonnets gliding out and in, and their dresses rustling; and now and then had to jump up and shake hands with some one who knew me, and asked after my papa and mamma. Then

Aunt Mary would give me a little smile again, and I slipped back to my window. She never seemed to mind. My mother would not have let me do it, I know. She would have remembered dozens of things there were to do. She would have sent me up-stairs to fetch something which I was quite sure she did not want, or down-stairs to carry some quite unnecessary message to the housemaid. She liked to keep me running about. Perhaps that was one reason why I was so fond of Aunt Mary's drawing-room, and the deep recess of the window, and the curtain that fell half over it, and the broad window-seat where one could collect so many things without being found fault with for untidiness. Whenever we had anything the matter with us in these days, we were sent to St Rule's to get up our strength. And this was my case at the time of which I am going to speak.

Everybody had said, since ever I learned to speak, that I was fantastic and fanciful and dreamy, and all the other words with which a girl who may happen to like poetry, and to be fond of thinking, is so often made uncomfortable. People don't know what they mean when they say fantastic. It sounds like Madge Wildfire* or something of that sort. My mother thought I should always be busy, to keep nonsense out of my head. But really I was not at all fond of nonsense. I was rather serious than otherwise. I would have been no trouble to anybody if I had been left to myself. It was only that I had a sort of second-sight, and was conscious of things to which I paid no attention. Even when reading the most interesting book, the things that were being talked about blew in to me; and I heard what the people were saying in the streets as they passed under the window. Aunt Mary always said I could do two or indeed three things at once—both read and listen, and see. I am sure that I did not listen much, and seldom looked out, of set purpose—as some people do who notice what bonnets the ladies in the street have on; but I did hear what I couldn't help hearing, even when I was reading my book, and I did see all sorts of things, though often for a whole half-hour I might never lift my eyes.

This does not explain what I said at the beginning, that there were many discussions about that window. It was, and still is, the last window in the

---

* Madge Wildfire is a character from Sir Walter Scott's novel *The Heart of Midlothian;* she is said to be "very giddy" and is essentially slightly mad.

row, of the College Library, which is opposite my aunt's house in the High Street. Yet it is not exactly opposite, but a little to the west, so that I could see it best from the left side of my recess. I took it calmly for granted that it was a window like any other till I first heard the talk about it which was going on in the drawing-room. "Have you never made up your mind, Mrs. Balcarres," said old Mr. Pitmilly, "whether that window opposite is a window or no?" He said Mistress Balcarres—and he was always called Mr. Pitmilly, Morton: which was the name of his place.

"I am never sure of it, to tell the truth," said Aunt Mary, "all these years."

"Bless me!" said one of the old ladies, "and what window may that be?"

Mr. Pitmilly had a way of laughing as he spoke, which did not please me; but it was true that he was not perhaps desirous of pleasing me. He said, "Oh, just the window opposite," with his laugh running through his words; "our friend can never make up her mind about it, though she has been living opposite it since—"

"You need never mind the date," said another; "the Leebrary window! Dear me, what should it be but a window? Up at that height it could not be a door."

"The question is," said my aunt, "if it is a real window with glass in it, or if it is merely painted, or if it once was a window, and has been built up. And the oftener people look at it, the less they are able to say."

"Let me see this window," said old Lady Carnbee, who was very active and strong-minded; and then they all came crowding upon me—three or four old ladies, very eager, and Mr. Pitmilly's white hair appearing over their heads, and my aunt sitting quiet and smiling behind.

"I mind the window very well," said Lady Carnbee; "ay: and so do more than me. But in its present appearance it is just like any other window; but has not been cleaned, I should say, in the memory of man."

"I see what ye mean," said one of the others. "It is just a very dead thing without any reflection in it; but I've seen as bad before."

"Ay, it's dead enough," said another, "but that's no rule; for these hizzies* of women-servants in this ill age—"

---

* A Scottish variant of "hussies"—a young, frivolous woman.

"Nay, the women are well enough," said the softest voice of all, which was Aunt Mary's. "I will never let them risk their lives cleaning the outside of mine. And there are no women-servants in the Old Library: there is maybe something more in it than that."

They were all pressing into my recess, pressing upon me, a row of old faces, peering into something they could not understand. I had a sense in my mind how curious it was, the wall of old ladies in their old satin gowns all glazed with age, Lady Carnbee with her lace about her head. Nobody was looking at me or thinking of me; but I felt unconsciously the contrast of my youngness to their oldness, and stared at them as they stared over my head at the Library window. I had given it no attention up to this time. I was more taken up with the old ladies than with the thing they were looking at.

"The framework is all right at least, I can see that, and pented black—"

"And the panes are pented black too. It's no window, Mrs Balcarres. It has been filled in, in the days of the window duties: you will mind, Leddy Carnbee."

"Mind!" said that oldest lady. "I mind when your mother was marriet, Jeanie: and that's neither the day nor yesterday. But as for the window, it's just a delusion: and that is my opinion of the matter, if you ask me."

"There's a great want of light in that muckle* room at the college," said another. "If it was a window, the Leebrary would have more light."

"One thing is clear," said one of the younger ones, "it cannot be a window to see through. It may be filled in or it may be built up, but it is not a window to give light."

"And who ever heard of a window that was no to see through?" Lady Carnbee said. I was fascinated by the look on her face, which was a curious scornful look as of one who knew more than she chose to say: and then my wandering fancy was caught by her hand as she held it up, throwing back the lace that dropped over it. Lady Carnbee's lace was the chief thing about her—heavy black Spanish lace with large flowers. Everything she wore was trimmed with it. A large veil of it hung over her old bonnet. But her hand coming out of this heavy lace was a curious thing to see. She had

_____
* A Scottish word meaning "large."

very long fingers, very taper, which had been much admired in her youth; and her hand was very white, or rather more than white, pale, bleached, and bloodless, with large blue veins standing up upon the back; and she wore some fine rings, among others a big diamond in an ugly old claw setting. They were too big for her, and were wound round and round with yellow silk to make them keep on: and this little cushion of silk, turned brown with long wearing, had twisted round so that it was more conspicuous than the jewels; while the big diamond blazed underneath in the hollow of her hand, like some dangerous thing hiding and sending out darts of light. The hand, which seemed to come almost to a point, with this strange ornament underneath, clutched at my half-terrified imagination. It too seemed to mean far more than was said. I felt as if it might clutch me with sharp claws, and the lurking, dazzling creature bite—with a sting that would go to the heart.

Presently, however, the circle of the old faces broke up, the old ladies returned to their seats, and Mr. Pitmilly, small but very erect, stood up in the midst of them, talking with mild authority like a little oracle among the ladies. Only Lady Carnbee always contradicted the neat, little, old gentleman. She gesticulated, when she talked, like a Frenchwoman, and darted forth that hand of hers with the lace hanging over it, so that I always caught a glimpse of the lurking diamond. I thought she looked like a witch among the comfortable little group which gave such attention to everything Mr. Pitmilly said.

"For my part, it is my opinion there is no window there at all," he said. "It's very like the thing that's called in scientific language an optical illusion. It arises generally, if I may use such a word in the presence of ladies, from a liver that is not just in the perfitt order and balance that organ demands—and then you will see things—a blue dog, I remember, was the thing in one case, and in another—"

"The man has gane gyte,"* said Lady Carnbee; "I mind the windows in the Auld Leebrary as long as I mind anything. Is the Leebrary itself an optical illusion too?"

---

* In Scottish dialect *gyte* means mad, demented.

"Na, na," and "No, no," said the old ladies; "a blue dogue would be a strange vagary: but the Library we have all kent from our youth," said one. "And I mind when the Assemblies were held there one year when the Town Hall was building," another said.

"It is just a great divert to me," said Aunt Mary: but what was strange was that she paused there, and said in a low tone, "now": and then went on again, "for whoever comes to my house, there are aye discussions about that window. I have never just made up my mind about it myself. Sometimes I think it's a case of these wicked window duties, as you said, Miss Jeanie, when half the windows in our houses were blocked up to save the tax.* And then, I think, it may be due to that blank kind of building like the great new buildings on the Earthen Mound in Edinburgh, where the windows are just ornaments. And then whiles I am sure I can see the glass shining when the sun catches it in the afternoon."

"You could so easily satisfy yourself, Mrs. Balcarres, if you were to—"

"Give a laddie a penny to cast a stone, and see what happens," said Lady Carnbee.

"But I am not sure that I have any desire to satisfy myself," Aunt Mary said. And then there was a stir in the room, and I had to come out from my recess and open the door for the old ladies and see them down-stairs, as they all went away following one another. Mr. Pitmilly gave his arm to Lady Carnbee, though she was always contradicting him; and so the tea-party dispersed. Aunt Mary came to the head of the stairs with her guests in an old-fashioned gracious way, while I went down with them to see that the maid was ready at the door. When I came back Aunt Mary was still standing in the recess looking out. Returning to my seat she said, with a kind of wistful look, "Well, honey: and what is your opinion?"

"I have no opinion. I was reading my book all the time," I said.

"And so you were, honey, and no' very civil; but all the same I ken well you heard every word we said."

---

* From 1696 to 1851 Great Britain enacted a window tax that taxed homeowners depending on the number of windows in their house. Although the tax was designed to ease the burden on the poor (whose smaller homes had less windows), it instead resulted in health issues as owners filled in their homes' windows; hence, the repeal in 1851.

Chapter II

It was a night in June; dinner was long over, and had it been winter the maids would have been shutting up the house, and my Aunt Mary preparing to go upstairs to her room. But it was still clear daylight, that daylight out of which the sun has been long gone, and which has no longer any rose reflections, but all has sunk into a pearly neutral tint—a light which is daylight yet is not day. We had taken a turn in the garden after dinner, and now we had returned to what we called our usual occupations. My aunt was reading. The English post had come in, and she had got her 'Times,' which was her great diversion. The 'Scotsman' was her morning reading, but she liked her 'Times' at night.

As for me, I too was at my usual occupation, which at that time was doing nothing. I had a book as usual, and was absorbed in it: but I was conscious of all that was going on all the same. The people strolled along the broad pavement, making remarks as they passed under the open window which came up into my story or my dream, and sometimes made me laugh. The tone and the faint sing-song, or rather chant, of the accent, which was "a wee Fifish,"* was novel to me, and associated with holiday, and pleasant; and sometimes they said to each other something that was amusing, and often something that suggested a whole story; but presently they began to drop off, the footsteps slackened, the voices died away. It was getting late, though the clear soft daylight went on and on. All through the lingering evening, which seemed to consist of interminable hours, long but not weary, drawn out as if the spell of the light and the outdoor life might never end, I had now and then, quite unawares, cast a glance at the mysterious window, which my aunt and her friends had discussed, as I felt, though I dared not say it even to myself, rather foolishly. It caught my eye without any intention on my part, as I paused, as it were, to take breath, in the flowing and current of undistinguishable thoughts and things from without and within which carried me along. First it occurred to me, with a little sensation of discovery, how absurd to say it was not a window, a living window, one to see through! Why, then, had they never seen it, these old folk? I saw as I

---

* That is, the accent of Fife, the eastern county of Scotland.

looked up suddenly the faint greyness as of visible space within—a room behind, certainly dim, as it was natural a room should be on the other side of the street—quite indefinite: yet so clear that if some one were to come to the window there would be nothing surprising in it. For certainly there was a feeling of space behind the panes which these old half-blind ladies had disputed about whether they were glass or only fictitious panes marked on the wall. How silly! when eyes that could see could make it out in a minute. It was only a greyness at present, but it was unmistakable, a space that went back into gloom, as every room does when you look into it across a street. There were no curtains to show whether it was inhabited or not; but a room—oh, as distinctly as ever room was! I was pleased with myself, but said nothing, while Aunt Mary rustled her paper, waiting for a favourable moment to announce a discovery which settled her problem at once. Then I was carried away upon the stream again, and forgot the window, till somebody threw unawares a word from the outer world, "I'm goin' hame; it'll soon be dark." Dark! what was the fool thinking of? it never would be dark if one waited out, wandering in the soft air for hours longer; and then my eyes, acquiring easily that new habit, looked across the way again.

Ah, now! nobody indeed had come to the window; and no light had been lighted, seeing it was still beautiful to read by—a still, clear, colourless light; but the room inside had certainly widened. I could see the grey space and air a little deeper, and a sort of vision, very dim, of a wall, and something against it; something dark, with the blackness that a solid article, however indistinctly seen, takes in the lighter darkness that is only space—a large, black, dark thing coming out into the grey. I looked more intently, and made sure it was a piece of furniture, either a writing-table or perhaps a large book-case. No doubt it must be the last, since this was part of the old library. I never visited the old College Library, but I had seen such places before, and I could well imagine it to myself. How curious that for all the time these old people had looked at it, they had never seen this before!

It was more silent now, and my eyes, I suppose, had grown dim with gazing, doing my best to make it out, when suddenly Aunt Mary said, "Will you ring the bell, my dear? I must have my lamp."

"Your lamp?" I cried, "when it is still daylight." But then I gave another look at my window, and perceived with a start that the light had indeed changed: for now I saw nothing. It was still light, but there was so much change in the light that my room, with the grey space and the large shadowy bookcase, had gone out, and I saw them no more: for even a Scotch night in June, though it looks as if it would never end, does darken at the last. I had almost cried out, but checked myself, and rang the bell for Aunt Mary, and made up my mind I would say nothing till next morning, when to be sure naturally it would be more clear.

Next morning I rather think I forgot all about it—or was busy: or was more idle than usual: the two things meant nearly the same. At all events I thought no more of the window, though I still sat in my own, opposite to it, but occupied with some other fancy. Aunt Mary's visitors came as usual in the afternoon; but their talk was of other things, and for a day or two nothing at all happened to bring back my thoughts into this channel. It might be nearly a week before the subject came back, and once more it was old Lady Carnbee who set me thinking; not that she said anything upon that particular theme. But she was the last of my aunt's afternoon guests to go away, and when she rose to leave she threw up her hands, with those lively gesticulations which so many old Scotch ladies have. "My faith!" said she, "there is that bairn there still like a dream. Is the creature bewitched, Mary Balcarres? and is she bound to sit there by night and by day for the rest of her days? You should mind that there's things about, uncanny for women of our blood."

I was too much startled at first to recognise that it was of me she was speaking. She was like a figure in a picture, with her pale face the colour of ashes, and the big pattern of the Spanish lace hanging half over it, and her hand held up, with the big diamond blazing at me from the inside of her uplifted palm. It was held up in surprise, but it looked as if it were raised in malediction; and the diamond threw out darts of light and glared and twinkled at me. If it had been in its right place it would not have mattered; but there, in the open of the hand! I started up, half in terror, half in wrath. And then the old lady laughed, and her hand dropped. "I've wakened you to life, and broke the spell," she said, nodding her old head at me, while the large black silk flowers of the lace waved and threatened. And she took my arm to go down-stairs, laughing and bidding me be steady, and no' tremble and shake like a broken reed. "You should be as steady as a rock at your age.

I was like a young tree," she said, leaning so heavily that my willowy girlish frame quivered—"I was a support to virtue, like Pamela,* in my time."

"Aunt Mary, Lady Carnbee is a witch!" I cried, when I came back.

"Is that what you think, honey? well: maybe she once was," said Aunt Mary, whom nothing surprised.

And it was that night once more after dinner, and after the post came in, and the 'Times,' that I suddenly saw the Library window again. I had seen it every day and noticed nothing; but to-night, still in a little tumult of mind over Lady Carnbee and her wicked diamond which wished me harm, and her lace which waved threats and warnings at me, I looked across the street, and there I saw quite plainly the room opposite, far more clear than before. I saw dimly that it must be a large room, and that the big piece of furniture against the wall was a writing-desk. That in a moment, when first my eyes rested upon it, was quite clear: a large old-fashioned escritoire, standing out into the room: and I knew by the shape of it that it had a great many pigeon-holes and little drawers in the back, and a large table for writing. There was one just like it in my father's library at home. It was such a surprise to see it all so clearly that I closed my eyes, for the moment almost giddy, wondering how papa's desk could have come here—and then when I reminded myself that this was nonsense, and that there were many such writing-tables besides papa's, and looked again—lo! it had all become quite vague and indistinct as it was at first; and I saw nothing but the blank window, of which the old ladies could never be certain whether it was filled up to avoid the window-tax, or whether it had ever been a window at all.

This occupied my mind very much, and yet I did not say anything to Aunt Mary. For one thing, I rarely saw anything at all in the early part of the day; but then that is natural: you can never see into a place from outside, whether it is an empty room or a looking-glass, or people's eyes, or anything else that is mysterious, in the day. It has, I suppose, something to do with the light. But in the evening in June in Scotland—then is the time to see. For it is daylight, yet it is not day, and there is a quality in it which I cannot describe, it is so clear, as if every object was a reflection of itself.

---

* A reference to Samuel Richardson's 1740 novel *Pamela; or, Virtue Rewarded*, about a fifteen-year-old servant who struggles to fend off her employer's advances.

I used to see more and more of the room as the days went on. The large escritoire stood out more and more into the space: with sometimes white glimmering things, which looked like papers, lying on it: and once or twice I was sure I saw a pile of books on the floor close to the writing-table, as if they had gilding upon them in broken specks, like old books. It was always about the time when the lads in the street began to call to each other that they were going home, and sometimes a shriller voice would come from one of the doors, bidding somebody to "cry upon the laddies" to come back to their suppers. That was always the time I saw best, though it was close upon the moment when the veil seemed to fall and the clear radiance became less living, and all the sounds died out of the street, and Aunt Mary said in her soft voice, "Honey! will you ring for the lamp?" She said honey as people say darling: and I think it is a prettier word.

Then finally, while I sat one evening with my book in my hand, looking straight across the street, not distracted by anything, I saw a little movement within. It was not any one visible—but everybody must know what it is to see the stir in the air, the little disturbance—you cannot tell what it is, but that it indicates some one there, even though you can see no one. Perhaps it is a shadow making just one flicker in the still place. You may look at an empty room and the furniture in it for hours, and then suddenly there will be the flicker, and you know that something has come into it. It might only be a dog or a cat; it might be, if that were possible, a bird flying across; but it is some one, something living, which is so different, so completely different, in a moment from the things that are not living. It seemed to strike quite through me, and I gave a little cry. Then Aunt Mary stirred a little, and put down the huge newspaper that almost covered her from sight, and said, "What is it, honey?" I cried "Nothing," with a little gasp, quickly, for I did not want to be disturbed just at this moment when somebody was coming! But I suppose she was not satisfied, for she got up and stood behind to see what it was, putting her hand on my shoulder. It was the softest touch in the world, but I could have flung it off angrily: for that moment everything was still again, and the place grew grey and I saw no more.

"Nothing," I repeated, but I was so vexed I could have cried. "I told you it was nothing, Aunt Mary. Don't you believe me, that you come to look—and spoil it all!"

I did not mean of course to say these last words; they were forced out of me. I was so much annoyed to see it all melt away like a dream: for it was no dream, but as real as—as real as—myself or anything I ever saw.

She gave my shoulder a little pat with her hand. "Honey," she said, "were you looking at something? Is't that? is't that?" "Is it what?" I wanted to say, shaking off her hand, but something in me stopped me: for I said nothing at all, and she went quietly back to her place. I suppose she must have rung the bell herself, for immediately I felt the soft flood of the light behind me, and the evening outside dimmed down, as it did every night, and I saw nothing more.

It was next day, I think, in the afternoon that I spoke. It was brought on by something she said about her fine work. "I get a mist before my eyes," she said; "you will have to learn my old lace stitches, honey—for I soon will not see to draw the threads."

"Oh, I hope you will keep your sight," I cried, without thinking what I was saying. I was then young and very matter-of-fact. I had not found out that one may mean something, yet not half or a hundredth part of what one seems to mean: and even then probably hoping to be contradicted if it is anyhow against one's self.

"My sight!" she said, looking up at me with a look that was almost angry; "there is no question of losing my sight—on the contrary, my eyes are very strong. I may not see to draw fine threads, but I see at a distance as well as ever I did—as well as you do."

"I did not mean any harm, Aunt Mary," I said. "I thought you said—But how can your sight be as good as ever when you are in doubt about that window? I can see into the room as clear as—" My voice wavered, for I had just looked up and across the street, and I could have sworn that there was no window at all, but only a false image of one painted on the wall.

"Ah!" she said, with a little tone of keenness and of surprise: and she half rose up, throwing down her work hastily, as if she meant to come to me: then, perhaps seeing the bewildered look on my face, she paused and hesitated—"Ay, honey!" she said, "have you got so far ben* as that?"

---

* In Scottish dialect, guileless, innocent.

What did she mean? Of course I knew all the old Scotch phrases as well as I knew myself; but it is a comfort to take refuge in a little ignorance, and I know I pretended not to understand whenever I was put out. "I don't know what you mean by 'far ben,'" I cried out, very impatient. I don't know what might have followed, but some one just then came to call, and she could only give me a look before she went forward, putting out her hand to her visitor. It was a very soft look, but anxious, and as if she did not know what to do: and she shook her head a very little, and I thought, though there was a smile on her face, there was something wet about her eyes. I retired into my recess, and nothing more was said.

But it was very tantalising that it should fluctuate so; for sometimes I saw that room quite plain and clear—quite as clear as I could see papa's library, for example, when I shut my eyes. I compared it naturally to my father's study, because of the shape of the writing-table, which, as I tell you, was the same as his. At times I saw the papers on the table quite plain, just as I had seen his papers many a day. And the little pile of books on the floor at the foot—not ranged regularly in order, but put down one above the other, with all their angles going different ways, and a speck of the old gilding shining here and there. And then again at other times I saw nothing, absolutely nothing, and was no better than the old ladies who had peered over my head, drawing their eyelids together, and arguing that the window had been shut up because of the old long-abolished window tax, or else that it had never been a window at all. It annoyed me very much at those dull moments to feel that I too puckered up my eyelids and saw no better than they.

Aunt Mary's old ladies came and went day after day while June went on. I was to go back in July, and I felt that I should be very unwilling indeed to leave until I had quite cleared up—as I was indeed in the way of doing—the mystery of that window, which changed so strangely and appeared quite a different thing, not only to different people, but to the same eyes at different times. Of course I said to myself it must simply be an effect of the light. And yet I did not quite like that explanation either, but would have been better pleased to make out to myself that it was some superiority in me, which made it so clear to me, if it were only the great superiority of young eyes over old—though that was not quite enough to satisfy me, seeing it was a superiority, which I shared with every little lass and lad in the street. I rather wanted, I believe, to think that there was some particular insight in me which gave clearness to my sight—which was a most impertinent assumption, but really did not mean half the harm it seems to mean when it is put down here in black and white. I had several times again, however, seen the room quite plain, and made out that it was a large room, with a great picture in a dim gilded frame hanging on the farther wall, and many other pieces of solid furniture making a blackness here and there, besides the great escritoire against the wall, which had evidently been placed near the window for the sake of the light. One thing became visible to me after another, till I almost thought I should end by being able to read the old lettering on one of the big volumes, which projected from the others and caught the light; but this was all preliminary to the great event which happened about Midsummer Day—the day of St John,* which was once so much thought of as a festival, but now means nothing at all in Scotland any more than any other of the saints' days: which I shall always think a great pity and loss to Scotland, whatever Aunt Mary may say.

CHAPTER III

It was about midsummer, I cannot say exactly to a day when, but near that time, when the great event happened. I had grown very well acquainted by this time with that large dim room. Not only the escritoire, which was very plain to me now, with the papers upon it, and the books at its foot, but the great picture that hung against the farther wall, and various other shadowy pieces of furniture, especially a chair, which one evening I saw had been moved into the space before the escritoire,—a little change which made my heart beat, for it spoke so distinctly of some one who must have been there, the some one who had already made me start, two or three times before, by some vague shadow of him or thrill of him which made a sort of movement in the silent space: a movement which made me sure that next

---

* The birthday of John the Baptist, still the occasion of festivals in many countries, including Spain and Lithuania.

minute I must see something or hear something, which would explain the whole—if it were not that something always happened outside to stop it, at the very moment of its accomplishment. I had no warning this time of movement or shadow. I had been looking into the room very attentively a little while before, and had made out everything almost clearer than ever; and then had bent my attention again on my book, and read a chapter or two at a most exciting period of the story: and consequently had quite left St Rule's, and the High Street, and the College Library, and was really in a South American forest, almost throttled by the flowery creepers, and treading softly lest I should put my foot on a scorpion or a dangerous snake. At this moment something suddenly calling my attention to the outside, I looked across, and then, with a start, sprang up, for I could not contain myself. I don't know what I said, but enough to startle the people in the room, one of whom was old Mr. Pitmilly. They all looked round upon me to ask what was the matter. And when I gave my usual answer of "Nothing," sitting down again shamefaced but very much excited, Mr. Pitmilly got up and came forward, and looked out, apparently to see what was the cause. He saw nothing, for he went back again, and I could hear him telling Aunt Mary not to be alarmed, for Missy had fallen into a doze with the heat, and had startled herself waking up, at which they all laughed: another time I could have killed him for his impertinence, but my mind was too much taken up now to pay any attention. My head was throbbing and my heart beating. I was in such high excitement, however, that to restrain myself completely, to be perfectly silent, was more easy to me then than at any other time of my life. I waited until the old gentleman had taken his seat again, and then I looked back. Yes, there he was! I had not been deceived. I knew then, when I looked across, that this was what I had been looking for all the time—that I had known he was there, and had been waiting for him, every time there was that flicker of movement in the room—him and no one else. And there at last, just as I had expected, he was. I don't know that in reality I ever had expected him, or any one: but this was what I felt when, suddenly looking into that curious dim room, I saw him there.

He was sitting in the chair, which he must have placed for himself, or which some one else in the dead of night when nobody was looking must have set for him, in front of the escritoire—with the back of his head towards me, writing. The light fell upon him from the left hand, and therefore upon his shoulders and the side of his head, which, however, was too much turned away to show anything of his face. Oh, how strange that there should be some one staring at him as I was doing, and he never to turn his head, to make a movement! If any one stood and looked at me, were I in the soundest sleep that ever was, I would wake, I would jump up, I would feel it through everything. But there he sat and never moved. You are not to suppose, though I said the light fell upon him from the left hand, that there was very much light. There never is in a room you are looking into like that across the street; but there was enough to see him by—the outline of his figure dark and solid, seated in the chair, and the fairness of his head visible faintly, a clear spot against the dimness. I saw this outline against the dim gilding of the frame of the large picture which hung on the farther wall.

I sat all the time the visitors were there, in a sort of rapture, gazing at this figure. I knew no reason why I should be so much moved. In an ordinary way, to see a student at an opposite window quietly doing his work might have interested me a little, but certainly it would not have moved me in any such way. It is always interesting to have a glimpse like this of an unknown life—to see so much and yet know so little, and to wonder, perhaps, what the man is doing, and why he never turns his head. One would go to the window—but not too close, lest he should see you and think you were spying upon him—and one would ask, Is he still there? is he writing, writing always? I wonder what he is writing! And it would be a great amusement: but no more. This was not my feeling at all in the present case. It was a sort of breathless watch, an absorption. I did not feel that I had eyes for anything else, or any room in my mind for another thought. I no longer heard, as I generally did, the stories and the wise remarks (or foolish) of Aunt Mary's old ladies or Mr. Pitmilly. I heard only a murmur behind me, the interchange of voices, one softer, one sharper; but it was not as in the time when I sat reading and heard every word, till the story in my book, and the stories they were telling (what they said almost always shaped into stories), were all mingled into each other, and the hero in the novel became somehow the hero (or more likely heroine) of them all. But I took no notice of what they were saying now. And it was not that there was anything very interesting to look at, except the fact that he was there. He did nothing to keep up the absorption of my thoughts. He moved just so much as a man will do when he is very busily writing, thinking of nothing else. There was a faint turn of his head as he went from one side to another of the page he was writing; but it appeared to be a long long page which never wanted turning. Just a little inclination when he was at the end of the line, outward, and then a little inclination inward when he began the next. That was little enough to keep one gazing. But I suppose it was the gradual course of events leading up to this, the finding out of one thing after another as the eyes got accustomed to the vague light: first the room itself, and then the writing-table, and then the other furniture, and last of all the human inhabitant who gave it all meaning. This was all so interesting that it was like a country which one had discovered. And then the extraordinary blindness of the other people who disputed among themselves whether it was a window at all! I did not, I am sure, wish to be disrespectful, and I was very fond of my Aunt Mary, and I liked Mr. Pitmilly well enough, and I was afraid of Lady Carnbee. But yet to think of the—I know I ought not to say stupidity—the blindness of them, the foolishness, the insensibility! discussing it as if a thing that your eyes could see was a thing to discuss! It would have been unkind to think it was because they were old and their faculties dimmed. It is so sad to think that the faculties grow dim, that such a woman as my Aunt Mary should fail in seeing, or hearing, or feeling, that I would not have dwelt on it for a moment, it would have seemed so cruel! And then such a clever old lady as Lady Carnbee, who could see through a millstone, people said—and Mr. Pitmilly, such an old man of the world. It did indeed bring tears to my eyes to think that all those clever people, solely by reason of being no longer young as I was, should have the simplest things shut out from them; and for all their wisdom and their knowledge be unable to see what a girl like me could see so easily. I was too much grieved for them to dwell upon that thought, and half ashamed, though perhaps half proud too, to be so much better off than they.

All those thoughts flitted through my mind as I sat and gazed across the street. And I felt there was so much going on in that room across the street! He was so absorbed in his writing, never looked up, never paused for a word, never turned round in his chair, or got up and walked about the room as my father did. Papa is a great writer, everybody says: but he would have come to the window and looked out, he would have drummed with his fingers on the pane, he would have watched a fly and helped it over a difficulty, and played with the fringe of the curtain, and done a dozen other nice, pleasant, foolish things, till the next sentence took shape. "My dear, I am waiting for a word," he would say to my mother when she looked at him, with a question why he was so idle, in her eyes; and then he would laugh, and go back again to his writing-table. But He over there never stopped at all. It was like a fascination. I could not take my eyes from him and that little scarcely perceptible movement he made, turning his head. I trembled with impatience to see him turn the page, or perhaps throw down his finished sheet on the floor, as somebody looking into a window like me once saw Sir Walter do, sheet after sheet.* I should have cried out if this Unknown had done that. I should not have been able to help myself, whoever had been present; and gradually I got into such a state of suspense waiting for it to be done that my head grew hot and my hands cold. And then, just when there was a little movement of his elbow, as if he were about to do this, to be called away by Aunt Mary to see Lady Carnbee to the door! I believe I did not hear her till she had called me three times, and then I stumbled up, all flushed and hot, and nearly crying. When I came out from the recess to give the old lady my arm (Mr. Pitmilly had gone away some time before), she put up her hand and stroked my cheek. "What ails the bairn?" she said; "she's fevered. You must not let her sit her lane in the window, Mary Balcarres. You and me know what comes of that." Her old fingers had a strange touch, cold like something not living, and I felt that dreadful diamond sting me on the cheek.

I do not say that this was not just a part of my excitement and suspense; and I know it is enough to make any one laugh when the excitement was

---

* Sir Walter Scott (1771–1832), the renowned author, was reportedly a tireless writer. One biographer, John Gibson Lockhart (Scott's son-in-law), wrote how in 1814 "a youthful friend of his own was irritated by the vision of a hand which he could see, while drinking his claret, through the window of a neighbouring house, unweariedly adding to a heap of manuscripts." The hand was later identified as Scott's, hard at work on his novel *Waverley*.

all about an unknown man writing in a room on the other side of the way, and my impatience because he never came to an end of the page. If you think I was not quite as well aware of this as any one could be! but the worst was that this dreadful old lady felt my heart beating against her arm that was within mine. "You are just in a dream," she said to me, with her old voice close at my ear as we went down-stairs. "I don't know who it is about, but it's bound to be some man that is not worth it. If you were wise you would think of him no more."

"I am thinking of no man!" I said, half crying. "It is very unkind and dreadful of you to say so, Lady Carnbee. I never thought of—any man, in all my life!" I cried in a passion of indignation. The old lady clung tighter to my arm, and pressed it to her, not unkindly.

"Poor little bird," she said, "how it's strugglin' and flutterin'! I'm not saying but what it's more dangerous when it's all for a dream."

She was not at all unkind; but I was very angry and excited, and would scarcely shake that old pale hand which she put out to me from her carriage window when I had helped her in. I was angry with her, and I was afraid of the diamond, which looked up from under her finger as if it saw through and through me; and whether you believe me or not, I am certain that it stung me again—a sharp malignant prick, oh full of meaning! She never wore gloves, but only black lace mittens, through which that horrible diamond gleamed.

I ran up-stairs—she had been the last to go and Aunt Mary too had gone to get ready for dinner, for it was late. I hurried to my place, and looked across, with my heart beating more than ever. I made quite sure I should see the finished sheet lying white upon the floor. But what I gazed at was only the dim blank of that window which they said was no window. The light had changed in some wonderful way during that five minutes I had been gone, and there was nothing, nothing, not a reflection, not a glimmer. It looked exactly as they all said, the blank form of a window painted on the wall. It was too much: I sat down in my excitement and cried as if my heart would break. I felt that they had done something to it, that it was not natural, that I could not bear their unkindness—even Aunt Mary. They thought it not good for me! not good for me! and they had done something—even Aunt Mary herself—and that wicked diamond that hid itself in Lady Carnbee's hand. Of course I knew all this was ridiculous as well as you could tell me; but I was exasperated by the disappointment and the sudden stop to all my excited feelings, and I could not bear it. It was more strong than I.

I was late for dinner, and naturally there were some traces in my eyes that I had been crying when I came into the full light in the dining-room, where Aunt Mary could look at me at her pleasure, and I could not run away. She said, "Honey, you have been shedding tears. I'm loth, loth that a bairn of your mother's should be made to shed tears in my house."

"I have not been made to shed tears," cried I; and then, to save myself another fit of crying, I burst out laughing and said, "I am afraid of that dreadful diamond on old Lady Carnbee's hand. It bites—I am sure it bites! Aunt Mary, look here."

"You foolish lassie," Aunt Mary said; but she looked at my cheek under the light of the lamp, and then she gave it a little pat with her soft hand. "Go away with you, you silly bairn. There is no bite; but a flushed cheek, my honey, and a wet eye. You must just read out my paper to me after dinner when the post is in: and we'll have no more thinking and no more dreaming for tonight."

"Yes, Aunt Mary," said I. But I knew what would happen; for when she opens up her 'Times,' all full of the news of the world, and the speeches and things which she takes an interest in, though I cannot tell why—she forgets. And as I kept very quiet and made not a sound, she forgot to-night what she had said, and the curtain hung a little more over me than usual, and I sat down in my recess as if I had been a hundred miles away. And my heart gave a great jump, as if it would have come out of my breast; for he was there. But not as he had been in the morning—I suppose the light, perhaps, was not good enough to go on with his work without a lamp or candles—for he had turned away from the table and was fronting the window, sitting leaning back in his chair, and turning his head to me. Not to me—he knew nothing about me. I thought he was not looking at any-thing; but with his face turned my way. My heart was in my mouth: it was so unexpected, so strange! though why it should have seemed strange I know not, for there was no communication between him and me that it should have moved me; and what could be more natural than that a man, wearied of his work, and feeling the want perhaps of more light, and yet that it was not dark enough to light a lamp, should turn round in his own chair, and rest a little, and think—perhaps of nothing at all? Papa always says he is thinking of nothing at all. He says things blow through his mind as if the doors were open, and he has no responsibility. What sort of things were blowing through this man's mind? or was he thinking, still thinking, of what he had been writing and going on with it still? The thing that troubled me most was that I could not make out his face. It is very difficult to do so when you see a person only through two windows, your own and his. I wanted very much to recognise him afterwards if I should chance to meet him in the street. If he had only stood up and moved about the room, I should have made out the rest of his figure, and then I should have known him again; or if he had only come to the window (as papa always did), then I should have seen his face clearly enough to have recognised him. But, to be sure, he did not see any need to do anything in order that I might recognise him, for he did not know I existed; and probably if he had known I was watching him, he would have been annoyed and gone away.

But he was as immovable there facing the window as he had been seated at the desk. Sometimes he made a little faint stir with a hand or a foot, and I held my breath, hoping he was about to rise from his chair—but he never did it. And with all the efforts I made I could not be sure of his face. I puckered my eyelids together as old Miss Jeanie did who was shortsighted, and I put my hands on each side of my face to concentrate the light on him: but it was all in vain. Either the face changed as I sat staring, or else it was the light that was not good enough, or I don't know what it was. His hair seemed to me light—certainly there was no dark line about his head, as there would have been had it been very dark—and I saw, where it came across the old gilt frame on the wall behind, that it must be fair: and I am almost sure he had no beard. Indeed I am sure that he had no beard, for the outline of his face was distinct enough; and the daylight was still quite clear out of doors, so that I recognised perfectly a baker's boy who was on the pavement opposite, and whom I should have known again whenever I had met him: as if it was of the least importance to recognise a baker's boy! There was one thing, however, rather curious about this boy. He had been throwing stones at something or somebody. In St Rule's they have a great way of throwing stones at each other, and I suppose there had been a battle. I suppose also that he had one stone in his hand left over from the battle, and his roving eye took in all the incidents of the street to judge where he could throw it with most effect and mischief. But apparently he found nothing worthy of it in the street, for he suddenly turned round with a flick under his leg to show his cleverness, and aimed it straight at the window. I remarked without remarking that it struck with a hard sound and without any breaking of glass, and fell straight down on the pavement. But I took no notice of this even in my mind, so intently was I watching the figure within, which moved not nor took the slightest notice, and remained just as dimly clear, as perfectly seen, yet as indistinguishable, as before. And then the light began to fail a little, not diminishing the prospect within, but making it still less distinct than it had been.

Then I jumped up, feeling Aunt Mary's hand upon my shoulder. "Honey," she said, "I asked you twice to ring the bell; but you did not hear me."

"Oh, Aunt Mary!" I cried in great penitence, but turning again to the window in spite of myself.

"You must come away from there: you must come away from there," she said, almost as if she were angry: and then her soft voice grew softer, and she gave me a kiss: "never mind about the lamp, honey; I have rung myself, and it is coming; but, silly bairn, you must not aye be dreaming—your little head will turn."

All the answer I made, for I could scarcely speak, was to give a little wave with my hand to the window on the other side of the street.

She stood there patting me softly on the shoulder for a whole minute or more, murmuring something that sounded like, "She must go away, she must go away." Then she said, always with her hand soft on my shoulder, "Like a dream when one awaketh." And when I looked again, I saw the blank of an opaque surface and nothing more.

Aunt Mary asked me no more questions. She made me come into the room and sit in the light and read something to her. But I did not know what I was reading, for there suddenly came into my mind and took possession of it, the thud of the stone upon the window, and its descent straight down, as if from some hard substance that threw it off: though I had myself seen it strike upon the glass of the panes across the way.

CHAPTER IV

I am afraid I continued in a state of great exaltation and commotion of mind for some time. I used to hurry through the day till the evening came, when I could watch my neighbour through the window opposite. I did not talk much to any one, and I never said a word about my own questions and wonderings. I wondered who he was, what he was doing, and why he never came till the evening (or very rarely); and I also wondered much to what house the room belonged in which he sat. It seemed to form a portion of the old College Library, as I have often said. The window was one of the line of windows which I understood lighted the large hall; but whether this room belonged to the library itself, or how its occupant gained access to it, I could not tell. I made up my mind that it must open out of the hall, and that the gentleman must be the Librarian or one of his assistants, perhaps kept busy all the day in his official duties, and only able to get to his desk and do his own private work in the evening. One has heard of so many things like that—a man who had to take up some other kind of work for his living, and then when his leisure-time came, gave it all up to something he really loved—some study or some book he was writing. My father himself at one time had been like that. He had been in the Treasury all day, and then in the evening wrote his books, which made him famous. His daughter, however little she might know of other things, could not but know that! But it discouraged me very much when somebody pointed out to me one day in the street an old gentleman who wore a wig and took a great deal of snuff, and said, "That's the Librarian of the old College." It gave me a great shock for a moment; but then I remembered that an old gentleman has generally assistants, and that it must be one of them.

Gradually I became quite sure of this. There was another small window above, which twinkled very much when the sun shone, and looked a very kindly bright little window, above that dullness of the other which hid so much. I made up my mind this was the window of his other room, and that these two chambers at the end of the beautiful hall were really beautiful for him to live in, so near all the books, and so retired and quiet, that nobody knew of them. What a fine thing for him! and you could see what use he made of his good fortune as he sat there, so constant at his writing for hours together. Was it a book he was writing, or could it be perhaps Poems? This was a thought which made my heart beat; but I concluded with much regret that it could not be Poems, because no one could possibly write Poems like that, straight off, without pausing for a word or a rhyme. Had they been Poems he must have risen up, he must have paced about the room or come to the window as papa did—not that papa wrote Poems: he always said, "I am not worthy even to speak of such prevailing mysteries," shaking his head—which gave me a wonderful admiration and almost awe of a Poet, who was thus much greater even than papa. But I could not believe that a Poet could have kept still for hours and hours like that. What could it be then? perhaps it was history; that is a great thing to work at, but you would not perhaps need to move nor to stride up and down, or look out upon the sky and the wonderful light.

He did move now and then, however, though he never came to the window. Sometimes, as I have said, he would turn round in his chair and turn his face towards it, and sit there for a long time musing when the light had begun to fail, and the world was full of that strange day which was night, that light without colour, in which everything was so clearly visible, and there were no shadows. "It was between the night and the day, when the fairy folk have power." This was the after-light of the wonderful, long, long summer evening, the light without shadows. It had a spell in it, and sometimes it made me afraid: and all manner of strange thoughts seemed to come in, and I always felt that if only we had a little more vision in our eyes we might see beautiful folk walking about in it, who were not of our world. I thought most likely he saw them, from the way he sat there looking out: and this made my heart expand with the most curious sensation, as if of pride that, though I could not see, he did, and did not even require to come to the window, as I did, sitting close in the depth of the recess, with my eyes upon him, and almost seeing things through his eyes.

I was so much absorbed in these thoughts and in watching him every evening—for now he never missed an evening, but was always there—that people began to remark that I was looking pale and that I could not be well, for I paid no attention when they talked to me, and did not care to go out, nor to join the other girls for their tennis, nor to do anything that others did; and some said to Aunt Mary that I was quickly losing all the ground I had gained, and that she could never send me back to my mother with a white face like that. Aunt Mary had begun to look at me anxiously for some time before that, and, I am sure, held secret consultations over me, sometimes with the doctor, and sometimes with her old ladies, who thought they knew more about young girls than even the doctors. And I could hear them saying to her that I wanted diversion, that I must be diverted, and that she must take me out more, and give a party, and that when the summer visitors began to come there would perhaps be a ball or two, or Lady Carnbee would get up a picnic. "And there's my young lord coming home," said the old lady whom they called Miss Jeanie, "and I never knew the young lassie yet that would not cock up her bonnet at the sight of a young lord."

But Aunt Mary shook her head. "I would not lippen much to the young lord," she said. "His mother is sore set upon siller* for him; and my poor bit honey has no fortune to speak of. No, we must not fly so high as the young lord; but I will gladly take her about the country to see the old castles and towers. It will perhaps rouse her up a little."

"And if that does not answer we must think of something else," the old lady said.

I heard them perhaps that day because they were talking of me, which is always so effective a way of making you hear—for latterly I had not been paying any attention to what they were saying; and I thought to myself how little they knew, and how little I cared about even the old castles and curious houses, having something else in my mind. But just about that time Mr Pitmilly came in, who was always a friend to me, and, when he heard them talking, he managed to stop them and turn the conversation into another channel. And after a while, when the ladies were gone away, he came up to my recess, and gave a glance right over my head. And then he asked my Aunt Mary if ever she had settled her question about the window opposite, "that you thought was a window sometimes, and then not a window, and many curious things," the old gentleman said.

My Aunt Mary gave me another very wistful look; and then she said, "Indeed, Mr Pitmilly, we are just where we were, and I am quite as

---

* Scottish dialect for *silver*—that is, he was meant for a woman of means.

unsettled as ever; and I think my niece she has taken up my views, for I see her many a time looking across and wondering, and I am not clear now what her opinion is."

"My opinion!" I said, "Aunt Mary." I could not help being a little scornful, as one is when one is very young. "I have no opinion. There is not only a window but there is a room, and I could show you—" I was going to say, "show you the gentleman who sits and writes in it," but I stopped, not knowing what they might say, and looked from one to another. "I could tell you—all the furniture that is in it," I said. And then I felt something like a flame that went over my face, and that all at once my cheeks were burning. I thought they gave a little glance at each other, but that may have been folly. "There is a great picture, in a big dim frame," I said, feeling a little breathless, "on the wall opposite the window".

"Is there so?" said Mr Pitmilly, with a little laugh. And he said, "Now I will tell you what we'll do. You know that there is a conversation party, or whatever they call it, in the big room to-night, and it will be all open and lighted up. And it is a handsome room, and two-three things well worth looking at. I will just step along after we have all got our dinner, and take you over to the pairty, madam—Missy and you—"

"Dear me!" said Aunt Mary. "I have not gone to a pairty for more years than I would like to say—and never once to the Library Hall." Then she gave a little shiver, and said quite low, "I could not go there."

"Then you will just begin again to-night, madam," said Mr Pitmilly, taking no notice of this, "and a proud man will I be leading in Mistress Balcarres that was once the pride of the ball!"

"Ah, once!" said Aunt Mary, with a low little laugh and then a sigh. "And we'll not say how long ago;" and after that she made a pause, looking always at me: and then she said, "I accept your offer, and we'll put on our braws;* and I hope you will have no occasion to think shame of us. But why not take your dinner here?"

That was how it was settled, and the old gentleman went away to dress, looking quite pleased. But I came to Aunt Mary as soon as he was gone, and besought her not to make me go. "I like the long bonnie night and the

---

* Scottish dialect for *fine clothes*, one's best apparel.

light that lasts so long. And I cannot bear to dress up and go out, wasting it all in a stupid party. I hate parties, Aunt Mary!" I cried, "and I would far rather stay here."

"My honey," she said, taking both my hands, "I know it will maybe be a blow to you, but it's better so."

"How could it be a blow to me?" I cried; "but I would far rather not go."

"You'll just go with me, honey, just this once: it is not often I go out. You will go with me this one night, just this one night, my honey sweet."

I am sure there were tears in Aunt Mary's eyes, and she kissed me between the words. There was nothing more that I could say; but how I grudged the evening! A mere party, a conversazione (when all the College was away, too, and nobody to make conversation!), instead of my enchanted hour at my window and the soft strange light, and the dim face looking out, which kept me wondering and wondering what was he thinking of, what was he looking for, who was he? all one wonder and mystery and question, through the long, long, slowly fading night!

It occurred to me, however, when I was dressing—though I was so sure that he would prefer his solitude to everything—that he might perhaps, it was just possible, be there. And when I thought of that, I took out my white frock though Janet had laid out my blue one—and my little pearl necklace which I had thought was too good to wear. They were not very large pearls, but they were real pearls, and very even and lustrous though they were small; and though I did not think much of my appearance then, there must have been something about me—pale as I was but apt to colour in a moment, with my dress so white, and my pearls so white, and my hair all shadowy perhaps, that was pleasant to look at: for even old Mr Pitmilly had a strange look in his eyes, as if he was not only pleased but sorry too, perhaps thinking me a creature that would have troubles in this life, though I was so young and knew them not. And when Aunt Mary looked at me, there was a little quiver about her mouth. She herself had on her pretty lace and her white hair very nicely done, and looking her best. As for Mr Pitmilly, he had a beautiful fine French cambric frill to his shirt, plaited in the most minute plaits, and with a diamond pin in it which sparkled as much as Lady Carnbee's ring; but this was a fine frank kindly stone, that looked you straight in the face and sparkled, with the light dancing in it as if it were pleased to see you, and to be shining on that old gentleman's honest and faithful breast: for he had been one of Aunt Mary's lovers in their early days, and still thought there was nobody like her in the world.

I had got into quite a happy commotion of mind by the time we set out across the street in the soft light of the evening to the Library Hall. Perhaps, after all, I should see him, and see the room which I was so well acquainted with, and find out why he sat there so constantly and never was seen abroad. I thought I might even hear what he was working at, which would be such a pleasant thing to tell papa when I went home. A friend of mine at St Rule's—oh, far, far more busy than you ever were, papa!—and then my father would laugh as he always did, and say he was but an idler and never busy at all.

The room was all light and bright, flowers wherever flowers could be, and the long lines of the books that went along the walls on each side, lighting up wherever there was a line of gilding or an ornament, with a little response. It dazzled me at first all that light: but I was very eager, though I kept very quiet, looking round to see if perhaps in any corner, in the middle of any group, he would be there. I did not expect to see him among the ladies. He would not be with them—he was too studious, too silent: but, perhaps among that circle of grey heads at the upper end of the room—perhaps—

No: I am not sure that it was not half a pleasure to me to make quite sure that there was not one whom I could take for him, who was at all like my vague image of him. No: it was absurd to think that he would be here, amid all that sound of voices, under the glare of that light. I felt a little proud to think that he was in his room as usual, doing his work, or thinking so deeply over it, as when he turned round in his chair with his face to the light.

I was thus getting a little composed and quiet in my mind, for now that the expectation of seeing him was over, though it was a disappointment, it was a satisfaction too—when Mr Pitmilly came up to me, holding out his arm. "Now," he said, "I am going to take you to see the curiosities." I thought to myself that after I had seen them and spoken to everybody I knew, Aunt Mary would let me go home, so I went very willingly, though I did not care for the curiosities. Something, however, struck me strangely as we walked up the room. It was the air, rather fresh and strong, from an open window at the east end of the hall. How should there be a window there? I hardly saw what it meant for the first moment, but it blew in my face as if there was some meaning in it, and I felt very uneasy without seeing why.

Then there was another thing that startled me. On that side of the wall which was to the street there seemed no windows at all. A long line of bookcases filled it from end to end. I could not see what that meant either, but it confused me. I was altogether confused. I felt as if I was in a strange country, not knowing where I was going, not knowing what I might find out next. If there were no windows on the wall to the street, where was my window? My heart, which had been jumping up and calming down again all this time, gave a great leap at this, as if it would have come out of me—but I did not know what it could mean.

Then we stopped before a glass case, and Mr Pitmilly showed me some things in it. I could not pay much attention to them. My head was going round and round. I heard his voice going on, and then myself speaking with a queer sound that was hollow in my ears; but I did not know what I was saying or what he was saying. Then he took me to the very end of the room, the east end, saying something that I caught—that I was pale, that the air would do me good. The air was blowing full on me, lifting the lace of my dress, lifting my hair, almost chilly. The window opened into the pale daylight, into the little lane that ran by the end of the building. Mr Pitmilly went on talking, but I could not make out a word he said. Then I heard my own voice, speaking through it, though I did not seem to be aware that I was speaking. "Where is my window?—where, then, is my window?" I seemed to be saying, and I turned right round, dragging him with me, still holding his arm. As I did this my eye fell upon something at last which I knew. It was a large picture in a broad frame, hanging against the farther wall.

What did it mean? Oh, what did it mean? I turned round again to the open window at the east end, and to the daylight, the strange light without any shadow, that was all round about this lighted hall, holding it like a bubble that would burst, like something that was not real. The real place was the room I knew, in which that picture was hanging, where the writing-table was, and where he sat with his face to the light. But where was the light and the window through which it came? I think my senses must have left me. I went up to the picture which I knew, and then I walked straight across the room, always dragging Mr Pitmilly, whose face was pale, but who did not struggle but allowed me to lead him, straight across to where the window was—where the window was not;—where there was no sign of it. "Where is my window?—where is my window?" I said. And all the time I was sure that I was in a dream, and these lights were all some theatrical illusion, and the people talking; and nothing real but the pale, pale, watching, lingering day standing by to wait until that foolish bubble should burst.

"My dear," said Mr Pitmilly, "my dear! Mind that you are in public. Mind where you are. You must not make an outcry and frighten your Aunt Mary. Come away with me. Come away, my dear young lady! and you'll take a seat for a minute or two and compose yourself; and I'll get you an ice or a little wine." He kept patting my hand, which was on his arm, and looking at me very anxiously. "Bless me! bless me! I never thought it would have this effect," he said.

But I would not allow him to take me away in that direction. I went to the picture again and looked at it without seeing it: and then I went across the room again, with some kind of wild thought that if I insisted I should find it. "My window—my window!" I said.

There was one of the professors standing there, and he heard me. "The window!" said he. "Ah, you've been taken in with what appears outside. It was put there to be in uniformity with the window on the stair. But it never was a real window. It is just behind that bookcase. Many people are taken in by it," he said.

His voice seemed to sound from somewhere far away, and as if it would go on for ever; and the hall swam in a dazzle of shining and of noises round me; and the daylight through the open window grew greyer, waiting till it should be over, and the bubble burst.

CHAPTER V

It was Mr Pitmilly who took me home; or rather it was I who took him, pushing him on a little in front of me, holding fast by his arm, not waiting for Aunt Mary or any one. We came out into the daylight again outside, I, without even a cloak or a shawl, with my bare arms, and uncovered head, and the pearls round my neck. There was a rush of the people about, and a baker's boy, that baker's boy, stood right in my way and cried, "Here's a braw ane!" shouting to the others: the words struck me somehow, as his stone had struck the window, without any reason. But I did not mind the people staring, and hurried across the street, with Mr Pitmilly half a step in advance. The door was open, and Janet standing at it, looking out to see what she could see of the ladies in their grand dresses. She gave a shriek when she saw me hurrying across the street; but I brushed past her, and pushed Mr Pitmilly up the stairs, and took him breathless to the recess, where I threw myself down on the seat, feeling as if I could not have gone another step farther, and waved my hand across to the window. "There! there!" I cried. Ah! there it was—not that senseless mob—not the theatre and the gas, and the people all in a murmur and clang of talking. Never in all these days had I seen that room so clearly. There was a faint tone of light behind, as if it might have been a reflection from some of those vulgar lights in the hall, and he sat against it, calm, wrapped in his thoughts, with his face turned to the window. Nobody but must have seen him. Janet could have seen him had I called her up-stairs. It was like a picture, all the things I knew, and the same attitude, and the atmosphere, full of quietness, not disturbed by anything. I pulled Mr Pitmilly's arm before I let him go,—"You see, you see!" I cried. He gave me the most bewildered look, as if he would have liked to cry. He saw nothing! I was sure of that from his eyes. He was an old man, and there was no vision in him. If I had called up Janet, she would have seen it all. "My dear!" he said. "My dear!" waving his hands in a helpless way. "He has been there all these nights," I cried, "and I thought you could tell me who he was and what he was doing; and that he might have taken me in to that room, and showed me, that I might tell papa. Papa would understand, he would like to hear. Oh, can't you tell me what work he is doing, Mr Pitmilly? He never lifts his head as long as the light throws a shadow, and then when it is like this he turns round and thinks, and takes a rest!"

Mr Pitmilly was trembling, whether it was with cold or I know not what. He said, with a shake in his voice, "My dear young lady—my dear—" and then stopped and looked at me as if he were going to cry. "It's peetiful, it's peetiful," he said; and then in another voice, "I am going across there again to bring your Aunt Mary home; do you understand, my poor little thing, I am going to bring her home—you will be better when she is here." I was glad when he went away, as he could not see anything: and I sat alone in the dark which was not dark, but quite clear light—a light like nothing I ever saw. How clear it was in that room! not glaring like the gas and the voices, but so quiet, everything so visible, as if it were in another world. I heard a little rustle behind me, and there was Janet, standing staring at me with two big eyes wide open. She was only a little older than I was. I called to her, "Janet, come here, come here, and you will see him,—come here and see him!" impatient that she should be so shy and keep behind. "Oh, my bonnie young leddy!" she said, and burst out crying. I stamped my foot at her, in my indignation that she would not come, and she fled before me with a rustle and swing of haste, as if she were afraid. None of them, none of them! not even a girl like myself, with the sight in her eyes, would understand. I turned back again, and held out my hands to him sitting there, who was the only one that knew. "Oh," I said, "say something to me! I don't know who you are, or what you are: but you're lonely and so am I; and I only—feel for you. Say something to me!" I neither hoped that he would hear, nor expected any answer. How could he hear, with the street between us, and his window shut, and all the murmuring of the voices and the people standing about? But for one moment it seemed to me that there was only him and me in the whole world.

But I gasped with my breath, that had almost gone from me, when I saw him move in his chair! He had heard me, though I knew not how. He rose up, and I rose too, speechless, incapable of anything but this mechanical movement. He seemed to draw me as if I were a puppet moved by his will. He came forward to the window, and stood looking across at me. I was sure that he looked at me. At last he had seen me: at last he had found out that somebody, though only a girl, was watching him, looking for him, believing in him. I was in such trouble and commotion of mind and trembling, that I could not keep on my feet, but dropped kneeling on the window-seat, supporting myself against the window, feeling as if my heart were being drawn out of me. I cannot describe his face. It was all dim, yet there was a light on it: I think it must have been a smile; and as closely as I looked at him he looked at me. His hair was fair, and there was a little quiver about his lips. Then he put his hands upon the window to open it. It was stiff and hard to move; but at last he forced it open with a sound that echoed all along the street. I saw that the people heard it, and several looked up. As for me, I put my hands together, leaning with my face against the glass, drawn to him as if I could have gone out of myself, my heart out of my bosom, my eyes out of my head. He opened the window with a noise that was heard from the West Port to the Abbey. Could any one doubt that?

And then he leaned forward out of the window, looking out. There was not one in the street but must have seen him. He looked at me first, with a little wave of his hand, as if it were a salutation—yet not exactly that either, for I thought he waved me away; and then he looked up and down in the dim shining of the ending day, first to the east, to the old Abbey towers, and then to the west, along the broad line of the street where so many people were coming and going, but so little noise, all like enchanted folk in an enchanted place. I watched him with such a melting heart, with such a deep satisfaction as words could not say; for nobody could tell me now that he was not there—nobody could say I was dreaming any more. I watched him as if I could not breathe—my heart in my throat, my eyes upon him. He looked up and down, and then he looked back to me. I was the first, and I was the last, though it was not for long: he did know, he did see, who it was that had recognised him and sympathised with him all the time. I was in a kind of rapture, yet stupor too; my look went with his look, following it as if I were his shadow; and then suddenly he was gone, and I saw him no more.

I dropped back again upon my seat, seeking something to support me, something to lean upon. He had lifted his hand and waved it once again to me. How he went I cannot tell, nor where he went I cannot tell; but in a moment he was away, and the window standing open, and the room fading into stillness and dimness, yet so clear, with all its space, and the great picture in its gilded frame upon the wall. It gave me no pain to see him go away. My heart was so content, and I was so worn out and satisfied—for what doubt or question could there be about him now? As I was lying back as weak as water, Aunt Mary came in behind me, and flew to me with a

little rustle as if she had come on wings, and put her arms round me, and
drew my head on to her breast. I had begun to cry a little, with sobs like a
child. "You saw him, you saw him!" I said. To lean upon her, and feel her so
soft, so kind, gave me a pleasure I cannot describe, and her arms round me,
and her voice saying "Honey, my honey!"—as if she were nearly crying too.
Lying there I came back to myself, quite sweetly, glad of everything. But
I wanted some assurance from them that they had seen him too. I waved
my hand to the window that was still standing open, and the room that
was stealing away into the faint dark. "This time you saw it all?" I said,
getting more eager. "My honey!" said Aunt Mary, giving me a kiss: and Mr
Pitmilly began to walk about the room with short little steps behind, as if
he were out of patience. I sat straight up and put away Aunt Mary's arms.
"You cannot be so blind, so blind!" I cried. "Oh, not to-night, at least not
to-night!" But neither the one nor the other made any reply. I shook myself
quite free, and raised myself up. And there, in the middle of the street,
stood the baker's boy like a statue, staring up at the open window, with
his mouth open and his face full of wonder—breathless, as if he could not
believe what he saw. I darted forward, calling to him, and beckoned him
to come to me. "Oh, bring him up! bring him, bring him to me!" I cried.

Mr Pitmilly went out directly, and got the boy by the shoulder. He
did not want to come. It was strange to see the little old gentleman, with
his beautiful frill and his diamond pin, standing out in the street, with his
hand upon the boy's shoulder, and the other boys round, all in a little
crowd. And presently they came towards the house, the others all following, gaping and wondering. He came in unwilling, almost resisting,
looking as if we meant him some harm. "Come away, my laddie, come
and speak to the young lady," Mr Pitmilly was saying. And Aunt Mary
took my hands to keep me back. But I would not be kept back.

"Boy," I cried, "you saw it too: you saw it: tell them you saw it! It is that
I want, and no more."

He looked at me as they all did, as if he thought I was mad. "What's she
wantin' wi' me?" he said; and then, "I did nae harm, even if I did throw a
bit stane at it—and it's nae sin to throw a stane."

"You rascal!" said Mr Pitmilly, giving him a shake; "have you been
throwing stones? You'll kill somebody some of these days with your stones."

The old gentleman was confused and troubled, for he did not understand what I wanted, nor anything that had happened. And then Aunt Mary, holding my hands and drawing me close to her, spoke. "Laddie," she said, "answer the young lady, like a good lad. There's no intention of finding fault with you. Answer her, my man, and then Janet will give ye your supper before you go."

"Oh speak, speak!" I cried; "answer them and tell them! You saw that window opened, and the gentleman look out and wave his hand?"

"I saw nae gentleman," he said, with his head down, "except this wee gentleman here."

"Listen, laddie," said Aunt Mary. "I saw ye standing in the middle of the street staring. What were ye looking at?"

"It was naething to make a wark about. It was just yon windy yonder in the library that is nae windy. And it was open as sure's death. You may laugh if you like. Is that a' she's wantin' wi' me?"

"You are telling a pack of lies, laddie," Mr Pitmilly said.

"I'm tellin' nae lees—it was standin' open just like ony ither windy. It's as sure's death. I couldna believe it mysel'; but it's true."

"And there it is," I cried, turning round and pointing it out to them with great triumph in my heart. But the light was all grey, it had faded, it had changed. The window was just as it had always been, a sombre break upon the wall.

I was treated like an invalid all that evening, and taken up-stairs to bed, and Aunt Mary sat up in my room the whole night through. Whenever I opened my eyes she was always sitting there close to me, watching. And there never was in all my life so strange a night. When I would talk in my excitement, she kissed me and hushed me like a child. "Oh, honey, you are not the only one!" she said. "Oh whisht, whisht, bairn! I should never have let you be there!"

"Aunt Mary, Aunt Mary, you have seen him too?"

"Oh whisht, whisht, honey!" Aunt Mary said: her eyes were shining—there were tears in them. "Oh whisht, whisht! Put it out of your mind, and try to sleep. I will not speak another word," she cried.

But I had my arms round her, and my mouth at her ear. "Who is he there?—tell me that and I will ask no more—"

"Oh honey, rest, and try to sleep! It is just—how can I tell you?—a dream, a dream! Did you not hear what Lady Carnbee said?—the women of our blood—"

"What? what? Aunt Mary, oh Aunt Mary—"

"I canna tell you," she cried in her agitation, "I canna tell you! How can I tell you, when I know just what you know and no more? It is a longing all your life after—it is a looking—for what never comes."

"He will come," I cried. "I shall see him to-morrow—that I know, I know!"

She kissed me and cried over me, her cheek hot and wet like mine. "My honey, try if you can sleep—try if you can sleep: and we'll wait to see what to-morrow brings."

"I have no fear," said I; and then I suppose, though it is strange to think of, I must have fallen asleep—I was so worn-out, and young, and not used to lying in my bed awake. From time to time I opened my eyes, and sometimes jumped up remembering everything: but Aunt Mary was always there to soothe me, and I lay down again in her shelter like a bird in its nest.

But I would not let them keep me in bed next day. I was in a kind of fever, not knowing what I did. The window was quite opaque, without the least glimmer in it, flat and blank like a piece of wood. Never from the first day had I seen it so little like a window. "It cannot be wondered at," I said to myself, "that seeing it like that, and with eyes that are old, not so clear as mine, they should think what they do." And then I smiled to myself to think of the evening and the long light, and whether he would look out again, or only give me a signal with his hand. I decided I would like that best: not that he should take the trouble to come forward and open it again, but just a turn of his head and a wave of his hand. It would be more friendly and show more confidence,—not as if I wanted that kind of demonstration every night.

I did not come down in the afternoon, but kept at my own window up-stairs alone, till the tea-party should be over. I could hear them making a great talk; and I was sure they were all in the recess staring at the window, and laughing at the silly lassie. Let them laugh! I felt above all that now. At dinner I was very restless, hurrying to get it over; and I think Aunt Mary was restless too. I doubt whether she read her 'Times' when it came; she opened it up so as to shield her, and watched from a corner. And I settled myself in the recess, with my heart full of expectation. I wanted nothing more than to see him writing at his table, and to turn his head and give me a little wave of his hand, just to show that he knew I was there. I sat from half-past seven o'clock to ten o'clock: and the daylight grew softer and softer, till at last it was as if it was shining through a pearl, and not a shadow to be seen. But the window all the time was as black as night, and there was nothing, nothing there.

Well: but other nights it had been like that: he would not be there every night only to please me. There are other things in a man's life, a great learned man like that. I said to myself I was not disappointed. Why should I be disappointed? There had been other nights when he was not there. Aunt Mary watched me, every movement I made, her eyes shining, often wet, with a pity in them that almost made me cry: but I felt as if I were more sorry for her than for myself. And then I flung myself upon her, and asked her, again and again, what it was, and who it was, imploring her to tell me if she knew? and when she had seen him, and what had happened? and what it meant about the women of our blood? She told me that how it was she could not tell, nor when: it was just at the time it had to be; and that we all saw him in our time—"that is," she said, "the ones that are like you and me." What was it that made her and me different from the rest? but she only shook her head and would not tell me. "They say," she said, and then stopped short. "Oh, honey, try and forget all about it—if I had but known you were of that kind! They say—that once there was one that was a Scholar, and liked his books more than any lady's love. Honey, do not look at me like that. To think I should have brought all this on you!"

"He was a Scholar?" I cried.

"And one of us, that must have been a light woman, not like you and me—But maybe it was just in innocence; for who can tell? She waved to him and waved to him to come over: and yon ring was the token: but he would not come. But still she sat at her window and waved and waved—till at last her brothers heard of it, that were stirring men; and then—oh, my honey, let us speak of it no more!"

"They killed him!" I cried, carried away. And then I grasped her with my hands, and gave her a shake, and flung away from her. "You tell me that to throw dust in my eyes—when I saw him only last night: and he as living as I am, and as young!"

"My honey, my honey!" Aunt Mary said.

After that I would not speak to her for a long time; but she kept close to me, never leaving me when she could help it, and always with that pity in her eyes. For the next night it was the same; and the third night. That third night I thought I could not bear it any longer. I would have to do something if only I knew what to do! If it would ever get dark, quite dark, there might be something to be done. I had wild dreams of stealing out of the house and getting a ladder, and mounting up to try if I could not open that window, in the middle of the night—if perhaps I could get the baker's boy to help me; and then my mind got into a whirl, and it was as if I had done it; and I could almost see the boy put the ladder to the window, and hear him cry out that there was nothing there. Oh, how slow it was, the night! and how light it was, and everything so clear no darkness to cover you, no shadow, whether on one side of the street or on the other side! I could not sleep, though I was forced to go to bed. And in the deep midnight, when it is dark dark in every other place, I slipped very softly down-stairs, though there was one board on the landing-place that creaked—and opened the door and stepped out. There was not a soul to be seen, up or down, from the Abbey to the West Port: and the trees stood like ghosts, and the silence was terrible, and everything as clear as day. You don't know what silence is till you find it in the light like that, not morning but night, no sunrising, no shadow, but everything as clear as the day.

It did not make any difference as the slow minutes went on: one o'clock, two o'clock. How strange it was to hear the clocks striking in that dead light when there was nobody to hear them! But it made no difference. The window was quite blank; even the marking of the panes seemed to have melted away. I stole up again after a long time, through the silent house, in the clear light, cold and trembling, with despair in my heart.

I am sure Aunt Mary must have watched and seen me coming back, for after a while I heard faint sounds in the house; and very early, when there had come a little sunshine into the air, she came to my bedside with a cup of tea in her hand; and she, too, was looking like a ghost. "Are you warm, honey—are you comfortable?" she said. "It doesn't matter," said I.

I did not feel as if anything mattered; unless if one could get into the dark somewhere—the soft, deep dark that would cover you over and hide you—but I could not tell from what. The dreadful thing was that there was nothing, nothing to look for, nothing to hide from—only the silence and the light.

That day my mother came and took me home. I had not heard she was coming; she arrived quite unexpectedly, and said she had no time to stay, but must start the same evening so as to be in London next day, papa having settled to go abroad. At first I had a wild thought I would not go. But how can a girl say I will not, when her mother has come for her, and there is no reason, no reason in the world, to resist, and no right! I had to go, whatever I might wish or any one might say. Aunt Mary's dear eyes were wet; she went about the house drying them quietly with her handkerchief, but she always said, "It is the best thing for you, honey—the best thing for you!" Oh, how I hated to hear it said that it was the best thing, as if anything mattered, one more than another! The old ladies were all there in the afternoon, Lady Carnbee looking at me from under her black lace, and the diamond lurking, sending out darts from under her finger. She patted me on the shoulder, and told me to be a good bairn. "And never lippen to what you see from the window," she said. "The eye is deceitful as well as the heart." She kept patting me on the shoulder, and I felt again as if that sharp wicked stone stung me. Was that what Aunt Mary meant when she said yon ring was the token? I thought afterwards I saw the mark on my shoulder. You will say why? How can I tell why? If I had known, I should have been contented, and it would not have mattered any more.

I never went back to St Rule's, and for years of my life I never again looked out of a window when any other window was in sight. You ask me did I ever see him again? I cannot tell: the imagination is a great deceiver, as Lady Carnbee said: and if he stayed there so long, only to punish the race that had wronged him, why should I ever have seen him again? for I had received my share. But who can tell what happens in a heart that often, often, and so long as that, comes back to do its errand? If it was he whom I have seen again, the anger is gone from him, and he means good and no longer harm to the house of the woman that loved him. I have seen his face looking at me from a crowd. There was one time when I came home a widow from India, very sad, with my little children: I am certain I saw him there among all the people coming to welcome their friends. There was nobody to welcome me—for I was not expected: and very sad was I, without a face I knew: when all at once I saw him, and he waved his hand to me. My heart leaped up again: I had forgotten who he was, but only that it was a face I knew, and I landed almost cheerfully, thinking here was some one who would help me. But he had disappeared, as he did from the window, with that one wave of his hand.

And again I was reminded of it all when old Lady Carnbee died—an old, old woman—and it was found in her will that she had left me that diamond ring. I am afraid of it still. It is locked up in an old sandal-wood box in the lumber-room in the little old country-house which belongs to me, but where I never live. If any one would steal it, it would be a relief to my mind. Yet I never knew what Aunt Mary meant when she said, "Yon ring was the token," nor what it could have to do with that strange window in the old College Library of St Rule's.

Mary Elizabeth Braddon (1835–1915), who frequently wrote as M. E. Braddon, was one of the literary celebrities of the Victorian age. Author of more than eighty novels, she is best remembered for *Lady Audley's Secret* (1862), a huge bestseller. Braddon also wrote one of the earliest detective novels in England, variously known as *Three Times Dead* or *Trail of the Serpent* (1860), as well as countless historical and sensational tales. In addition, she wrote several well-regarded novels of supernatural fiction and countless short stories, including this frequently-collected tale. The story harkens back to the legends of the Hungarian Countess Elizabeth Bathory, said to have murdered dozens of young women and bathed in their blood to retain her youthful appearance. It first appeared in the *Strand Magazine* for February 1896.

Good Lady Ducayne
by Mary Elizabeth Braddon

CHAPTER I

Bella Rolleston had made up her mind that her only chance of earning her bread and helping her mother to an occasional crust was by going out into the great unknown world as companion to a lady. She was willing to go to any lady rich enough to pay her a salary and so eccentric as to wish for a hired companion. Five shillings* told off reluctantly from one of those sovereigns which were so rare with the mother and daughter, and which

---

* John H. Watson's wound pension, of the same era, was eleven shillings per day. Five shillings in 1896 is the equivalent of an income of about £110 today, a serious amount of money to invest in finding a job.

melted away so quickly, five solid shillings, had been handed to a smartly-dressed lady in an office in Harbeck Street, W.,[*] in the hope that this very Superior Person would find a situation and a salary for Miss Rolleston.

The Superior Person glanced at the two half-crowns as they lay on the table where Bella's hand had placed them, to make sure they were neither of them florins,[†] before she wrote a description of Bella's qualifications and requirements in a formidable-looking ledger.

"Age?" she asked curtly.

"Eighteen, last July."

"Any accomplishments?"

"No; I am not at all accomplished. If I were I should want to be a governess—a companion seems the lowest stage."

"We have some highly accomplished ladies on our books as companions, or chaperon companions."

"Oh, I know!" babbled Bella, loquacious in her youthful candour. "But that is quite a different thing. Mother hasn't been able to afford a piano since I was twelve years old, so I'm afraid I've forgotten how to play. And I have had to help mother with her needlework, so there hasn't been much time to study."

"Please don't waste time upon explaining what you can't do, but kindly tell me anything you can do," said the Superior Person, crushingly, with her pen poised between delicate fingers waiting to write. "Can you read aloud for two or three hours at a stretch? Are you active and handy, an early riser, a good walker, sweet tempered, and obliging?"

"I can say yes to all those questions except about the sweetness. I think I have a pretty good temper, and I should be anxious to oblige anybody who paid for my services. I should want them to feel that I was really earning my salary."

---

[*] A fictitious street, though of course the West End was the fashionable part of London.

[†] In this context, the old English coin that was valued at six shillings. A "half-crown" is two shillings, sixpence. The Superior Person was considering whether Bella had paid extra to secure employment faster; having paid only the exact amount required, she earned no special treatment.

"The kind of ladies who come to me would not care for a talkative companion," said the Person, severely, having finished writing in her book. "My connection lies chiefly among the aristocracy, and in that class considerable deference is expected."

"Oh, of course," said Bella; "but it's quite different when I'm talking to you. I want to tell you all about myself once and for ever."

"I am glad it is to be only once!" said the Person, with the edges of her lips.

The Person was of uncertain age, tightly laced in a black silk gown. She had a powdery complexion and a handsome clump of somebody else's hair on the top of her head. It may be that Bella's girlish freshness and vivacity had an irritating effect upon nerves weakened by an eight hours day in that over-heated second floor in Harbeck Street. To Bella the official apartment, with its Brussels carpet,* velvet curtains and velvet chairs, and French clock, ticking loud on the marble chimney-piece, suggested the luxury of a palace, as compared with another second floor in Walworth† where Mrs. Rolleston and her daughter had managed to exist for the last six years.

"Do you think you have anything on your books that would suit me?" faltered Bella, after a pause.

"Oh, dear, no; I have nothing in view at present," answered the Person, who had swept Bella's half-crowns into a drawer, absentmindedly, with the tips of her fingers. "You see, you are so very unformed—so much too young to be companion to a lady of position. It is a pity you have not enough education for a nursery governess; that would be more in your line."

"And do you think it will be very long before you can get me a situation?" asked Bella, doubtfully.

"I really cannot say. Have you any particular reason for being so impatient—not a love affair, I hope?"

"A love affair!" cried Bella, with flaming cheeks. "What utter nonsense. I want a situation because mother is poor, and I hate being a burden to her. I want a salary that I can share with her."

---

* A type of carpet (rather than the place of manufacture) known for its heavy linen backing and thick pile formed of uncut loops.

† A district of South London, south of the Thames, in Southwark—a shabby, commercial area. Beresford Street, on which Bella and her mother live, is now John Ruskin Street.

"There won't be much margin for sharing in the salary you are likely to get at your age—and with your—very—unformed manners," said the Person, who found Bella's peony cheeks, bright eyes, and unbridled vivacity more and more oppressive.

"Perhaps if you'd be kind enough to give me back the fee I could take it to an agency where the connection isn't quite so aristocratic," said Bella, who—as she told her mother in her recital of the interview—was determined not to be sat upon.

"You will find no agency that can do more for you than mine," replied the Person, whose harpy fingers never relinquished coin. "You will have to wait for your opportunity. Yours is an exceptional case: but I will bear you in mind, and if anything suitable offers I will write to you. I cannot say more than that."

The half-contemptuous bend of the stately head, weighted with borrowed hair, indicated the end of the interview. Bella went back to Walworth—tramped sturdily every inch of the way in the September afternoon—and 'took off'* the Superior Person for the amusement of her mother and the landlady, who lingered in the shabby little sitting-room after bringing in the tea-tray, to applaud Miss Rolleston's "taking off."

"Dear, dear, what a mimic she is!" said the landlady. "You ought to have let her go on the stage, mum. She might have made her fortune as a hactress."

CHAPTER II

Bella waited and hoped, and listened for the postman's knocks which brought such store of letters for the parlours and the first floor, and so few for that humble second floor, where mother and daughter sat sewing with hand and with wheel and treadle, for the greater part of the day.

Mrs Rolleston was a lady by birth and education; but it had been her bad fortune to marry a scoundrel; for the last half-dozen years she had been that worst of widows, a wife whose husband had deserted her. Happily, she

---

* Mimicked.

was courageous, industrious, and a clever needle-woman; and she had been able just to earn a living for herself and her only child, by making mantles and cloaks for a West-end house. It was not a luxurious living. Cheap lodgings in a shabby street off the Walworth Road, scanty dinners, homely food, well-worn raiment, had been the portion of mother and daughter; but they loved each other so dearly, and Nature had made them both so light-hearted, that they had contrived somehow to be happy. But now this idea of going out into the world as companion to some fine lady had rooted itself into Bella's mind, and although she idolized her mother, and although the parting of mother and daughter must needs tear two loving hearts into shreds, the girl longed for enterprise and change and excitement, as the pages of old longed to be knights, and to start for the Holy Land to break a lance with the infidel.

She grew tired of racing downstairs every time the postman knocked, only to be told "nothing for you, miss," by the smudgy-faced drudge who picked up the letters from the passage floor.

"Nothing for you, miss," grinned the lodging-house drudge, till at last Bella took heart of grace and walked up to Harbeck Street, and asked the Superior Person how it was that no situation had been found for her.

"You are too young," said the Person, "and you want a salary."

"Of course I do," answered Bella; "don't other people want salaries?"

"Young ladies of your age generally want a comfortable home."

"I don't," snapped Bella; "I want to help mother."

"You can call again this day week," said the Person; "or, if I hear of anything in the meantime, I will write to you."

No letter came from the Person, and in exactly a week Bella put on her neatest hat, the one that had been seldomest caught in the rain, and trudged off to Harbeck Street.

It was a dull October afternoon, and there was a greyness in the air which might turn to fog before night. The Walworth Road shops gleamed brightly through that grey atmosphere, and though to a young lady reared in Mayfair or Belgravia such shop-windows would have been unworthy of a glance, they were a snare and temptation for Bella. There were so many things that she longed for, and would never be able to buy.

Harbeck Street is apt to be empty at this dead season of the year, a long, long street, an endless perspective of eminently respectable houses. The

Person's office was at the further end, and Bella looked down that long, grey vista almost despairingly, more tired than usual with the trudge from Walworth. As she looked, a carriage passed her, an old-fashioned, yellow chariot, on cee springs,* drawn by a pair of high grey horses, with the stateliest of coachmen driving them, and a tall footman sitting by his side.

"It looks like the fairy god-mother's coach," thought Bella. "I shouldn't wonder if it began by being a pumpkin."

It was a surprise when she reached the Person's door to find the yellow chariot standing before it, and the tall footman waiting near the doorstep. She was almost afraid to go in and meet the owner of that splendid carriage. She had caught only a glimpse of its occupant as the chariot rolled by, a plumed bonnet, a patch of ermine.

The Person's smart page ushered her upstairs and knocked at the official door. "Miss Rolleston," he announced, apologetically, while Bella waited outside.

"Show her in," said the Person, quickly; and then Bella heard her murmuring something in a low voice to her client.

Bella went in fresh, blooming, a living image of youth and hope, and before she looked at the Person her gaze was riveted by the owner of the chariot.

Never had she seen anyone as old as the old lady sitting by the Person's fire: a little old figure, wrapped from chin to feet in an ermine mantle; a withered, old face under a plumed bonnet—a face so wasted by age that it seemed only a pair of eyes and a peaked chin. The nose was peaked, too, but between the sharply pointed chin and the great, shining eyes, the small, aquiline nose was hardly visible. "This is Miss Rolleston, Lady Ducayne."

Claw-like fingers, flashing with jewels, lifted a double eyeglass to Lady Ducayne's shining black eyes, and through the glasses Bella saw those unnaturally bright eyes magnified to a gigantic size, and glaring at her awfully.

"Miss Torpinter has told me all about you," said the old voice that belonged to the eyes. "Have you good health? Are you strong and active,

---

* Carriage springs were named for their shapes. C-shaped springs dated to the previous century, and though they were still in use in 1896, this was no modern carriage.

able to eat well, sleep well, walk well, able to enjoy all that there is good in life?"

"I have never known what it is to be ill, or idle," answered Bella.

"Then I think you will do for me."

"Of course, in the event of references being perfectly satisfactory," put in the Person.

"I don't want references. The young woman looks frank and innocent. I'll take her on trust."

"So like you, dear Lady Ducayne," murmured Miss Torpinter.

"I want a strong young woman whose health will give me no trouble."

"You have been so unfortunate in that respect," cooed the Person, whose voice and manner were subdued to a melting sweetness by the old woman's presence.

"Yes, I've been rather unlucky," grunted Lady Ducayne.

"But I am sure Miss Rolleston will not disappoint you, though certainly after your unpleasant experience with Miss Tomson, who looked the picture of health—and Miss Blandy, who said she had never seen a doctor since she was vaccinated—"

"Lies, no doubt," muttered Lady Ducayne, and then turning to Bella, she asked, curtly, "You don't mind spending the winter in Italy, I suppose?"

In Italy! The very word was magical. Bella's fair young face flushed crimson.

"It has been the dream of my life to see Italy," she gasped.

From Walworth to Italy! How far, how impossible such a journey had seemed to that romantic dreamer.

"Well, your dream will be realized. Get yourself ready to leave Charing Cross by the train deluxe this day week at eleven. Be sure you are at the station a quarter before the hour. My people will look after you and your luggage."

Lady Ducayne rose from her chair, assisted by her crutch-stick, and Miss Torpinter escorted her to the door.

"And with regard to salary?" questioned the Person on the way.

"Salary, oh, the same as usual—and if the young woman wants a quarter's pay in advance you can write to me for a cheque," Lady Ducayne answered, carelessly.

Miss Torpinter went all the way downstairs with her client, and waited to see her seated in the yellow chariot. When she came upstairs again she was slightly out of breath, and she had resumed that superior manner which Bella had found so crushing.

"You may think yourself uncommonly lucky, Miss Rolleston," she said. "I have dozens of young ladies on my books whom I might have recommended for this situation—but I remembered having told you to call this afternoon—and I thought I would give you a chance. Old Lady Ducayne is one of the best people on my books. She gives her companion a hundred a year, and pays all travelling expenses. You will live in the lap of luxury."

"A hundred a year! How too lovely! Shall I have to dress very grandly? Does Lady Ducayne keep much company?"

"At her age! No, she lives in seclusion—in her own apartments—her French maid, her footman, her medical attendant, her courier."

"Why did those other companions leave her?" asked Bella.

"Their health broke down!"

"Poor things, and so they had to leave?"

"Yes, they had to leave. I suppose you would like a quarter's salary in advance?"

"Oh, yes, please. I shall have things to buy."

"Very well, I will write for Lady Ducayne's cheque, and I will send you the balance—after deducting my commission for the year."

"To be sure, I had forgotten the commission."

"You don't suppose I keep this office for pleasure."

"Of course not," murmured Bella, remembering the five shillings entrance fee; but nobody could expect a hundred a year and a winter in Italy for five shillings.

CHAPTER III

"From Miss Rolleston, at Cap Ferrino,* to Mrs. Rolleston, in Beresford Street, Walworth.

---

* A fictitious location.

"How I wish you could see this place, dearest; the blue sky, the olive woods, the orange and lemon orchards between the cliffs and the sea—sheltering in the hollow of the great hills—and with summer waves dancing up to the narrow ridge of pebbles and weeds which is the Italian idea of a beach! Oh, how I wish you could see it all, mother dear, and bask in this sunshine, that makes it so difficult to believe the date at the head of this paper. November! The air is like an English June—the sun is so hot that I can't walk a few yards without an umbrella. And to think of you at Walworth while I am here! I could cry at the thought that perhaps you will never see this lovely coast, this wonderful sea, these summer flowers that bloom in winter. There is a hedge of pink geraniums under my window, mother—a thick, rank hedge, as if the flowers grew wild—and there are Dijon roses climbing over arches and palisades all along the terrace—a rose garden full of bloom in November! Just picture it all! You could never imagine the luxury of this hotel.

"It is nearly new, and has been built and decorated regardless of expense. Our rooms are upholstered in pale blue satin, which shows up Lady Ducayne's parchment complexion; but as she sits all day in a corner of the balcony basking in the sun, except when she is in her carriage, and all the evening in her armchair close to the fire, and never sees anyone but her own people, her complexion matters very little.

"She has the handsomest suite of rooms in the hotel. My bedroom is inside hers, the sweetest room—all blue satin and white lace—white enamelled furniture, looking-glasses on every wall, till I know my pert little profile as I never knew it before. The room was really meant for Lady Ducayne's dressing-room, but she ordered one of the blue satin couches to be arranged as a bed for me—the prettiest little bed, which I can wheel near the window on sunny mornings, as it is on castors and easily moved about. I feel as if Lady Ducayne were a funny old grandmother, who had suddenly appeared in my life, very, very rich, and very, very kind.

"She is not at all exacting. I read aloud to her a good deal, and she dozes and nods while I read.

"Sometimes I hear her moaning in her sleep—as if she had troublesome dreams. When she is tired of my reading she orders Francine, her maid, to read a French novel to her, and I hear her chuckle and groan now and then, as if she were more interested in those books than in Dickens or Scott. My French is not good enough to follow Francine, who reads very quickly. I have a great deal of liberty, for Lady Ducayne often tells me to run away and amuse myself; I roam about the hills for hours. Everything is so lovely. I lose myself in olive woods, always climbing up and up towards the pine woods above—and above the pines there are the snow mountains that just show their white peaks above the dark hills. Oh, you poor dear, how can I ever make you understand what this place is like—you, whose poor, tired eyes have only the opposite side of Beresford Street? Sometimes I go no farther than the terrace in front of the hotel, which is a favourite lounging-place with everybody. The gardens lie below, and the tennis courts where I sometimes play with a very nice girl, the only person in the hotel with whom I have made friends. She is a year older than I, and has come to Cap Ferrino with her brother, a doctor—or a medical student, who is going to be a doctor. He passed his M.B. exam at Edinburgh* just before they left home, Lotta told me. He came to Italy entirely on his sister's account. She had a troublesome chest attack last summer and was ordered to winter abroad. They are orphans, quite alone in the world, and so fond of each other. It is very nice for me to have such a friend as Lotta. She is so thoroughly respectable. I can't help using that word, for some of the girls in this hotel go on in a way that I know you would shudder at. Lotta was brought up by an aunt, deep down in the country, and knows hardly anything about life. Her brother won't allow her to read a novel, French or English, that he has not read and approved.

"'He treats me like a child,' she told me, 'but I don't mind, for it's nice to know somebody loves me, and cares about what I do, and even about my thoughts.'"

"Perhaps this is what makes some girls so eager to marry—the want of someone strong and brave and honest and true to care for them and order them about. I want no one, mother darling, for I have you, and you are all

---

* A "Bachelor of Medicine" degree was all the education required to practice medicine— doctorates were uncommon and more suitable for academics. Edinburgh University had a renowned school of medicine, and Arthur Conan Doyle received his bachelor of medicine degree from the university in 1881.

the world to me. No husband could ever come between us two. If I ever were to marry he would have only the second place in my heart. But I don't suppose I ever shall marry, or even know what it is like to have an offer of marriage. No young man can afford to marry a penniless girl nowadays. Life is too expensive.

"Mr. Stafford, Lotta's brother, is very clever, and very kind. He thinks it is rather hard for me to have to live with such an old woman as Lady Ducayne, but then he does not know how poor we are—you and I—and what a wonderful life this seems to me in this lovely place. I feel a selfish wretch for enjoying all my luxuries, while you, who want them so much more than I, have none of them—hardly know what they are like—do you, dearest?—for my scamp of a father began to go to the dogs soon after you were married, and since then life has been all trouble and care and struggle for you."

This letter was written when Bella had been less than a month at Cap Ferrino, before the novelty had worn off the landscape, and before the pleasure of luxurious surroundings had begun to cloy. She wrote to her mother every week, such long letters as girls who have lived in closest companionship with a mother alone can write; letters that are like a diary of heart and mind. She wrote gaily always; but when the new year began Mrs. Rolleston thought she detected a note of melancholy under all those lively details about the place and the people.

"My poor girl is getting homesick," she thought. "Her heart is in Beresford Street."

It might be that she missed her new friend and companion, Lotta Stafford, who had gone with her brother for a little tour to Genoa and Spezzia, and as far as Pisa. They were to return before February; but in the meantime Bella might naturally feel very solitary among all those strangers, whose manners and doings she described so well.

The mother's instinct had been true. Bella was not so happy as she had been in that first flush of wonder and delight which followed the change from Walworth to the Riviera. Somehow, she knew not how, lassitude had crept upon her. She no longer loved to climb the hills, no longer flourished her orange stick in sheer gladness of heart as her light feet skipped over the rough ground and the coarse grass on the mountain side. The odour of rosemary and thyme, the fresh breath of the sea, no longer filled her with rapture. She thought of Beresford Street and her mother's face with a sick longing. They were so far—so far away! And then she thought of Lady Ducayne, sitting by the heaped-up olive logs in the over-heated salon—thought of that wizened-nut-cracker profile, and those gleaming eyes, with an invincible horror.

Visitors at the hotel had told her that the air of Cap Ferrino was relaxing—better suited to age than to youth, to sickness than to health. No doubt it was so. She was not so well as she had been at Walworth; but she told herself that she was suffering only from the pain of separation from the dear companion of her girlhood, the mother who had been nurse, sister, friend, flatterer, all things in this world to her. She had shed many tears over that parting, had spent many a melancholy hour on the marble terrace with yearning eyes looking westward, and with her heart's desire a thousand miles away.

She was sitting in her favourite spot, an angle at the eastern end of the terrace, a quiet little nook sheltered by orange trees, when she heard a couple of Riviera habitués talking in the garden below. They were sitting on a bench against the terrace wall.

She had no idea of listening to their talk, till the sound of Lady Ducayne's name attracted her, and then she listened without any thought of wrong-doing. They were talking no secrets—just casually discussing an hotel acquaintance.

They were two elderly people whom Bella only knew by sight. An English clergyman who had wintered abroad for half his lifetime; a stout, comfortable, well-to-do spinster, whose chronic bronchitis obliged her to migrate annually.

"I have met her about Italy for the last ten years," said the lady; "but have never found out her real age.

"I put her down at a hundred—not a year less," replied the parson. "Her reminiscences all go back to the Regency. She was evidently then in her zenith; and I have heard her say things that showed she was in Parisian society when the First Empire was at its best—before Josephine was divorced."*

---

* Joséphine du Beauharnais, later Empress Joséphine, married Napoleon Bonaparte. When she bore him no children, he had the marriage annulled (in 1810).

"She doesn't talk much now."

"No; there's not much life left in her. She is wise in keeping herself secluded. I only wonder that wicked old quack, her Italian doctor, didn't finish her off years ago."

"I should think it must be the other way, and that he keeps her alive."

"My dear Miss Manders, do you think foreign quackery ever kept anybody alive?"

"Well, there she is—and she never goes anywhere without him. He certainly has an unpleasant countenance."

"Unpleasant," echoed the parson, "I don't believe the foul fiend himself can beat him in ugliness. I pity that poor young woman who has to live between old Lady Ducayne and Dr. Parravicini."

"But the old lady is very good to her companions."

"No doubt. She is very free with her cash; the servants call her good Lady Ducayne. She is a withered old female Croesus,* and knows she'll never be able to get through her money, and doesn't relish the idea of other people enjoying it when she's in her coffin. People who live to be as old as she is become slavishly attached to life. I daresay she's generous to those poor girls—but she can't make them happy. They die in her service."

"Don't say they, Mr. Carton; I know that one poor girl died at Mentone last spring."

"Yes, and another poor girl died in Rome three years ago. I was there at the time. Good Lady Ducayne left her there in an English family. The girl had every comfort. The old woman was very liberal to her—but she died. I tell you, Miss Manders, it is not good for any young woman to live with two such horrors as Lady Ducayne and Parravicini." They talked of other things—but Bella hardly heard them. She sat motionless, and a cold wind seemed to come down upon her from the mountains and to creep up to her from the sea, till she shivered as she sat there in the sunshine, in the shelter of the orange trees in the midst of all that beauty and brightness.

---

* Croesus was the King of Lydia (now Turkey) in the sixth century BCE and was known for his great wealth, which was said to have come from the gold that resulted when Midas washed his hands in the River Pactolus.

Yes, they were uncanny, certainly, the pair of them—she so like an aristocratic witch in her withered old age; he of no particular age, with a face that was more like a waxen mask than any human countenance Bella had ever seen. What did it matter? Old age is venerable, and worthy of all reverence; and Lady Ducayne had been very kind to her. Dr. Parravicini was a harmless, inoffensive student, who seldom looked up from the book he was reading. He had his private sitting-room, where he made experiments in chemistry and natural science—perhaps in alchemy.

What could it matter to Bella? He had always been polite to her, in his far-off way. She could not be more happily placed than she was—in this palatial hotel, with this rich old lady.

No doubt she missed the young English girl who had been so friendly, and it might be that she missed the girl's brother, for Mr. Stafford had talked to her a good deal—had interested himself in the books she was reading, and her manner of amusing herself when she was not on duty.

"You must come to our little salon when you are 'off,' as the hospital nurses call it, and we can have some music. No doubt you play and sing?" upon which Bella had to own with a blush of shame that she had forgotten how to play the piano ages ago.

"Mother and I used to sing duets sometimes between the lights,* without accompaniment," she said, and the tears came into her eyes as she thought of the humble room, the half-hour's respite from work, the sewing-machine standing where a piano ought to have been, and her mother's plaintive voice, so sweet, so true, so dear.

Sometimes she found herself wondering whether she would ever see that beloved mother again. Strange forebodings came into her mind. She was angry with herself for giving way to melancholy thoughts.

One day she questioned Lady Ducayne's French maid about those two companions who had died within three years.

"They were poor, feeble creatures," Francine told her. "They looked fresh and bright enough when they came to Miladi; but they ate too much and they were lazy. They died of luxury and idleness. Miladi was too kind

---

* That is, at twilight.

to them. They had nothing to do; and so they took to fancying things; fancying the air didn't suit them, that they couldn't sleep."

"I sleep well enough, but I have had a strange dream several times since I have been in Italy."

"Ah, you had better not begin to think about dreams, or you will be like those other girls. They were dreamers—and they dreamt themselves into the cemetery."

The dream troubled her a little, not because it was a ghastly or frightening dream, but on account of sensations which she had never felt before in sleep—a whirring of wheels that went round in her brain, a great noise like a whirlwind, but rhythmical like the ticking of a gigantic clock: and then in the midst of this uproar as of winds and waves she seemed to sink into a gulf of unconsciousness, out of sleep into far deeper sleep—total extinction. And then, after that blank interval, there had come the sound of voices, and then again the whirr of wheels, louder and louder—and again the blank—and then she knew no more till morning, when she awoke, feeling languid and oppressed.

She told Dr. Parravicini of her dream one day, on the only occasion when she wanted his professional advice. She had suffered rather severely from the mosquitoes before Christmas—and had been almost frightened at finding a wound upon her arm which she could only attribute to the venomous sting of one of these torturers. Parravicini put on his glasses, and scrutinized the angry mark on the round, white arm, as Bella stood before him and Lady Ducayne with her sleeve rolled up above her elbow.

"Yes, that's rather more than a joke," he said, "he has caught you on the top of a vein. What a vampire! But there's no harm done, signorina, nothing that a little dressing of mine won't heal.

"You must always show me any bite of this nature. It might be dangerous if neglected. These creatures feed on poison and disseminate it."

"And to think that such tiny creatures can bite like this," said Bella; "my arm looks as if it had been cut by a knife."

"If I were to show you a mosquito's sting under my microscope you wouldn't be surprised at that," replied Parravicini.

Bella had to put up with the mosquito bites, even when they came on the top of a vein, and produced that ugly wound. The wound recurred now and then at longish intervals, and Bella found Dr. Parravicini's dressing a speedy cure. If he were the quack his enemies called him, he had at least a light hand and a delicate touch in performing this small operation.

"Bella Rolleston to Mrs. Rolleston—April 14th.

"Ever Dearest—Behold the cheque for my second quarter's salary—five and twenty pounds.[*]

"There is no one to pinch off a whole tenner for a year's commission as there was last time, so it is all for you, mother, dear. I have plenty of pocket-money in hand from the cash I brought away with me, when you insisted on my keeping more than I wanted. It isn't possible to spend money here—except on occasional tips to servants, or sous to beggars and children—unless one had lots to spend, for everything one would like to buy—tortoise-shell, coral, lace—is so ridiculously dear that only a millionaire ought to look at it. Italy is a dream of beauty: but for shopping, give me Newington Causeway.[†]

"You ask me so earnestly if I am quite well that I fear my letters must have been very dull lately. Yes, dear, I am well—but I am not quite so strong as I was when I used to trudge to the West-end to buy half a pound of tea—just for a constitutional walk—or to Dulwich to look at the pictures.[‡] Italy is relaxing; and I feel what the people here call 'slack.' But I fancy I can see your dear face looking worried as you read this. Indeed, and indeed, I am not ill. I am only a little tired of this lovely scene—as I suppose one might get tired of looking at one of Turner's pictures[§] if it hung on a wall that was always opposite one. I think of you every hour in every day—think

---

[*] A generous amount—we learn, in Arthur Conan Doyle's "A Case of Identity," that the young woman Mary Sutherland earns £100 per year as a typewritist, employment that required more education and skills than Bella had attained. In terms of relative income this is a modern equivalent of about £76,000 per year—quite a bit for a mere "companion," especially with room and board included!

[†] A road (and shopping district) in Southwark, between the Elephant and Castle and Borough High Street.

[‡] Dulwich Village, in Southwark, features the Dulwich Picture Gallery, a collection of portraits and British Old Masters.

[§] J. M. W. Turner (1775–1851), the renowned English painter of seascapes and other natural settings.

of you and our homely little room—our dear little shabby parlour, with the armchairs from the wreck of your old home, and Dick singing in his cage over the sewing-machine. Dear, shrill, maddening Dick, who, we flattered ourselves, was so passionately fond of us. Do tell me in your next that he is well.

"My friend Lotta and her brother never came back after all. They went from Pisa to Rome.

"Happy mortals! And they are to be on the Italian lakes in May; which lake was not decided when Lotta last wrote to me. She has been a charming correspondent, and has confided all her little flirtations to me. We are all to go to Bellaggio* next week—by Genoa and Milan. Isn't that lovely? Lady Ducayne travels by the easiest stages—except when she is bottled up in the train de luxe. We shall stop two days at Genoa and one at Milan. What a bore I shall be to you with my talk about Italy when I come home.

"Love and love—and ever more love from your adoring, Bella."

CHAPTER IV

Herbert Stafford and his sister had often talked of the pretty English girl with her fresh complexion, which made such a pleasant touch of rosy colour among all those sallow faces at the Grand Hotel. The young doctor thought of her with a compassionate tenderness—her utter loneliness in that great hotel where there were so many people, her bondage to that old, old woman, where everybody else was free to think of nothing but enjoying life. It was a hard fate; and the poor child was evidently devoted to her mother, and felt the pain of separation—"only two of them, and very poor, and all the world to each other," he thought.

Lotta told him one morning that they were to meet again at Bellaggio. "The old thing and her court are to be there before we are," she said. "I shall be charmed to have Bella again. She is so bright and gay—in spite of an occasional touch of homesickness. I never took to a girl on a short acquaintance as I did to her."

---

* Properly Belagio, a village on Lake Como in the north of Italy.

"I like her best when she is homesick," said Herbert; "for then I am sure she has a heart."

"What have you to do with hearts, except for dissection? Don't forget that Bella is an absolute pauper. She told me in confidence that her mother makes mantles for a West-end shop. You can hardly have a lower depth than that."

"I shouldn't think any less of her if her mother made match-boxes."

"Not in the abstract—of course not. Match-boxes are honest labour. But you couldn't marry a girl whose mother makes mantles."

"We haven't come to the consideration of that question yet," answered Herbert, who liked to provoke his sister.

In two years' hospital practice he had seen too much of the grim realities of life to retain any prejudices about rank. Cancer, phthisis,* gangrene, leave a man with little respect for the outward differences which vary the husk of humanity. The kernel is always the same—fearfully and wonderfully made—a subject for pity and terror.

Mr. Stafford and his sister arrived at Bellaggio in a fair May evening. The sun was going down as the steamer approached the pier; and all that glory of purple bloom which curtains every wall at this season of the year flushed and deepened in the glowing light. A group of ladies were standing on the pier watching the arrivals, and among them Herbert saw a pale face that startled him out of his wonted composure.

"There she is," murmured Lotta, at his elbow, "but how dreadfully changed. She looks a wreck."

They were shaking hands with her a few minutes later, and a flush had lighted up her poor pinched face in the pleasure of meeting.

"I thought you might come this evening," she said. "We have been here a week."

She did not add that she had been there every evening to watch the boat in, and a good many times during the day. The Grand Bretagne† was close by, and it had been easy for her to creep to the pier when the boat bell rang.

---

* Pulmonary tuberculosis.

† This once-beautiful hotel, opened in 1861, has fallen into ruin but plans are in place for a restoration.

She felt a joy in meeting these people again; a sense of being with friends; a confidence which Lady Ducayne's goodness had never inspired in her.

"Oh, you poor darling, how awfully ill you must have been," exclaimed Lotta, as the two girls embraced.

Bella tried to answer, but her voice was choked with tears.

"What has been the matter, dear? That horrid influenza, I suppose?"

"No, no, I have not been ill—I have only felt a little weaker than I used to be. I don't think the air of Cap Ferrino quite agreed with me."

"It must have disagreed with you abominably. I never saw such a change in anyone. Do let Herbert doctor you. He is fully qualified, you know. He prescribed for ever so many influenza patients at the Londres.* They were glad to get advice from an English doctor in a friendly way."

"I am sure he must be very clever!" faltered Bella, "but there is really nothing the matter. I am not ill, and if I were ill, Lady Ducayne's physician—"

"That dreadful man with the yellow face? I would as soon one of the Borgias prescribed for me.† I hope you haven't been taking any of his medicines."

"No, dear, I have taken nothing. I have never complained of being ill."

This was said while they were all three walking to the hotel. The Staffords' rooms had been secured in advance, pretty ground-floor rooms, opening into the garden. Lady Ducayne's statelier apartments were on the floor above.

"I believe these rooms are just under ours," said Bella.

"Then it will be all the easier for you to run down to us," replied Lotta, which was not really the case, as the grand staircase was in the centre of the hotel.

"Oh, I shall find it easy enough," said Bella. "I'm afraid you'll have too much of my society.

---

* Probably the Hotel de Londres y de Ingleterres, a first-class beachfront hotel in San Sebastian. An influenza pandemic ran in Europe from 1889 to 1890 and killed almost one million people. While this was a few years later, influenza outbreaks still had devastating effect.

† The Borgias were of course renowned poisoners.

"Lady Ducayne sleeps away half the day in this warm weather, so I have a good deal of idle time; and I get awfully moped thinking of mother and home."

Her voice broke upon the last word. She could not have thought of that poor lodging which went by the name of home more tenderly had it been the most beautiful that art and wealth ever created. She moped and pined in this lovely garden, with the sunlit lake and the romantic hills spreading out their beauty before her. She was homesick and she had dreams: or, rather, an occasional recurrence of that one bad dream with all its strange sensations—it was more like a hallucination than dreaming—the whirring of wheels; the sinking into an abyss; the struggling back to consciousness. She had the dream shortly before she left Cap Ferrino, but not since she had come to Bellaggio, and she began to hope the air in this lake district suited her better, and that those strange sensations would never return.

Mr. Stafford wrote a prescription and had it made up at the chemist's near the hotel. It was a powerful tonic, and after two bottles, and a row or two on the lake, and some rambling over the hills and in the meadows where the spring flowers made earth seem paradise, Bella's spirits and looks improved as if by magic.

"It is a wonderful tonic," she said, but perhaps in her heart of hearts she knew that the doctor's kind voice and the friendly hand that helped her in and out of the boat, and the watchful care that went with her by land and lake, had something to do with her cure.

"I hope you don't forget that her mother makes mantles," Lotta said, warningly.

"Or match-boxes: it is just the same thing, so far as I am concerned."

"You mean that in no circumstances could you think of marrying her?"

"I mean that if ever I love a woman well enough to think of marrying her, riches or rank will count for nothing with me. But I fear—I fear your poor friend may not live to be any man's wife."

"Do you think her so very ill?"

He sighed, and left the question unanswered.

One day, while they were gathering wild hyacinths in an upland meadow, Bella told Mr. Stafford about her bad dream.

"It is curious only because it is hardly like a dream," she said. "I daresay you could find some common-sense reason for it. The position of my head on my pillow, or the atmosphere, or something."

And then she described her sensations; how in the midst of sleep there came a sudden sense of suffocation; and then those whirring wheels, so loud, so terrible; and then a blank, and then a coming back to waking consciousness.

"Have you ever had chloroform given you—by a dentist, for instance?"

"Never—Dr. Parravicini asked me that question one day."

"Lately?"

"No, long ago, when we were in the train de luxe."

"Has Dr. Parravicini prescribed for you since you began to feel weak and ill?"

"Oh, he has given me a tonic from time to time, but I hate medicine, and took very little of the stuff. And then I am not ill, only weaker than I used to be. I was ridiculously strong and well when I lived at Walworth, and used to take long walks every day. Mother made me take those tramps to Dulwich or Norwood, for fear I should suffer from too much sewing-machine; sometimes—but very seldom—she went with me. She was generally toiling at home while I was enjoying fresh air and exercise. And she was very careful about our food—that, however plain it was, it should be always nourishing and ample. I owe it to her care that I grew up such a great, strong creature."

"You don't look great or strong now, you poor dear," said Lotta.

"I'm afraid Italy doesn't agree with me."

"Perhaps it is not Italy, but being cooped up with Lady Ducayne that has made you ill."

"But I am never cooped up. Lady Ducayne is absurdly kind, and lets me roam about or sit in the balcony all day if I like. I have read more novels since I have been with her than in all the rest of my life."

"Then she is very different from the average old lady, who is usually a slave-driver," said Stafford. "I wonder why she carries a companion about with her if she has so little need of society."

"Oh, I am only part of her state. She is inordinately rich—and the salary she gives me doesn't count. Apropos of Dr. Parravicini, I know he is a clever doctor, for he cures my horrid mosquito bites."

"A little ammonia would do that, in the early stage of the mischief. But there are no mosquitoes to trouble you now."

"Oh, yes, there are, I had a bite just before we left Cap Ferrino."

She pushed up her loose lawn sleeve, and exhibited a scar, which he scrutinized intently, with a surprised and puzzled look.

"This is no mosquito bite," he said.

"Oh, yes it is—unless there are snakes or adders at Cap Ferrino."

"It is not a bite at all. You are trifling with me. Miss Rolleston—you have allowed that wretched Italian quack to bleed you.* They killed the greatest man in modern Europe that way, remember. How very foolish of you."

"I was never bled in my life, Mr. Stafford."

"Nonsense! Let me look at your other arm. Are there any more mosquito bites?"

"Yes; Dr. Parravicini says I have a bad skin for healing, and that the poison acts more virulently with me than with most people."

Stafford examined both her arms in the broad sunlight, scars new and old.

"You have been very badly bitten, Miss Rolleston," he said, "and if ever I find the mosquito I shall make him smart. But, now tell me, my dear girl, on your word of honour, tell me as you would tell a friend who is sincerely anxious for your health and happiness—as you would tell your mother if she were here to question you—have you no knowledge of any cause for these scars except mosquito bites—no suspicion even?"

"No, indeed! No, upon my honour! I have never seen a mosquito biting my arm. One never does see the horrid little fiends. But I have heard them trumpeting under the curtains, and I know that I have often had one of the pestilent wretches buzzing about me."

Later in the day Bella and her friends were sitting at tea in the garden, while Lady Ducayne took her afternoon drive with her doctor.

---

* Blood-letting remained a highly controversial medical treatment until the early twentieth century. George Washington may well have died from overly aggressive blood-letting, though Mr Stafford probably has Lord Byron in mind, who allegedly died from sepsis that was carried by the instruments used in letting his blood when he grew ill in Turkey.

"How long do you mean to stop with Lady Ducayne, Miss Rolleston?" Herbert Stafford asked, after a thoughtful silence, breaking suddenly upon the trivial talk of the two girls.

"As long as she will go on paying me twenty-five pounds a quarter."

"Even if you feel your health breaking down in her service?"

"It is not the service that has injured my health. You can see that I have really nothing to do—to read aloud for an hour or so once or twice a week; to write a letter once in a way to a London tradesman. I shall never have such an easy time with anybody else. And nobody else would give me a hundred a year."

"Then you mean to go on till you break down; to die at your post?"

"Like the other two companions? No! If ever I feel seriously ill—really ill—I shall put myself in a train and go back to Walworth without stopping."

"What about the other two companions?"

"They both died. It was very unlucky for Lady Ducayne. That's why she engaged me; she chose me because I was ruddy and robust. She must feel rather disgusted at my having grown white and weak. By-the-bye, when I told her about the good your tonic had done me, she said she would like to see you and have a little talk with you about her own case."

"And I should like to see Lady Ducayne. When did she say this?"

"The day before yesterday."

"Will you ask her if she will see me this evening?"

"With pleasure. I wonder what you will think of her? She looks rather terrible to a stranger; but Dr. Parravicini says she was once a famous beauty."

It was nearly ten o'clock when Mr. Stafford was summoned by message from Lady Ducayne, whose courier came to conduct him to her ladyship's salon. Bella was reading aloud when the visitor was admitted; and he noticed the languor in the low, sweet tones, the evident effort.

"Shut up the book," said the querulous old voice. "You are beginning to drawl like Miss Blandy."

Stafford saw a small, bent figure crouching over the piled-up olive logs; a shrunken old figure in a gorgeous garment of black and crimson brocade, a skinny throat emerging from a mass of old Venetian lace, clasped with diamonds that flashed like fire-flies as the trembling old head turned towards him.

The eyes that looked at him out of the face were almost as bright as the diamonds—the only living feature in that narrow parchment mask. He had seen terrible faces in the hospital—faces on which disease had set dreadful marks—but he had never seen a face that impressed him so painfully as this withered countenance, with its indescribable horror of death outlived, a face that should have been hidden under a coffin-lid years and years ago.

The Italian physician was standing on the other side of the fireplace, smoking a cigarette, and looking down at the little old woman brooding over the hearth as if he were proud of her.

"Good evening, Mr. Stafford; you can go to your room, Bella, and write your everlasting letter to your mother at Walworth," said Lady Ducayne. "I believe she writes a page about every wild flower she discovers in the woods and meadows. I don't know what else she can find to write about," she added, as Bella quietly withdrew to the pretty little bedroom opening out of Lady Ducayne's spacious apartment. Here, as at Cap Ferrino, she slept in a room adjoining the old lady's.

"You are a medical man, I understand, Mr. Stafford."

"I am a qualified practitioner, but I have not begun to practise."

"You have begun upon my companion, she tells me."

"I have prescribed for her, certainly, and I am happy to find my prescription has done her good; but I look upon that improvement as temporary. Her case will require more drastic treatment."

"Never mind her case. There is nothing the matter with the girl—absolutely nothing—except girlish nonsense; too much liberty and not enough work."

"I understand that two of your ladyship's previous companions died of the same disease," said Stafford, looking first at Lady Ducayne, who gave her tremulous old head an impatient jerk, and then at Parravicini, whose yellow complexion had paled a little under Stafford's scrutiny.

"Don't bother me about my companions, sir," said Lady Ducayne. "I sent for you to consult you about myself—not about a parcel of anæmic girls. You are young, and medicine is a progressive science, the newspapers tell me. Where have you studied?"

"In Edinburgh—and in Paris."

"Two good schools. And you know all the new-fangled theories, the modern discoveries—that remind one of the mediæval witchcraft, of Albertus Magnus,* and George Ripley;† you have studied hypnotism—electricity?"

"And the transfusion of blood," said Stafford, very slowly, looking at Parravicini.

"Have you made any discovery that teaches you to prolong human life—any elixir—any mode of treatment? I want my life prolonged, young man. That man there has been my physician for thirty years. He does all he can to keep me alive—after his lights. He studies all the new theories of all the scientists—but he is old; he gets older every day—his brain-power is going—he is bigoted—prejudiced—can't receive new ideas—can't grapple with new systems. He will let me die if I am not on my guard against him."

"You are of an unbelievable ingratitude, Ecclenza,"‡ said Parravicini.

"Oh, you needn't complain. I have paid you thousands to keep me alive. Every year of my life has swollen your hoards; you know there is nothing to come to you when I am gone. My whole fortune is left to endow a home for indigent women of quality who have reached their ninetieth year. Come, Mr. Stafford, I am a rich woman. Give me a few years more in the sunshine, a few years more above ground, and I will give you the price of a fashionable London practice—I will set you up at the West-end."

"How old are you, Lady Ducayne?"

"I was born the day Louis XVI was guillotined."§

"Then I think you have had your share of the sunshine and the pleasures of the earth, and that you should spend your few remaining days in repenting your sins and trying to make atonement for the young lives that have been sacrificed to your love of life."

---

* Albertus Magnus was a thirteenth-century Catholic Dominican friar who later became St. Albert the Great; he was rumored to have investigated alchemy and discovered the philosopher's stone.

† George Ripley was a sixteenth-century English alchemist.

‡ We learn later that Lady Ducayne's first name was "Adeline." Therefore, we can deduce that this is a typographical error for *Excellenza* (Excellency), an honorific.

§ January 21, 1793.

"What do you mean by that, sir?"

"Oh, Lady Ducayne, need I put your wickedness and your physician's still greater wickedness in plain words? The poor girl who is now in your employment has been reduced from robust health to a condition of absolute danger by Dr. Parravicini's experimental surgery; and I have no doubt those other two young women who broke down in your service were treated by him in the same manner. I could take upon myself to demonstrate—by most convincing evidence, to a jury of medical men—that Dr. Parravicini has been bleeding Miss Rolleston, after putting her under chloroform, at intervals, ever since she has been in your service. The deterioration in the girl's health speaks for itself; the lancet marks upon the girl's arms are unmistakable; and her description of a series of sensations, which she calls a dream, points unmistakably to the administration of chloroform while she was sleeping. A practice so nefarious, so murderous, must, if exposed, result in a sentence only less severe than the punishment of murder."

"I laugh," said Parravicini, with an airy motion of his skinny fingers; "I laugh at once at your theories and at your threats. I, Parravicini Leopold, have no fear that the law can question anything I have done."

"Take the girl away, and let me hear no more of her," cried Lady Ducayne, in the thin, old voice, which so poorly matched the energy and fire of the wicked old brain that guided its utterances. "Let her go back to her mother—I want no more girls to die in my service. There are girls enough and to spare in the world, God knows."

"If you ever engage another companion—or take another English girl into your service, Lady Ducayne, I will make all England ring with the story of your wickedness."

"I want no more girls. I don't believe in his experiments. They have been full of danger for me as well as for the girl—an air bubble,* and I should be gone. I'll have no more of his dangerous quackery. I'll find some new

---

* Blood transfusions were still a relatively young procedure when this story was written—it wouldn't be until five years after this story was written that the major human blood groups were identified—and an air embolism caused by an air bubble in the IV tube would have been a real concern.

man—a better man than you, sir, a discoverer like Pasteur, or Virchow,[*] a genius—to keep me alive. Take your girl away, young man. Marry her if you like.

"I'll write her a cheque for a thousand pounds, and let her go and live on beef and beer, and get strong and plump again. I'll have no more such experiments. Do you hear, Parravicini?" she screamed, vindictively, the yellow, wrinkled face distorted with fury, the eyes glaring at him.

The Staffords carried Bella Rolleston off to Varese[†] next day, she very loath to leave Lady Ducayne, whose liberal salary afforded such help for the dear mother. Herbert Stafford insisted, however, treating Bella as coolly as if he had been the family physician, and she had been given over wholly to his care.

"Do you suppose your mother would let you stop here to die?" he asked. "If Mrs. Rolleston knew how ill you are, she would come post haste to fetch you."

"I shall never be well again till I get back to Walworth," answered Bella, who was low-spirited and inclined to tears this morning, a reaction after her good spirits of yesterday.

"We'll try a week or two at Varese first," said Stafford. "When you can walk half-way up Monte Generoso[‡] without palpitation of the heart, you shall go back to Walworth."

"Poor mother, how glad she will be to see me, and how sorry that I've lost such a good place."

This conversation took place on the boat when they were leaving Bellaggio. Lotta had gone to her friend's room at seven o'clock that morning, long before Lady Ducayne's withered eyelids had opened to the daylight, before even Francine, the French maid, was astir, and had helped to pack

---

[*] The French microbiologist Louis Pasteur (1822–1895) is remembered today for his discovery of "pasteurization," the process of killing bacteria in milk, as well as the benefits of vaccination. The German physician Rudolf Virchow (1821–1902), however, has no such visibility outside professional circles, where he is known as the "father of modern pathology" and social medicine.

[†] An Italian town in the north of Italy, near the lake region.

[‡] An Alpine mountain of almost 1,800 meters, with a view of Varese and Lake Como.

a Gladstone bag* with essentials, and hustled Bella downstairs and out of doors before she could make any strenuous resistance.

"It's all right," Lotta assured her. "Herbert had a good talk with Lady Ducayne last night and it was settled for you to leave this morning. She doesn't like invalids, you see."

"No," sighed Bella, "she doesn't like invalids. It was very unlucky that I should break down, just like Miss Tomson and Miss Blandy."

"At any rate, you are not dead, like them," answered Lotta, "and my brother says you are not going to die."

It seemed rather a dreadful thing to be dismissed in that off-hand way, without a word of farewell from her employer.

"I wonder what Miss Torpinter will say when I go to her for another situation," Bella speculated, ruefully, while she and her friends were breakfasting on board the steamer.

"Perhaps you may never want another situation," said Stafford.

"You mean that I may never be well enough to be useful to anybody?"

"No, I don't mean anything of the kind."

It was after dinner at Varese, when Bella had been induced to take a whole glass of Chianti, and quite sparkled after that unaccustomed stimulant, that Mr. Stafford produced a letter from his pocket.

"I forgot to give you Lady Ducayne's letter of adieu," he said.

"What, did she write to me? I am so glad—I hated to leave her in such a cool way; for after all she was very kind to me, and if I didn't like her it was only because she was too dreadfully old."

She tore open the envelope. The letter was short and to the point:

"Goodbye, child. Go and marry your doctor. I enclose a farewell gift for your trousseau†—Adeline Ducayne."

"A hundred pounds, a whole year's salary—no—why, it's for a—a cheque for a thousand!" cried Bella. "What a generous old soul! She really is the dearest old thing."

"She just missed being very dear to you, Bella," said Stafford.

---

* A small suitcase that opened into two sections.

† A dowry.

He had dropped into the use of her Christian name while they were on board the boat. It seemed natural now that she was to be in his charge till they all three went back to England.

"I shall take upon myself the privileges of an elder brother till we land at Dover," he said; "after that—well, it must be as you please."

The question of their future relations must have been satisfactorily settled before they crossed the Channel, for Bella's next letter to her mother communicated three startling facts.

First, that the enclosed cheque for £1,000 was to be invested in debenture stock* in Mrs. Rolleston's name, and was to be her very own, income and principal, for the rest of her life.

Next, that Bella was going home to Walworth immediately.

And last, that she was going to be married to Mr. Herbert Stafford in the following autumn.

"And I am sure you will adore him, mother, as much as I do," wrote Bella. "It is all good Lady Ducayne's doing. I never could have married if I had not secured that little nest-egg for you.

"Herbert says we shall be able to add to it as the years go by, and that wherever we live there shall be always a room in our house for you. The word 'mother-in-law' has no terrors for him."

---

* A type of stock that pays out regular, fixed amounts.

Vernon Lee (1856–1935) was the pen name of the British writer Violet Paget. Paget's supernatural fiction has been compared to that of M. R. James by Montague Summers, while scholar and critic Everett Bleiler noted that her stories "are really in a category by themselves . . . they deserve more than the passing attention that they have attracted." Paget began writing at fifteen, but in 1875, she adopted the pen name in order to be taken seriously as an art critic and a philosopher. Childhood friends with the renowned painter John Singer Sargent, he painted her in men's clothing in 1881. Paget was openly involved in romantic relationships with several women, including her longtime lover Clementina "Kit" Anstruther-Thomson, with whom she wrote an important essay on art. When the pair were accused of plagiarism, their relationship crumbled. Paget wrote the following in 1900 (too early to have been influenced by James) but did not collect it until 1927, in her volume *For Maurice: Five Unlikely Stories* (dedicated to Maurice Baring). It reflects her love of Greek mythology.

Marsyas in Flanders *

by Vernon Lee

(1900)

---

* In Greek mythology Marsyas was a satyr who was said to have invented flute music. He arrogantly challenged the god Apollo to a music contest, which Apollo won by besting Marsyas's flute with his lyre. To punish Marsyas for his hubris, Apollo flayed him alive. There are a number of statues depicting Marsyas in agony, including one from the third century BCE (now displayed in the Istanbul Archaeology Museum) in which the arms are missing.

I

"You are right. This is not the original crucifix at all. Another one has been put instead. *Il y a eu substitution*,"* and the little old Antiquary† of Dunes nodded mysteriously, fixing his ghostseer's eyes upon mine.

He said it in a scarce audible whisper. For it happened to be the vigil of the Feast of the Crucifix,‡ and the once famous church was full of semi-clerical persons decorating it for the morrow, and of old ladies in strange caps, clattering about with pails and brooms. The Antiquary had brought me there the very moment of my arrival, lest the crowd of faithful should prevent his showing me everything next morning.

The famous crucifix was exhibited behind rows and rows of unlit candles, and surrounded by strings of paper flowers and coloured muslin, and garlands of sweet resinous maritime pine; and two lighted chandeliers illumined it.

"There has been an exchange," he repeated, looking round that no one might hear him. *"Il y a eu substitution."*

For I had remarked, as anyone would have done, at the first glance, that the crucifix had every appearance of French work of the thirteenth century, boldly realistic, whereas the crucifix of the legend, which was a work of St. Luke,§ which had hung for centuries in the Holy Sepulchre at Jerusalem and been miraculously cast ashore at Dunes¶ in 1195, would

---

* "There was a substitution."

† An antiquary is a recorder or custodian of antiquities.

‡ Also known as the Feast of the Cross or the Feast of the Exaltation of the Holy Cross, this Catholic observance is dedicated to commemoration of the cross used in Christ's crucifixion, and occurs on September 14. Parts of the actual cross are claimed to be held by a number of churches, who display them in reliquaries, which are usually ornate crucifixes.

§ St. Luke the Evangelist not only wrote much of the New Testament but was also an artist who painted some of the earliest religious icons.

¶ Much of the Belgian coast is lined with dunes, but this seems to be a fictitious name Lee is using.

surely have been a more or less Byzantine image, like its miraculous companion of Lucca.[*]

"But why should there have been a substitution?" I inquired innocently. "Hush, hush," answered the Antiquary, frowning, "not here—later, later—"

He took me all over the church, once so famous for pilgrimages; but from which, even like the sea which has left it in a salt marsh beneath the cliffs, the tide of devotion has receded for centuries. It is a very dignified little church, of charmingly restrained and shapely Gothic, built of a delicate pale stone, which the sea damp has picked out, in bases and capitals and carved foliation, with stains of a lovely bright green. The Antiquary showed me where the transept[†] and belfry had been left unfinished when the miracles had diminished in the fourteenth century. And he took me up to the curious warder's chamber, a large room up some steps in the triforium;[‡] with a fireplace and stone seats for the men who guarded the precious crucifix day and night. There had even been beehives in the window, he told me, and he remembered seeing them still as a child.

"Was it usual, here in Flanders,[§] to have a guardroom in churches containing important relics?" I asked, for I could not remember having seen anything similar before.

"By no means," he answered, looking round to make sure we were alone, "but it was necessary here. You have never heard in what the chief miracles of this church consisted?"

"No," I whispered back, gradually infected by his mysteriousness, "unless you allude to the legend that the figure of the Saviour broke all the crosses until the right one was cast up by the sea?"

He shook his head but did not answer, and descended the steep stairs into the nave, while I lingered a moment looking down into it from the

---

[*] The Holy Face of Lucca is an eight-foot tall carving of Christ crucified that dates back to at least the ninth century CE.

[†] In churches built in a cross shape the transept runs crosswise across the nave or main body.

[‡] A triforium is a gallery set above the arches and the main floor of a church.

[§] The Dutch-speaking northern part of Belgium.

warder's chamber. I have never had so curious an impression of a church. The chandeliers on either side of the crucifix swirled slowly round, making great pools of light which were broken by the shadows of the clustered columns, and among the pews of the nave moved the flicker of the sacristan's lamp. The place was full of the scent of resinous pine branches, evoking dunes and mountainsides; and from the busy groups below rose a subdued chatter of women's voices, and a splash of water and clatter of pattens.* It vaguely suggested preparations for a witches' sabbath.

"What sort of miracles did they have in this church?" I asked, when we had passed into the dusky square, "and what did you mean about their having exchanged the crucifix—about a *substitution?*"

It seemed quite dark outside. The church rose black, a vague lopsided mass of buttresses and high-pitched roofs, against the watery, moonlit sky; the big trees of the churchyard behind wavering about in the seawind; and the windows shone yellow, like flaming portals, in the darkness.

"Please remark the bold effect of the gargoyles," said the Antiquary pointing upwards.

They jutted out, vague wild beasts, from the roof-line; and, what was positively frightening, you saw the moonlight, yellow and blue through the open jaws of some of them. A gust swept through the trees, making the weathercock clatter and groan.

"Why, those gargoyle wolves seem positively to howl," I exclaimed.

The old Antiquary chuckled. "Aha," he answered, "did I not tell you that this church has witnessed things like no other church in Christendom? And it still remembers them! There—have you ever known such a wild, savage church before?"

And as he spoke there suddenly mingled with the sough of the wind and the groans of the weather-vane, a shrill quavering sound as of pipers inside.

"The organist trying his vox humana† for tomorrow," remarked the Antiquary.

---

* Wooden shoes or clogs.

† An organ stop which supposedly resembles a human voice.

II

Next day I bought one of the printed histories of the miraculous crucifix which they were hawking all round the church; and next day also, my friend the Antiquary was good enough to tell me all that he knew of the matter. Between my two informants, the following may be said to be the true story.

In the autumn of 1195, after a night of frightful storm, a boat was found cast upon the shore of Dunes, which was at that time a fishing village at the mouth of the Nys,* and exactly opposite a terrible sunken reef.

The boat was broken and upset; and close to it, on the sand and bent grass, lay a stone figure of the crucified Saviour, without its cross and, as seems probable, also without its arms, which had been made of separate blocks. A variety of persons immediately came forward to claim it; the little church of Dunes, on whose glebe† it was found; the Barons of Cröy, who had the right of jetsam on that coast, and also the great Abbey of St. Loup of Arras,‡ as possessing the spiritual over-lordship of the place. But a holy man who lived close by in the cliffs, had a vision which settled the dispute. St Luke in person appeared and told him that he was the original maker of the figure; that it had been one of three which had hung round the Holy Sepulchre of Jerusalem; that three knights, a Norman, a Tuscan, and a man of Arras, had with the permission of Heaven stolen them from the Infidels and placed them on unmanned boats; that one of the images had been cast upon the Norman coast near Salenelles; that the second had run aground not far from the city of Lucca, in Italy, and that this third was the one which had been embarked by the knight from Artois. As regarded its final resting place, the hermit, on the authority of St Luke, recommended that the statue should be left to decide the matter itself. Accordingly, the crucified figure was solemnly cast back into the sea. The very next day it was found once more in the same spot, among the sand and bent grass at the mouth of the Nys. It was therefore deposited in the little church of

---

* This seems to be a fictitious river name.

† Lands or fields, usually belonging to a church.

‡ There is an Abbey of St. Loup in Troyes but not in Arras (Arras is in northern France, not far south of the Belgian border).

Dunes; and very soon indeed the flocks of pious persons who brought it offerings from all parts made it necessary and possible to rebuild the church thus sanctified by its presence.

The Holy Effigy of Dunes—*Sacra Dunarum Effigies* as it was called—did not work the ordinary sort of miracles. But its fame spread far and wide by the unexampled wonders which became the constant accompaniment of its existence. The Effigy, as above mentioned, had been discovered without the cross to which it had evidently been fastened, nor had any researches or any subsequent storms brought the missing blocks to light, despite the many prayers which were offered for the purpose. After some time therefore, and a deal of discussion, it was decided that a new cross should be provided for the effigy to hang upon. And certain skilful stonemasons of Arras were called to Dunes for this purpose. But behold! The very day after the cross had been solemnly erected in the church, an unheard of and terrifying fact was discovered. The Effigy, which had been hanging perfectly straight the previous evening, had shifted its position, and was bent violently to the right, as if in an effort to break loose.

This was attested not merely by hundreds of laymen, but by the priests of the place, who notified the fact in a document, existing in the episcopal archives of Arras until 1790, to the Abbot of St. Loup their spiritual overlord.

This was the beginning of a series of mysterious occurrences which spread the fame of the marvellous crucifix all over Christendom. The Effigy did not remain in the position into which it had miraculously worked itself: it was found, at intervals of time, shifted in some other manner upon its cross, and always as if it had gone through violent contortions. And one day, about ten years after it had been cast up by the sea, the priests of the church and the burghers of Dunes discovered the Effigy hanging in its original outstretched, symmetrical attitude, but O wonder! With the cross, broken in three pieces, lying on the steps of its chapel.

Certain persons, who lived in the end of the town nearest the church, reported to have been roused in the middle of the night by what they had taken for a violent clap of thunder, but which was doubtless the crash of the cross falling down; or perhaps, who knows? The noise with which the terrible Effigy had broken loose and spurned the alien cross from it. For that was the secret: the Effigy, made by a saint and come to Dunes by miracle, had evidently found some trace of unholiness in the stone to which it had been fastened. Such was the ready explanation afforded by the Prior of the church, in answer to an angry summons of the Abbot of St. Loup, who expressed his disapproval of such unusual miracles. Indeed, it was discovered that the piece of marble had not been cleaned from sinful human touch with the necessary rites before the figure was fastened on; a most grave, though excusable oversight. So a new cross was ordered, although it was noticed that much time was lost about it; and the consecration took place only some years later.

Meanwhile the Prior had built the warder's chamber, with the fireplace and recess, and obtained permission from the Pope himself that a clerk in orders should watch day and night, on the score that so wonderful a relic might be stolen. For the relic had by this time entirely cut out all similar crucifixes, and the village of Dunes, through the concourse of pilgrims, had rapidly grown into a town, the property of the now fabulously wealthy Priory of the Holy Cross.

The Abbots of St. Loup, however, looked upon the matter with an unfavourable eye. Although nominally remaining their vassals, the Priors of Dunes had contrived to obtain gradually from the Pope privileges which rendered them virtually independent, and in particular, immunities which sent to the treasury of St. Loup only a small proportion of the tribute money brought by the pilgrims. Abbot Walterius in particular, showed himself actively hostile. He accused the Prior of Dunes of having employed his warders to trump up stories of strange movements and sounds on the part of the still crossless Effigy, and of suggesting, to the ignorant, changes in its attitude which were more credulously believed in now that there was no longer the straight line of the cross by which to verify. So finally the new cross was made, and consecrated, and on Holy Cross Day of the year, the Effigy was fastened to it in the presence of an immense concourse of clergy and laity. The Effigy, it was now supposed, would be satisfied, and no unusual occurrences would increase or perhaps fatally compromise its reputation for sanctity.

These expectations were violently dispelled. In November, 1293, after a year of strange rumours concerning the Effigy, the figure was again discovered to have moved, and continued moving, or rather (judging from the position on the cross) writhing; and on Christmas Eve of the same year, the cross was a second time thrown down and dashed in pieces. The priest on duty was, at the same time, found, it was thought, dead, in his warder's chamber. Another cross was made and this time privately consecrated and put in place, and a hole in the roof made a pretext to close the church for a while, and to perform the rites of purification necessary after its pollution by workmen. Indeed, it was remarked that on this occasion the Prior of Dunes took as much trouble to diminish and if possible to hide away the miracles, as his predecessor had done his best to blazon the preceding ones abroad. The priest who had been on duty on the eventful Christmas Eve disappeared mysteriously, and it was thought by many persons that he had gone mad and was confined in the Prior's prison, for fear of the revelations he might make. For by this time, and not without some encouragement from the Abbots at Arras, extraordinary stories had begun to circulate about the goings-on in the church of Dunes. This church, be it remembered, stood a little above the town, isolated and surrounded by big trees. It was surrounded by the precincts of the Priory and, save on the water side, by high walls. Nevertheless, persons there were who affirmed that, the wind having been in that direction, they had heard strange noises come from the church of nights. During storms, particularly, sounds had been heard which were variously described as howls, groans, and the music of rustic dancing. A master mariner affirmed that one Halloween, as his boat approached the mouth of the Nys, he had seen the church of Dunes brilliantly lit up, its immense windows flaming.* But he was suspected of being drunk and of having exaggerated the effect of the small light shining from the warder's chamber. The interest of the townsfolk of Dunes coincided with that of the Priory, since they prospered greatly by the pilgrimages, so these tales were promptly hushed up. Yet they undoubtedly reached the ear of the Abbot of St. Loup. And at last there came an event which brought them all back to the surface.

---

* A common folklore belief throughout the UK and Brittany was that on Halloween a visitor to a church would see the windows lit and packed with the souls of those who were to die in the coming year.

For, on the Vigil of All Saints,* 1299, the church was struck by lightning. The new warder was found dead in the middle of the nave, the cross broken in two; and oh, horror! the Effigy was missing. The indescribable fear which overcame everyone was merely increased by the discovery of the Effigy lying behind the high altar, in an attitude of frightful convulsion, and, it was whispered, blackened by lightning.

This was the end of the strange doings at Dunes.

An ecclesiastical council was held at Arras, and the church shut once more for nearly a year. It was opened this time and re-consecrated by the Abbot of St. Loup, whom the Prior of Holy Cross served humbly at mass. A new chapel had been built, and in it the miraculous crucifix was displayed, dressed in more splendid brocade and gems than usual, and its head nearly hidden by one of the most gorgeous crowns ever seen before; a gift, it was said, of the Duke of Burgundy.

All this new splendour, and the presence of the great Abbot himself, was presently explained to the faithful, when the Prior came forward to announce that a last and greatest miracle had now taken place. The original cross, on which the figure had hung in the Church of the Holy Sepulchre, and for which the Effigy had spurned all others made by less holy hands, had been cast on the shore of Dunes, on the very spot where, a hundred years before, the figure of the Saviour had been discovered in the sands. "This," said the Prior, "was the explanation of the terrible occurrences which had filled all hearts with anguish. The Holy Effigy was now satisfied, it would rest in peace and its miraculous powers would be engaged only in granting the prayers of the faithful." One half of the forecast came true: from that day forward the Effigy never shifted its position; but from that day forward also, no considerable miracle was ever registered; the devotion of Dunes diminished, other relics threw the Sacred Effigy into the shade; and the pilgrimages dwindling to mere local gatherings, the church was never brought to completion.

What had happened? No one ever knew, guessed, or perhaps even asked. But, when in 1790 the Archiepiscopal palace of Arras was sacked, a certain notary of the neighbourhood bought a large portion of the archives

---

* Halloween, in other words.

at the price of waste paper, either from historical curiosity, or expecting to obtain thereby facts which might gratify his aversion to clergy. These documents lay unexamined for many years, till my friend the Antiquary bought them. Among them taken helter skelter from the Archbishop's palace, were sundry papers referring to the suppressed Abbey of St. Loup of Arras, and among these latter, a series of notes concerning the affairs of the church of Dunes; they were, so far as their fragmentary nature explained, the minutes of an inquest made in 1309, and contained the deposition of sundry witnesses. To understand their meaning it is necessary to remember that this was the time when witch trials had begun, and when the proceedings against the Templars had set the fashion of inquests which could help the finances of the country* while furthering the interests of religion.

What appears to have happened is that after the catastrophe of the Vigil of All Saints, October, 1299, the Prior, Urbain de Luc, found himself suddenly threatened with a charge of sacrilege and witchcraft, of obtaining miracles of the Effigy by devilish means, and of converting his church into a chapel of the Evil One.

Instead of appealing to high ecclesiastical tribunals, as the privileges obtained from the Holy See would have warranted, Prior Urbain guessed that this charge came originally from the wrathful Abbot of St. Loup, and, dropping all his pretensions in order to save himself, he threw himself upon the mercy of the Abbot whom he had hitherto flouted. The Abbot appears to have been satisfied by his submission, and the matter to have dropped after a few legal preliminaries, of which the notes found among the archiepiscopal archives of Arras represented a portion. Some of these notes my friend the Antiquary kindly allowed me to translate from the Latin, and I give them here, leaving the reader to make what he can of them.

"Item. The Abbot expresses himself satisfied that His Reverence the Prior has had no personal knowledge of or dealings with the Evil One (Diabolus). Nevertheless, the gravity of the charge requires . . ."—here the page is torn.

---

* Because property was confiscated from those found guilty.

"Hugues Jacquot, Simon le Couvreur, Pierre Denis, burghers of Dunes, being interrogated, witness:

"That the noises from the Church of the Holy Cross always happened on nights of bad storms, and foreboded shipwrecks on the coast; and were very various, such as terrible rattling, groans, howls as of wolves, and occasional flute playing. A certain Jehan, who has twice been branded and flogged for lighting fires on the coast and otherwise causing ships to wreck at the mouth of the Nys, being promised immunity, after two or three slight pulls on the rack, witnesses as follows: That the band of wreckers to which he belongs always knew when a dangerous storm was brewing, on account of the noises which issued from the church of Dunes. Witness has often climbed the walls and prowled round in the churchyard, waiting to hear such noises. He was not unfamiliar with the howlings and roarings mentioned by the previous witnesses. He has heard tell by a countryman who passed in the night that the howling was such that the countryman thought himself pursued by a pack of wolves, although it is well known that no wolf has been seen in these parts for thirty years. But the witness himself is of the opinion that the most singular of all the noises, and the one which always accompanied or foretold the worst storms, was a noise of flutes and pipes (*quod vulgo dicuntur flustes er musettes*)* so sweet that the King of France could not have sweeter at his Court. Being interrogated whether he had ever seen anything? the witness answers:

"That he has seen the church brightly lit up from the sands; but on approaching found all dark, save the light from the warder's chamber. That once, by moonlight, the piping and fluting and howling being uncommonly loud, he thought he had seen wolves, and a human figure on the roof, but that he ran away from fear, and cannot be sure."

"Item. His Lordship the Abbot desires the Right Reverend Prior to answer truly, placing his hand on the Gospels, whether or not he had himself heard such noises.

"The Right Reverend Prior denies ever having heard anything similar. But, being threatened with further proceedings (the rack?)

---

* "What is commonly referred to as flutes and pipes."

acknowledges that he had frequently been told of these noises by the Warder on duty.

"*Query:* Whether the Right Reverend Prior was ever told anything else by the Warder?

"*Answer:* Yes; but under the seal of confession. The last Warder, moreover, the one killed by lightning, had been a reprobate priest, having committed the greatest crimes and obliged to take asylum, whom the Prior had kept there on account of the difficulty of finding a man sufficiently courageous for the office.

"*Query:* Whether the Prior has ever questioned previous Warders?

"*Answer:* That the Warders were bound to reveal only in confession whatever they had heard; that the Prior's predecessors had kept the seal of confession inviolate, and that though unworthy, the Prior himself desired to do alike.

"*Query:* What had become of the Warder who had been found in a swoon after the occurrences of Halloween?

"*Answer:* That the Prior does not know. The Warder was crazy. The Prior believes he was secluded for that reason."

A disagreeable surprise had been, apparently, arranged for Prior Urbain de Luc. For the next entry states that:

"Item. By order of His Magnificence the Lord Abbot, certain servants of the Lord Abbot aforesaid introduce Robert Baudouin, priest, once Warder in the Church of the Holy Cross, who has been kept ten years in prison by His Reverence the Prior, as being of unsound mind. Witness manifests great terror on finding himself in the presence of their Lordships, and particularly of His Reverence the Prior. And refuses to speak, hiding his face in his hands and uttering shrieks. Being comforted with kind words by those present, nay even most graciously by My Lord the Abbot himself, *etiam** threatened with the rack if he continue obdurate, this witness deposes as follows, not without much lamentation, shrieking and senseless jabber after the manner of mad men.

"*Query:* Can he remember what happened on the Vigil of All Saints, in the church of Dunes, before he swooned on the floor of the church?

---

* "And."

"*Answer:* He cannot. It would be sin to speak of such things before great spiritual Lords. Moreover he is but an ignorant man, and also mad. Moreover his hunger is great.

"Being given white bread from the Lord Abbot's own table, witness is again cross-questioned.

"*Query:* What can he remember of the events of the Vigil of All Saints?

"*Answer:* Thinks he was not always mad. Thinks he has not always been in prison. Thinks he once went in a boat on sea, etc.

"*Query:* Does witness think he has ever been in the church of Dunes?

"*Answer:* Cannot remember. But is sure that he was not always in prison.

"*Query:* Has witness ever heard anything like that? (My Lord the Abbot having secretly ordered that a certain fool in his service, an excellent musician, should suddenly play the pipes behind the arras.*)

"At which sound witness began to tremble and sob and fall on his knees, and catch hold of the robe even of My Lord the Abbot, hiding his head therein.

"*Query:* Wherefore does he feel such terror, being in the fatherly presence of so clement a prince as the Lord Abbot?

"*Answer:* That witness cannot stand that piping any longer. That it freezes his blood. That he has told the Prior many times that he will not remain any longer in the warder's chamber. That he is afraid for his life. That he dare not make the sign of the Cross nor say his prayers for fear of the Great Wild Man. That the Great Wild Man took the Cross and broke it in two and played at quoits† with it in the nave. That all the wolves trooped down from the roof howling, and danced on their hind legs while the Great Wild Man played the pipes on the high altar. That witness had surrounded himself with a hedge of little crosses, made of broken rye straw, to keep off the Great Wild Man from the warder's chamber. Ah—ah—ah! He is piping again! The wolves are howling! He is raising the tempest.

"*Item:* That no further information can be extracted from witness, who falls on the floor like one possessed and has to be removed from the presence of His Lordship the Abbot and His Reverence the Prior.

---

* A rich tapestry.

† A game in which a ring is thrown onto an upright peg.

III

Here the minutes of the inquest break off. Did those great spiritual dignitaries ever get to learn more about the terrible doings in the church of Dunes? Did they ever guess at their cause?

"For there was a cause," said the Antiquary, folding his spectacles after reading me these notes, "or more strictly the cause still exists. And you will understand, though those learned priests of six centuries ago could not."

And rising, he fetched a key from a shelf and preceded me into the yard of his house, situated on the Nys, a mile below Dunes.

Between the low steadings one saw the salt marsh, lilac with sea lavender, the Island of Birds, a great sandbank at the mouth of the Nys, where every kind of sea fowl gathers; and beyond, the angry white-crested sea under an angry orange afterglow. On the other side, inland, and appearing above the farm roofs, stood the church of Dunes, its pointed belfry and jagged outlines of gables and buttresses and gargoyles and wind-warped pines black against the easterly sky of ominous livid red.

"I told you," said the Antiquary, stopping with the key in the lock of a big outhouse, "that there had been a *substitution;* that the crucifix at present at Dunes is not the one miraculously cast up by the storm of 1195. I believe the present one may be identified as a life-size statue, for which a receipt exists in the archives of Arras, furnished to the Abbot of St. Loup by Estienne Le Mas and Guillaume Pernel, stonemasons, in the year 1299, that is to say the year of the inquest and of the cessation of all supernatural occurrences at Dunes. As to the original effigy, you shall see it and understand everything."

The Antiquary opened the door of a sloping, vaulted passage, lit a lantern and led the way. It was evidently the cellar of some mediæval building; and a scent of wine, of damp wood, and of fir branches from innumerable stacked up faggots, filled the darkness among thickset columns.

"Here," said the Antiquary, raising his lantern, "he was buried beneath this vault and they had run an iron stake through his middle, like a vampire, to prevent his rising."

The Effigy was erect against the dark wall, surrounded by brush-wood. It was more than life-size, nude, the arms broken off at the shoulders, the head, with stubbly beard and clotted hair, drawn up with an effort, the face contracted with agony; the muscles dragged as of one hanging crucified, the feet bound together with a rope. The figure was familiar to me in various galleries. I came forward to examine the ear: it was leaf-shaped.

"Ah, you have understood the whole mystery," said the Antiquary.

"I have understood," I answered, not knowing how far his thought really went, "that this supposed statue of Christ is an antique satyr, a Marsyas awaiting his punishment."

The Antiquary nodded. "Exactly," he said drily, "that is the whole explanation. Only I think the Abbot and the Prior were not so wrong to drive the iron stake through him when they removed him from the church."

Gertrude Atherton (1857–1948) began to pursue writing at twenty-five, partly in response to an unhappy marriage. After she was widowed at thrity and left with a daughter to support, she became a prolific and successful author whose acquaintances included Ambrose Bierce and Kenneth Rexroth. Her most famous novels were *Mrs. Belfame* (1916) and *Black Oxen* (1923), both of which were adapted into silent movies. As an author, she was sometimes compared to Edith Wharton and Helen Hunt Jackson; privately, she was a suffragist and an anti-Communist. "The Dead and the Countess" originally appeared in the August 1902 issue of *The Smart Set*; it was later reprinted in the collection *The Bell in the Fog and Other Stories* (1905), which was dedicated to one of Atherton's literary heroes, Henry James.

The Dead and the Countess

by Gertrude Atherton

I t was an old cemetery, and they had been long dead. Those who died nowadays were put in the new burying-place on the hill, close to the Bois d'Amour* and within sound of the bells that called the living to mass. But the little church where the mass was celebrated stood faithfully beside the older dead; a new church, indeed, had not been built in that forgotten corner of Finisterre† for centuries, not since the calvary on its pile of stones had been raised in the tiny square, surrounded then, as now, perhaps, by gray naked cottages; not since the castle with its round tower, down on

---

* The "Wood of Love" is on the Île-Tudy, in Finistère.

† Finistère ("Land's End") is a French department in the northwest of the region of Brittany, the northwesternmost part of the country.

the river, had been erected for the Counts of Croisac. But the stone walls enclosing that ancient cemetery had been kept in good repair, and there were no weeds within, nor toppling headstones. It looked cold and gray and desolate, like all the cemeteries of Brittany, but it was made hideous neither by tawdry gewgaws nor the license of time.

And sometimes it was close to a picture of beauty. When the village celebrated its yearly *pardon*,* a great procession came out of the church—priests in glittering robes, young men in their gala costume of black and silver, holding flashing standards aloft, and many maidens in flapping white head-dress and collar, black frocks and aprons flaunting with ribbons and lace. They marched, chanting, down the road beside the wall of the cemetery, where lay the generations that in their day had held the banners and chanted the service of the *pardon*. For the dead were peasants and priests—the Croisacs had their burying-place in a hollow of the hills behind the castle—old men and women who had wept and died for the fishermen that had gone to the *grande pêche*† and returned no more, and now and again a child, slept there. Those who walked past the dead at the *pardon*, or after the marriage ceremony, or took part in any one of the minor religious festivals with which the Catholic village enlivens its existence—all, young and old, looked grave and sad. For the women from childhood know that their lot is to wait and dread and weep, and the men that the ocean is treacherous and cruel, but that bread can be wrung from no other master. Therefore the living have little sympathy for the dead who have laid down their crushing burden; and the dead under their stones slumber contentedly enough. There is no envy among them for the young who wander at evening and pledge their troth in the Bois d'Amour, only pity for the groups of women who wash their linen in the creek that flows to the river. They look like pictures in the green quiet book of nature, these women, in their glistening white head-gear and deep collars; but the dead know better than to envy them, and the women—and the lovers—know better than to pity the dead.

---

* A Catholic festival of penance, usually accompanied by a procession. This is a Breton tradition, though it is similar to a St. Patrick's Day parade.

† Literally, the "great fishing-place," a proverbial heavenly place of eternal rest.

The dead lay at rest in their boxes and thanked God they were quiet and had found everlasting peace.

And one day even this, for which they had patiently endured life, was taken from them.

The village was picturesque and there was none quite like it, even in Finisterre. Artists discovered it and made it famous. After the artists followed the tourists, and the old creaking *diligence* became an absurdity. Brittany was the fashion for three months of the year, and wherever there is fashion there is at least one railway. The one built to satisfy the thousands who wished to visit the wild, sad beauties of the west of France was laid along the road beside the little cemetery of this tale.

It takes a long while to awaken the dead. These heard neither the voluble working-men nor even the first snort of the engine. And, of course, they neither heard nor knew of the pleadings of the old priest that the line should be laid elsewhere. One night he came out into the old cemetery and sat on a grave and wept. For he loved his dead and felt it to be a tragic pity that the greed of money, and the fever of travel, and the petty ambitions of men whose place was in the great cities where such ambitions were born, should shatter forever the holy calm of those who had suffered so much on earth. He had known many of them in life, for he was very old; and although he believed, like all good Catholics, in heaven and purgatory and hell, yet he always saw his friends as he had buried them, peacefully asleep in their coffins, the souls lying with folded hands like the bodies that held them, patiently awaiting the final call. He would never have told you, this good old priest, that he believed heaven to be a great echoing palace in which God and the archangels dwelt alone waiting for that great day when the elected dead should rise and enter the Presence together, for he was a simple old man who had read and thought little; but he had a zigzag of fancy in his humble mind, and he saw his friends and his ancestors' friends as I have related to you, soul and body in the deep undreaming sleep of death, but sleep, not a rotted body deserted by its affrighted mate; and to all who sleep there comes, sooner or later, the time of awakening.

He knew that they had slept through the wild storms that rage on the coast of Finisterre, when ships are flung on the rocks and trees crash down in the Bois d'Amour. He knew that the soft, slow chantings of the *pardon* never struck a chord in those frozen memories, meagre and monotonous as their store had been; nor the bagpipes down in the open village hall—a mere roof on poles—when the bride and her friends danced for three days without a smile on their sad brown faces.

All this the dead had known in life and it could not disturb nor interest them now. But that hideous intruder from modern civilization, a train of cars with a screeching engine, that would shake the earth, which held them and rend the peaceful air with such discordant sounds that neither dead nor living could sleep! His life had been one long unbroken sacrifice, and he sought in vain to imagine one greater, which he would cheerfully assume could this disaster be spared his dead.

But the railway was built, and the first night the train went screaming by, shaking the earth and rattling the windows of the church, he went out and sprinkled every grave with holy-water.

And thereafter, twice a day, at dawn and at night, as the train tore a noisy tunnel in the quiet air, like the plebeian upstart it was, he sprinkled every grave, rising sometimes from a bed of pain, at other times defying wind and rain and hail. And for a while he believed that his holy device had deepened the sleep of his dead, locked them beyond the power of man to awake. But one night he heard them muttering.

It was late. There were but a few stars on a black sky. Not a breath of wind came over the lonely plains beyond, or from the sea. There would be no wrecks to-night, and all the world seemed at peace. The lights were out in the village. One burned in the tower of Croisac, where the young wife of the count lay ill. The priest had been with her when the train thundered by, and she had whispered to him:

"Would that I were on it! Oh, this lonely lonely land! this cold echoing château, with no one to speak to day after day! If it kills me, *mon père*, make him lay me in the cemetery by the road, that twice a day I may hear the train go by—the train that goes to Paris! If they put me down there over the hill, I will shriek in my coffin every night."

The priest had ministered as best he could to the ailing soul of the young noblewoman, with whose like he seldom dealt, and hastened back to his dead. He mused, as he toiled along the dark road with rheumatic legs, on the fact that the woman should have the same fancy as himself.

"If she is really sincere, poor young thing," he thought aloud, "I will forbear to sprinkle holy-water on her grave. For those who suffer while alive should have all they desire after death, and I am afraid the count neglects her. But I pray God that my dead have not heard that monster to-night." And he tucked his gown under his arm and hurriedly told his rosary.

But when he went about among the graves with the holy-water he heard the dead muttering.

"Jean-Marie," said a voice, fumbling among its unused tones for forgotten notes, "art thou ready? Surely that is the last call."

"Nay, nay," rumbled another voice, "that is not the sound of a trumpet, François. That will be sudden and loud and sharp, like the great blasts of the north when they come plunging over the sea from out the awful gorges of Iceland. Dost thou remember them, François? Thank the good God they spared us to die in our beds with our grandchildren about us and only the little wind sighing in the Bois d'Amour. Ah, the poor comrades that died in their manhood, that went to the *grande pêche* once too often! Dost thou remember when the great wave curled round Ignace like his poor wife's arms, and we saw him no more? We clasped each other's hands, for we believed that we should follow, but we lived and went again and again to the *grande pêche*, and died in our beds. *Grâce à Dieu!*"

"Why dost thou think of that now—here in the grave where it matters not, even to the living?"

"I know not; but it was of that night when Ignace went down that I thought as the living breath went out of me. Of what didst thou think as thou layest dying?"

"Of the money I owed to Dominique and could not pay. I sought to ask my son to pay it, but death had come suddenly and I could not speak. God knows how they treat my name to-day in the village of St. Hilaire."

"Thou art forgotten," murmured another voice. "I died forty years after thee and men remember not so long in Finisterre. But thy son was my friend and I remember that he paid the money."

"And my son, what of him? Is he, too, here?"

"Nay; he lies deep in the northern sea. It was his second voyage, and he had returned with a purse for the young wife, the first time. But he returned no more, and she washed in the river for the dames of Croisac, and by-and-by she died. I would have married her, but she said it was enough to lose one husband. I married another, and she grew ten years in every three that I went to the *grande pêche*. Alas for Brittany, she has no youth!"

"And thou? Wert thou an old man when thou camest here?"

"Sixty. My wife came first, like many wives. She lies here. Jeanne!"

"Is't thy voice, my husband? Not the Lord Jesus Christ's? What miracle is this? I thought that terrible sound was the trump of doom."

"It could not be, old Jeanne, for we are still in our graves. When the trump sounds we shall have wings and robes of light, and fly straight up to heaven. Hast thou slept well?"

"Ay! But why are we awakened? Is it time for purgatory? Or have we been there?"

"The good God knows. I remember nothing. Art frightened? Would that I could hold thy hand, as when thou didst slip from life into that long sleep thou didst fear, yet welcome."

"I am frightened, my husband. But it is sweet to hear thy voice, hoarse and hollow as it is from the mould of the grave. Thank the good God thou didst bury me with the rosary in my hands," and she began telling the beads rapidly.

"If God is good," cried François, harshly, and his voice came plainly to the priest's ears, as if the lid of the coffin had rotted, "why are we awakened before our time? What foul fiend was it that thundered and screamed through the frozen avenues of my brain? Has God, perchance, been vanquished and does the Evil One reign in His stead?"

"Tut, tut! Thou blasphemest! God reigns, now and always. It is but a punishment He has laid upon us for the sins of earth."

"Truly, we were punished enough before we descended to the peace of this narrow house. Ah, but it is dark and cold! Shall we lie like this for an eternity, perhaps? On earth we longed for death, but feared the grave. I would that I were alive again, poor and old and alone and in pain. It were better than this. Curse the foul fiend that woke us!"

"Curse not, my son," said a soft voice, and the priest stood up and uncovered and crossed himself, for it was the voice of his aged predecessor. "I cannot tell thee what this is that has rudely shaken us in our graves and freed our spirits of their blessed thraldom, and I like not the consciousness of this narrow house, this load of earth on my tired heart. But it is right, it must be right, or it would not be at all—ah, me!"

For a baby cried softly, hopelessly, and from a grave beyond came a mother's anguished attempt to still it.

"Ah, the good God!" she cried. "I, too, thought it was the great call, and that in a moment I should rise and find my child and go to my Ignace, my Ignace whose bones lie white on the floor of the sea. Will he find them, my father, when the dead shall rise again? To lie here and doubt!—that were worse than life."

"Yes, yes," said the priest; "all will be well, my daughter."

"But all is not well, my father, for my baby cries and is alone in a little box in the ground. If I could claw my way to her with my hands—but my old mother lies between us."

"Tell your beads!" commanded the priest, sternly—"tell your beads, all of you. All ye that have not your beads, say the 'Hail Mary!' one hundred times."

Immediately a rapid, monotonous muttering arose from every lonely chamber of that desecrated ground. All obeyed but the baby, who still moaned with the hopeless grief of deserted children. The living priest knew that they would talk no more that night, and went into the church to pray till dawn. He was sick with horror and terror, but not for himself. When the sky was pink and the air full of the sweet scents of morning, and a piercing scream tore a rent in the early silences, he hastened out and sprinkled his graves with a double allowance of holy-water. The train rattled by with two short derisive shrieks, and before the earth had ceased to tremble the priest laid his ear to the ground. Alas, they were still awake!

"The fiend is on the wing again," said Jean-Marie; "but as he passed I felt as if the finger of God touched my brow. It can do us no harm."

"I, too, felt that heavenly caress!" exclaimed the old priest. "And I!" "And I!" "And I!" came from every grave but the baby's.

The priest of earth, deeply thankful that his simple device had comforted them, went rapidly down the road to the castle. He forgot that he had not broken his fast nor slept. The count was one of the directors of the railroad, and to him he would make a final appeal.

It was early, but no one slept at Croisac. The young countess was dead. A great bishop had arrived in the night and administered extreme unction. The priest hopefully asked if he might venture into the presence of the bishop. After a long wait in the kitchen, he was told that he could speak with *Monsieur l'Évêque.** He followed the servant up the wide spiral stair of the tower, and from its twenty-eighth step entered a room hung with purple cloth stamped with golden fleurs-de-lis. The bishop lay six feet above the floor on one of the splendid carved cabinet beds that are built against the walls in Brittany. Heavy curtains shaded his cold white face. The priest, who was small and bowed, felt immeasurably below that august presence, and sought for words.

"What is it, my son?" asked the bishop, in his cold weary voice. "Is the matter so pressing? I am very tired."

Brokenly, nervously, the priest told his story, and as he strove to convey the tragedy of the tormented dead he not only felt the poverty of his expression—for he was little used to narrative—but the torturing thought assailed him that what he said sounded wild and unnatural, real as it was to him. But he was not prepared for its effect on the bishop. He was standing in the middle of the room, whose gloom was softened and gilded by the waxen lights of a huge candelabra; his eyes, which had wandered unseeingly from one massive piece of carved furniture to another, suddenly lit on the bed, and he stopped abruptly, his tongue rolling out. The bishop was sitting up, livid with wrath.

"And this was thy matter of life and death, thou prating madman!" he thundered. "For this string of foolish lies I am kept from my rest, as if I were another old lunatic like thyself! Thou art not fit to be a priest and have the care of souls. To-morrow—"

But the priest had fled, wringing his hands.

As he stumbled down the winding stair he ran straight into the arms of the count. Monsieur de Croisac had just closed a door behind him. He opened it, and, leading the priest into the room, pointed to his dead countess, who lay high up against the wall, her hands clasped, unmindful for evermore of the six feet of carved cupids and lilies that upheld her. On

---

* *L'Eveque* means "the bishop."

high pedestals at head and foot of her magnificent couch the pale flames rose from tarnished golden candlesticks. The blue hangings of the room, with their white fleurs-de-lis, were faded, like the rugs on the old dim floor; for the splendor of the Croisacs had departed with the Bourbons.* The count lived in the old château because he must; but he reflected bitterly to-night that if he had made the mistake of bringing a young girl to it, there were several things he might have done to save her from despair and death.

"Pray for her," he said to the priest. "And you will bury her in the old cemetery. It was her last request."

He went out, and the priest sank on his knees and mumbled his prayers for the dead. But his eyes wandered to the high narrow windows through which the countess had stared for hours and days, stared at the fishermen sailing north for the *grande pêche*, followed along the shore of the river by wives and mothers, until their boats were caught in the great waves of the ocean beyond; often at naught more animate than the dark flood, the wooded banks, the ruins, the rain driving like needles through the water. The priest had eaten nothing since his meagre breakfast at twelve the day before, and his imagination was active. He wondered if the soul up there rejoiced in the death of the beautiful restless body, the passionate brooding mind. He could not see her face from where he knelt, only the waxen hands clasping a crucifix. He wondered if the face were peaceful in death, or peevish and angry as when he had seen it last. If the great change had smoothed and sealed it, then perhaps the soul would sink deep under the dark waters, grateful for oblivion, and that cursed train could not awaken it for years to come. Curiosity succeeded wonder. He cut his prayers short, got to his weary swollen feet and pushed a chair to the bed. He mounted it and his face was close to the dead woman's. Alas! it was not peaceful. It was stamped with the tragedy of a bitter renunciation. After all, she had been young, and at the last had died unwillingly. There was still a fierce tenseness about the nostrils, and her upper lip was curled as if her last word had been an imprecation. But she was very beautiful, despite the emaciation of

---

* Although there are still living descendents of the royal House of Bourbon, this French dynasty is usually thought to have originated in 1272 and have been finally overthrown in the July Revolution of 1830.

her features. Her black hair nearly covered the bed, and her lashes looked too heavy for the sunken cheeks.

"*Pauvre petite!*"* thought the priest. "No, she will not rest, nor would she wish to. I will not sprinkle holy-water on her grave. It is wondrous that monster can give comfort to any one, but if he can, so be it."

He went into the little oratory adjoining the bedroom and prayed more fervently. But when the watchers came an hour later they found him in a stupor, huddled at the foot of the altar.

When he awoke he was in his own bed in his little house beside the church. But it was four days before they would let him rise to go about his duties, and by that time the countess was in her grave.

The old housekeeper left him to take care of himself. He waited eagerly for the night. It was raining thinly, a gray quiet rain that blurred the landscape and soaked the ground in the Bois d'Amour. It was wet about the graves, too; but the priest had given little heed to the elements in his long life of crucified self, and as he heard the remote echo of the evening train he hastened out with his holy-water and had sprinkled every grave but one when the train sped by.

Then he knelt and listened eagerly. It was five days since he had knelt there last. Perhaps they had sunk again to rest. In a moment he wrung his hands and raised them to heaven. All the earth beneath him was filled with lamentation. They wailed for mercy, for peace, for rest; they cursed the foul fiend who had shattered the locks of death; and among the voices of men and children the priest distinguished the quavering notes of his aged predecessor; not cursing, but praying with bitter entreaty. The baby was screaming with the accents of mortal terror and its mother was too frantic to care.

"Alas," cried the voice of Jean-Marie, "that they never told us what purgatory was like! What do the priests know? When we were threatened with punishment of our sins not a hint did we have of this. To sleep for a few hours, haunted with the moment of awakening! Then a cruel insult from the earth that is tired of us, and the orchestra of hell. Again! and again! and again! Oh God! How long? How long?"

---

* "Poor little thing!"

The priest stumbled to his feet and ran over graves and paths to the mound above the countess. There he would hear a voice praising the monster of night and dawn, a note of content in this terrible chorus of despair, which he believed would drive him mad. He vowed that on the morrow he would move his dead, if he had to un-bury them with his own hands and carry them up the hill to graves of his own making.

For a moment he heard no sound. He knelt and laid his ear to the grave, then pressed it more closely and held his breath. A long rumbling moan reached it, then another and another. But there were no words.

"Is she moaning in sympathy with my poor friends?" he thought; "or have they terrified her? Why does she not speak to them? Perhaps they would forget their plight were she to tell them of the world they have left so long. But it was not their world. Perhaps that it is which distresses her, for she will be lonelier here than on earth. Ah!"

A sharp horrified cry pierced to his ears, then a gasping shriek, and another; all dying away in a dreadful smothered rumble.

The priest rose and wrung his hands, looking to the wet skies for inspiration.

"Alas!" he sobbed, "she is not content. She has made a terrible mistake. She would rest in the deep sweet peace of death, and that monster of iron and fire and the frantic dead about her are tormenting a soul so tormented in life. There may be rest for her in the vault behind the castle, but not here. I know, and I shall do my duty—now, at once."

He gathered his robes about him and ran as fast as his old legs and rheumatic feet would take him towards the château, whose lights gleamed through the rain. On the bank of the river he met a fisherman and begged to be taken by boat. The fisherman wondered, but picked the priest up in his strong arms, lowered him into the boat, and rowed swiftly towards the château. When they landed he made fast.

"I will wait for you in the kitchen, my father," he said; and the priest blessed him and hurried up to the castle.

Once more he entered through the door of the great kitchen, with its blue tiles, its glittering brass and bronze warming-pans which had comforted nobles and monarchs in the days of Croisac splendor. He sank into a chair beside the stove while a maid hastened to the count. She returned while the priest was still shivering, and announced that her master would see his holy visitor in the library.

It was a dreary room where the count sat waiting for the priest, and it smelled of musty calf, for the books on the shelves were old. A few novels and newspapers lay on the heavy table, a fire burned on the andirons, but the paper on the wall was very dark and the fleurs-de-lis were tarnished and dull. The count, when at home, divided his time between this library and the water, when he could not chase the boar or the stag in the forests. But he often went to Paris, where he could afford the life of a bachelor in a wing of his great hotel; he had known too much of the extravagance of women to give his wife the key of the faded salons. He had loved the beautiful girl when he married her, but her repinings and bitter discontent had alienated him, and during the past year he had held himself aloof from her in sullen resentment. Too late he understood, and dreamed passionately of atonement. She had been a high-spirited brilliant eager creature, and her unsatisfied mind had dwelt constantly on the world she had vividly enjoyed for one year. And he had given her so little in return!

He rose as the priest entered, and bowed low. The visit bored him, but the good old priest commanded his respect; moreover, he had performed many offices and rites in his family. He moved a chair towards his guest, but the old man shook his head and nervously twisted his hands together.

"Alas, *monsieur le comte*," he said, "it may be that you, too, will tell me that I am an old lunatic, as did *Monsieur l'Évêque*. Yet I must speak, even if you tell your servants to fling me out of the château."

The count had started slightly. He recalled certain acid comments of the bishop, followed by a statement that a young *curé* should be sent, gently to supersede the old priest, who was in his dotage. But he replied suavely:

"You know, my father, that no one in this castle will ever show you disrespect. Say what you wish; have no fear. But will you not sit down? I am very tired."

The priest took the chair and fixed his eyes appealingly on the count.

"It is this, monsieur." He spoke rapidly, lest his courage should go. "That terrible train, with its brute of iron and live coals and foul smoke and screeching throat, has awakened my dead. I guarded them with holy-water and they heard it not, until one night when I missed—I was with madame as the train shrieked by shaking the nails out of the coffins. I hurried back, but the mischief was done, the dead were awake, the dear sleep of eternity was shattered. They thought it was the last trump and wondered why they still were in their graves. But they talked together and it was not so bad at the first. But now they are frantic. They are in hell, and I have come to beseech you to see that they are moved far up on the hill. Ah, think, think, monsieur, what it is to have the last long sleep of the grave so rudely disturbed—the sleep for which we live and endure so patiently!"

He stopped abruptly and caught his breath. The count had listened without change of countenance, convinced that he was facing a madman. But the farce wearied him, and involuntarily his hand had moved towards a bell on the table.

"Ah, monsieur, not yet! not yet!" panted the priest. "It is of the countess I came to speak. I had forgotten. She told me she wished to lie there and listen to the train go by to Paris, so I sprinkled no holy-water on her grave. But she, too, is wretched and horror-stricken, monsieur. She moans and screams. Her coffin is new and strong, and I cannot hear her words, but I have heard those frightful sounds from her grave to-night, monsieur; I swear it on the cross. Ah, monsieur, thou dost believe me at last!"

For the count, as white as the woman had been in her coffin, and shaking from head to foot, had staggered from his chair and was staring at the priest as if he saw the ghost of his countess.

"You heard—?" he gasped.

"She is not at peace, monsieur. She moans and shrieks in a terrible, smothered way, as if a hand were on her mouth—"

But he had uttered the last of his words. The count had suddenly recovered himself and dashed from the room. The priest passed his hand across his forehead and sank slowly to the floor.

"He will see that I spoke the truth," he thought, as he fell asleep, "and to-morrow he will intercede for my poor friends."

The priest lies high on the hill where no train will ever disturb him, and his old comrades of the violated cemetery are close about him. For the

Count and Countess of Croisac, who adore his memory, hastened to give him in death what he most had desired in the last of his life. And with them all things are well, for a man, too, may be born again, and without descending into the grave.

Published frequently as **Josephine Dodge Daskam, Bacon** (1876–1961) wrote juvenile mysteries, poetry, and more serious works, including dozens of short stories. Born in Connecticut, she attended Smith College, graduating in 1898, a few years after Georgia Wood Pangborn, and her first work of fiction, based on her collegiate experiences, was titled simply *Smith College Stories* (1900). Bacon was prolific, publishing more than forty books during her lifetime and contributing to numerous magazines. Like many writers of her era, she refused to be limited to a single genre, and the following is not exactly a ghost story. It first appeared in *Harper's Monthly* for August 1909 and was included in her 1913 collection *The Strange Cases of Dr. Stanchon*.

The Children

by Josephine Daskam Bacon

I t all came over me, as you might say, when I began to tell the new housemaid about the work. Not that I hadn't known before, of course, what a queer sort of life was led in that house; it was hard enough the first months, goodness knows. But then, a body can get used to anything. And there was no harm in it—I'll swear that to my dying day! Although a lie's a lie, any way you put it, and if all I've told—but I'll let you judge for yourself.

As I say, it was when I began to break Margaret in, that it all came over me, and I looked about me, in a way of speaking, for how I should put it to her. She'd been house-parlor-maid in a big establishment in the country and knew what was expected of her well enough, and I saw from the first she'd fit in nicely with us; a steady, quiet girl, like the best of the

Scotch, looking to save her wages, and get to be housekeeper herself, some day, perhaps.

But when Hodges brought the tray with the porringers* on it and the silver mug, for me to see, and said, "I suppose this young lady'll take these up, Miss Umbleby?" and when Margaret looked surprised and said, "I didn't know there were children in the family—am I supposed to wait on them, too?"—then, as I say, it all came over me, and for the first time in five years I really saw where I stood, like.

I stared at Hodges and then at the girl, and the tray nearly went down amongst us.

"Do you mean to say you haven't told her, Sarah?" says Hodges (and that was the first time that ever he called me by my given name).

"She's told me nothing," Margaret answers rather short, "and if it's invalid children or feeble-minded, I take it most unkind, Miss Umbleby, for I've never cared for that sort of thing, and could have had my twenty-five dollars a month this long time, if I'd wanted to go out as nurse."

"Take the tray up this time, yourself, Mr. Hodges, please," I said, "and I'll have a little talk with Margaret," and I sat down and smoothed my black silk skirt (I always wore black silk of an afternoon) nervously enough, I'll be bound.

The five years rolled away like yesterday—as they do now—as they do now—

I saw myself, in my mind's eye, new to the place, and inclined to feel strange, as I always did when I made a change, though I was twenty-five and no chicken, but rather more settled than most, having had my troubles early and got over them. I'd just left my place—chambermaid and seamstress—in a big city house, and though it was September, I was looking out for the country, for I was mortal tired of the noise and late hours and excitement that I saw ahead of me. It was parties and balls every night and me sitting up to undress the young ladies, for they kept no maid, like so many rich Americans, and yet some one must do for them. There was no housekeeper either, and the mistress was not very strong and we had to use our own responsibility more than I liked—for I wasn't paid for that, do you see, and that's what they forget in this country.

---

* Small bowls, usually for soup or stew.

"I think I've got you suited at last, Sarah," the head of the office had said to me, "a nice, quiet place in the country, good pay and light work, but everything as it should be, you understand. Four in help besides the housekeeper and only one in family. Church within a mile and every other Sunday for yourself."

That was just what I wanted, and I packed my box thankfully and left New York for good, I hoped, and I got my wish, for I've never seen the inside of it since.

A middle-aged coachman in good, quiet country livery, met me at the little station, and though he was a still-mouthed fellow and rather reserved, I made out quite a little idea of the place on the way. The mistress, Mrs. Childress, was a young widow, deep in her mourning, so there was no company. The housekeeper was her old nurse, who had brought her up. John, who drove me, was coachman-gardener, and the cook was his wife—both Catholics. Everything went on very quiet and regular and it was hoped that the new upstairs maid wouldn't be one for excitement and gaiety. The inside man had been valet to Mr. Childress and was much trusted and liked by the family. I could see that old John was a bit jealous in that direction.

We drove in through a black iron gate with cut stone posts and old black iron lanterns on top, and the moment we were inside the gates I began to take a fancy to the place. It wasn't kept up like the places at home, but it was neat enough to show that things were taken thought for, and the beds of asters and dahlias and marigolds as we got near the house seemed so home-like and bright to me, I could have cried for comfort. Childerstone was the name of the place; it was carved on a big boulder by the side of the entrance, and just as we drove up to the door John stopped to pick some dahlias for the house (being only me in the wagon) and I took my first good look at my home for twenty years afterward.

There was something about it that went to my heart. It was built of grey cut stone in good-sized blocks, square, with two windows each side the hall door. To some it might have seemed cold-looking, but not to me, for one side was all over ivy, and the thickness of the walls and the deep sills looked solid and comfortable after those nasty brown-stone things all glued to each other in the city. It looked old and respectable and settled, like, and the sun, just at going down, struck the windows like fire and the clean panes shone. There was that yellow light over everything and that stillness, with now and then a leaf or so dropping quietly down, that makes the fall of the year so pleasant, to my mind.

The house stood in beeches and the trunks of them were grey like the house and the leaves all light lemon-coloured, like the sky, and that's the way I always think of Childerstone—grey and yellow and clean and still. Just a few rooks (you call them crows here), went over the house, and except for their cry as they flew, there wasn't a sound about the place. I can see how others might have found it sad, but it never seemed so to me.

John set me down at the servants' entrance and there, before ever I'd got properly into the hall, the strangeness began. The cook in her check apron was kneeling on the floor in front of the big French range with the tears streaming down her face, working over her rosary beads and gabbling to drive you crazy. Over her stood a youngish but severe-appearing man in a white linen coat like a ship's steward, trying to get her up.

"Come, Katey," he was saying, "come, woman, up with you and help—she'll do no harm, the poor soul! Look after her, now, and I'll send for the doctor and see to madam—it's only a fit, most like!"

Then he saw me and ran forward to give a hand to my box.

"You're the chambermaid, Miss, I'm sure," he said. "I'm sorry to say you'll find us a bit upset. The housekeeper's down with a stroke of some sort and the madam's none too strong herself. Are you much of a hand to look after the sick?"

"I'm not so clumsy as some," I said. "Let me see her," and so we left the cook to her prayers and he carried my box to my room.

I got into a print dress and apron and went to the housekeeper's room. She was an elderly person and it looked to me as if she was in her last sickness. She didn't know any one and so I was as good as another, and I had her tidy and comfortable in bed by the time the doctor came. He said she would need watching through the night and left some medicine, but I could see he had little hope for her. I made up a bed in the room and all that night she chattered and muttered and took me for different ones, according as her fever went and came. Towards morning she got quiet, and as I thought, sensible again.

"Are you a nurse?" she says to me.

"Yes, Mrs. Shipman, be still and rest," I told her, to soothe her.

"I'm glad the children are sent away," she went on, after a bit. "'Twould break their mother's heart if they got the fever. Are the toys packed?"

"Yes, yes," I answered, "all packed and sent."

"Be sure there's enough frocks for Master Robertson," she begged me. "He's so hard on them and his aunties are so particular. And my baby must have her woolly rabbit at night or her darling heart will be just broken!"

"The rabbit is packed," I said, "and I saw to the frocks myself."

There's but one way with the sick when they're like that, and that's to humour them, you see. So she slept and I got a little nap for myself. I was glad the children were away by next morning, for she was worse, the cook lost her head, and managed to break the range so that the water-back* leaked and John and Hodges were mopping and mending all day. The madam herself had a bad turn and the doctor (a New York doctor for madam, you may be sure!) brought out a handsome, dark woman, the trained hospital nurse, with him. Madam wasn't allowed to know how bad her old nurse was.

So it turned out that I'd been a week in the house without ever seeing my mistress. The nurse and I would meet on the stairs and chat a little, evenings, and once I took a turn in the grounds with her. She was a sensible sort of girl, not a bit above herself, as our English nursing-sisters are, sometimes, but very businesslike, as they say, and a good, brisk way with her. She saw a lot more than she spoke of, Miss Jessop did, I'll warrant!

"It's a good thing the children are sent away," I said. "They always add to the bother when there's sickness."

"Why, are there children?" says she.

"Oh, yes, a boy and a girl," I answered, "poor old Mrs. Shipman is forever talking about them. She thinks she's their nurse, it seems, as she was their mother's."

"I wish they were here, then," says she, "for I don't like the looks of my patient at all. She doesn't speak seven words a day, and there's really little or nothing the matter with her, that I can see. She's nervous and she's low and she wants cheering, that's all. I wonder the doctor doesn't see it."

---

* A reservoir at the back of a stove or range, the heat of which would keep the water hot.

That night, after both patients were settled, she came up to my room and took a glance at the old lady, who was going fast.

"Mrs. Childress will soon have to know about this," she said and then, suddenly, "Are you sure about the children, Sarah?"

"Sure about them?" I repeated after her. "In what way, Miss Jessop?"

"That there are any," says she.

"Why, of course," I answered, "Mrs. Shipman talks of nothing else. They're with their aunty, in New Jersey, somewhere. It's a good thing there are some, for from what she says when she's rambling, the house and all the property would go out of the family otherwise. It's been five generations in the Childress family, but the nearest now is a cousin who married a Jew, and the family hate her for it. But Master Robertson makes it all safe, Mrs. Shipman says."

"That's a queer thing," said she. "I took in a dear little picture of the boy and girl this afternoon, to cheer her up a bit, and told her to try to think they were the real ones, who'd soon be with her, for that matter, and so happy to see their dear mamma, and she went white as a sheet and fainted in my arms. Of course, I didn't refer to it again. She's quiet now, holding the picture, but I feared they were dead and you hadn't known."

"Oh, no," said I. "I'm sure not," and then I remembered that I'd been told there was but one in family. However, that's often said when there's a nurse to take care of small children (though it's not quite fair, perhaps), and I was certain of the children, anyway, for there were toys all about Mrs. Shipman's room and some seed-cookies and "animal-crackers," as they call those odd little biscuits, in a tin on her mantel.

However, we were soon to learn something that made me, at least, all the more curious. The doctor came that morning and told Miss Jessop that her services would be no longer required, after he had seen her patient.

"Mrs. Childress is perfectly recovered," he said, "and she has unfortunately conceived a grudge against you, my dear girl. I need you, anyway, in town. Poor old Shipman can't last the night now, and I want all that business disposed of very quietly. I have decided not to tell Mrs. Childress until it is all over and the funeral done with. She is in a very morbid state, and as I knew her husband well I have taken this step on my own responsibility. Hodges seems perfectly able to run things, and to tell the truth, it would do your mistress far more good to attend to that herself," he said, turning to me.

"It would be a good thing for the poor woman to have some one about her, Dr. Stanchon," the nurse put in quietly. "If there were children in the house, now—"

"Children!" he cried, pulling himself up and staring at her. "Did you speak to her about them? Then that accounts for it! I should have warned you."

"Then they did die?" she asked him. "That's what I thought."

"I'm afraid not," he said, shaking his head with a queer sort of sad little smile. "I forgot you were strange here. Why, Miss Jessop, didn't you know that—"

"Excuse me, sir, but there's no sign of your mare about—did you tie her?" says Hodges, coming in in a great hurry, and the doctor swore and ran off and I never heard the end of the sentence.

Well, I'm running on too long with these little odds and ends, as I'm sure Margaret felt when I started telling her all about it. The truth is I dreaded then, just as I dread now, to get at the real story and look our conduct straight in the face. But I'll get on more quickly now.

Old Mrs. Shipman died very quiet in her sleep and madam wasn't told, which I didn't half like. The doctor was called out of those parts to attend on his father, very suddenly, and Hodges managed the funeral and all. It was plain to see he was a very trusty, silent fellow, devoted to the family. I took as much off him as I could, and I was dusting the drawing-room the day of the funeral, when I happened to pick up a photograph in a silver frame of the same little fellow in the picture the nurse had shown me—a dear little boy in short kilts.

"That's Master Robertson, isn't it?" I said, very carelessly, not looking at him—I will own I was curious. He gave a start.

"Yes—yes, certainly, that's Master Robertson—if you choose to put it that way," he said, and I saw him put his hand up to his eyes and his mouth twitched and he left the room.

I didn't question him again, naturally; he was a hard man to cross and very haughty, was William Hodges, and no one in the house but respected him.

That day I saw Mrs. Childress for the first time. She was a sweet, pretty thing, about my own age, but younger looking, fair, with grey eyes. She was in heavy crêpe and her face all fallen and saddened like, with grief and hopelessness—I felt for her from the moment I saw her. And all the more that I'd made up my mind what her trouble was: I thought that the children were idiots, maybe, or feeble-minded, anyhow, and so the property would go to the Jew in the end and that his family were hating her for it! Folly, of course, but women will have fancies, and that seemed to fit in with all I'd heard.

She'd been told that Shipman was away with some light, infectious fever, and she took it very mildly, and said there was no need to get any one in her place, at present.

"Hodges will attend to everything," she said, in her pretty, tired way; "not that there's much to do—for one poor woman."

"Things may mend, ma'am, and you'll feel more like having some friends about you, most likely, later on," I said, to cheer her a bit.

She shook her head sadly.

"No, no, Sarah—if I can't have my own about me, I'll have no others," she said, and I thought I saw what she meant and said no more.

That night the doctor and the legal gentleman that looked after the family affairs were with us and my mistress kept them for dinner. I helped Hodges with the serving and was in the butler's pantry after Mrs. Childress had left them with their coffee and cigars, and as Hodges had left the door ajar I couldn't help catching a bit of the talk now and then.

"The worst of it is this trouble about the children," said the doctor. "She will grieve herself into a decline, I'm afraid."

"I suppose there's no hope?" said the other gentleman.

"No hope?" the doctor burst out. "Why, man, Robertson's been dead six months!"

"To be sure—I'd forgotten it was so long. Well, well, it's too bad, too bad," and Hodges came back and closed the door.

I must say I was thoroughly put out with the doctor. Why should he have told me a lie? And it was mostly from that that I deliberately disobeyed him that night, for I knew from the way he had spoken to the nurse that he didn't wish the children mentioned. But I couldn't help it, for when I came to her room to see if I could help her, she was sitting in her black bedroom gown with her long hair in two braids, crying over the children's picture. "Hush, hush, ma'am," I said, kneeling by her and soothing her head, "if they were here, you may be sure they wouldn't wish it."

"Who? Who?" she answers me, quite wild, but not angry at all. I saw this and spoke it out boldly, for it was plain that she liked me.

"Your children, ma'am," I said, softly but very firm, "and you should control yourself and be cheerful and act as if they *were* here—as if it had pleased God to let you have them and not *Himself*!"

Such a look as she gave me! But soon she seemed to melt, like, and put out her arm over my shoulders.

"What a beautiful way to put it, Sarah!" says she, in a dreamy kind of way. "Do you really think God has them—somewhere?"

"Why, of course, ma'am," said I, shocked in good earnest. "Who else?"

"Then you think I might love them, just as if—just as if—" here she began to sob.

"Why, Mrs. Childress," I said, "where is your belief? That's all that's left to mothers. I know, for I've lost two, and their father to blame for it, which you need never say," I told her.

She patted my shoulder very kindly. "But oh, Sarah, if only they *were* here!" she cried, "really, really here!"

"I know, I know," I said, "it's very hard. But try to think it, ma'am—it helped me for weeks. Think they're in the room next you, here, and you'll sleep better for it."

"Shall I?" she whispered, gripping my hand hard. "I believe I would—how well you understand me, Sarah! And will you help me to believe it?"

I saw she was feverish and I knew what it means to get one good refreshing night without crying, and so I said, "Of course I will, ma'am; see, I'll open the door into the next room and you can fancy them in their cribs, and I'll sleep in there as if it was to look after them, like."

Well, she was naught but a child herself, the poor dear, and she let me get her into bed like a lamb and put her cheek into her hand and went off like a baby. It almost scared me, to see how easy she was to manage, if one did but get hold of the right way. She looked brighter in the morning and as Hodges had told me that Shipman used to do for her, I went in and dressed her—not that I was ever a lady's maid, mind you, but I've always been one to turn my hand easily to anything I had a mind to, and I was growing very fond of my poor lady—and then, I was a little proud, I'll own, of being able to do more for her than her own medical man, who couldn't trust a sensible woman with the truth!

She clung to me all the morning, and after my work was done, I persuaded her to come out for the air. The doctor had ordered it long ago, but she was obstinate, and would scarcely go at all. That day, however, she took a good stroll with me and it brought a bit of colour into her cheeks. Just as we turned toward the house she sat down on a big rock to rest herself, and I saw her lip quiver and her eyes begin to fill. I followed her look and there was a child's swing, hung from two ropes to a low bough. It must have been rotted with the rains, for it looked very old and the board seat was cracked and worn. All around—it hung in a sort of little glade—were small piles of stones and bits of oddments that only children get together, like the little magpies they are.

There's no use to expect any one but a mother or one who's had the constant care of little ones to understand the tears that come to your eyes at a sight like that. What they leave behind is worse than what they take with them; their curls and their fat legs and the kisses they gave you are all shut into the grave, but what they used to play with stays there and mourns them with you.

I saw a wild look come into her eyes, and I determined to quiet her at any cost.

"There, there, ma'am," I said quickly, "'tis only their playthings. Supposing they were there, now, and enjoying them! You go in and take your nap, as the doctor ordered, and leave me behind . . ."

She saw what I meant in a twinkling and the colour jumped into her face again. She turned and hurried in and just as she went out of sight she looked over her shoulder, timid like, and waved her hand—only a bit of a wave, but I saw it.

Under a big stone in front of me, for that part of the grounds was left wild, like a little grove, I saw a rusty tin biscuit box, and as I opened it, curiously, to pass the time, I found it full of little tin platters and cups. Hardly thinking what I did, I arranged them as if laid out for tea, on a flat stone, and left them there. When I went to awaken her for lunch, I started, for some more of those platters were on the table by her bed and a white woolly rabbit and a picture book! She blushed, but I took no notice, and after her luncheon I spied her going quickly back to the little grove.

"Madam's taking a turn for the better, surely," Hodges said to me that afternoon. "She's eating like a Christian now. What have you done to her, Miss Umbleby?" (I went as "Miss" for it's much easier to get a place so.)

"Mr. Hodges," I said, facing him squarely, "the doctors don't know everything. You know as well as I that it's out of nature not to mention children, where they're missed every hour of the day and every day of the month. It's easing the heart that's wanted—not smothering it."

"What d'you mean?" he says, staring at me.

"I mean toys and such like," I answered him, very firm, "and talk of them that's not here to use them, and even pretending that they are, if that will bring peace of mind, Mr. Hodges."

He rubbed his clean shaven chin with his hand.

"Well, well!" he said at last. "Well, well, well! You're a good girl, Miss Umbleby, and a kind one, that's certain. I never thought o' such a thing. Maybe it's all right, though. But who could understand a woman, anyway?"

"That's not much to understand," said I, shortly, and left him staring at me.

She came in late in the afternoon with the rabbit under her arm and there was Mr. Hodges in the drawing-room laying out the tea—we always had everything done as if the master was there, and guests, for the matter of that; she insisted on it. He knew his place as well as any man, but his eye fell on the rabbit and he looked very queer and nearly dropped a cup. She saw it and began to tremble and go white, and it came over me then that now or never was the time to clinch matters or she'd nearly die from shame and I couldn't soothe her any more.

"Perhaps Hodges had better go out and bring in the rest of the toys, ma'am," I says, very careless, not looking at her. "It's coming on for rain. And he can take an umbrella . . . shall he?"

She stiffened up and gave a sort of nod to him.

"Yes, Hodges, go," she said, half in a whisper, and he bit his lip, and swallowed hard and said, "Very good, madam," and went.

Well, after that, you can see how it would be, can't you? One thing led to another, and one time when she was not well for a few days and rather low, I actually got the two little cribs down from the garret and ran up some white draperies for them. She'd hardly let me leave her, and indeed there was not so much work that I couldn't manage very well. She gave all her orders through me and I was well pleased to do for her and let Mr. Hodges manage things, which he did better than poor old Shipman, I'll be bound. By the time we told her about Shipman's death, she took it very easy—indeed, I think, she'd have minded nothing by that time, she had grown so calm and almost healthy.

Mr. Hodges would never catch my eye and I never talked private any more with him, but that was the only sign he didn't approve, and he never spoke for about a month, but joined in with me by little and little and never said a word but to shrug his shoulders when I ordered up a tray with porringers on it for the nursery (she had a bad cold and got restless and grieving). I left her in the nursery with the tray and went out to him, for I saw he wished to speak to me at last.

"Dr. Stanchon would think well of this, if he was here. Is that your idea, Miss Umbleby?" he said to me, very dry. (The doctor had never come back, but gone to be head of a big asylum out in the west.)

"I'm sure I don't know, Mr. Hodges," I answered. "I think any doctor couldn't but be glad to see her gaining every day, and when she feels up to it and guests begin to come again, she'll get willing to see them and forget the loss of the poor little things."

"The loss of *what*?" says he, frowning at me.

"Why, the children," I answered.

"What children?"

"Master Robertson, of course, and Miss Winifred," I said, quite vexed with his obstinacy. (I had asked her once if the baby was named after her and she nodded and went away quickly.)

"See here, my girl," says he, "there's no good keeping this up for my benefit. *I'm* not going into a decline, you know. I know as well as you do that she couldn't lose what she never had!"

"Never had!" I gasped. "She never had any children?"

"Of course not," he said, steadying me, for my knees got weak all of a sudden. "That's what's made all the trouble—that's what's so unfortunate! D'you mean to say you didn't know?"

I sank right down on the stairs. "But the pictures!" I burst out.

"If you mean that picture of Mr. Robertson Childress when he was a little lad and the other one of him and his sister that died when a baby, and chose to fancy they was *hers*," says he, pointing upstairs, "it's no fault of mine, Miss Umbleby."

And no more it was. What with poor old Shipman's ramblings and the doctor's words that I had twisted into what they never meant, I had got myself into a fine pickle.

"But what shall I do, Mr. Hodges?" I said, stupid-like, with the surprise and the shock of it. "It'd kill her, if I stopped now."

"That's for you to decide," said he, in his reserved, cold way, "I have my silver to do."

Well, I did decide. I lay awake all night at it, and maybe I did wrong, but I hadn't the heart to see the red go out of her cheek and the little shy smile off her pretty mouth. It hurt no one, and the mischief was done, anyway—there'd be no heir to Childerstone, now. For five generations it had been the same—a son and a daughter to every pair, and the old place about as dear to each son, as I made out, as ever his wife or child could be. General Washington had stopped the night there, and some great French general that helped the Americans had come there for making plans to attack the British, and Colonel Robertson Childress that then was had helped him. They had plenty of English kin and some in the Southern States, but no friends near them, on account of my mistress's husband having to live in Switzerland for his health and his father dying young (as he did) so that his mother couldn't bear the old place. But as soon as Mr. Robertson was told he was cured and could live where he liked, he made for Childerstone and brought his bride there—a stranger from an American family in Switzerland—and lived but three months. If anybody was ever alone, it was that poor lady, I'm sure. There was no big house like theirs anywhere about—no county families, as you might say—and those that had called from the village she wouldn't see, in her mourning. And yet out of that house she would not go, because he had loved it so; it was pitiful.

There's no good argle-bargling over it, as my mother used to say, I'd do the same again! For I began it with the best of motives, and as innocent as a babe, myself, of the real truth, you see.

I can shut my eyes, now, and it all comes back to me as it was in the old garden, of autumn afternoons—I always think of Childerstone in the autumn, somehow. There was an old box hedge there, trimmed into balls and squares, and beds laid out in patterns, with asters and marigolds and those little rusty chrysanthemums that stand the early frosts so well. A wind-break of great evergreens all along two sides kept it warm and close, and from the south and west the sun streamed in onto the stone dial that the Childress of General Washington's time had had brought over from home. It was set for Surrey, Hodges told me once, and no manner of use, consequently, but very settled and home-like to see, if you understand me. In the middle was an old stone basin, all mottled and chipped, and the water ran out from a lion's mouth in some kind of brown metal, and trickled down its mane and jaws and splashed away. We cleaned it out, she and I, one day, *pretending we had help*, and Hodges went to town and got us some gold fish for it. They looked very handsome there. Old John kept the turf clipped and clean and routed out some rustic seats for us—all grey they were and tottery, but he strengthened them, and I smartened them up with yellow chintz cushions I found in the garret—and I myself brought out two tiny arm-chairs, painted wood, from the loft in the coach house. We'd sit there all the afternoon in September, talking a little, me mending and my mistress embroidering on some little frocks I cut out for her. We talked about the children, of course. They got to be as real to me as to her, almost. Of course at first it was all what they *would* have been (for she was no fool, Mrs. Childress, though you may be thinking so) but by little and little it got to be what they *were*. It couldn't be helped.

Hodges would bring her tea out there and she'd eat heartily, for she never was much of a one for a late dinner, me sewing all the time, for I always knew my place, though I believe in her kind heart she'd have been willing for me to eat with her, bless her! Then she'd look at me so wistful-like, and say, "I'll leave you now, Sarah—eat your tea and don't keep out too late. Good-bye—good-bye. . . ." Ah, dear me!

I'd sit and think, with the leaves dropping quiet and yellow around me and the water dripping from the lion's mouth and sometimes I'd close my eyes and—I'll swear I could hear them playing quietly beyond me! They were never noisy children. I'll say now something I never mentioned, even to her, and I'd say it if my life hung by it. More than once I've left the metal tea-set shut in the biscuit box and found it spread out of mornings. My mistress slept in the room next me with the door open, and am I to think that William Hodges, or Katey, crippled with rheumatism, or that lazy old John came down and set them out? I've taken a hasty run down to that garden (we called it the children's garden, after a while) because she took an idea, and seen the swing just dying down, and not a breath stirring. That's the plain gospel of it. And I've lain in my bed, just off the two cribs, and held my breath at what I felt and heard. She knew it, too. But never heard so much as I, and often cried for it. I never knew why that should be, nor Hodges, either.

There was one rainy day I went up in the garret and pulled the old rocking-horse out and dusted it and put it out in the middle and set the doors open and went away. It was directly over our heads as we sat sewing, and—ah, well, it's many years ago now, a many and a many, and it's no good raking over too much what's past and gone, I know. And as Hodges said, afterward, the rain on the roof was loud and steady. . . .

I don't know why I should have thought of the rocking-horse, and she not that was always thinking and planning for them. Hodges said it was because I had had children. But I could never have afforded them any such toy as that. Still, perhaps he was right. It was odd his saying that (he knew the facts about me, of course, by that time) being such a dry man, with no fancy about him, you might say, and disliking the whole subject, as he always did, but so it was. Men will often come out with something like that, and quite astonish one.

He never made a hint of objection when I was made housekeeper, and that was like him, too, though I was, to say so, put over him. But he knew my respect for him, black silk afternoons or no black silk, and how we all leaned on him, really.

And then Margaret came, as I said, and it was all to tell, and a fine mess I made of it and William Hodges that settled it, after all.

For Margaret wanted to pack her box directly and get off, and said she'd never heard of such doings and had no liking for people that weren't right.

"Not right?" says Hodges, "not right? Don't you make any such mistake, my girl. Madam attends to all her law business and is at church regularly, and if she's not for much company—why, all the easier for us. Her cheques are as sensible as any one's, I don't care who the man is, and a lady has a right to her fancies. I've lived with very high families at home, and if I'm suited, you may depend upon it the place is a good one. Go or stop, as you like, but don't set up above your elders, young woman."

So she thought it over and the end of it all was that she was with us till the last. And gave me many a black hour, too, poor child, meaning no harm, but she admired Hodges, it was plain, and being younger than I and far handsomer in a dark, Scotch way, it went hard with me, for he made no sign, and I was proud and wouldn't have showed my feelings for my life twice over.

Well, it went on three years more. I made my little frocks longer and the gold fish grew bigger and we set out new marigolds every year, that was all. It was like some quiet dream, when I've gone back and seemed a girl again in the green lanes at home, with mother clear-starching* and the rector's daughter hearing my catechism and Master Lawrence sent off to school for bringing me his first partridge. Those dreams seem long and short at one and the same time, and I wake years older, and yet it has not been years that passed but only minutes. So it was at Childerstone. The years went by like the hours went in the children's garden, all hedged in, like, and quiet and leaving no mark. We all seemed the same to each other and one day was like another, full, somehow, and busy and happy, too, in a quiet, gentle way.

When old Katey lay dying she spoke of these days for the first time to me. She'd sent up the porringers and set out glasses of milk and made cookies in heart shapes with her mouth tight shut for all that time, and we never knowing if she sensed it rightly or not. But on her deathbed she told me that she felt the Blessed Mary (as she called her) had given those days to my poor mistress to make up to her for all she'd lost and all she'd

---

* This means, not surprisingly, stiffening linen cloth with clear or colorless starch.

never had, and that she'd confessed her part in it and been cleared, long ago. I never loved any time better, looking back, nor Hodges either. One season the Christmas greens would be up, and then before we knew it the ice would be out of the brooks and there would be crocuses and daffodils for Mr. Childress's grave.

She and I took all the care of it and the key to the iron gate of it lay out on her low work table, and one or other of us always passing through, but one afternoon in summer when I went with a basket of June roses, she being not quite up to it that day, there on the flat stone I saw with my own eyes a little crumpled bunch of daisies—all nipped off short, such as children pick, and crushed and wilted in their hot little hands! And on no other tomb but his. But I was used to such as that, by then. . . .

Margaret was handy with her needle, and I remember well the day she made the linen garden hat with a knot of rose-colour under the brim.

"You don't think this will be too old, do you, ma'am?" she said when she showed it to my mistress, and the dear lady was that pleased!

"Not a bit, Margaret," she said and I carried it off to Miss Winifred's closet. Many's the time I missed it after that, and knew too much to hunt. It was hunting that spoiled all, for we tried it. . . .

And yet we didn't half believe. Heaven help us, we knew, but we didn't believe: St. Thomas* was nothing to us!

Margaret was with us three years when the new family came. Hodges told us that Hudson River property was looking up and land was worth more every year. Anyway, in one year two families built big houses within a mile of us and we went to call, of course, as in duty bound. John grumbled at getting out the good harness and having the carriage re-lined, but my mistress knew what was right, and he had no choice. I dressed her very carefully, and we watched her off from the door, a thought too pale in her black, but sweet as a flower, and every inch full of breeding, as Hodges said.

I never knew what took place at that visit, but she came back with a bright red circle in each cheek and her head very high, and spent all the evening in the nursery. Alone, of course, for I heard little quick sounds on

---

* St. Thomas the Apostle is the source of the phrase "Doubting Thomas" because he at first refused to believe in the resurrection of Christ.

the piano in the drawing-room, and the fairy books were gone from the children's book-shelves, and Margaret found them in front of the fire and brought them to me. . . .

It was only three days before the new family called on us (a pair of ponies to a basket phaeton—very neat and a nice little groom) and my heart jumped into my mouth when I saw there were two children in with the lady: little girls of eight and twelve, I should say. 'Twas the first carriage callers that ever I'd seen in the place, and Hodges says to me as he goes toward the hall,

"This is something like, eh, Miss Umbleby?"

But I felt odd and uncertain, and when from behind the library door I heard the lady say, "You see I've kept my word and brought my babies, Mrs. Childress—my son is hardly old enough for yours—only four—but Helena and Lou can't wait—they are so impatient to see your little girl!"— when I heard that, I saw what my poor mistress had been at, and the terrible situation we were in (and had been in for years) flashed over me and my hands got cold as ice.

"Where is she?" the lady went on.

At that I went boldly into the library and stood by my mistress's chair—I couldn't desert her then, after all those years.

"Where? where?" my poor lady repeated, vague-like and turning her eyes so piteous at me that I looked the visitor straight in the face and getting between her and my mistress I said very calmly,

"I think Miss Winifred is in the children's garden, madam; shall I take the young ladies there?"

For my thought was to get the children out of the way, before it all came out, you see.

Oh, the look of gratitude she gave me! And yet it was a mad thing to do. But I couldn't desert her—I couldn't.

"There, you see, mamma!" cried the youngest, and the older one said,

"We can find our way, thank you," very civil, to me.

"Children have sharp eyes," said the lady, laughing. "One can't hide them from each other—haven't you found it so?"

"Now what the devil does she mean by that?" Hodges muttered to me as he passed by me with the tray. He always kept the silver perfect, and it did one's heart good to see his tray: urn and sugar and cream just twinkling and the toast in a covered dish—old Chelsea it was*—and new cakes and jam and fresh butter, just as they have at home.

I don't know what they talked of, for I couldn't find any excuse to stop in the room, and she wouldn't have had it, anyway. I went around to the front to catch the children when they should come back, and quiet them, but they didn't come, and I was too thankful to think much about it.

After about half an hour I saw the oldest one coming slowly along by herself, looking very sulky.

"Where's your sister, dear?" I said, all in a tremble, for I dreaded how she might put it.

"She's too naughty—I can't get her to leave," she said pettishly, and burst into the library ahead of me. My mistress's face was scarlet and her eyes like two big stars—for the first time I saw that she was a beauty. Her breath came very quick and I knew as well as if I'd been there all the time that she'd been letting herself go, as they say, and talked to her heart's content about what she'd never have a chance to talk again to any guest. She was much excited and the other woman knew it and was puzzled, I could see, from the way she looked at her.

Now the girl burst into the talk.

"Mamma, Lou is so naughty!" she cried. "I saw the ponies coming up the drive, and I told her it was time, but she won't come!"

"Gently, daughter, gently," said the lady, and put her arm around her and smoothed her hair. "Why won't Lou come?"

I can see that room now, as plain as any picture in a frame: the setting sun all yellow on the gilt of the rows of books, the streak of light on the waxed oak floor, the urn shining in the last rays. There was the mother patting the big girl, there was Hodges with his hand on the tray, and there was me standing behind my mistress, with her red cheeks and her poor heaving bosom.

"Why won't Lou come?" she asked the girl again.

"Because," she says, still fretful, and very loud and clear, "because she is taking a pattern of the little girl's hat and trying to twist hers into that shape! I told her you wouldn't like it."

---

* Chelsea china was a treasured possession, porcelain made in the eighteenth century.

My mistress sprang up and the chair fell down with a crash behind her. I turned (Hodges says) as white as a sheet and moved nearer her.

"Hat!" she gasped. "What hat? *whose hat*?"

There seemed to be a jingling, like sleighbells, all through the air, and I thought I was going crazy till I saw that it came from the tray, where Hodges's hand was shaking so, and yet he couldn't take it off.

"The hat with the rose-coloured ribbon on it," said the girl, "the one we saw as we drove in, you know, mamma. It's so becoming."

"Sarah! Sarah! did you hear? Did you hear?" shrieked my mistress. "She saw, Sarah, *she saw*!"

Then the colour went out of her like when you blow out a candle, and she put her hand to her heart.

"Oh, oh, what pain!" she said very quickly, and Hodges cried, "My God, she's gone!" and I caught her as she fell and we went down together, for my knees were shaking.

When I opened my eyes there was only Margaret there, wetting my forehead, for William had gone for a doctor. Not that it was of any use, for she never breathed. But the smile on her face was lovely.

We got her on her bed and the sight of her there brought the tears to me and I cried out, "Oh, dear, oh, dear! she was all I had in the world, and now—"

"Now you've got me, my girl, and isn't that worth anything to you, Sarah?"

That was William Hodges, and he put his arm over my shoulder, right before Margaret, and looked so kind at me, so kind—I saw in a moment that no one else was anything to him and that he had always cared for me. And that, coming so sudden, when I had given up all hope of it, was too much for me, weak as I was, and I fainted off again and woke up raving hot with fever and half out of my mind, but not quite, for I kept begging them to put off the funeral till I should be able to be up.

But this, of course, was not done, and by the time I was out of hospital the turf was all in place on her dear grave.

William had managed everything and had picked out all the little keepsakes I should have chosen—the heirs were most kind, though Jews. Indeed, I've felt different to that sort of people ever since, for they not caring for the house on account of its being lonely, to their way of thinking, made it into a children's home for those of their belief as were poor and orphaned, and whatever may have been, the old place will never lack for children now.

I never stepped foot in the grounds again, for William Hodges, though the gentlest and fairest of men, never thwarted me but once, and it was in just that direction. Moreover, he forbade me to speak of what only he and I knew for a certainty, and he was one of that sort that when a command is laid, it's best kept.

We've two fine children—girl and boy—and he never murmured at the names I chose for them. Indeed, considering what my mistress's will left me and what his master had done for him, he was as pleased as I.

"They're named after our two best friends, Sarah," he said, looking hard at me, once.

And I nodded my head, but if she saw me, in heaven, she knew who were in my heart when I named them!

The American writer **Alice Brown** (1857–1948) is another whose popularity waned in the early twentieth century, though she published a book a year until 1935. Her output included novels, poetry, and plays, but she is often regarded today only as a "regional" writer of "local color" tales. The following is set far from her native New England and first appeared in *Scribner's Magazine* for June 1911; it was later reprinted in her collection *The Flying Teuton and Other Stories*.

The Tryst

by Alice Brown

That a man nearing forty is far from being in his right mind when he even contemplates an excursion with two recently married couples, one of the brides being she whom he has not been able to cease loving with an ardor intensified by the certainty that he had been denied his chance with her by circumstance only, bare circumstance, a matter of staying in a place eight and three-quarters days instead of nine, thereby missing her by a train—this is pathologically evident. I was the man. I was at Naples, with no more idea that Julia and her young husband were there for an ecstatic minute of their bridal tour than I had that I should be dining with them in a kind of enraged content, being offered fruit from her soft finger-tips I would have died to kiss—I let myself go now in the telling of it as I let myself go mentally at that incredible dinner, since, after all, there has to be a moment's delirium even for a man of forty who has got his wound. I had met them face to face in the street, I absurdly chaffering for corals I didn't want, only to spur the vendor's verbal acrobatics, and then meaning to go on to the Aquarium* and pretend I had an interest in fins and octopi, when they came on me, the radiant four of them, she and her Jack, Billy Petersham and his new wife, who had been a widow, over-corseted and creaking. She always, in spite of decency, made you think of her stays, and I never saw her without a vague nautical memory that stays are something a boat is warped into or warped out of, and I never could resist the certainty that she had got in and stayed warped. They greeted me, three of them, with the hilarious ecstasy of the inordinately joyous crowded up one more notch of bliss by the spectacle of the enforcedly abstemious for whom the cupboard is bare of "syrops tinct with cinnamon"† and the heavenly manna of verified illusion.

"Dine with us, old boy," Jack said at once, and mentioned the gilded hotel on the height where I had been too tame-spirited to go.

I looked at him a second before I answered, looked him up and down perhaps, for I had a chance to think how fresh-colored his face was, how hued by blood so good and so new that it might have run from heavenly founts, how white his teeth were, and how his honest eyes met me with their old clarity and kindness, but more—a challenge, perhaps, to note how happy he was, and what a conqueror. I noted his exquisite clothes, too, his lilac tie—I knew the stockings matched it, if only the eye could have got at them—his general look of something flowered out in the spring. He was a splendor, no mistake, I must have hesitated, for before I answered, Julia was holding out her hand, that slender hand I knew in all its gloved seclusion, in its slim, lovely length as it fed her beautiful lips—she held it out to me, and I took it and forgot Jack's question and his tie. I only stood and stared into that face I had so hungered for—and yet I had seen it night upon night, framed in the black wall of darkness, or against the moving tapestry of my shut eyes—I had been seeing it, I thought, "every day i' the hour"‡ since she had been reft away by her Jack; but only God He knew how horribly I had been longing to set eyes once more upon its fair reality.

---

* The Zoological Station in Campania, founded in 1872 by Anton Dohrn, is the oldest aquarium in Italy.

† From John Keats's poem "The Eve of St. Agnes," written in 1819, first published in 1820.

‡ Now Olmstead thinks of a line from Shakespeare's *Romeo and Juliet*, Act III, Scene V.

She was above all women beautiful, not because I loved her, but chiefly that she was so kind. The faint flush, the fineness of her cheek, the glory of hair all gold and rarer, the wistful look of her blue eyes: these a lover, if he had been also a poet, might inadequately have sung. But nobody in this generation, nobody but a dead and gone cavalier who clapped his sword in scabbard to write a lyric explaining why swords must be out and love-knots temporarily put by, only he could have hit off that human look of hers, of sympathy, of compassion, of knowing exactly how the under dog felt, with even a surprising hint of having been herself, at some time, desperately at odds with fortune and now remembering it. This was not for me, I thought, as I stood stupidly worshipping her. Julia Dove never had, I was sure, the least suspicion of my love for her. How could she, when she was engaged the day I met her, and I must have looked to her a dry old *hortus siccus** of emotions as I was, pelting round after historical data, even more desiccated than was entirely just, seen through the lilac mists of Jack's ties and hose and his beaming glance. But now her look seemed to say inexplicably: "Dear man, be comforted. You are shockingly lonesome. So am I."

There I pulled myself up in my unlawful imaginings. She couldn't be. The candid glance meant only so she once had been before she found him and twined her soul with his. But all she really said, independently of her kind eyes, was this, oh, in the dearest voice:

"Do, Mr. Olmstead. Do come."

I dropped her hand.

"Thank you," said I, with the abruptness of one recalled. "I will."

So we five dined together in the splendor of the Bertolini,[†] and sat on the terrace afterward like funny modern gods on Olympus, and watched the lights flaming out and twinkling out below, and heard faint touches of music, and knew the multitudinous life of the city was dancing itself blind and mad, and doing the little tasks that bought its bread, and playing its pageant because its blood ran so fast it couldn't help it, and yet thriftily, since the foreigners paid for piping. Mrs. Billy and I did most of

---

* An arrangement of dried plants.

† Hotel Bertolini, also known as Bertolini's Palace Hotel, was the finest in Naples—long closed.

the talking. I fancied she was rather glad of a prosaic new element, she who was almost forty herself, and getting painfully attached to succulent dishes and talk about reducing one's self and, on this occasion, my immunity from care because nature turned me out so lean. Her husband smoked and stared at her through the dusk, glorifying her into the eternal beautiful, I have no doubt, because she was new and his; and Julia looked at the city and said nothing. It was my one hour, not to shine, not to acquire, not to do in any sense a memorable deed, but to sit in the same visible universe with Julia Dove. Once I got a little drunk with it, the wonder of it, the ineffable compassion of the upper powers to allow me this heavenly anodyne before my heart beat itself out with lonesome misery, and I found myself repeating idiotically:

"'Only to kiss the air—'" There I stopped, and got hold of myself for a fool; but Mrs. Billy clacked in with her complacent note, perfectly ready for all challenges of give or take:

"What's that, Mr. Olmstead? Is it a new song?"

"Not absolutely new," said I stupidly, "though it's for all time. It's been running in my head. I've been trying to get the last line."

"Why, I know it," said Julia, with no hesitation in her clear young voice:

'Only to kiss that air
That lately kissed thee.'"

I know it all."

---

* These are lines from a song by Robert Herrick (1591–1674), one of many he titled "To Electra." The Victorian poet Swinburne called Herrick "the greatest song-writer ever born of English race." Here is the full song:

I dare not ask to kiss,
I dare not beg a smile,
Lest having that, or this,
I might grow proud the while.

No, no, the utmost share
Of my desire shall be
Only to kiss the air
That lately kissèd thee.

And then, as if the immortals loved me, and meant to accord me one more blissful cup to live on till I died of surfeit and despair, she sat here with the lights of Naples below her in a seemly humbleness and the stars shining like her own galaxy, and repeated it all.

"Shall I write it down for you?" she asked, at the end.

"No," said I. "I shall remember." I got on my feet. I'd had all I could carry. "Good-night," I said.

Then I was wishing them joy all round—joy and a fortunate trip, in a manner that, I hope, satisfied the lightly conventional; but Jack, for some reason, would not hear of losing me.

"Breakfast with us," he said. I have had an idea since that because I was staying at a meagre *pension** below he had confirmed his estimate of my poverty. "Then come on to Pompeii."

I didn't want Pompeii, or any further spectacle of marital felicity. I remembered the gentle eternal sunlit gloom of the dead city, as I had seen it before, and it appeared to me that, superadded to my own grounded sense that life itself was pretty well over, I should as soon choose an after-dinner stroll in the catacombs.

"Awfully good of you," I said, "but I'm due at Capri. I'm afraid I shall have to be leaving rather early in the morning to make it."

I was due there because I had to have a pretext, and that would serve as well as any.

"Who's at Capri?" inquired Mrs. Billy skittishly, and I tried dismally to look as if somebody very fetching indeed might be there; whereupon she forgot she was mated and settled again, and bridled in the old way. "Well, we'll let you off from Pompeii," she conceded, "but you simply must meet us at Pæstum."†

Immediately, not because she said it, for what she said meant to me, as it did to every man save Billy, less than the crackling of thorns under a pot—for I suppose a sufficient crackling might boil the dinner, and Billy is the raw material that boils easily—but for some reason hidden

---

* A boarding house or small hotel.

† Pæstum was a major Greek city in ancient times, in the province of Salerno, Italy. It is famous today for the ruins of three Doric temples.

even from that inner self which is forever hearing unexpected calls and challenges, immediately I felt mad to go to Pæstum.

"Yes," said Jack, from his perennial desire to challenge everybody to "come on" whither he is going, "yes, come on to Pæstum. That'll be Thursday. We make it from La Cava."*

I knew Cava of the Tyrrhenians, all blue mountain and silent valley and hills and hollow distances and balconies moonlighted. And now it was full moon, and my merciless fancy pictured me Julia in the sea of it, and Jack—commonplace Jack, yet he was young!—he adoring her. I would have none of Cava. But Pæstum was still drawing me; it had me with an iron grip.

"We're doomed to Pæstum because Julia wants it," said Jack fondly, with the husband's young pride of being under dominion. "Think it over, Jule. It's as full of malaria† as it can stick. Come on to Capri with Olmstead, and I'll give you a black pearl."‡

"I'm sorry," said Julia, in her dear voice pierced with a thrill of something I had never heard in it—resistance, maybe, not of him but for the sake of what she was obliged to do. "I have to go there."

"Have to, child? Why have you?"

I looked at her and wondered why: not from wilfulness, for that wasn't in her, but for some reason so rigid that not only could she not permit it to be withstood, but she herself, from its unknown power, could not withstand it. Now the fair territory of her face was unfeignedly perplexed.

"I don't know," she owned. "I have to go, that's all. I know I have to."

"Gammon,"§ said Jack, still fondly. If it had been less than a lover's acquiescent pride I couldn't have suffered him. "What if we let you go alone?"

---

* The town of Cava dei Tirreni, near Campagnia, in the Salerno province, a popular tourist attraction of the day.

† The disease, often fatal, was thought to be caused by "bad air" (*mala aria* in medieval Italian). It was only in the 1880s that parasites were found in the blood of infected victims, and not until 1897 were mosquitos identified as the most common carrier.

‡ A rare gem—the "Black Pearl of the Borgias" features in Conan Doyle's Holmes story "The Adventure of the Six Napoleons" (1904).

§ Jack is being figurative here: A *gammon* is a victory in the game of backgammon, in which the winner removes all of the player's pieces before the other removes any. Thus, Julia has defeated Jack soundly by declaring that "I've got to go."

"I should have to, then," she said, in the same serious wistfulness of wonder. "I can't bear to be so obstinate; but truly I've got to go."

Jack laughed. He liked her sudden tyranny, and took her hand and swung it back and forth.

"All right then," said he, "we've got to go. Olmstead, how about you? Can't you reconsider?"

"Assuredly," I said, with no volition, it seemed to me afterward, to say that particular thing. "I've got to go, too. I'll meet you there."

So we looked at times and trains and made our final pact. I had privately decided that, for all my mythical engagement at Capri, I should probably stay on at Naples up to the point of being due at Pæstum—for due there I was, I solemnly knew, for other reason than that I had vowed to meet the lately married there. But what the reason was, I could no more say than Julia could, of hers. Only there was a reason.

The few days passed, and I occupied them as well as I could for thinking of the moon at Cava, in running back over my own life, meagre though it was of incident, to see, once for all, whether I could have made it different. I didn't find that I could. At every point where other men score, in the brave crisis, the big distances, I had slipped a cog. When a man was needed at the vital spot, I simply couldn't be there. When life demanded testimony of me, I might have it to offer, but court was never sitting that day. The whole thing was consistent. It had happened to me over and over. It wasn't that I was faint-hearted and weak-backed, or that my legs were not strong enough to make a pace. I was becalmed in some zone of the soul. Information never reached me. Boats couldn't get into my latitude with the news of the battles that were going to be, or the great treaties that would prevent my striking futile blows for a quarrel that was lost. It had all been like a retribution for some misdeed of mine. I felt that strongly, for I believed in the justice that dogs us like a loving hound, and I knew it was part of the beneficent scheme of things that if we are hit over the head, it is that we have at some time bought the blow. Only, how had I deserved precisely this? Why was I "come-tardy-of"* in all the games of life? How had it been managed that I shouldn't find Julia three months before the fresh-colored Jack brought his

---

* To fall short—a phrase that appears in Shakespeare's *Hamlet*, Act III, Scene 2.

conquering cravats into the field? I hadn't even had a chance—and why? I felt it would help me for the home stretch, which had, after all, to be run with ardor, even if to a decreed ignominy, to know.

The morning came, and all fell out as we had said. We met at Pæstum station, the five of us, they with little canvas bags of luncheon from the paternal Hotel de Londres,* an extra portion for me. There was not a single tourist beside ourselves—"a single, blooming tourist," Billy said—and the sky was Italian blue, and a light wind moving to welcome us, when between dry fields where wild larkspur bloomed we walked toward the temple—and I, by what seemed some fated chance, walked with Julia, while Jack leaped the low walls to bring her larkspur and crowd it into her hands. She was silent, and I seemed to know it was because the moment, the day, meant something to her nobody could share—nobody but me, perhaps, for I, too, knew it meant tremendously. And then we were in face of the great yellow-pillared splendor, and we dared to enter and wander up and down its ruined aisles. The gods were there, I knew perfectly well, and said so; but I chanced to say it was Apollo,† for I heard him, and Mrs. Billy kept chirping:

"But why do you say Apollo, Mr. Olmstead, when this is the Temple of Neptune? Don't you know it's the Temple of Neptune, Mr. Olmstead? Isn't it Neptune you mean?"

And then I got meek and patient because there was no other way of hushing her, and said, "Yes, I did mean Neptune." But about this time we all began to notice Julia. She had stayed apart from us, in our wandering up and down, our profane feet where priests had ministered, and now she was hurrying back and forth, peering out between columns, even so far as the line of distant saline blue, and her face had piteously changed. It was gray-pale and her eyes were black and anguished. Her husband saw it about as soon as I did, and started for her over grassy gulfs between the slabs. But when he would have touched her, she waved him off. She almost pushed him.

---

* A fine hotel in Cava dei Tirreni that operated until the mid-twentieth century and a favorite of English-speaking tourists.

† Leader of the Muses, the god of music and poetry.

"What is it, darling?" I heard him say, and she looked so unfriended that I was glad the tender word was ready for her. "Lost something?"

She started and looked at him, not, I could have sworn, knowing him at all, and then put both her hands to her head in an unaffected gesture of wild perplexity.

"I don't know," she said. "I don't know." And then, "Where is the ship?"

He took her by the arm and led her along perforce and made her sit.

"She feels the heat," I heard him say to Mrs. Billy who was staring. "Get the apollinaris,* Bill. Wet a handkerchief in it, somebody."

But there was really no heat to feel. The little breeze was still doing its kindest for us. Julia laughed out now. Her color had come back as if, having got into another part of the temple, she had escaped an especial territory of influence.

"What are you giving me apollinaris for?" she asked. "Jack, you're dripping that handkerchief over Mrs. Billy's dress. Want it on my head? Of course I don't want a great wet dab on my head! Come, let's read the guide-book and then have luncheon."

So we avoided looking at one another, the rest of us, and went rather hastily into activities, as if we had witnessed some special madness that had blessedly passed, and must never be thought of any more. And in due time we had our luncheon, and fed the lean dogs that came, evidently by habit, to yearn for bits, and then it was in the air that the Temple of Ceres must be visited, and everybody, well primed by Jack's conscientious perorations from the guide-book, rose to go. All but me, and, for a moment, all but Julia.

"Come, come," said Jack to her. It was impatient, but the impatience of a solicitude most tender. "Get a move on, missus. The day's 'most over."

She shook her head. The puzzled look had come back to her.

"I don't believe I can," she said, and she spoke with some difficulty, as they do who have imperfectly rehearsed their subject-matter. "I might be late."

He gave her arm a little shake.

---

* Bottled water, a brand now controlled by Coca-Cola but then manufactured in Germany, with the slogan "The Queen of Table Waters." By 1911 it was selling nearly forty million bottles per year.

"Come, come, dear," said he. "You're not going to worry me again?"

That seemed to bring her back with a wrench to what we are pleased to call reasonableness, and she laughed and turned with him obediently enough. They were midway out of the temple, all of them, when they remembered me.

"Come along, Olmstead," Jack threw back at me. He was entirely good-natured now he had his own special prize under convoy. "You mustn't keep Ceres waiting. They don't like it."

"I'm not going," I said. "I'll take a nap. See you at the train."

At that, Julia, his wife, stopped short and gave me that puzzled but now almost recognizing look; but he reminded her by a touch on the arm, and she went on with him, patient, I could see, and droopingly. And Billy tossed me a cigar, and Mrs. Billy shook her parasol at me, and they were gone, and had left me to the oblivion I candidly knew I wanted. I put my head back on the calm old pillar—I was conscious of wishing I were as old, so that I could perhaps be as indifferent—and shut my eyes. I was horribly tired, and at the same time most unbearably excited with it all. With what? I didn't know. Was this panic? Was I Pan-struck, as one might well be on this ground of colossal shadowy deities? I felt that I was nervous as a green girl, and threw all sorts of obloquy at my senile state for admitting such a thing. And I kept my eyes shut to rest them from the vision of things seen, and so they stayed until I heard a voice. It was a woman's voice, a voice I could have sworn was Julia's, and it spoke my name. Now I am not going to tell what my name is, because it is Greek, and old, and funny when I sign it to a reply to a dinner invitation, though it does very well for a scholar who has dry conclusions to make upon living facts. My father was a scholar, and he gave it to me, and perhaps for that reason, perhaps for some unknown other, I have always been content with it. I have had, indeed, connected with it, a certain inevitable feeling I can't describe, as if nothing else could ever possibly have been my name. But when I opened my eyes I saw it could not have been I who was called. The tourists indeed were upon me, a man and a woman, both young, and they walked together outside the temple, and talked together with a trouble and haste I could hardly forbear to share, even by an eye-beam, it was in itself so passionate. It seemed to draw lesser intelligences to it, as the sun compels the earth. I thought I knew who they were, this from their costume. They were in white, the flowing robes of an ancient time, and I guessed at once that they were out of a troupe of actors of classical Greek plays, who had been going about London and Paris, during my stay there, in the free beauty of their borrowed dress. But I began to hear them speak, and took no shame in listening. I seemed, indeed, to be there to listen, to share, to partake with them of the tragic imminence of their fate. They spoke rapidly, but in the melody of a majestic tongue which was not mine. Yet, though I could not that night transcribe a word of it, I followed it with the ease of a leaf on a flowing river. She was entreating him, this man of my name, to undo some irrevocable deed. What it was I could not at first determine. Then, from her heart-broken reproaches, and his hurlings back of the "No!" that seemed inevitable, I gradually gathered knowledge. He had sold the state's secret—some secret—he had been paid by the enemy—some enemy—and what he had been paid was to enrich him to the point of seizing her from the arms of the hated lover she was decreed to, and fleeing with her in the enemy's ship. And the ship was out there across the blue line.

But the girl would not go. She was adjuring him, in the name of all the gods, to deliver himself up to justice, to inevitable death. Here was where she had appointed their meeting, here by the sacred temple, here where their whisperings might be heard, the better that they should, that priests and gods combined might slay them both and so hasten his expiation. As they walked back and forth in the sunlight, and once she set her foot unconsciously on a snake and I saw it did not move even by a tremor of its shining length, my eyes dwelt with a love and pity I cannot measure upon the filleted gold of her small head. I seemed to partake with her of anguish lest he fail, yet to know it was a foregone fate, and my sadness settled into the acquiescence of despair. He desired nothing but to save her, yet he would not save them both, as they do who play for honors, by giving up himself. And as if I were in his skin I saw why. He loved her too fervidly, too passionately, as earth is tempting, forcing, pushing us to love, and as the big law we only now and then catch a glimpse of, will not have us. And curiously from that far time, from the misty gates of it, my mind leaped with a throb, a vault down the centuries, to the cavalier who made an immortal discovery and wrote it in immortal words:

> I could not love thee, Dear, so much,
> Loved I not Honor more. [*]

This, in substance, she represented to him in the passion of her noble phrases, unconsidered, born like tears out of a breaking heart. She was his dearest, she said, she thanked the gods, but nevertheless the gods themselves must be still dearer to him, they and the state. What was it compared with the dishonor he had bought that her poor body should be stained by the mastery of a hated spouse? At that he cried aloud, and she hushed him while my mind had time to flash aside to another mandate made for perpetuity concerning them that kill the body and have not power to kill the soul. [†] Her voice continued in its lyric rise and fall. There was no help for either of them, she told him, he in his present disaster and she before her coming slavery, no help save death, and that might happily be now. But all the same, while the bright rapiers of their argument were glancing, I knew he would not yield: that they were to be discovered, that since she must not go with him, he would snatch at her with the force of love run wild, and, trusting in the ship, resolve in his madness to bear her to it across the parching leagues. That she would cry out to the gods to save them and they would be saved—he by the knife at his throat and she to sink into so ill a mind that no man would take her to him with her bright beauty faded.

All this I seemed indubitably and with a high sadness to know, and athwart the web of it, like something sharply remembered, I heard other voices, insistently familiar ones of the common day. Some one was calling, Jack, Billy, and Mrs. Billy, she waving her parasol up and down, in a pump-handle fashion, across the bright vista through which

---

[*] From Richard Lovelace's 1649 poem "To Lucasta, Going to the Warres."

[†] Matthew 10:28: "And fear not them which kill the body, but are not able to kill the soul: but rather fear him which is able to destroy both soul and body in hell."

they ran. Did they shock the other visitants to a scene beloved and throw them out of the aura where they were for the moment visible? Had the time been preeminently ripe and right that they—these two beautiful young beings—had returned for a fleeting hour of a day no longer existent, to play their parts again in faithful rigor to a vanished past, or had I, incalculably endowed, seen but the picture of them, woven for all time into the waving tapestry of the air? However it was, they were gone, not of a sudden, not either walking away or vanishing, but in some quite familiar and convincing fashion, as if I had seen beautiful young lovers go thus, as conclusively as if it were through a gate. And at the instant that I felt they were gone, and knew myself to be in some way the richer, the more complete for having seen them, I heard a cry—not from those three chorusing on behind, but a light, hurried call in a voice I knew. Yet never had I heard it so moved, so jubilant, so full of life. And as I turned to it, she came—Julia came, flying. Her face was pink like dawn, and her glad eyes hailed me. She made no hesitant pause or pretense that it was anything but me and what I stood for she had come to find. Both hands out, she rushed to me, and I with my two hands received her. Standing so, palm to palm, she looked up in my face, one glad smile of recognition. So might the girl I had just seen have looked at her lover if she had, instead of dooming him to death, beckoned him to life with her.

"Am I too late?" she was imploring me, yet with the sweetest certainty that she was not. "Oh, don't tell me I'm too late!"

"No, no," I answered her, worship on my lips, in my eyes, I felt, as in my heart. "No. I was here. I saw them. What difference whether it was you or I?"

"What difference!" she echoed out of a deep-breathed, heavenly tranquillity of happiness. "Oh, what difference!" Then she looked at me for a long minute, as if she saw behind my lean old face what jocund youth I should have been the last to understand, but not to believe. I knew and believed it all. "It is the last now," she said. She was growing fragmentary, like one recalled to an existence not yet comprehended, and only able to stay in it for a minute, and now, the minute over, fading out of it as the two others had faded to my eyes. But I understood. The last parting, she had meant to say. "Next time"—she stammered sweetly, in her lovely hesitancy, like a child of heaven learning the new language and as yet imperfect in it. And then I saw her—the one who had looked at me, who had spoken, who had known the hour was nearly accomplished, and next time, in whatever age and whatever star, would see the bridegroom claim his bride—I saw her fading out into Julia Dove, the young mate of Jack, who was anxiously hailing her as he ran: for she, in that wonder of predestined flight, had outstripped them all. And I did not care. I did not care that she was to return with him to moonlight and bells at Cava, for that, too, must be mysteriously accomplished. He was beside her now, and I dropped her hands. She looked down at them, as I did it, surprised a little, it seemed, to know why I had been holding them.

"What is it?" Jack was insisting, out of a rage of anxious love. "What in thunder is it, dear?"

Mrs. Billy came up, panting and creaking, and her parasol might have dinted the sacred stones, so did she punctuate her haste.

"What is what, dear?" Julia echoed, lightly and most honestly. "Did I hurry? I was bidding Mr. Olmstead good-by."

"Come along then," said Jack, mopping his smooth young brow, and almost a little fractious at having been fretted into more perplexities. "That train will be in in about three minutes and a half. Come along, Olmstead."

"No," said I. "I'm not going."

I felt light-headed, drunk with the delirium and the certainty of it.

"Not going? You won't get anywhere tonight."

"I don't want to," said I. "I'm somewhere now. There'll be some kind of a little hostelry."

"Don't be a fool, man," said Billy, and Mrs. Billy shrieked "Malaria!" italicising with her parasol.

"Well, there's a minute gone, and we can't stop here," said Jack, and I didn't blame him. One doesn't lightly subject wives to even a mythical malaria. "Come on, Olmstead. We're off."

Julia turned willingly and obediently with him; but at ten paces she stopped. She ran back toward me. The other look fleeted into her face. "Don't you smell them," she cried. "Roses!"

"Yes," I said, afire with my exultation, and again my mind challenged my own century and found the right word from another man's pen: "'Roses from Pæstan rosaries!'"*

"Next time"—she faltered, as if she herself least of all understood what she might be saying. The look had faded.

"Julia! Julia!" Jack was calling, and Mrs. Billy piped me out one more warning:

"Malaria, Mr. Olmstead! Remember!"

But I stood there happier, younger, more at peace than anything, I believed, on earth. I could think of but one word to call: the word any man would be likest to leave in the keeping of his dearest, if they were to be parted for a lifetime or two. Mrs. Billy thought it was her word; but it was Julia's, to her soul alone, though it meant no more to her, with the memory washed out of her face, than if a butterfly had settled for an instant on her gown, and she, flying with Jack, had had no eyes for it. I called it after them, and Mrs. Billy, thinking it the echo of her own, shook her parasol despairingly. Out of my kingdom of youth regained and love inalienably assured I called, and it rang splendidly:

"Remember!"

---

* *Roses of Paestum* by Edward McCurdy is a book of essays first published in 1900. In a 1904 reprint edited by Thomas Mosher, the first (titular) essay is described: "[McCurdy] pens with a delicate blending of fact-and-fable which presently becomes exquisitely allegorical in its treatment of the deathless Greek roses transplanted oversea into Italian flower gardens. Thenceforth the stream of thought widens and we are bid behold a second flowering of Beauty—that marvellous reincarnation of the antique world of Art which came into life when the actual roses of Paestum had ages ago faded 'from Paestan rosaries,' and with their lovers of old time and the city of their delight was only a muted memory in the minds of men."

Georgia Wood Pangborn (1872–1955), the mother of science-fiction writer Edgar Pangborn, was primarily known for her horror and supernatural fiction. A New Yorker by birth and by choice, she attended Smith College and soon became part of the New York literary scene. A frequent contributor of short stories and poetry to *Scribner's, Harper's, Cosmopolitan, Collier's, The Bookman*, and others, she wrote only one novel, *Roman Biznet*, published in 1902. This haunting tale first appeared in August 1911 in *Scribner's Magazine* and was collected in her 1911 *Interventions*.

Broken Glass

by Georgia Wood Pangborn

I can't stay but a minute," said Mrs. Waring, spreading her long hands above the wood blaze. "I was taking my evening constitutional over the moors. *Did* you see the sunset? And the firelight dancing in your open windows was so dear and sweet and homy I had to come. Babies in bed?"

"Oh, yes. Such perfectly good six-o'clock babies! I can tuck them up myself and still have time to dress safe from sticky fingers. Delia is such a blessing. So big and soft and without any nerves, and really and truly fond of them. When she leaves me for a day I am perfectly wild and lost."

"What is the matter with us women," said Mrs. Waring frowningly, "that we can't take care of our own children and run our own houses, to say nothing of spinning and weaving as our grandmothers did? My grandmother was a Western pioneer and brought up six without help, and—buried three. Think of it! To *lose* a child—" A strong shudder went through her delicate body. "How can a woman live after that? We can gasp through the bearing—you and I know that—but to lose—" She covered her face with her ringed hands.

"But, my dear," said the sleek woman by the fire, "your babies are such little Samsons! That nightmare ought not to bother you now."

"No. It oughtn't. That it does so only shows the more our modern unfitness."

"I suppose our grandmothers must have been more of the Delia type."

"And yet we think the Delia type inferior. It's solid and quiet and stupid—not always honest, but it succeeds with children. You and I are reckoned among the cultured. We read in three languages—and write magazine verse. Your nocturne is to be given in concert next week—yet I think that Delia and her type rather despise us because we are wrecks after spending an afternoon trying to keep a creeping baby from choking and bumping and burning and taking cold, or reading Peter Rabbit the fiftieth time to Miss Going-on-Three."

"The question is," said Mrs. Waring, coiling bonelessly in the Morris chair,* "what will our children be? You and I may be inferior, but," she caught her lower lip in her teeth, "my babies came to me after I was thirty, and I know their value, as your Delia type or your grandmother type doesn't for all her motherliness. When women are mothers in the early twenties they don't know. They can't. My music filled in those years. Filled them! It served to express the despair of a barren woman—that was all. Since they came fools have condoled with me because I have had to give up my 'career' for their sake. Career!" She threw back her head and stood up with her hands in her coat pocket. "Here," her voice grew gentle and humorous as she took out the tatters of a little book gay with red and green, "give me some paste. I promised to mend it. She has read it to pieces at last. I thought I could rhyme about sunsets and love and death, but nobody ever loved my rhymes as she loves this. Let's write some children's verses, you and I—

"'Goldilocks was naughty, she began to sulk and pout;
She threw aside her playthings—'

---

* An armchair with a hinged back that can be moved to allow for reclining.

"That's the way, you see, not—

"'When from the sessions of sweet silent thought.'"

She had seated herself at the big flat-topped desk as she spoke and was deftly pasting and mending.

"I've written one; or Tommy has. We were sitting up with his first double tooth. We had taken a go-cart ride in the early moonlight and I was taking cows as an example of people who chew properly. So we got up a song—(past one o'clock it was and a dark and stormy morning)—

"'The moon goes sailing through the sky,
The cows are chewing—chewing—'"

"He liked that but when he'd had it fifty times he changed it—

"'The cows go sailing through the sky
The moon is chewing—chewing—'"

"And it is better that way; I can recommend it as a lullaby."
"Thanks, but I've some of my own pretty nearly as good. A Norwegian maid left me a legacy—

"'Go away du Fisker mand
Catch a pretty fish fish—sh—sh
Bring it home to baby boy
Quicker than a wish—wish—shsh.'"

"That's not bad; I'll remember it when the moon's chewing palls . . .
"As I was saying," said Mrs. Waring, "you and I know the value of our children even if our type is inferior to the Delia type; and if we were bereft everything of our Delias and didn't have to dress for dinner and had no time to read we should show up quite as well as the Delias.
"We use the Delias for them because we want them to have everything of the best. Delias *are* best when they're little. We enter later on. We couldn't

nurse our babies. All that part of us was metamorphosed into brain—thanks to a mistaken education. Very well; we must nourish them with our brains. We can. And we go and get the best service we can, maids and nurses; we bring them home to our nests like cats bringing mice—for the babies . . .

"But I'm afraid I've got to let Aileen go. She told Martha a story about Indians carrying off children and nearly scared the child to death. And when I went to find them yesterday afternoon over by the empty Taylor cottage, they were playing where a window had been broken and there was broken glass everywhere. It was like dancing on knives. My spine shivers with it still. And there sat Aileen—so lost in a dream that I had to put my hand on her shoulder to rouse her. 'Oh,' said she, when I showed her the glass, 'I thought it was ice!' She cried when I told her what a terribly dangerous thing she had done. Her tears come easily enough. A pretty little thing, but *so* stupid. I must do better for Martha."

"I thought," said Mrs. Blake hesitatingly, "that she didn't seem very warmly dressed the other day."

"I don't know why she shouldn't be. I gave her a very good coat. Come to think of it, she hasn't worn it. I wonder why?"

"My Delia told me she had a sister. Perhaps—"

"Sponging on her. Poor child! I like her—but, Martha dancing on broken glass. . . . There, that's done. Now, Martha can read it a hundred times more—'Goldilocks was naughty.'

"Now I must go—and dress. Symbol of degeneracy, as women; but of all that raises us above the Delias, if we *are* above them."

The road was icy and ill kept. Some half-dozen cottages with boarded windows showed silent and black against the red band of sunset and the gray, waving line of moors. The pound of winter surf was like distant hoof-beats over the frozen land. The only cottages that were open had children in them. Air; air is what we give them now. Air and careful food for the rearing of the best of the next generation. And for that purpose the half-dozen cottages on that island kept their warmth and life all winter, just for the sake of properly reddening the cheeks of a dozen little children for whom city streets and parks are not supposed to furnish the proper brand of air.

"Lovely—lovely," thought Mrs. Waring as she walked crisply toward her own fair window. "The moors and the winter storms shall make up to them for having a middle-aged mother. They shall have all the youth and vigor that I had not—that I had not."

Suddenly she faced about. It was not a footfall or a sigh or a spoken word though it gave the impression of all three. Something behind her had betrayed its presence. . . .

No. There was nothing.

"The wind in the dead grass," she thought, but was not satisfied. A caretaker had been murdered on the other side of the island the winter before. Being the mother of a Martha makes one a coward. If there were no Martha one would go striding anywhere, disregarding fantastic dangers, but *when* there is a Martha, who waits at home for a mother to read the story of Goldilocks one hundred times more, why, a mother must not let the least shadow of danger come near her. Because there are so many ways besides reading Goldilocks in which a mother may be useful.

Therefore she thought sharply about the dead care-taker and vowed that on her next constitutional she would carry a pistol in her pocket—for Martha's sake. The black hedges with their white spots of snow gave no sign; the road behind and in front showed empty but for the gleam of frozen puddles. The wind rattled lightly in the frozen grass. . . .

"I hope ye'll excuse me, mum—" The voice was deprecatory and, thank Heaven! A woman's; though where she had come from out of all that emptiness—

"Ah!" gasped Martha's mother.

"I didn't want to scare ye, mum."

"I can't stop," said Mrs. Waring. "If you want to talk to me come to the house. I must get home to—to—"

"Yes, mum; I know, mum, to your little girl. But I can keep pace with you, by your leave, mum, for I was wishin' to speak to you about Aileen—"

"My nurse maid?"

"The same. I was hearin' she was not givin' ye satisfaction, mum, and would like to speak a word for her—widout offence."

"I have not complained of Aileen. It is true she is sometimes thoughtless. May I ask—"

The woman's figure was so shrouded and huddled that Mrs. Waring, looking all she could, might not distinguish the features. She fancied a resemblance to Mrs. Magillicuddy who came every week to help with the washing. No doubt it was Mrs. Magillicuddy. That would account for her knowledge of Aileen.

Mrs. Waring felt a twinge of annoyance at the thought of Aileen's complaining to Mrs. Magillicuddy. She walked on rapidly, but the other kept as close as her shadow.

"You mean, I suppose, about the broken glass."

"It was very bad, mum; so bad that . . . yet there's worse than broken glass in the world. There's other things that seems no more than the glitter of harmless ice and is really daggers for your heart's blood . . . an' so I was wishin' to speak to ye a word about Aileen. As to the glass, mum, there was no real harm done, an' could ye have seen the lass cryin' her eyes out in her little room that night. . . . Not because ye'd scolded her, but because she'd been that careless. And she could not sleep the night, that tender heart, for seein' the baby welterin' in gore that never was shed at all. Och—those eyes wid tears in them! Surely, mum—surely, ye must have noticed the eyes of her when she looks up at ye wid the hope in them that maybe she has pleased ye? Remember this is her first place and that she was reared gently among the sisters, orphanage as it was, and knows as little of the world as a fine lady-girl when she comes out from *her* convent school. She is not yet used to the rough ways of servants. . . .

"But she will be soon. Ah, wirra, wirra, she will be soon. . . .

"I would like her to stay wid ye . . . I little thought, ten years ago, that she would be eatin' the bitter bread of service, for bitter it must be, however soft the life; bitter and dangerous for a young girl that is all alone and knows nothin' at all of the world's wickedness. . . . Do ye blame her for not seein' the broken glass? Can ye not guess that the eyes of her were blind with tears for a harsh word ye had given her about mixin' up the big baby's stockings wid the little one's? Do ye mind that each of your children has two dozen little rolled up balls of stockings to be looked after and that they are very near of a size—very near? My Aileen—she never had but two pairs at a time and she washes out the wan pair at night so she can change to the other. And do ye mind that hers are thin cotton—twelve cints the pair they are—and her feet are cold to break yer heart as she sits in the cold wind watchin' your little girl at play, so warm in her English woollen stockings and leggins. And have ye ever been into Aileen's room? Do ye know that the fine gilt radiator in it is never warm and that she has but one thin blanket and a comforter so ragged your dog would scorn it? And when she had a bit of a cough ye were afraid it might be consumption, ye said, and if so ye couldn't have her with the children—"

"You seem to know my house and my servants remarkably well, Mrs. Magillicuddy. I will see to Aileen's room at once. I have been very busy, but—really—"

"Ah, save yer anger, mum, for one that desarves it. He's not far away. I am not angry with you, mum, though well I might be. I know with what love ye love yer own. But the world is so large and in such need of the kind and wise that, when one is truly kind and wise like you, mum, it is accounted a sin to let your kindness and wisdom go no further than the soft small heads that are your own. There are so many children without any mothers at all . . . as yours might be had I been what you feared but now. . . .

"Broken glass! Is it not worse than broken glass for a young thing like that, as white-souled as that bit of snow on the hedge—have ye ever heard the talk of house servants? And the only place she can go to get away from it when ye do not want her for your children is her own little room that is so cold.

"She does not understand as yet, the whiteness in her is so white, and the servants' hall is warm and pleasant and full of the laughter that ye sometimes hear and frown about. She knows no more than you do of the black heart beneath the white coat of the rascal that is so soft stepping and pleasant and keeps your silver so clean and bright an' says 'Very good, sir,' to everything the boss says to him—"

"You mean—impossible!"

"Does it not happen every day? Do men and women leave off bein' men and women because they do your housework for you? Hearts as well as platters can break in the kitchen, and who cares what goes on among the help so long as your house is clean and quiet?

"Broken glass. . . ." Her voice rose with the rising wind, thinly. . . . "Wirra, wirra—an' a colleen as innocent of the danger of it as your baby that danced upon it unharmed—praise the saints!—unharmed. . . ."

"I do not understand," said Mrs. Waring, shivering without knowing why. She leaned forward to pluck at the shawl which the other held about her head. At the moment a shaft of light, probably the searchlight from some vessel close inshore—or was it something else?—fell upon the woman's face. It was gone so quickly that Mrs. Waring could not afterward swear to what she had seen. No. Not Mrs. Magillicuddy's face, but similar. Lined and worn but singularly noble.

"*Who are you?*" cried out Mrs. Waring.

"Do ye ask me *that?*" said the Voice.

The flash of light having passed, it seemed so dark that now Mrs. Waring could not even distinguish the film of shadow that had showed where the woman stood.

"Do ye ask me that, mother that loves her children? What would *ye* do, then, if ye were dead, and your children's tears fell upon ye in purgatory? What would ye do if the feet of your own colleen were standing among broken glass that is broken glass indeed?"

"Who are you?" whimpered Mrs. Waring. But the little moon had risen now and showed the moor empty except for the silent lights of the cottages where little children were.

As she stumbled at her own doorstep her butler opened the door with obsequious concern, and obvious amazement when she cried out— "Aileen—where is she?"

"In her room, I think, m'm; the children being asleep. Shall I call her, m'm?"

"*No!*"

She hurried to the attic room and knocked. The door was locked. Something stirred softly and it opened. Aileen's frightened eyes sought her mistress's face. Mrs. Waring read dread of something having been stolen, of some terrible oversight in the nursery, of instant dismissal.

The girl coughed and shivered. She was wearing her coat but her little cap and apron were ready for instant duty. Mrs. Waring remembered with a shock of contrition that Martha had cried because Aileen's hands were cold as she dressed her.

"Aileen—" sobbed Mrs. Waring. . . ."Oh, you poor *little* thing—come down, child, where it is warm!"

Mary Amelia St. Clair (1863–1946), who wrote as May Sinclair, was a popular British writer of two dozen novels and many short stories. She was an active suffragette. Her older siblings were all quite ill, and so beginning in 1896, she wrote to support herself and her mother. Sinclair was interested in psychology and philosophy and wrote frequently on those topics as well as literature, in which field she became a well-regarded critic. Agatha Christie and George Orwell were great admirers of her 1913 novel *The Combined Maze*, and her two volumes of supernatural fiction, *Uncanny Stories* (1923) and *The Intercessor and Other Stories* (1931), were praised by scholars of the genre. The following first appeared in *The English Review* for October 1922 and was included in *Uncanny Stories*.

Where Their Fire Is Not Quenched

by May Sinclair

There was nobody in the orchard. Harriott Leigh went out, carefully, through the iron gate into the field. She had made the latch slip into its notch without a sound.

The path slanted widely up the field from the orchard gate to the stile under the elder tree. George Waring waited for her there.

Years afterwards, when she thought of George Waring she smelt the sweet, hot, wine-scent of the elder flowers. Years afterwards, when she smelt elder flowers she saw George Waring, with his beautiful, gentle face, like a poet's or a musician's, his black-blue eyes, and sleek, olive-brown hair. He was a naval lieutenant.

Yesterday he had asked her to marry him and she had consented. But her father hadn't, and she had come to tell him that and say good-bye before he left her. His ship was to sail the next day.

He was eager and excited. He couldn't believe that anything could stop their happiness, that anything he didn't want to happen could happen.

"Well?" he said.

"He's a perfect beast, George. He won't let us. He says we're too young."

"I was twenty last August," he said, aggrieved.

"And I shall be seventeen in September."

"And this is June. We're quite old, really. How long does he mean us to wait?"

"Three years."

"Three years before we can be engaged even—why, we might be dead."

She put her arms round him to make him feel safe. They kissed; and the sweet, hot, wine-scent of the elder flowers mixed with their kisses. They stood, pressed close together, under the elder tree.

Across the yellow fields of charlock* they heard the village clock strike seven. Up in the house a gong clanged.

"Darling, I must go," she said.

"Oh stay—stay *five* minutes."

He pressed her close. It lasted five minutes, and five more. Then he was running fast down the road to the station, while Harriott went along the field-path, slowly, struggling with her tears.

"He'll be back in three months," she said. "I can live through three months."

But he never came back. There was something wrong with the engines of his ship, the *Alexandra*. Three weeks later she went down in the Mediterranean, and George with her.

Harriott said she didn't care how soon she died now. She was quite sure it would be soon, because she couldn't live without him.

Five years passed.

The two lines of beech trees stretched on and on, the whole length of the Park, a broad green drive between. When you came to the middle they branched off right and left in the form of a cross, and at the end of the right

---

* Field-mustard.

arm there was a white stucco pavilion with pillars and a three-cornered pediment like a Greek temple. At the end of the left arm, the west entrance to the Park, double gates and a side door.

Harriott, on her stone seat at the back of the pavilion, could see Stephen Philpotts the very minute he came through the side door.

He had asked her to wait for him there. It was the place he always chose to read his poems aloud in. The poems were a pretext. She knew what he was going to say. And she knew what she would answer.

There were elder bushes in flower at the back of the pavilion, and Harriott thought of George Waring. She told herself that George was nearer to her now than he could ever have been, living. If she married Stephen she would not be unfaithful, because she loved him with another part of herself. It was not as though Stephen were taking George's place. She loved Stephen with her soul, in an unearthly way.

But her body quivered like a stretched wire when the door opened and the young man came towards her down the drive under the beech trees.

She loved him; she loved his slenderness, his darkness and sallow whiteness, his black eyes lighting up with the intellectual flame, the way his black hair swept back from his forehead, the way he walked, tiptoe, as if his feet were lifted with wings.

He sat down beside her. She could see his hands tremble. She felt that her moment was coming; it had come.

"I wanted to see you alone because there's something I must say to you. I don't quite know how to begin. . . ."

Her lips parted. She panted lightly.

"You've heard me speak of Sybill Foster?"

Her voice came stammering, "N-o, Stephen. Did you?"

"Well, I didn't mean to, till I knew it was all right. I only heard yesterday."

"Heard what?"

"Why, that she'll have me. Oh, Harriott—do you know what it's like to be terribly happy?"

She knew. She had known just now, the moment before he told her. She sat there, stone-cold and stiff, listening to his raptures, listening to her own voice saying she was glad.

Ten years passed.

Harriott Leigh sat waiting in the drawing-room of a small house in Maida Vale.* She had lived there ever since her father's death two years before.

She was restless. She kept on looking at the clock to see if it was four, the hour that Oscar Wade had appointed. She was not sure that he would come, after she had sent him away yesterday.

She now asked herself, why, when she had sent him away yesterday, she had let him come to-day. Her motives were not altogether clear. If she really meant what she had said then, she oughtn't to let him come to her again. Never again.

She had shown him plainly what she meant. She could see herself, sitting very straight in her chair, uplifted by a passionate integrity, while he stood before her, hanging his head, ashamed and beaten; she could feel again the throb in her voice as she kept on saying that she couldn't, she couldn't; he must see that she couldn't, that no, nothing would make her change her mind; she couldn't forget he had a wife; that he must think of Muriel.

To which he had answered savagely: "I needn't. That's all over. We only live together for the look of the thing."

And she, serenely, with great dignity: "And for the look of the thing, Oscar, we must leave off seeing each other. Please go."

"Do you mean it?"

"Yes. We must never see each other again." And he had gone then, ashamed and beaten.

She could see him, squaring his broad shoulders to meet the blow. And she was sorry for him. She told herself she had been unnecessarily hard. Why shouldn't they see each other again, now he understood where they must draw the line? Until yesterday the line had never been very clearly drawn. To-day she meant to ask him to forget what he had said to her. Once it was forgotten, they could go on being friends as if nothing had happened.

It was four o'clock. Half-past. Five. She had finished tea and given him up when, between the half-hour and six o'clock, he came.

---

* An affluent London neighborhood.

He came as he had come a dozen times, with his measured, deliberate, thoughtful tread, carrying himself well braced, with a sort of held-in arrogance, his great shoulders heaving. He was a man of about forty, broad and tall, lean-flanked and short-necked, his straight, handsome features showing small and even in the big square face and in the flush that swamped it. The close-clipped, reddish-brown moustache bristled forwards from the pushed-out upper lip. His small, flat eyes shone, reddish-brown, eager and animal.

She liked to think of him when he was not there, but always at the first sight of him she felt a slight shock. Physically, he was very far from her admired ideal. So different from George Waring and Stephen Philpotts.

He sat down, facing her.

There was an embarrassed silence, broken by Oscar Wade.

"Well, Harriott, you said I could come." He seemed to be throwing the responsibility on her. "So I suppose you've forgiven me," he said.

"Oh, yes, Oscar, I've forgiven you."

He said she'd better show it by coming to dine with him somewhere that evening. She could give no reason to herself for going. She simply went.

He took her to a restaurant in Soho. Oscar Wade dined well, even extravagantly, giving each dish its importance. She liked his extravagance. He had none of the mean virtues.

It was over. His flushed, embarrassed silence told her what he was thinking. But when he had seen her home, he left her at her garden gate. He had thought better of it.

She was not sure whether she were glad or sorry. She had had her moment of righteous exaltation and she had enjoyed it. But there was no joy in the weeks that followed. She had given up Oscar Wade because she didn't want him very much; and now she wanted him furiously, perversely, because she had given him up. Though he had no resemblance to her ideal, she couldn't live without him.

She dined with him again and again, till she knew Schnebler's Restaurant by heart, the white panelled walls picked out with gold; the white pillars, and the curling gold fronds of their capitals; the Turkey carpets, blue and crimson, soft under her feet, the thick crimson velvet cushions, that clung to her skirts; the glitter of silver and glass on the innumerable white circles of the tables. And the faces of the diners, red, white, pink, brown, grey and sallow, distorted and excited; the curled mouths that twisted as they ate; the convoluted electric bulbs pointing, pointing down at them, under the red, crinkled shades. All shimmering in a thick air that the red light stained as wine stains water.

And Oscar's face, flushed with his dinner. Always, when he leaned back from the table and brooded in silence she knew what he was thinking. His heavy eyelids would lift, she would find his eyes fixed on hers, wondering, considering.

She knew now what the end would be. She thought of George Waring, and Stephen Philpotts, and of her life, cheated. She hadn't chosen Oscar, she hadn't really wanted him; but now he had forced himself on her she couldn't afford to let him go. Since George died no man had loved her, no other man ever would. And she was sorry for him when she thought of him going from her, beaten and ashamed.

She was certain, before he was, of the end. Only she didn't know when and where and how it would come. That was what Oscar knew.

It came at the close of one of their evenings when they had dined in a private sitting-room. He said he couldn't stand the heat and noise of the public restaurant.

She went before him, up a steep, red-carpeted stair to a white door on the second landing.

From time to time they repeated the furtive, hidden adventure. Sometimes she met him in the room above Schnebler's. Sometimes, when her maid was out, she received him at her house in Maida Vale. But that was dangerous, not to be risked too often.

Oscar declared himself unspeakably happy. Harriott was not quite sure. This was love, the thing she had never had, that she had dreamed of, hungered and thirsted for; but now she had it she was not satisfied. Always she looked for something just beyond it, some mystic, heavenly rapture, always beginning to come, that never came. There was something about Oscar that repelled her. But because she had taken him for her lover, she couldn't bring herself to admit that it was a certain coarseness. She looked another way and pretended it wasn't there. To justify herself, she fixed her mind on his good qualities, his generosities, his strength, the way he had built up his engineering business. She made him take her over his works, and show her his great dynamos. She made him lend her the books he read. But always, when she tried to talk to him, he let her see that *that* wasn't what she was there for.

"My dear girl, we haven't time," he said. "It's waste of our priceless moments."

She persisted. "There's something wrong about it all if we can't talk to each other."

He was irritated. "Women never seem to consider that a man can get all the talk he wants from other men. What's wrong is our meeting in this unsatisfactory way. We ought to live together. It's the only sane thing. I would, only I don't want to break up Muriel's home and make her miserable."

"I thought you said she wouldn't care."

"My dear, she cares for her home and her position and the children. You forget the children." Yes. She had forgotten the children. She had forgotten Muriel. She had left off thinking of Oscar as a man with a wife and children and a home.

He had a plan. His mother-in-law was coming to stay with Muriel in October and he would get away. He would go to Paris, and Harriott should come to him there. He could say he went on business. No need to lie about it; he *had* business in Paris.

He engaged rooms in an hotel in the Rue de Rivoli. They spent two weeks there.

For three days Oscar was madly in love with Harriott and Harriott with him. As she lay awake she would turn on the light and look at him as he slept at her side. Sleep made him beautiful and innocent; it laid a fine, smooth tissue over his coarseness; it made his mouth gentle; it entirely hid his eyes.

In six days reaction had set in. At the end of the tenth day, Harriott, returning with Oscar from Montmartre, burst into a fit of crying. When questioned, she answered wildly that the Hotel Saint Pierre was too hideously ugly; it was getting on her nerves. Mercifully Oscar explained her state as fatigue following excitement. She tried hard to believe that she was miserable because her love was purer and more spiritual than Oscar's; but all the time she knew perfectly well she had cried from pure boredom. She was in love with Oscar, and Oscar bored her. Oscar was in love with her, and she bored him. At close quarters, day in and day out, each was revealed to the other as an incredible bore. At the end of the second week she began to doubt whether she had ever been really in love with him.

Her passion returned for a little while after they got back to London. Freed from the unnatural strain which Paris had put on them, they persuaded themselves that their romantic temperaments were better fitted to the old life of casual adventure.

Then, gradually, the sense of danger began to wake in them. They lived in perpetual fear, face to face with all the chances of discovery. They tormented themselves and each other by imagining possibilities that they would never have considered in their first fine moments. It was as though they were beginning to ask themselves if it were, after all, worth while running such awful risks, for all they got out of it. Oscar still swore that if he had been free he would have married her. He pointed out that his intentions at any rate were regular. But she asked herself: Would I marry *him?* Marriage would be the Hotel Saint Pierre all over again, without any possibility of escape. But, if she wouldn't marry him, was she in love with him? That was the test. Perhaps it was a good thing he wasn't free. Then she told herself that these doubts were morbid, and that the question wouldn't arise.

One evening Oscar called to see her. He had come to tell her that Muriel was ill. "Seriously ill?"

"I'm afraid so. It's pleurisy. May turn to pneumonia. We shall know one way or another in the next few days."

A terrible fear seized upon Harriott. Muriel might die of her pleurisy; and if Muriel died, she would have to marry Oscar. He was looking at her queerly, as if he knew what she was thinking, and she could see that the same thought had occurred to him and that he was frightened too.

Muriel got well again; but their danger had enlightened them. Muriel's life was now inconceivably precious to them both; she stood between them and that permanent union, which they dreaded and yet would not have the courage to refuse.

After enlightenment the rupture.

It came from Oscar, one evening when he sat with her in her drawing-room. "Harriott," he said, "do you know I'm thinking seriously of settling down?"

"How do you mean, settling down?"

"Patching it up with Muriel, poor girl. . . . Has it never occurred to you that this little affair of ours can't go on for ever?"

"You don't want it to go on?"

"I don't want to have any humbug about it. For God's sake, let's be straight. If it's done, it's done. Let's end it decently."

"I see. You want to get rid of me."

"That's a beastly way of putting it."

"Is there any way that isn't beastly? The whole thing's beastly. I should have thought you'd have stuck to it now you've made it what you wanted. When I haven't an ideal, I haven't a single illusion, when you've destroyed everything you didn't want."

"What didn't I want?"

"The clean, beautiful part of it. The part *I* wanted."

"My part at least was real. It was cleaner and more beautiful than all that putrid stuff you wrapped it up in. You were a hypocrite, Harriott, and I wasn't. You're a hypocrite now if you say you weren't happy with me."

"I was never really happy. Never for one moment. There was always something I missed. Something you didn't give me. Perhaps you couldn't."

"No. I wasn't spiritual enough," he sneered.

"You were not. And you made me what you were."

"Oh, I noticed that you were always very spiritual *after* you'd got what you wanted."

"What I wanted?" she cried. "Oh, my God—"

"If you ever knew what you wanted."

"What—I—wanted," she repeated, drawing out her bitterness.

"Come," he said, "why not be honest? Face facts. I was awfully gone on you. You were awfully gone on me—once. We got tired of each other and it's over. But at least you might own we had a good time while it lasted."

"A good time?"

"Good enough for me."

"For you, because for you love only means one thing. Everything that's high and noble in it you dragged down to that, till there's nothing left for us but that. *That's* what you made of love."

Twenty years passed.

⊶⟶⊷

It was Oscar who died first, three years after the rupture. He did it suddenly one evening, falling down in a fit of apoplexy.[*]

His death was an immense relief to Harriott. Perfect security had been impossible as long as he was alive. But now there wasn't a living soul who knew her secret.

Still, in the first moment of shock Harriott told herself that Oscar dead would be nearer to her than ever. She forgot how little she had wanted him to be near her, alive. And long before the twenty years had passed she had contrived to persuade herself that he had never been near to her at all. It was incredible that she had ever known such a person as Oscar Wade. As for their affair, she couldn't think of Harriott Leigh as the sort of woman to whom such a thing could happen. Schnebler's and the Hotel Saint Pierre ceased to figure among prominent images of her past. Her memories, if she had allowed herself to remember, would have clashed disagreeably with the reputation for sanctity which she had now acquired.

For Harriott at fifty-two was the friend and helper of the Reverend Clement Farmer, Vicar of St. Mary the Virgin, Maida Vale. She worked as a deaconess in his parish, wearing the uniform of a deaconess, the semi-religious gown, the cloak, the bonnet and veil, the cross and rosary, the holy smile. She was also secretary to the Maida Vale and Kilbum Home for Fallen Girls.

Her moments of excitement came when Clement Farmer, the lean, austere likeness of Stephen Philpotts, in his cassock and lace-bordered surplice, issued from the vestry, when he mounted the pulpit, when he stood before the altar rails and lifted up his arms in the Benediction; her moments of ecstasy when she received the Sacrament from his hands. And

---

[*] A stroke.

she had moments of calm happiness when his study door closed on their communion. All these moments were saturated with a solemn holiness.

And they were insignificant compared with the moment of her dying.

She lay dozing in her white bed under the black crucifix with the ivory Christ. The basins and medicine bottles had been cleared from the table by her pillow; it was spread for the last rites. The priest moved quietly about the room, arranging the candles, the Prayer Book and the Holy Sacrament. Then he drew a chair to her bedside and watched with her, waiting for her to come up out of her doze.

She woke suddenly. Her eyes were fixed upon him. She had a flash of lucidity. She was dying, and her dying made her supremely important to Clement Farmer.

"Are you ready?" he asked.

"Not yet. I think I'm afraid. Make me not afraid."

He rose and lit the two candles on the altar. He took down the crucifix from the wall and stood it against the foot-rail of the bed.

She sighed. That was not what she had wanted. "You will not be afraid now," he said.

"I'm not afraid of the hereafter. I suppose you get used to it. Only it may be terrible just at first."

"Our first state will depend very much on what we are thinking of at our last hour."

"There'll be my—confession," she said.

"And after it you will receive the Sacrament. Then you will have your mind fixed firmly upon God and your Redeemer. . . . Do you feel able to make your confession now, Sister? Everything is ready."

Her mind went back over her past and found Oscar Wade there. She wondered: Should she confess to him about Oscar Wade? One moment she thought it was possible; the next she knew that she couldn't. She could not. It wasn't necessary. For twenty years he had not been part of her life. No. She wouldn't confess about Oscar Wade. She had been guilty of other sins.

She made a careful selection.

"I have cared too much for the beauty of this world. . . . I have failed in charity to my poor girls. Because of my intense repugnance to their sin. . . . I have thought, often, about—people I love, when I should have been thinking about God."

After that she received the Sacrament.

"Now," he said, "there is nothing to be afraid of."

"I won't be afraid if—if you would hold my hand."

He held it. And she lay still a long time, with her eyes shut. Then he heard her murmuring something. He stooped close.

"This—is—dying. I thought it would be horrible. And it's bliss. . . . Bliss."

The priest's hand slackened, as if at the bidding of some wonder. She gave a weak cry. "Oh—don't let me go."

His grasp tightened.

"Try," he said, "to think about God. Keep on looking at the crucifix."

"If I look," she whispered, "you won't let go my hand?"

"I will not let you go."

He held it till it was wrenched from him in the last agony.

⚬———⚬

She lingered for some hours in the room where these things had happened.

Its aspect was familiar and yet unfamiliar, and slightly repugnant to her. The altar, the crucifix, the lighted candles, suggested some tremendous and awful experience the details of which she was not able to recall. She seemed to remember that they had been connected in some way with the sheeted body on the bed; but the nature of the connection was not clear; and she did not associate the dead body with herself. When the nurse came in and laid it out, she saw that it was the body of a middle-aged woman. Her own living body was that of a young woman of about thirty-two.

Her mind had no past and no future, no sharp-edged, coherent memories, and no idea of anything to be done next.

Then, suddenly, the room began to come apart before her eyes, to split into shafts of floor and furniture and ceiling that shifted and were thrown by their commotion into different planes. They leaned slanting at every possible angle; they crossed and overlaid each other with a transparent mingling of dislocated perspectives, like reflections fallen on an interior seen behind glass.

The bed and the sheeted body slid away somewhere out of sight. She was standing by the door that still remained in position.

She opened it and found herself in the street, outside a building of yellowish-brick and freestone, with a tall slated spire. Her mind came together with a palpable click of recognition. This object was the Church of St. Mary the Virgin, Maida Vale. She could hear the droning of the organ. She opened the door and slipped in.

She had gone back into a definite space and time, and recovered a certain limited section of coherent memory. She remembered the rows of pitch-pine benches, with their Gothic peaks and mouldings; the stone-coloured walls and pillars with their chocolate stencilling; the hanging rings of lights along the aisles of the nave; the high altar with its lighted candles, and the polished brass cross, twinkling. These things were somehow permanent and real, adjusted to the image that now took possession of her.

She knew what she had come there for. The service was over. The choir had gone from the chancel; the sacristan moved before the altar, putting out the candles. She walked up the middle aisle to a seat that she knew under the pulpit. She knelt down and covered her face with her hands. Peeping sideways through her fingers, she could see the door of the vestry on her left at the end of the north aisle. She watched it steadily.

Up in the organ loft the organist drew out the Recessional, slowly and softly, to its end in the two solemn, vibrating chords.

The vestry door opened and Clement Farmer came out, dressed in his black cassock. He passed before her, close, close outside the bench where she knelt. He paused at the opening. He was waiting for her. There was something he had to say.

She stood up and went towards him. He still waited. He didn't move to make way for her. She came close, closer than she had ever come to him, so close that his features grew indistinct. She bent her head back, peering short-sightedly, and found herself looking into Oscar Wade's face.

He stood still, horribly still, and close, barring her passage.

She drew back, his heaving shoulders followed her. He leaned forward, covering her with his eyes. She opened her mouth to scream and no sound came.

She was afraid to move lest he should move with her. The heaving of his shoulders terrified her.

One by one the lights in the side aisles were going out. The lights in the middle aisle would go next. They had gone. If she didn't get away she would be shut up with him there, in the appalling darkness.

She turned and moved towards the north aisle, groping, steadying herself by the book ledge. When she looked back, Oscar Wade was not there.

Then she remembered that Oscar Wade was dead. Therefore, what she had seen was not Oscar; it was his ghost. He was dead; dead seventeen years ago. She was safe from him for ever.

When she came out on to the steps of the church she saw that the road it stood in had changed. It was not the road she remembered. The pavement on this side was raised slightly and covered in. It ran under a succession of arches. It was a long gallery walled with glittering shop windows on one side; on the other a line of tall grey columns divided it from the street.

She was going along the arcades of the rue de Rivoli. Ahead of her she could see the edge of an immense grey pillar jutting out. That was the porch of the Hotel Saint Pierre. The revolving glass doors swung forward to receive her; she crossed the grey, sultry vestibule under the pillared arches. She knew it. She knew the porter's shining, wine-coloured, mahogany pen on her left, and the shining, wine-coloured, mahogany barrier of the clerk's bureau on her right; she made straight for the great grey carpeted staircase; she climbed the endless flights that turned round and round the caged-in shaft of the well, past the latticed doors of the lift, and came up on to a landing that she knew, and into the long, ash-grey, foreign corridor lit by a dull window at one end.

It was there that the horror of the place came on her. She had no longer any memory of St. Mary's Church, so that she was unaware of her backward course through time. All space and time were here.

She remembered she had to go to the left, the left.

But there was something there; where the corridor turned by the window; at the end of all the corridors. If she went the other way she would escape it.

The corridor stopped there. A blank wall. She was driven back past the stairhead to the left.

At the corner, by the window, she turned down another long ash-grey corridor on her right, and to the right again where the night-light sputtered on the table-flap at the turn.

This third corridor was dark and secret and depraved. She knew the soiled walls, and the warped door at the end. There was a sharp-pointed streak of light at the top. She could see the number on it now, 107.

Something had happened there. If she went in it would happen again. Oscar Wade was in the room waiting for her behind the closed door. She felt him moving about in there. She leaned forward, her ear to the key-hole, and listened. She could hear the measured, deliberate, thoughtful footsteps. They were coming from the bed to the door.

She turned and ran; her knees gave way under her; she sank and ran on, down the long grey corridors and the stairs, quick and blind, a hunted beast seeking for cover, hearing his feet coming after her.

The revolving doors caught her and pushed her out into the street.

The strange quality of her state was this, that it had no time. She remembered dimly that there had once been a thing called time; but she had forgotten altogether what it was like. She was aware of things happening and about to happen; she fixed them by the place they occupied, and measured their duration by the space she went through.

So now she thought: If I could only go back and get to the place where it hadn't happened. To get back farther—

She was walking now on a white road that went between broad grass borders.

To the right and left were the long raking lines of the hills, curve after curve, shimmering in a thin mist.

The road dropped to the green valley. It mounted the humped bridge over the river. Beyond it she saw the twin gables of the grey house pricked up over the high, grey garden wall. The tall iron gate stood in front of it between the ball-topped stone pillars.

And now she was in a large, low-ceilinged room with drawn blinds. She was standing before the wide double bed. It was her father's bed. The dead body, stretched out in the middle under the drawn white sheet, was her father's body.

The outline of the sheet sank from the peak of the upturned toes to the shin bone, and from the high bridge of the nose to the chin.

She lifted the sheet and folded it back across the breast of the dead man. The face she saw then was Oscar Wade's face, stilled and smoothed in the innocence of sleep, the supreme innocence of death. She stared at it, fascinated, in a cold, pitiless joy.

Oscar was dead.

She remembered how he used to lie like that beside her in the room in the Hotel Saint Pierre, on his back with his hands folded on his waist, his mouth half open, his big chest rising and falling. If he was dead, it would never happen again. She would be safe.

The dead face frightened her, and she was about to cover it up again when she was aware of a light heaving, a rhythmical rise and fall. As she drew the sheet up tighter, the hands under it began to struggle convulsively, the broad ends of the fingers appeared above the edge, clutching it to keep it down. The mouth opened; the eyes opened; the whole face stared back at her in a look of agony and horror.

Then the body drew itself forwards from the hips and sat up, its eyes peering into her eyes; he and she remained for an instant motionless, each held there by the other's fear.

Suddenly she broke away, turned and ran, out of the room, out of the house. She stood at the gate, looking up and down the road, not knowing by which way she must go to escape Oscar. To the right, over the bridge and up the hill and across the downs she would come to the arcades of the rue de Rivoli and the dreadful grey corridors of the hotel. To the left the road went through the village.

If she could get further back she would be safe, out of Oscar's reach. Standing by her father's death-bed she had been young, but not young enough. She must get back to the place where she was younger still, to the Park and the green drive under the beech trees and the white pavilion at the cross. She knew how to find it. At the end of the village the high road ran right and left, east and west, under the Park walls; the south gate stood there at the top looking down the narrow street.

She ran towards it through the village, past the long grey barns of Goodyer's farm, past the grocer's shop, past the yellow front and blue sign of the "Queen's Head," past the post office, with its one black window blinking under its vine, past the church and the yew-trees in the churchyard, to where the south gate made a delicate black pattern on the green grass.

These things appeared insubstantial, drawn back behind a sheet of air that shimmered over them like thin glass. They opened out, floated past and away from her; and instead of the high road and Park walls she saw a London street of dingy white façades, and instead of the south gate the swinging glass doors of Schnebler's Restaurant.

⊶

The glass doors swung open and she passed into the restaurant. The scene beat on her with the hard impact of reality: the white and gold panels, the white pillars and their curling gold capitals, the white circles of the tables, glittering, the flushed faces of the diners, moving mechanically.

She was driven forward by some irresistible compulsion to a table in the corner, where a man sat alone. The table napkin he was using hid his mouth, and jaw, and chest; and she was not sure of the upper part of the face above the straight, drawn edge. It dropped; and she saw Oscar Wade's face. She came to him, dragged, without power to resist; she sat down beside him, and he leaned to her over the table; she could feel the warmth of his red, congested face; the smell of wine floated towards her on his thick whisper.

"I knew you would come."

She ate and drank with him in silence, nibbling and sipping slowly, staving off the abominable moment it would end in.

At last they got up and faced each other. His long bulk stood before her, above her; she could almost feel the vibration of its power.

"Come," he said. "Come."

And she went before him, slowly, slipping out through the maze of the tables, hearing behind her Oscar's measured, deliberate, thoughtful tread. The steep, red-carpeted staircase rose up before her.

She swerved from it, but he turned her back. "You know the way," he said.

At the top of the flight she found the white door of the room she knew. She knew the long windows guarded by drawn muslin blinds; the gilt looking-glass over the chimney-piece that reflected Oscar's head and shoulders grotesquely between two white porcelain babies with bulbous limbs and garlanded loins, she knew the sprawling stain on the drab carpet by the table, the shabby, infamous couch behind the screen.

They moved about the room, turning and turning in it like beasts in a cage, uneasy, inimical, avoiding each other.

At last they stood still, he at the window, she at the door, the length of the room between.

"It's no good your getting away like that," he said. "There couldn't be any other end to it—to what we did."

"But that was ended."

"Ended there, but not here."

"Ended for ever. We've done with it for ever."

"We haven't. We've got to begin again. And go on. And go on."

"Oh, no. No. Anything but that."

"There isn't anything else."

"We can't. We can't. Don't you remember how it bored us?"

"Remember? Do you suppose I'd touch you if I could help it? . . . That's what we're here for. We must. We must."

"No. No. I shall get away—now." She turned to the door to open it.

"You can't," he said. "The door's locked."

"Oscar—what did you do that for?"

"We always did it. Don't you remember?"

She turned to the door again and shook it; she beat on it with her hands.

"It's no use, Harriott. If you got out now you'd only have to come back again. You might stave it off for an hour or so, but what's that in an immortality?"

"Immortality?"

"That's what we're in for."

"Time enough to talk about immortality when we're dead. . . . Ah—"

They were being drawn towards each other across the room, moving slowly, like figures in some monstrous and appalling dance, their heads thrown back over their shoulders, their faces turned from the horrible approach. Their arms rose slowly, heavy with intolerable reluctance; they stretched them out towards each other, aching, as if they held up an over-powering weight. Their feet dragged and were drawn.

Suddenly her knees sank under her; she shut her eyes; all her being went down before him in darkness and terror.

It was over. She had got away, she was going back, back, to the green drive of the Park, between the beech trees, where Oscar had never been, where he would never find her. When she passed through the south gate her memory became suddenly young and clean. She forgot the Rue de Rivoli and the Hotel Saint Pierre, she forgot Schnebler's Restaurant and the room at the top of the stairs. She was back in her youth. She was Harriott Leigh going to wait for Stephen Philpotts in the pavilion opposite the west gate. She could feel herself, a slender figure moving fast over the grass between the lines of the great beech trees. The freshness of her youth was upon her.

She came to the heart of the drive where it branched right and left in the form of a cross. At the end of the right arm the white Greek temple, with its pediment and pillars, gleamed against the wood.

She was sitting on their seat at the back of the pavilion, watching the side door that Stephen would come in by.

The door was pushed open; he came towards her, light and young, skimming between the beech trees with his eager, tiptoeing stride. She rose up to meet him. She gave a cry.

"Stephen!"

It had been Stephen. She had seen him coming. But the man who stood before her between the pillars of the pavilion was Oscar Wade.

And now she was walking along the field-path that slanted from the orchard door to the stile, further and further back, to where young George Waring waited for her under the elder tree. The smell of the elder flowers came to her over the field. She could feel on her lips and in all her body the sweet, innocent excitement of her youth.

"George, oh, George?"

As she went along the field-path she had seen him. But the man who stood waiting for her under the elder tree was Oscar Wade.

"I told you it's no use getting away, Harriott. Every path brings you back to me. You'll find me at every turn."

"But how did you get here?"

"As I got into the pavilion. As I got into your father's room, on to his death bed. Because I was there. I am in all your memories."

"My memories are innocent. How could you take my father's place, and Stephen's, and George Waring's? You?"

"Because I did take them."

"Never. My love for them was innocent."

"Your love for me was part of it. You think the past affects the future. Has it never struck you that the future may affect the past? In your innocence there was the beginning of your sin. You were what you were to be."

"I shall get away," she said.

"And, this time, I shall go with you."

The stile, the elder tree, and the field floated away from her. She was going under the beech trees down the Park drive towards the south gate and the village, slinking close to the right-hand row of trees. She was aware that Oscar Wade was going with her under the left-hand row, keeping even with her, step by step, and tree by tree. And presently there was grey pavement under her feet and a row of grey pillars on her right hand. They were walking side by side down the rue de Rivoli towards the hotel.

They were sitting together now on the edge of the dingy white bed. Their arms hung by their sides, heavy and limp, their heads drooped, averted. Their passion weighed on them with the unbearable, unescapable boredom of immortality.

"Oscar—how long will it last?"

"I can't tell you. I don't know whether this is one moment of eternity, or the eternity of one moment."

"It must end some time," she said. "Life doesn't go on for ever. We shall die."

"Die? We *have* died. Don't you know what this is? Don't you know where you are? This is death. We're dead, Harriott. We're in hell."

"Yes. There can't be anything worse than this."

"This isn't the worst. We're not quite dead yet, as long as we've life in us to turn and run and get away from each other; as long as we can escape into our memories. But when you've got back to the farthest memory of all and there's nothing beyond it—when there's no memory but this—

"In the last hell we shall not run away any longer; we shall find no more roads, no more passages, no more open doors. We shall have no need to look for each other.

"In the last death we shall be shut up in this room, behind that locked door, together. We shall lie here together, for ever and ever, joined so fast that even God can't put us asunder. We shall be one flesh and one spirit, one sin repeated for ever, and ever; spirit loathing flesh, flesh loathing spirit; you and I loathing each other."

"Why? Why?" she cried.

"Because that's all that's left us. That's what you made of love."

<hr />

The darkness came down swamping, it blotted out the room. She was walking along a garden path between high borders of phlox and larkspur and lupin. They were taller than she was, their flowers swayed and nodded above her head. She tugged at the tall stems and had no strength to break them. She was a little thing.

She said to herself then that she was safe. She had gone back so far that she was a child again; she had the blank innocence of childhood. To be a child, to go small under the heads of the lupins, to be blank and innocent, without memory, was to be safe.

The walk led her out through a yew hedge on to a bright green lawn. In the middle of the lawn there was a shallow round pond in a ring of rockery cushioned with small flowers, yellow and white and purple. Gold-fish swam in the olive brown water. She would be safe when she saw the gold-fish swimming towards her. The old one with the white scales would come up first, pushing up his nose, making bubbles in the water.

At the bottom of the lawn there was a privet hedge cut by a broad path that went through the orchard. She knew what she would find there; her mother was in the orchard. She would lift her up in her arms to play with the hard red balls of the apples that hung from the tree. She had got back to the farthest memory of all; there was nothing beyond it.

There would be an iron gate in the wall of the orchard. It would lead into a field.

Something was different here, something that frightened her. An ash-grey door instead of an iron gate.

She pushed it open and came into the last corridor of the Hotel Saint Pierre.

Zora Neale Hurston (1890–1961) was one of the shining figures of the Harlem Renaissance. Her best-known work is the novel *Their Eyes Were Watching God* (1937), though she wrote anthropological studies, copious amounts of fiction (four novels and dozens of short stories), and made several films. Born in the South, she lived in Eatonville, Florida, one of the nation's first self-governed, all-Black communities. Hurston attended Howard University, where she made an important connection with Alain Locke, the doyen of the university's literary club. Subsequently, she studied anthropology at Barnard College and Columbia University. Hurston's literary talent was recognized by contemporaries including Langston Hughes and Countee Cullen. She published a few pieces of poetry and a short story or two in Black journals, but her "breakthrough" occurred when the following story, which first appeared in the June 1925 issue of *Opportunity: A Journal of Negro Life*, was selected to appear in *The New Negro: An Interpretation* (1925), edited by her mentor Alain Locke. The anthology collected fiction, poetry, and essays celebrating African and Afro-American culture and is regarded as the definitive work of the Harlem Renaissance. The story reflects Hurston's interest in folklore and villages like Eatonville, as well as her determination to portray the lives of the Black lower classes. It also foreshadows her later extensive anthropological work to discover and record folktales of the South and the Caribbean. Sadly, Hurston's literary work fell from sight after the 1930s until a revival occurred in the mid-1970s, when Alice Walker (later the author of *The Color Purple* [1982]) wrote a story for *Ms. Magazine* about Hurston's life and work.

Spunk

by Zora Neale Hurston

A giant of a brown-skinned man sauntered up the one street of the Village and out into the palmetto thickets with a small pretty woman clinging lovingly to his arm.

"Looka theah, folkses!" cried Elijah Mosley, slapping his leg gleefully. "Theah they go, big as life an' brassy as tacks."

All the loungers in the store tried to walk to the door with an air of nonchalance but with small success.

"Now pee-eople!" Walter Thomas gasped. "Will you look at 'em!"

"But that's one thing Ah likes about Spunk Banks—he ain't skeered of nothin' on God's green footstool—nothin'! He rides that log down at saw-mill jus' like he struts 'round wid another man's wife—jus' don't give a kitty. When Tes' Miller got cut to giblets on that circle-saw, Spunk steps right up and starts ridin'. The rest of us was skeered to go near it."

A round-shouldered figure in overalls much too large, came nervously in the door and the talking ceased. The men looked at each other and winked.

"Gimme some soda-water. Sass'prilla Ah reckon," the newcomer ordered, and stood far down the counter near the open pickled pig-feet tub to drink it.

Elijah nudged Walter and turned with mock gravity to the new-comer.

"Say, Joe, how's everything up yo' way? How's yo' wife?"

Joe started and all but dropped the bottle he held in his hands. He swallowed several times painfully and his lips trembled.

"Aw 'Lige, you oughtn't to do nothin' like that," Walter grumbled. Elijah ignored him.

"She jus' passed heah a few minutes ago goin' theta way," with a wave of his hand in the direction of the woods.

Now Joe knew his wife had passed that way. He knew that the men lounging in the general store had seen her, moreover, he knew that the men knew he knew. He stood there silent for a long moment staring blankly, with his Adam's apple twitching nervously up and down his throat. One could actually see the pain he was suffering, his eyes, his face, his hands and even the dejected slump of his shoulders. He set the bottle down upon the counter. He didn't bang it, just eased it out of his hand silently and fiddled with his suspender buckle.

"Well, Ah'm goin' after her to-day. Ah'm goin' an' fetch her back. Spunk's done gone too fur."

He reached deep down into his trouser pocket and drew out a hollow ground razor,* large and shiny, and passed his moistened thumb back and forth over the edge.

"Talkin' like a man, Joe. Course that's yo' fambly affairs, but Ah like to see grit in anybody."

Joe Kanty laid down a nickel and stumbled out into the street.

Dusk crept in from the woods. Ike Clarke lit the swinging oil lamp that was almost immediately surrounded by candle-flies. The men laughed boisterously behind Joe's back as they watched him shamble woodward.

"You oughtn't to said whut you did to him, Lige—look how it worked him up," Walter chided.

"And Ah hope it did work him up. 'Tain't even decent for a man to take and take like he do."

"Spunk will sho' kill him."

"Aw, Ah doan't know. You never kin tell. He might turn him up an' spank him fur gettin' in the way, but Spunk wouldn't shoot no unarmed man. Dat razor he carried outa heah ain't gonna run Spunk down an' cut him, an' Joe ain't got the nerve to go up to Spunk with it knowing he totes that Army 45. He makes that break outa heah to bluff us. He's gonna hide that razor behind the first likely palmetto root an' sneak back home to bed. Don't tell me nothin' 'bout that rabbit-foot colored man. Didn't he meet Spunk an' Lena face to face one day las' week an' mumble sumthin' to Spunk 'bout lettin' his wife alone?"

"What did Spunk say?" Walter broke in—"Ah like him fine but 'tain't right the way he carries on wid Lena Kanty, jus' cause Joe's timid 'bout fightin'."

"You wrong theah, Walter. 'Tain't cause Joe's timid at all, it's cause Spunk wants Lena. If Joe was a passle of wile cats Spunk would tackle the job just the same. He'd go after anything he wanted the same way. As Ah wuz sayin' a minute ago, he tole Joe right to his face that Lena was his. 'Call her,' he says to Joe. 'Call her and see if she'll come. A woman knows her boss an' she answers when he calls.' 'Lena, ain't I yo' husband?' Joe sorter whines out. Lena looked at him real disgusted but she don't answer and

---

* A hollow ground razor has the sharpest grade of blade.

she don't move outa her tracks. Then Spunk reaches out an' takes hold of her arm an' says: 'Lena, youse mine. From now on Ah works for you an' fights for you an' Ah never wants you to look to nobody for a crumb of bread, a stitch of close or a shingle to go over yo' head, but me long as Ah live. Ah'll git the lumber foh owah house to-morrow. Go home an' git yo' things together!'

" 'Thass mah house,' Lena speaks up. 'Papa gimme that.'

"'Well,' says Spunk, 'doan give up whut's yours, but when youse inside don't forgit youse mine, an' let no other man git outa his place wid you!'

"Lena looked up at him with her eyes so full of love that they wuz runnin' over, an' Spunk seen it an' Joe seen it too, and his lip started to tremblin' and his Adam's apple was galloping up and down his neck like a race horse. Ah bet he's wore out half a dozen Adam's apples since Spunk's been on the job with Lena. That's all he'll do. He'll be back heah after while swallowin' an' workin' his lips like he wants to say somethin' an' can't."

"But didn't he do nothin' to stop 'em?"

"Nope, not a frazzlin' thing—jus' stood there. Spunk took Lena's arm and walked off jus' like nothin' ain't happened and he stood there gazin' after them till they was outa sight. Now you know a woman don't want no man like that. I'm jus' waitin' to see whut he's goin' to say when he gits back."

II

But Joe Kanty never came back, never. The men in the store heard the sharp report of a pistol somewhere distant in the palmetto thicket and soon Spunk came walking leisurely, with his big black Stetson set at the same rakish angle and Lena clinging to his arm, came walking right into the general store. Lena wept in a frightened manner.

"Well," Spunk announced calmly, "Joe come out there wid a meatax an' made me kill him."

He sent Lena home and led the men back to Joe—Joe crumpled and limp with his right hand still clutching his razor.

"See mah back? Mah cloes cut clear through. He sneaked up an' tried to kill me from the back, but Ah got him, an' got him good, first shot," Spunk said.

The men glared at Elijah, accusingly.

"Take him up an' plant him in 'Stoney lonesome,'" Spunk said in a care-less voice. "Ah didn't wanna shoot him but he made me do it. He's a dirty coward, jumpin' on a man from behind."

Spunk turned on his heel and sauntered away to where he knew his love wept in fear for him and no man stopped him. At the general store later on, they all talked of locking him up until the sheriff should come from Orlando, but no one did anything but talk.

A clear case of self-defense, the trial was a short one, and Spunk walked out of the court house to freedom again. He could work again, ride the dangerous log-carriage that fed the singing, snarling, biting, circle-saw; he could stroll the soft dark lanes with his guitar. He was free to roam the woods again; he was free to return to Lena. He did all of these things.

III

"Whut you reckon, Walt?" Elijah asked one night later. "Spunk's gittin' ready to marry Lena!"

"Naw! Why, Joe ain't had time to git cold yit. Nohow Ah didn't figger Spunk was the marryin' kind."

"Well, he is," rejoined Elijah. "He done moved most of Lena's things—and her along wid 'em—over to the Bradley house. He's buying it. Jus' like Ah told yo' all right in heah the night Joe wuz kilt. Spunk's crazy 'bout Lena. He don't want folks to keep on talkin' 'bout her—thass reason he's rushin' so. Funny thing 'bout that bob-cat, wan't it?"

"What bob-cat, 'Lige? Ah ain't heered 'bout none."

"Ain't cher? Well, night befo' las' was the fust night Spunk an' Lena moved together an' jus' as they was goin' to bed, a big black bob-cat,* black all over, you hear me, black, walked round and round that house and howled like forty, an' when Spunk got his gun an' went to the winder to shoot it he says it stood right still an' looked him in the eye, an' howled right at him.

---

* Black (melanistic) bobcats are extremely rare—only twelve have been recorded in North America, with ten of those being found in Florida.

The thing got Spunk so nervoused up he couldn't shoot. But Spunk says twan't no bob-cat nohow. He says it was Joe done sneaked back from Hell!"

"Humph!" sniffed Walter, "he oughter be nervous after what he done. Ah reckon Joe come back to dare him to marry Lena, or to come out an' fight. Ah bet he'll be back time and agin, too. Know what Ah think? Joe wuz a braver man than Spunk."

There was a general shout of derision from the group.

"Thass a fact," went on Walter. "Lookit whut he done took a razor an' went out to fight a man he knowed toted a gun an' wuz a crack shot, too; 'nother thing Joe wuz skeered of Spunk, skeered plumb stiff! But he went jes' the same. It took him a long time to get his nerve up. 'Tain't nothin' for Spunk to fight when he ain't skeered of nothin'. Now, Joe's done come back to have it out wid the man that's got all he ever had. Y'll know Joe ain't never had nothin' nor wanted nothin' besides Lena. It musta been a h'ant cause ain' nobody never seen no black bob-cat."

"Nother thing," cut in one of the men, "Spunk wuz cussin' a blue streak to-day 'cause he 'lowed dat saw wuz wobblin'—almos' got 'im once. The machinist come, looked it over an' said it wuz alright. Spunk musta been leanin' t'wards it some. Den he claimed somebody pushed 'im but 'twant nobody close to 'im. Ah wuz glad when knockin' off time come. I'm skeered of dat man when he gits hot. He'd beat you full of button holes as quick as he's look atcher."

IV

The men gathered the next evening in a different mood, no laughter. No badinage this time.

"Look, 'Lige, you goin' to set up wid Spunk?"

"New, Ah reckon not, Walter. Tell yuh the truth, Ah'm a lil bit skittish. Spunk died too wicket—died cussin' he did. You know he thought he wuz done outa life."

"Good Lawd, who'd he think done it?"

"Joe."

"Joe Kanty? How come? "

"Walter, Ah b'leeve Ah will walk up theta way an' set. Lena would like it Ah reckon."

"But whut did he say, 'Lige?"

Elijah did not answer until they had left the lighted store and were strolling down the dark street.

"Ah wuz loadin' a wagon wid scantlin'* right near the saw when Spunk fell on the carriage but 'fore Ah could git to him the saw got him in the body—awful sight. Me an' Skint Miller got him off but it was too late. Anybody could see that. The fust thing he said wuz: 'He pushed me, 'Lige—the dirty hound pushed me in the back!'—He was spittin' blood at ev'ry breath. We laid him on the sawdust pile with his face to the East so's he could die easy. He helt mah han' till the last, Walter, and said: 'It was Joe, 'Lige—the dirty sneak shoved me . . . he didn't dare come to mah face . . . but Ah'll git the son-of-a-wood louse soon's Ah get there an' make hell too hot for him. . . . Ah felt him shove me. . .!' Thass how he died."

"If spirits kin fight, there's a powerful tussle goin' on somewhere ovah Jordan 'cause Ah b'leeve Joe's ready for Spunk an' ain't skeered anymore—yes, Ah b'leeve Joe pushed 'im mahself."

They had arrived at the house. Lena's lamentations were deep and loud. She had filled the room with magnolia blossoms that gave off a heavy sweet odor. The keepers of the wake tipped about whispering in frightened tones. Everyone in the village was there, even old Jeff Kanty, Joe's father, who a few hours before would have been afraid to come within ten feet of him, stood leering triumphantly down upon the fallen giant as if his fingers had been the teeth of steel that laid him low.

The cooling board† consisted of three sixteen-inch boards on saw horses, a dingy sheet was his shroud.

The women ate heartily of the funeral baked meats and wondered who would be Lena's next. The men whispered coarse conjectures between guzzles of whiskey.

---

* Scraps.

† In the rural South, it was a common practice to place bodies on cooling boards as the coffin was built. Because of the rate of decomposition, the coffin construction and family viewing had to be completed within a day.

Acknowledgements

My biggest thanks are to the readers who enjoyed our first volume enough to allow us to return. I'd also like to thank Donald Maass, Claiborne, and everyone at Pegasus, my constantly-astonishing partner Les Klinger, and my weird man Ricky Grove.

—Lisa

Thanks again to Rebecca Baumann, who let us "borrow" the title from her brilliant *Frankenstein* exhibition at the Lilly Library. Special thanks to our publisher Claiborne Hancock for believing in this project enough to let us produce a second volume! Lisa Morton is amazing—in truth, she did the lioness's share of the work on this book, and I'm deeply grateful that she said "yes" when I first conceived of our partnership. This is our third book together, and each one has been a delight! Finally, all of my writing is inspired by and cheered on by *the* "weird woman" in my life, my wife Sharon. I am ever indebted to her for her constant support.

—Les